THE OPERATION IS A GO!

Colonel Beall stood frozen for a moment, the enormity of the situation seemingly overwhelming him.

Finally, Captain Dawson, the senior officer present, could wait no more. "Colonel, we need to do something and we need to do it now."

Reluctantly, Beall picked up the bat phone and within seconds had General Walters on the line.

"Sir. We have just received disturbing photos from the F-14 TARP's mission over the Operation Roundup LZ. It looks like there are men deployed in the hills. We have indications that they may have Stingers. We think we may have a mission abort, sir."

"I will *not* abort. This mission is a go."

The entire Watch Team Bravo stood in shocked silence, knowing that Americans would be on the ground in this "friendly" country, fighting for their lives.

For Naval Intelligence Officer Laura Peters, it was a nightmare come true.

THE
CORONADO
CONSPIRACY

GEORGE GALDORISI

AVON BOOKS ◆ NEW YORK

This is a work of fiction. Names, characters, places, and incidents either are the product of the author's imagination or are used fictitiously. Any resemblance to actual events, locales, organizations, or persons, living or dead, is entirely coincidental and beyond the intent of either the author or the publisher.

AVON BOOKS, INC.
1350 Avenue of the Americas
New York, New York 10019

Copyright © 1998 by George Galdorisi and Bill Bleich
Inside cover author photo by Becky Galdorisi
Published by arrangement with the author
Visit our website at **http://www.AvonBooks.com**
Library of Congress Catalog Card Number: 97-94937
ISBN: 0-380-79893-X

First Avon Books Printing: September 1998

AVON TRADEMARK REG. U.S. PAT. OFF. AND IN OTHER COUNTRIES, MARCA REGISTRADA, HECHO EN U.S.A.

Printed in the U.S.A.

WCD   10 9 8 7 6 5 4 3 2 1

*This book is dedicated to
the two best teachers any writer could have:
to my late mother,
who taught me that writing was important,
and to my father,
who taught me the value of hard work.
No two people ever tried harder
to help one person succeed.*

Acknowledgments

No effort of this magnitude reaches closure without a great degree of help and encouragement.

First and foremost, my wife, Becky, provided the encouragement to take this project on, the guidance to keep it in perspective, the reassurance that it was achievable, and oh, by the way, was my number one sounding board, chief grammarian, proofreader, and confidante.

Next, and critical to the success of this work, was my chief collaborator and friend Bill Bleich. We concocted this idea jointly and he provided continuing, years-long infectious enthusiasm regarding the prospects for this project. No one I've ever known, or known of, combines as much raw talent, creative imagination, and ability to see the big picture. Most importantly for the eventual completion of this project, more so than anyone else, including myself, he believed.

CHAPTER 1

CORONADO'S BOW ROSE, HESITATED, THEN CRASHED back into the sea, sending green water rushing along her fo'c'sle, then running back in a thousand rivulets out through the scuppers and back into the roiling ocean. The eighteen-thousand-ton Landing Platform Dock, or LPD, flagship for Joint Task Force Eight, pounded rhythmically through the eastern Pacific west of Panama, rising and falling in sync with the cadence of the sea, her massive bulk shuddering with each rise and fall. *Coronado* was not a sleek-looking greyhound, she was a workhorse—a blue-collar ship, as many of her crew fondly called her. Her bulk, and particularly her broad beam, seemed to crush the waves beneath her, rather than slice through them like her small, sleek brethren.

On the bridge, high above the surface of the sea, it was business as usual on the 2000-to-2400 watch. The faint glow of the radar repeaters and the green digital readouts of the Global Positioning System at the navigator's chart table provided the only light on this moonless night. With no moon and few stars, there was no line between sea and sky, just the seamless murky background that the sailors on the bridge had dubbed the "inside of the inkwell." The faint background static of a half-dozen radios tuned to receive incoming transmissions on the circuits guarded by *Coronado* provided a constant drone of white noise that, when combined with the measured cadence of the ship's rise and fall, threatened to lull the watchstanders to sleep, or at least into a sense of lethargy not uncommon on a watch like this.

The conning officer, Ensign Mike Powers, was being drawn into that lethargy, but was broken out of it abruptly by the commanding voice of the officer of the deck, Lieutenant Bill Miller:

"Powers, has Radio Central transmitted our evening SITREP yet?"

"I'll check again," replied Powers dutifully. He pressed the button to Radio Central on the "bitch box," Navy slang for the ship's intercom, one of the last remaining pieces of original equipment on this thirty-year-old flagship and former amphibious ship, now configured with the most up-to-date communications and intelligence wizardry in the military inventory.

The response from watch supervisor Radioman First Class Frank Rodriquez was the same one that Powers had heard throughout the course of his watch. "No sir. Volume of traffic to and from the staff has been incredible, mostly op immediate and flash. SITREP is in the queue but it'll probably be a while."

Miller didn't like what he heard one bit. The captain's night orders—his instructions to his watch team to be followed to the letter while he slept—were insistent. The SITREP goes out on time, unless *Coronado* wants a loud, undesired blast from the squadron commander in Norfolk. The SITREP, the Navy's shorthand for situation report, was a daily, ponderous collection of minutiae sent back to the ship's administrative commander in Norfolk containing everything from how much fuel they had burned in the last twenty-four hours, to what spare parts they needed from the supply system, to how many of *Coronado*'s four-hundred-plus sailors had needed treatment at sick bay that day. If the embarked Joint Task Force Eight staff was, for some unknown reason, sending a high volume of op immediate and flash traffic—code words for the highest priority messages, which "bumped" all normal traffic—his SITREP would just have to wait. Miller considered jumping in and responding directly to Rodriquez, but thought better of it. He allowed Powers to reply to Radio Central with a simple "Bridge, aye."

Miller was a seasoned officer and had been attached to the flagship long enough to know that something way out of the ordinary was going on. True, the hundred-plus-man JTF Eight staff generated and received a large amount of message traffic, but most of it was routine, just as their mission had been for the past two months. Joint Task Force Eight, commanded by Army Brigadier General Ashley Lovelace, was the Pentagon's anti-drug task force, charged with drawing together the resources of all services within the Department of Defense as well as federal anti-drug agencies. Their embarkation aboard *Coronado* allowed them to go close to the action, the littoral waters off of Central and South America, where the flow of drugs into the United States by air and sea was still at epidemic proportions. The President had made stopping the flow of drugs into the United States a major campaign theme and Brigadier General Lovelace was rumored to have been his personal pick for this high-visibility assignment.

The volume of message traffic to and from the JTF Eight staff, coupled with a noticeable decrease in the presence of staff officers at normal wardroom functions ranging from meals, to movies, to daily workouts, all suggested to Miller that a big operation was definitely in the offing. Curiously, the JTF Eight staff had been circumspect about discussing their activities with ship's company officers, and the usual amiable banter in the wardroom had been replaced by stony silence and a rush to get back to their staff spaces.

Miller surveyed the sea with his Navy-regulation binoculars—the damn things felt like a brick around his neck—thinking of his family thousands of miles away, when the bitch box squawked again. "Bridge, staff watch officer."

"Bridge, aye," responded Miller, moving the junior Powers aside so that he, as the more senior officer, could deal directly with the watch officer of the embarked JTF Eight staff.

"Staff navigation wants you to come easterly to a course of 120 true."

"We've got a much easier ride here at 030," countered Miller. "The ship will be abeam the swells at 120." Miller, knowing that often junior staff watch officers came up with "orders" for the ship that reflected their own whims and not the desires of their leaders, wanted to let the majority of *Coronado*'s sailors spend most of the night restfully, and not have to wedge themselves into their racks as the ship rolled incessantly from side to side in the long, deep Pacific swells.

"Roger that," replied the watch officer. "We've worked this out down here; just make it so."

Miller tried again. "Okay, but maybe if we just come about halfway—" but immediately regretted it, as the unmistakable gruff voice of the JTF Eight chief of staff, Colonel Conrad Hicks, boomed in over the now-resonating bitch box.

"Lieutenant, if you can't execute the order I'll have your captain relieve you with someone who can!"

Miller was stunned by the ferocity of the command.

"Right full rudder, steer course 120," chimed Powers, trying to help the shaken Miller recover his composure by at least responding to Hicks's order with alacrity.

"Helmsman, aye, right full rudder, make my course 120," replied the shaken helmsman.

"Aye, aye, Colonel, coming right to course 120 now, sir. I'll inform the captain," said Miller, as all the bridge watchstanders became a little more aware that the JTF Eight staff, indeed, had clandestine plans for *Coronado* and her crew.

As her sleeping sailors braced themselves reflexively against the ship's rolls, *Coronado* shuddered as full rudder brought her around toward a new course.

Eight decks below the bridge, in *Coronado*'s weight room, dozens of barbells rocked in their racks with the ship's new movement, and the men lifting weights tried to keep their balance. This interruption was an occupational hazard of lifting weights aboard a moving ship, but pumping iron was one of the only ways of getting a workout aboard *Coronado* other than running in endless circles around the flight deck during those sporadic times when helicopter flight operations were not in progress.

Coronado's weight room bore absolutely no resemblance to the glitzy gyms ashore. Crammed into a corner of Lower Vehicle Stow, the usual location for amphibious vehicles in years past when *Coronado* had been a "straight stick" amphibious ship, this relatively inaccessible part of the ship lived in musty negligence with poor ventilation, low hanging overheads, gritty bulkheads, missing lights, and a general veneer of grit so common aboard most steamships past a quarter-century in age. Consequently, only a hardy few, those most dedicated fitness fanatics, frequented this murky place.

Chief Petty Officer Rick Holden was one of them. He was a special weapons and communications expert with the embarked Navy SEAL team, and physical fitness for Holden was not just a hobby but an occupational necessity. In fact, he was such a regular in the weight room that the few ships company and more numerous staff officers who frequented it carried on an easy banter with the enlisted man whom they would normally deal with far more formally if they encountered him several decks above.

"Hey Holden, you know, you SEALs really have a racket. The Navy actually pays you good money to keep all buff and cut." Commander Ben Malgrave, staff communications officer and another weight room regular, rarely missed an opportunity to give Holden a hard time about being in a line of work where he was paid to do what he enjoyed anyway.

"That's right, Commo," replied Rick. "And all I'm trying to do is give the Navy their money's worth." One needed only to glance at him to see that he was right. Even among a group of SEALs, who were known for their incredible level of fitness, Rick stood out. A full six feet two inches tall and a finely muscled 180 pounds, Rick looked like a model for a Greek or Roman sculptor's subject of a perfect human body. With blond hair perilously close to violating Navy grooming standards, a bushy walrus mustache, and deep-set, penetrating green eyes, Rick should have been on a recruiting poster.

"Way those young lieutenants are driving this ship, lucky we get a workout at all," answered Malgrave.

"All this rock and roll got you skipping workouts, or are you just getting too lazy, Commander?" said Rick.

"Just too busy. Radio traffic has been hot and heavy, and you-know-who's the point man on that," replied Malgrave, straining for just one more 220-pound bench press.

"The powers that be just must be bored. I guess they

figure they got to help us operators by checking up on us and having us tell them everything that we're doing every minute of the day."

"No, this is different. Mostly P-4s going back and forth between General Lovelace and either SouthCom or the Joint Chiefs in the Pentagon. You know how high-vis this anti-drug stuff is and you know how my general's got a notion he can stop the flow all by his lonesome. Some of the traffic has gone SPECAT, so even yours truly hasn't seen it."

His communications knowledge alerted Holden to the fact that *Coronado*'s hitherto routine anti-drug deployment had reached a different level. P-4s were "personal for" messages exchanged between flag and general officers that allowed them to communicate directly in plain language unencumbered by the bureaucratic structure and jargon of most military messages. SPECATs, or special category messages, were those of such a highly sensitive nature that only a specially designated senior radioman and the person to whom the message was addressed were allowed to view them. Holden could sense that Commander Ben Malgrave was more than a little annoyed at being out of the loop.

"You mean more than one SPECAT?" asked Holden.

"More in one day than I've seen on a full deployment," responded Malgrave.

"Can't believe that this anti-drug caper has that much interest. We haven't done a significant op in a month and a half."

"True, but I can feel the momentum building. Staff's been having a lot of meetings, just the heavies, general, chief of staff, not the minions like this LDO."

As an LDO, or limited duty officer, Malgrave had worked his way up through the system, starting out as a radioman and then earning a commission and rising through the ranks in his highly technical specialty. LDOs were vital to the operations of any staff but were not typically in the inner circle and certainly not privy to the important decision-making processes.

Malgrave was initially surprised that a SEAL, one of those folk primarily concerned with going out into the bush and killing people, would know so much about all of this complex communications gear and be completely conversant with Navy communications circuits and procedures. But as the leading communicator for his SEALs team, Holden was in Radio Central frequently and was eager to help, and—damn the Navy drawdown—Malgrave was so short-handed that he welcomed the extra help repairing gear, setting up circuits, and the like. Conveniently, Holden had all of the proper compartmentalized clearances needed to work on and operate some of Malgrave's most sophisticated gear. All this kept Rick in good stead with the staff Commo.

"Well, Commo, I guess that they'll let us know when they let us know."

"That's the Navy way. Probably just a routine operation, just trying to make it seem more important to give everyone a sense that we're doing something that matters."

But Holden suspected that it was more than just routine. He remembered feeling this way before—before he resurfaced as a Navy chief petty officer, before he'd erected and maintained the illusion of coincidence that he was a SEAL, a communications expert, and also assigned to *Coronado*.

As was their habit after their workout, Rick and Malgrave climbed the eight decks of ladders from *Coronado*'s gym to radio and check on the action prior to returning to their respective "homes": Rick to the three-tier chief's berthing compartment—or "goat locker," in Navy parlance—Malgrave to his small but personalized commander's stateroom.

"Come on, Commander. Way you're pumping iron down below, you should be sprinting up these steps," said Rick.

"Just wait until you get a few more years on you, Holden. Seagoing life takes its toll. I've probably got more years at sea than you have in the Navy," replied Malgrave.

Rick thought how true that was. He was about to change the subject as they rounded a corner and started down the athwartship passageway outside of Radio Cen-

tral, but then Colonel Conrad Hicks emerged in his
starched khakis and his chief-of-staff loop.

Hicks barely looked up at them as he snarled, "Make
a hole," and breezed past.

As Malgrave and Holden entered Radio Central, Petty
Officer First Class Rodriquez and the rest of his watch
team looked as perplexed as Holden and Malgrave did.

CHAPTER 2

GENERAL WALTERS SAT AT HIS LARGE DESK IN HIS IM-
posing headquarters at Quarry Heights in the Republic of
Panama. As head of the U.S. Southern Command—
SouthCom—he was one of the military's eight top leaders
in the Unified Command, with broad powers over all he
surveyed. On paper, General Walters was responsible for
U.S. military activities in South America and in Central
America south of Mexico; an area of responsibility en-
compassing nineteen countries, representing about one-
sixth of the world's landmass, covering about seven
million square miles and stretching six thousand miles
from the Mexican-Guatemalan border to the southern tip
of South America. In his own mind, he was responsible
for a great deal more. It was a responsibility that would
give most men pause. General Charles Bigelow Walters
took it all in stride.

Tall, trim, and tan, General Walters appeared the perfect warrior. His athletic build belied his fifty-seven years
and he looked more ready to take on the world than men
half his age. His six-foot two-inch frame and hardened
185-pound body, his square jaw, his penetrating blue eyes,
all conveyed a sense of, at once, overwhelming power,
unsurpassed confidence, and the absolute ability to get
things done when, where, and how he wanted them done.
It was a look he cultivated.

He thought about the unlikely sequence of events leading up to this moment: the election, the long-anticipated

and -feared changes, the meeting, his "surprise" appointment as SouthCom commander, the sudden selection of Brigadier General Lovelace to command Operation Roundup. It was all unfolding as planned, and not a moment too soon. The nation . . . his nation . . . the one he had sworn to defend and that he had defended for the past thirty-four years, was in mortal danger. Only he could save it now.

One would have to know General Walters only casually to understand that he could believe he held the fate of the nation in his hands. Born into a prominent banking family and educated at Phillips Exeter Academy in Exeter, New Hampshire, as the third son of an overbearing father, he refused to be the fourth most prominent banker in the family and instead went to the U.S. Military Academy at West Point. Deputy brigade commander of the Corps of Cadets, all-American squash player, Rhodes Scholar—his career had taken off like a rocket and he had remained a fast-tracker since then. Vietnam, Europe, Grenada, Desert Storm, he had always been in the field at the right place at the right time.

But the field had not been where Walters had made his mark. Certainly he had distinguished himself there, but his field assignments were always brief and seemed to end just as the exciting action did. It was inside the beltway that Walters had made a name for himself. While other officers toiled in obscure offices in the bowels of the Pentagon where they were intimately involved in the minutiae of some Army program or some budgetary battle, Walters had always secured the most coveted high-vis assignments. National Security Council, Office of Legislative Affairs, military aide to the Vice President, executive assistant to the chairman of the Joint Chiefs of Staff—these assignments and others had assured him of early recognition as an up-and-comer. Just as importantly, they had enabled him to build a network of contacts in Washington that assured him access to information few possessed. He was accustomed to getting things done, accustomed to being at the nexus of critical decision making. As he rose in seniority, the chances of him being out of the loop on any major decision involving the national security of the United States grew more and more remote.

He was certainly in the loop now, inextricably bound up with his long associate, General Howard Campbell. Walters would give the order, the field commander would begin his operation, things would begin to go awry, his orders to withdraw would not—could not—be obeyed, and all the rest would fall into place. But he would give the order. It was to be a historic moment. His historic moment.

He could rationalize the matter, Walters once thought. He was not directly involved. There would be no smoking gun, no direct link back to him and the other coconspirators, particularly not to General Campbell.

The phone had rung early in General Walters's SouthCom quarters that day. He was accustomed to that; in fact, he had insisted on it. His key subordinates knew that failure to wake the general on important matters would, at a minimum, evoke the severest possible public dressing-down at the morning staff meeting. If the failure to alert him involved a matter that he considered vital, he was famous for the unpleasant chain of career-ending events he could set in motion against the offending officer or noncom.

The hum of the air-conditioning had made it difficult to hear General Campbell on the other end of the line, but the cool air was preferable to the hot, steamy Panama nights. Anyway, he knew what the call would be about and even at 0400 his agile mind was racing with the possibilities. The only words that he needed to hear from his friend and confidant were "President" and "go." He would dutifully pass the order down the chain of command and General Lovelace would set the operation in motion. What would inevitably happen to Lovelace then was no concern of his. There were larger issues at stake. This was the opportunity that they had waited for. He was about to set Operation Roundup in motion. As he tossed away the covers and bounded from bed, he wondered how long it would take to ruin the man who had made such a shallow mockery of his and his fellow officers' careers and of what they had once hoped they could be.

CHAPTER 3

"THERE! HIT IT!" WITH THAT, DETECTIVE FRED KALAS, Washington PD, gunned the 1993 Ford Taurus away from the curb on New York Avenue just east of Mount Vernon Square and he and his partner, Detective Mike Wyncoop, took off after a beat-up light brown Nissan 280Z that had just wheeled out of Kim's Auto Body Shop.

Wyncoop called it in to the precinct. "Base, unit six, have finally waited out Cooper. He's heading east on New York. We've just passed the corner of New Jersey Avenue. We're in loose trail behind him. Tell us what you want us to do." The narcotics detectives had been staked out for several days trying to locate Harvey "Penny" Cooper, a midlevel drug dealer of some notoriety in the District, who was wanted for questioning in a major case they were working. Now they needed to get instructions as to whether to pick him up or just follow him. Awaiting a response, they passed North Capitol Street and entered the northeast section of the District. Cooper continued to speed along, past two- and three-story row houses, a number of which had a wide variety of chain-link fences and humble little gardens. Many of these houses were now boarded up, their former occupants driven from this once-prestigious neighborhood by the blight, by the crime, by the drugs pushed by people like Cooper. As the detectives noted the New York Avenue Car Wash disappearing behind them, the radio came alive. The directive from base didn't satisfy either of them.

"Unit six, base. Stay close but try to remain unseen. However, don't, repeat, don't lose him. We've got questions he's got to answer."

"Great," snarled Kalas, "that's a bureaucratic answer for you. Damned if we do and damned if we don't."

"Yeah," responded Wyncoop. "Maybe if those station house geeks would go out on a real operation once in a while they wouldn't be sitting there in their easy chairs giving us such half-assed instructions."

Both detectives were venting their frustrations in this most thankless of jobs. Washington, D.C., had the dubious distinction of annually being one of the top murder cities in the United States. Kalas and Wyncoop both knew that this epidemic was primarily due to the brisk drug trade in the city, but while the murder rate received national and even international attention, the anti-drug efforts received, at best, lip service and almost laughable funding. They were doing the best they could, but sometimes it seemed almost hopeless.

"Guess we better close it up a bit," said Wyncoop, and with that, Kalas moved into the passing lane on this wide avenue and cut down the distance between their Taurus and Cooper's Z. Cooper slowed down and Kalas responded in kind before he suddenly hung a right on First Street NE and screamed south toward the heart of the Capitol District. "This doesn't look good," said Wyncoop.

"I know," said Kalas, "but we got to stay with him. Maybe he hasn't seen us yet."

He had. They saw Cooper swivel his head and look back toward their Taurus. Then he hit the accelerator.

"This is it," shouted Kalas. "Hit the light, Mike."

With that, Wyncoop took the red light from under his seat, activated it, and placed it on the roof of the Taurus.

Cooper accelerated even more and continued to burn south on First Street, past empty lots surrounded by chain-link fences topped by barbed wire. The streets were littered everywhere with trash—boxes, used tires, newspaper. He continued past the six-story Woodward and Lothrop warehouse on the left, crossing L Street, swerving to avoid hitting people crossing the street to get to the Greyhound bus terminal. Kalas followed, and as Cooper approached K Street he whipped the Z into a right-hand turn. Tires screeching, Cooper sped up, going back to the west along K Street. Kalas closed, but Cooper stepped on the brakes and wheeled his Z right again, onto North Capitol Street. Accelerating, he sped past Kaiser

Permanente, North Capitol Medical Center, and the Mount Airy Baptist Church, then the D.C. Housing Authority Headquarters. Every time Kalas closed the distance a bit, Cooper accelerated even more.

"Damn, I hate this," said Kalas. "The shit thinks that he can outrun us. I hate this part. I just hate it."

Wyncoop hated it too and called it in. "Base, unit six. In pursuit of a brown Nissan 280Z. Traveling at high speed north on North Capitol Street. We're in pursuit. How about some backup?"

"Roger, unit six," intoned the faceless base radio operator. "All units, officers need assistance. In pursuit of a brown Nissan 280Z traveling north on North Capitol Street. All units in the vicinity respond."

Kalas started to drive more aggressively. His Taurus was the souped-up police version of the standard Ford sedan, and although he wasn't driving as recklessly as the clearly panicked Cooper, he was closing the distance rapidly. Cooper continued to weave in and out of traffic, crossing New York Avenue through the underpass. Suddenly he slowed again and wheeled left on P Street, speeding up again as he passed small shops with their pull-down gratings, Checkpoint Charlies against the seemingly endless crime in this area of town; past Cook Elementary School; past the small two-story row houses on either side of P Street, some with tiny gardens, some with Astroturf, most with metal lawn furniture whose large chains securing them from theft destroyed whatever ambience they might have provided. Cooper was driving more carelessly now and smacked against a pickup truck parked outside of the Armstrong Adult Education Center on the left.

Cooper turned hard right onto Third Street NW. Kalas followed, now with a death grip on the steering wheel and a determined look on his face. Wyncoop had never seen his partner like this. Kalas seemed to be taking the chase now as a personal challenge. He had to swerve radically to avoid hitting a pedestrian just starting to cross the street, while Cooper whipped right onto Q Street NW. He sped up, blew through a red light on First Street NW, slid sideways right through the busy intersection where Q Street, Florida Avenue, and North Capitol Street all came together, then screeched right again, now onto Bates Street, nearly in the shadow of Dunbar High School.

Cooper wasn't an idiot. He was trying to outpace the police sedan, but he wasn't just mindlessly speeding around Washington. He was clearly seeking out familiar turf, spiraling into a neighborhood well-known to him were he could avoid the police by moving on his own ground and on his own terms. Both Kalas and Wyncoop knew exactly where they were, in the heart of the capital's most notorious collection of crack houses. There must be more drugs bought and sold in these few square blocks than anywhere else in the world. Kalas had a strong hunch Cooper would take off on foot here. Cooper slowed to turn left into the first alley paralleling North Capitol Street, moving as quickly as he could over the broken roadway lined with tiny backyards, high chain-link fences—many festooned with barbed wire—and an endless stream of decrepit cars.

Kalas and Wyncoop were now almost on top of him. Still in the alley, he crossed P Street and continued in the next alley, careening off a broken sofa on his left, passing Cook Elementary School on his right. He was on familiar turf here, all right, thought Kalas and Cooper. They were afraid they would loose him if he got out and ran for it.

Kalas's instincts took over. As Cooper screeched to a stop, Kalas shouted to Wyncoop, "Hang on." With that, he slammed into Cooper's stopped car, hoping to shake him up enough to daze him before he could run off. But it was too late. Cooper half-jumped, half-rolled out of his now-wrecked car and, without even looking at his pursuers, took off like a shot. Kalas jumped from the Taurus and went after him.

Wyncoop grabbed the radio for one quick transmission. "All units, unit six. Pursuing suspect on foot, request backup now!" Not waiting for acknowledgment, he followed his partner, now almost halfway down the street.

Cooper's fear kept him running at high speed, but a few dozen yards back, the detectives sensed that he was also looking for a house he knew, some warren he could duck into to elude them.

Then Cooper suddenly stopped and jumped up on a

ten-foot-high chain-link fence at the back of a two-story brick house. The light, lithe Cooper was already clamboring down the other side as the winded Kalas and Wyncoop reached the fence and tried to grab at him through the chain links.

"Stop, you asshole," shouted Kalas, but the desperate Cooper didn't even look back. He just ran toward the house, a decrepit building. As Kalas and Wyncoop scaled the fence, Cooper flung open the iron grate door and entered the back of 1304 North Capitol Street, long since abandoned, the neighborhood less than two miles from the dome of the U.S. Capitol but looking more like Beirut than Beirut itself.

The detectives dropped down from the fence just as the iron door fell shut behind Cooper.

"Dammit, we've lost him," hissed Wyncoop.

"No we haven't," said Kalas, winking at his partner. "Just follow me. We'll flush him." Then, pressing his head close to Wyncoop's, he whispered softly, "Mike, say we've lost him really loud—and sound really disappointed."

Wyncoop complied, saying loudly, "Dammit, we've lost him. Let's call it in. I'm not hanging around here."

"No," said Kalas, "he's here, I can *smell* him."

"What . . . how?" said the still bewildered Wyncoop. But Kalas put his index finger to his lips, signaling Wyncoop to be quiet. He stalked a few feet each way, up and down from the place where they were standing, muttering under his breath, "Mr. Cooper, oh Mr. Cooper, oh why don't you just come out now?"

Wyncoop just froze, staring in bewilderment at the seemingly crazed Kalas. But there was a method to his partner's madness.

"Oh Mr. Cooper, *Mr. Cooper,* now you're going to make me start shooting at where I think you might be!"

Kalas drew his service revolver. Oh no, thought Wyncoop. There were rules. You just couldn't do that.

Kalas cocked the trigger. That was all it took. The terrified Cooper could stand no more. He bolted from his position just inside the door and started noisily through the house and up the stairs. Kalas and Wyncoop followed. First one flight, then another, Cooper was going for the roof. Desperately, Kalas started taking steps three at a time.

Then Cooper looked back. It was a tragic mistake, as it slowed him down ever so slightly. In one desperate lunge Kalas tackled the fleeing drug dealer at the top of the third landing.

It was not much of a struggle. The 220-pound Kalas merely laid on top on the wiry Cooper until Wyncoop caught up seconds later. They had him frisked and in cuffs in less than a minute.

Kalas dragged him to his feet. "This your coop, *Mr. Cooper*?"

"Hey man, I got nothing to say."

"I think it's your coop, *man*. Now, what do you think we'll find? Think we'll find any drugs here, my man?"

"Hey, look, I ain't done nothin', man. You can't go searching no place, you got no warrant or nothin', man."

"Well, *man*, maybe this is your place." Wyncoop swiveled his head, and at the end of the hallway he saw light under a doorway. A nod to Kalas and they moved toward it, dragging the reluctant Cooper with them.

Two loud knocks on the door by Wyncoop: no answer, but furious scuffling inside. This might or might not be Mr. Cooper's place, but it sure sounded interesting. Wyncoop nodded to Kalas and the detective used Cooper as a ready battering ram, slamming him against the door and springing it wide open. The window was open and one man was scrambling out to the fire escape while two women were screaming, both too startled to move. "Don't shoot, man, don't shoot." Their eyes showed genuine terror as each stared directly at the hulking Kalas.

Kalas ran to the window, but it was too late to catch the fleeing man. He and Wyncoop surveyed the scene before them, stooping over the stunned Cooper as they did. This was a crack house, there was no doubt about it. All of the typical paraphernalia littered every available space in the tiny one-bedroom apartment. The place was a total disaster. Pressed up against the wall of the living room, the two hysterical females, longtime crack addicts from the look of their emaciated bodies, just shook and glanced furtively at the officers, then at the writhing Cooper. They truly looked as if they thought the detectives might shoot them. It was a familiar scene that both detectives had witnessed scores of times. While Wyncoop held Cooper and the women at bay, Kalas turned the corner into the bedroom, his service revolver at the ready, determined not to be ambushed the way so many of his fellow officers had been in this dangerous duty. He was in the bedroom for only seconds before coming out. He looked straight at Wyncoop.

"Mike, I'll cover them. You need to look in there."

Wyncoop didn't know what to expect, but as soon as Kalas had his weapon pointed at the three in the living room he went into the bedroom. What he saw staggered him. There, slumped against the wall, was a pretty young girl, sixteen, maybe seventeen at the outside. And in her cheerleader outfit—that of classy Langley High in the very upscale suburb of McLean. Home to the power brokers of Washington.

Wyncoop approached the girl. She had a crack vial at her side. He felt for a pulse. There was none. He lifted her pupils. No sign of life. The girl was dead. She'd come from classy McLean to this . . . this sewer, to smoke crack, and she had paid the ultimate price. Wyncoop came out of the room with a look of rage on his face. He started moving toward the two women. There was renewed terror in their eyes.

"Hey, look, mister detective . . . we didn't do nothing. She bought some stuff on the street, just wanted to come in there and smoke it. Hey, I said, okay honey, come on in here. We were just trying to help her out."

"We didn't sell her stuff," protested the other.

"Why?" screamed Wyncoop, and he moved menacingly toward one of the women. Kalas grabbed his arm.

"Mike, no. Look, find out who she is. I'll get backup up here."

Kalas called base on his mobile radio while Wyncoop forced himself to go back into the bedroom. He found her small Dooney and Bourke purse and pulled out her wallet. Christen Chamberlain. Nice name. Nice girl. Dead. What was this drug thing coming to?

*   *   *

Within fifteen minutes, the apartment was jammed. Virtually all of the backups Kalas had called for were still there, as well as the Washington, D.C., medical examiner, a bevy of other detectives, a contingent from the forensics lab, another from the homicide squad, and a host of others. The chase had attracted other attention too, especially since all emergency calls are monitored by many, especially by the media. Quietly, and essentially unnoticed, Joe Hache of the *Washington Star* had wormed his way into the apartment. The police weren't paying attention to him, nor if they had been could they come up with any reason to make him leave, as he snapped several pictures of the girl in her cheerleader outfit, slumped dead against the wall of this decrepit brownstone. It was only a local story, but it was a good local story, thought Hache.

CHAPTER 4

"DAMN DISAPPOINTING, I MEAN *DAMN DISAPPOINTING*," boomed President Taylor Calhoun as he leaped out of his Kevlar-backed chair and threw the copy of the latest approval polls against the thick, bulletproof window of the Oval Office. He was usually a man of exceptionally calm demeanor and not given to outbursts, and this reaction caught his staffers off guard. "Ray, they got their head up their ass out there? Why the hell can't your people do a better job at spin control? You just gonna watch me sink, or tie an anvil to my ass to make me go down faster?"

Ray Weaver, the President's press secretary and one of his closet political advisors, didn't know how to respond. He had worked for the President since his earliest days in Georgia politics and, in all humility, assigned himself great credit for the President's success, especially his long-shot quest for the White House. He knew that Taylor Calhoun did not intend for his outburst to be a personal rebuke, but Weaver felt responsible nonetheless.

"Mr. President, clearly we're not where we want to be

in the ratings . . . but you're making tough choices and, hell, we can't keep everyone happy."

Here in the Oval Office, sitting at his large desk, beneath the seal of the United States, with the tall, narrow windows filled with five inches of pale green bulletproof glass framed by the gold-colored damask draperies behind him, Taylor Calhoun should have been satisfied, polls or not. But he was not. He snapped at Weaver, who was sitting on one of the two chairs that flanked his desk.

"Everyone? *Everyone?* Ray, we're not keeping anyone happy. Hell, we came into the White House with a mandate and now they wish we weren't here." Calhoun almost shot out of his chair as he responded, his six-foot four-inch frame and 230 pounds now looming above the others in the room. Taylor Calhoun had clear blue eyes, bushy eyebrows, a still-full head of sandy brown hair, a prominent nose, and large jowls. Those features had given him the appropriate good ol' boy look so helpful in the South and particularly in southern politics, but they were far less effective for a national figure.

Weaver pondered his next response. He was torn between telling his longtime friend the truth and telling him what he wanted to hear. The truth was that Calhoun was sinking in the approval ratings because he had done virtually nothing as President. He had finally reached a position where he was out of his element.

His two-decade rise through the political maze had been carefully orchestrated to capitalize on his strengths and protect his weaknesses. Calhoun was a brilliant man, and Weaver and the President's other close advisors had polished that brilliance to make it shine. They had propelled him from the Georgia legislature, where they found the right issues for him to take on, to the U.S. House of Representatives, where he represented the district of Savannah and brought thousands of jobs to his constituents with the construction of the submarine base. Weaver and the others in the inner circle had recognized that Calhoun had a natural flair for the often pedantic details of military force structures, weapons throw weights, naval ship characteristics, and the like, and fashioned a successful Senate campaign around his bringing the same military largesse to the entire state. As a senator, Calhoun had done just that, finding his niche as a defense expert and gaining additional credibility nationwide as a spokesman for defense matters. His success in delivering military bases and contracts to Georgia communities while elsewhere bases closed and defense contracts dried up had inspired the grateful citizens of that state to send him back to the Senate for an additional two terms.

As his party's nominee for President, Calhoun had waged a competent campaign against an incumbent President mortally wounded by personal scandal. Weaver and his other long-term advisors had successfully taken the pulse of the nation and had built his platform on the twin pillars of capitalizing on his military expertise and "enfranchising the disenfranchised," not being particularly careful regarding who was promised what. As a result, Calhoun had arrived in the White House with a seeming mandate. But that is where it ended. Calhoun had no personal national agenda and no real sense of where he wanted to take the nation. Special interest groups held sway and the best that could pass for an agenda was the *cause de jour*. With such an aimless agenda, it was no surprise that his popularity in the polls was at a low ebb as he neared the end of his third year in office.

.Weaver had seen all this coming and had cast about for a cause to seize on. After sifting through many dead ends he returned to one of the President's key campaign themes—the drug war. Calhoun was energized when he spoke out against drugs and it was one of his most compelling messages. The death of young Christen Chamberlain in that sewer of a crack house in the District could supply the exclamation point on that message. Calhoun could be eloquent when speaking about something he believed in passionately, and speaking out against the scourge that had destroyed that beautiful misguided girl was right up his alley. Yes! He would use this regrettable incident to shape the President's message and to focus the nation's efforts in "winning the war against drugs."

But the reality of winning the drug war involved eliminating the demand. This was something Calhoun couldn't do in two terms, let alone one, for the necessary education at all levels, as well as the comprehensive prevention and treatment programs, required more time than that to take hold. The results were also hard to gauge with any accuracy at all. But the supply side—that was a different matter. Stepping up the pressure there, by increasing the use of military forces left over from the Cold War, might give the President a chance to capitalize on his military expertise and perhaps even garner a big win for the administration.

Calhoun was a cautious man and his staff recognized that he couldn't commit to a plan to attack the supply side of the drug trade unless he sensed that he had a well-above-average chance of garnering a win. Weaver and some of the other White House staffers had floated this trial balloon with the Defense Department. Although it had received somewhat lukewarm support within the office of the Secretary of Defense, they had found strong support on the Joint Chiefs of Staff, particularly from the chairman himself and the Joint Chiefs J-3, the director of operations.

The Joint Chiefs, headed by General Howard Campbell, had prepared the usual plethora of position papers heavy with military jargon and short of clear-cut recommendations. Calhoun found the damn things indifferent at best, sop at worst. However, the chairman of the Joint Chiefs, General Campbell, had requested an appointment with the President to discuss the matter directly with him. After some juggling of his calendar, the President invited the chairman to meet with him at Camp David the following weekend.

It was a productive meeting that pleased both men. The President was in slacks and a turtleneck when General Campbell arrived at Camp David. The President had asked Campbell to come without his military aide and the President returned the courtesy by receiving Campbell with only two Secret Service men discreetly in the background.

"General, welcome to Camp David. Your first time out here, I'm told."

"Yes, Mr. President, it is indeed. I'm struck by the

beauty of this place. It must be particularly difficult to come back to Washington after a weekend here."

"Oh, it has its attractions, surely," continued the President, working hard to put the general at ease—and finding himself also at ease with him. Although the general looked sharp and precise in his military uniform, covered with seemingly countless ribbons and decorations, his black Army corfam shoes mirror-bright, his five-foot ten-inch height and wiry frame inspired trust rather than fear. He wore his hair long by military standards and the graying at his temples conveyed a sense of solid middle-class virtue. His soft brown eyes seemed to convey understanding, not menace, and his fluid gestures had the effect of relaxing others in his presence. It was an effect Campbell cultivated, for his many tours inside the Washington beltway had taught him that the civilian leadership had more than enough hardened warriors that they could use and then expend. What they were looking for were senior officers who made them feel comfortable. He had worked mightily at conveying that image and had surprised even himself at how successful he had been.

"General, I'll come right to the point. The position papers your staff sent over regarding our proposed anti-drug efforts were pretty noncommittal, yet I hear tell that you yourself favor such a plan. I suppose that's why you asked for this meeting. Now, just what is your position?"

"Mr. President, those position papers were designed to present all sides of the issue. We spend an incredible amount of time in our command and staff colleges teaching our staff officers to do just that: present all sides of the issue in a cogent fashion so that the decision maker can make an informed decision. I think that they've done a good job at that."

"That's all well and good, General, and your system makes sense. And I appreciate having a wide range of options. But I'd like you to tell me what *you* think. I expect that you wanted an opportunity to do just that—to tell me whether you think we have a chance to get out in front of this drug scourge."

"Yes I did, Mr. President. You see, sir, there are some things that just don't lend themselves directly to position papers. Those are good as far as they go, but Mr. President, they really can't present the full picture. Your advisors have hit upon a good idea—no, a really capital idea—and I believe that we can execute it with our military forces."

"General, I'm not talking about executing some minor drug bust. I'm talking about going after the big fish, about shutting this thing down. We want action. We want a big win!" Calhoun was almost shouting now, not in anger but with enthusiasm, hoping it would be contagious and affect the general.

"Yes Mr. President, I see. I think we are on the same page here," replied Campbell. This could be the opportunity he had waited for.

"I want to make sure we are, General. I want you to take some time and think about it. We want this to be a defining moment in the war against drugs."

"Mr. President, you know that you have my support. Now that I know where you want to go with this, I know we can get you the win you want."

"I know you can," responded the President. As he showed General Howard Campbell out, the President felt he had won a key ally to his war against drugs.

And Howard Campbell felt he had taken the first important step in a war of his own.

CHAPTER 5

THE STATELY JOINT CHIEFS OF STAFF CONFERENCE Room, dubbed, the "tank" or sometimes, the "gold room"—in recognition of its exquisite gold carpet—was not far from the Pentagon's river entrance. The flag of the United States, as well as the flags of each of the military services, dominated one end of the room, while twin video projection screens dominated the other. The dark paneling on the lower walls and the stark white upper walls—with their impressive pictures all around—conveyed an air

of importance and purposefulness. The large polished table and soft leather chairs were occupied by only six people, as only the principals—the chairman, the vice
chairman, and the heads of the Army, Navy, Air Force,
and Marine Corps—were in attendance. Missing were the
usual entourage of deputies, assistants, and aides who
were typically charged with knowing the issues, backing
up their respective bosses, and generally doing the
"stubby pencil work" whenever the Joint Chiefs met.
Even the operations deputies were missing—a clear signal
that matters of extreme sensitivity were being discussed.

As the other Joint Chiefs took their seats, Howard
Campbell reflected on the uniqueness of his office and the
break with his predecessors of previous decades. Military
miscues throughout the 1970s and early 1980s, the collapse
in Vietnam, the Mayaguez incident, the failed Iranian hostage rescue raid at Desert One, and others, had revealed
serious systemic flaws in the organization of the Department of Defense. One of the most glaring weaknesses was
the lack of power of the Joint Chiefs and particularly the
lack of power of the chairman, leaving him as little more
than an arbiter of the conflicting views of his colleagues,
merely the person who had to present a watered-down
consensus to the Secretary of Defense and the President.
So the Goldwater-Nichols Defense Reorganization Act
had stripped power from the individual service secretaries
and their military heads of service and vested it in the
Joint Chiefs of Staff, and particularly in the person of the
chairman himself. Now the chairman had direct and unprecedented access to the Secretary of Defense and the
President and was, in every sense of the word, the most
important and most visible military man in the nation.
Campbell had aspired to this position for the four decades
since his graduation from the U.S. Military Academy at
West Point and he envisioned this final assignment as the
crowning achievement of his distinguished military career.

But Howard Campbell was not satisfied—he was terrified. A visceral, all-encompassing terror gripped him, a
terror far greater than that which he had felt as a company
commander in Vietnam, on the front lines of the Cold
War in Germany and Korea, during skirmishes in Gre-

nada and Panama, or even during the "great encircle-
ment" during Desert Storm when his forces almost outran
their logistics support and opened themselves up to counterattack by the Iraqi army. The terror he felt had nothing
to do with men in battle, but was the result of the profound changes the President was making in the U.S. military.

President Taylor Calhoun had campaigned on a popu-
list platform that included sweeping societal changes, including unprecedented changes in the U.S. military.
Vignettes from the campaign were still vivid in Campbell's
mind almost three years after the election:

"Senator Calhoun, now that the Cold War is over, what
are your views on our security arrangements and your
views on the role of our military forces?"

The question by the *Wall Street Journal* reporter gave
the then-ranking member of the Senate Armed Services
Committee the desired opening to hammer away at many
of his key themes.

"While the Cold War has passed into history we have
another war to fight, a war for economic survival. We
need to restructure our military to help us win that war.
Certainly our overall military force structure will decrease.
I envision a total force about half its size, and one that is
more representative of all Americans."

"What changes, then, Senator, would that entail?"

"Clearly, profound changes," replied Calhoun. "The
current coterie of military leaders has been vocal about
their opinions regarding gays and lesbians serving in the
military. These citizens have served in the military with
honor throughout our history, and if the current uniformed leaders have trouble dealing with that, then they
need to be replaced with officers who can work with soldiers and sailors of all persuasions."

Calhoun was gathering momentum, and the reporters
were being particularly compliant, recognizing that Calhoun's highly visible service on various military committees and subcommittees had made him the Senate's de
facto expert on military affairs.

The *Washington Post* reporter provided the next opening. "Senator, what new missions do you envision for this

smaller, and more egalitarian, military that you are pro-
posing?"

"We're not going to fight another world war, you know
that. Hell, we can't even find a major regional contingency
that's worth worrying about, now that North Korea has
been isolated by her Pacific Rim neighbors and Iraq and
Iran have bled each other dry in a second major war that
made their first conflict pale by comparison. We can cut
our force structure, well, in half at least, and those troops
don't need to be deployed overseas by the tens of
thousands. There's real work to be done right here at
home. Those Navy amphibious ships with all that room
can tie up in many of our major coastal cities—New York,
Los Angeles, Miami, San Francisco, for example—and
provide a bed and warm meals for our homeless. Those
Army trucks and bulldozers and other heavy equipment
can build roads in some of our rural areas where we still
have good folks driving on dirt roads. And all those Air
Force transport planes ought to be helping our Postal Service move the mail better and help out our park rangers
when they're fightin' fires in inaccessible places. What we
really need is more of a paramilitary force, not the antique
legions that are leftovers from the Cold War. 'Bout the
only truly military action I can envision them doing is finally getting serious about stopping the drugs flowing into
this country from some of our neighbors to the south."

One didn't need to be a Clausewitz to see that Calhoun's proposals would result in an emasculated military
that would become a vehicle for social experimentation
and would not be capable of defending the nation. But
Calhoun believed most of what he was preaching, and the
subject allowed him to demonstrate his expertise in security and military matters and gain the high ground
against his opposition during the campaign for the White
House.

After the election, the special interest groups that had
ensured Calhoun's victory were quick to demand payback
for their support. Without consulting his key military advisors, such as Campbell, President Calhoun crafted proposed legislation that was designed to make the
egalitarian paramilitary force he proposed a reality. Hav-

ing gays and lesbians serve, in numbers, was only the tip of the iceberg. Calhoun would restructure the military to provide something for everyone. Unemployed, unwed mothers could be put to work on military bases, and unused buildings on these bases could become day-care centers for their children. Handicapped citizens shouldn't be denied the right to serve and jobs within the military should be found for them. Inner-city youths needed jobs too, and since these youngsters had such a disadvantaged background, they shouldn't be subjected to the full rigors of military discipline, but should be shepherded along with a "softer" approach. Furthermore, he had directed all segments of the Executive Branch, from Interior, to Commerce, to Treasury, and many subagencies, from FEMA, to the EPA, to the BLM, to come up with aggressive plans to utilize military forces to help them in their daily operations. Across the board, these agencies, their budgets constrained by a burgeoning federal debt, were eager to take advantage of this "free" assistance offered by the military.

This, then, was Howard Campbell's nightmare. Profound and unprecedented social and structural changes to the U.S. military that the President, basking in a solid electoral majority immediately after the presidential election, was pushing through a Congress dominated by his party. This was the inexorable force he was determined to derail.

As the last of the Joint Chiefs settled into his plush leather chair, General Campbell cleared his throat. "Gentlemen! You know why we are here. We have an opportunity to take a really proactive role in the anti-drug war. I've charged the head of SouthCom, General Charlie Walters, to draw up a plan to push this along. Dan, tell us what Charlie has in mind."

"Mr. Chairman, General Walters thinks that he can put a big dent in the drug traffic coming out of Central America, maybe totally disrupt it for up to a year or more," replied Admiral Dan Bell, the JCS vice chairman. Bell had that rugged look of an old sea dog, short in stature but tough, with close-cropped red hair and freckles that looked somehow menacing, his face lean and leathered from countless hours on the bridges of Navy ships.

Campbell swiveled in his massive chair, thinking of his predecessors in this job, his personal and professional heroes, wondering if any of them would have made such a bold stroke. He dared not make eye contact with Dan Bell because he might reveal what was the only thing he found distasteful about what he was doing—he had to lie to his fellow Joint Chiefs, lie to his fellow officers who, collectively, had served their nation and supported and defended the Constitution for almost two centuries. Only a cause that could decide the fate of the nation could make him do this.

Admiral Dan Bell continued, "Mr. Chairman, SouthCom, General Walters, has an outstanding feel for the dynamics in Latin America. He believes that the time is right to move against the Maradona drug cartel."

"Why now?" asked Campbell.

"As you know, Mr. Chairman," continued Admiral Bell, "General Walters has been tracking the drug problem ever since he was J-3—the Operations Director—here with the Joint Chiefs. He senses a great opportunity here. As he sees it, Maradona has been systematically wiping out many of the small drug suppliers from Yucatán down to Panama. Seems that, as he's been doing that, he's been going into a bit of a defensive stance, consolidating most of his people, weapons, drugs, and supplies at his ranch on the Polara Mesa. Not usually a good move business-wise, but he's worried about the small and midsize guys lashing back. He also figures a dormant period will drive up the street price and set him up for huge profits down the line. Charlie figures that we have maybe a month or two, three tops, before he breaks out of this fallback position and resumes his normal routine again, pushing the large supply of drugs he's hoarding north up into California and Texas. That's why he's anxious to strike against Maradona soon."

Campbell continued to question his right-hand man, wanting it to appear that his decision to move forward was not already a foregone conclusion. "What kind of risks does Charlie see if we go forward with this?"

"Really minimal, Mr. Chairman. His informers tell him that Maradona has stashed away incredible amounts of drugs and the largest cache of weapons we have ever heard about, but that he has just a few people around him—he has the rest of them out setting up new markets, recruiting new runners, that sort of thing. Costa Rica is doing little to deter him. Although the Ortiz administration has gone on record denouncing all of the drug cartels, there's not much that they can do, and most of what they seem to be doing is for show anyway. Maradona seems to have a cozy arrangement with the local gendarmes and they treat his estate almost like a presidential palace, denying access to anyone who even approaches it from afar—let alone gets near enough to pose a real threat."

"Fine, but how would the Ortiz government feel about an intervention by a third party?" asked Campbell.

"That's really State Department turf, Mr. Chairman," offered Air Force Chief of Staff General Hank Paxton. The tall, thin Paxton, with his steel-gray eyes, eagle-beak nose, and silver hair, looked every bit the warrior who would rather be flying a tactical jet than sitting in a meeting room.

"That's fine, Hank, but they're on board with this too. Their hands are tied, but they interpose no objection to our running with it—off the record, of course," replied the chairman tersely, letting Paxton know that now was not the time for interruptions. The knowing smiles of the other Joint Chiefs in response to this slam of the State Department told Campbell he was winning them over. He wanted to keep the briefing on track. "Please continue, Dan."

"They'd like to do something about Maradona, but they don't really have the wherewithal. He and his cartel are giving the country an increasingly visible international black eye. They'd just as soon be rid of him but lack the forces and the popular mandate to do it themselves. If some outside force made it a fait accompli, they could have the best of both worlds—put on a public face that they were glad their country was rid of the drug cartel, but not encourage the drug lords to go on an assassination spree against public officials.

"They're not shy about that assassination stuff, are they, Walt?" said Campbell, turning toward Army Chief of Staff Walt Prestridge.

The heavyset general cleared his throat. He was definitely one of Campbell's favorites. Big, almost hulking, with the frame of an aging athlete, a bald head, and bland features, Prestridge presented no threat to Campbell—perhaps that's why the chairman liked him so much.

"No Mr. Chairman, I can see why they're hesitant to act—and why they'd welcome our taking the lead," he replied, smiling self-assuredly, knowing that his response was exactly what his boss wanted to hear.

"Well, Charlie has done his usual thorough job looking at all facets of this situation—and he has the best instincts of any soldier I know. Maybe we shouldn't stand in the way of something that could have such a big payoff. After all, our Commander in Chief has made it clear that this is his number one military priority."

Campbell could not help but congratulate himself on how well he was weaving this plan. He had played a believable devil's advocate to the other Joint Chiefs in questioning General Charlie Walters's plan. He had given the go-ahead only after the virtual insistence of Admiral Dan Bell. None of the other Joint Chiefs could guess that this evolving plan had been put together by Campbell and Walters months earlier. Nor could they guess what else lay in store and how complete their planning had been.

The plan was born almost coincidentally after a round of golf at the Army-Navy Country Club in Arlington, Virginia. There, on a warm, sunny Saturday morning, sitting on the balcony of the golf clubhouse looking out on the well-kept acres of the club, two decades-long friends rehashed their golf game and their years of service—almost three-quarters of a century between the two of them. Of course, it might not have been, except for a split-second judgment made by Cadet Campbell almost four decades ago at West Point.

Cadets First Class Howard Campbell and Neil Beattie were in charge of a squad of first-year cadets, Charles Walters among them, who were marching off their demerits for various minor offenses committed at the Academy. Campbell was captain of the squash team and had taken a bit of a big-brotherly interest in Walters, who was the star of the plebe, or freshman, squash team and who seemed destined to help the Academy rebuild its struggling squash team, which had lost to archrival Navy in three of the last four years. When Walters arrived in formation at the appointed hour, Beattie was in a foul mood and had gotten in the hapless plebe's face.

"Mister, you look like shit. You're a disgrace to the Corps of Cadets," said Beattie to the heavily perspiring Walters.

"Sir, yes sir." Walters knew this was the only acceptable response in such cases.

"You look like a bum. I'm going to run your dead ass out of here. Why do you look like a bag of shit?" continued Beattie, clearly enjoying haranguing Walters in front of Campbell. Beattie wasn't a jock, and the opportunity to abuse a jock in front of Campbell—especially a squash jock—was just too good to pass up.

"No excuse, sir," replied Walters, who was beginning to wilt under the interrogation. Campbell looked on with some concern, but was letting Beattie handle it for now, knowing that putting first-year cadets under enormous strain was the essence of the rite of passage at West Point.

"There is no excuse for you, you maggot. Why, I'll bet you haven't even polished your belt buckle. You know I told you to do that the last time you were here and told you I'd fry your ass if you didn't do it. How's twenty demerits sound, mister?"

Walters had polished the belt buckle recently, but not today. But he was wilting under the barrage of epithets and saw yet another weekend of these grillings if he racked up another twenty demerits. For a split second he lost his composure and thought he'd stretch the truth a bit. "Yes sir, I have polished it."

"You what? You want me to believe that you polished that gross piece of shit? What did you polish it with?"

"With brasso, sir."

With that, Beattie grabbed the buckle and literally ripped it off Walters's belt and pulled it up to his nose.

"I can't smell any damn brasso, can you?" And with that, he shoved the buckle under Walters's nose.

"No sir, I mean, I think so, sir, I mean . . ."

Beattie leaped at the opening. "So did you brasso it or are you lying?"

"No, I did, sir, I—"

"Then there'll be a wet cloth with brasso down in your room, right, *Mr. Walters*?" The interrogation was now intense and Campbell sensed that Walters had lied. But the kid had not done it with malice aforethought, he had just folded up under an intense, one-sided barrage by the crazed Beattie. It didn't seem fair and this was a hell of a way to lose a good squash player—for lying was an honor offense that called for immediate dismissal from West Point. Campbell knew that if there wasn't a wet cloth with brasso on it sitting in Walters's room, the kid was as good as gone within days.

"Yes sir, there will be, sir, yes sir," stammered Walters.

"Well, I don't think so, mister, but I'm sure as hell going to find out." Beattie was on a roll now, clearly playing to the crowd, a shocked and completely cowered group of hapless plebes who seemed to be trying to edge away from Walters and away from the now-seething Beattie.

"Tell you what, classmate," said Campbell, "I'll head on down to his room and have a look-see myself. Then we'll know if he's telling the truth."

Beattie wanted to make the final discovery himself, but the much bigger Campbell did not phrase it as a request and his body language conveyed the idea that he intended to do it—and that was that.

Beattie recovered as best he could. "I think your ass is grass, son. In about five minutes, Cadet Campbell is going to confirm that you're a damn liar!"

"Sir, no sir," responded Walters, now almost on the verge of tears.

Howard Campbell turned the corner and headed for Walters's room. Beattie was really being a total ass about this. Walters had always been a totally honest kid as long as Campbell had known him. Hell, anyone could foul up under the pressure Beattie was putting on him. Why did that geek Beattie single him out? He hoped he'd find evidence that the belt buckle had been shined. He continued down the long hallway, looking for Walters's room. Here it was, Walters and Currie. Campbell entered the room, looked around, and found his cleaning gear in the proper place—everything at West Point was always in the proper place—and it was bone dry. Walters was finished. Then some instinct—maybe it was humanity, maybe it was justice, maybe it was an athlete's camaraderie—overcame Cadet First Class Howard Campbell and he reached for the brasso and splashed it liberally over the cleaning cloth, dropping some on the desk for good measure. There, that's done, he thought. Now I've done it and I can't go back on it.

As he returned to the formation, Campbell walked directly up to Beattie. "Looks like this kid told the truth, but he got more brasso on his desk than on the belt. That's probably why it looks like hell. Have a look yourself if you like." Then, turning to Walters to keep up the facade, he said, "Your room looks like crap, mister. Take ten demerits."

"Sir, yes sir," stammered the relieved Walters. His head was swimming with a mixture of disbelief and relief. He hadn't brassoed the belt, but Cadet Campbell had said he found a wet cloth with brasso on it. Could he have gone to the wrong room? Or could he be helping Beattie bait him?

Beattie turned to Campbell and said, "Well, Mr. Campbell, you seem to have taken over. Dismiss the formation." He stormed off, disappointed that he had not been able to administer his own brand of rough justice. After he left, Walters looked at Campbell.

"Sir, I, well . . ."

"That's all, mister. You're dismissed, with ten demerits."

"Yes sir, but—"

"I said you're dismissed, mister. Get the shit out of your ears. Now haul your ass back to your room and clean up that shithole you live in."

Howard Campbell knew that Walters wanted to thank him, for Campbell had put his own career in jeopardy by going way out on a limb for him. He didn't know why he had done it, he just had. Several times in the next few weeks, usually during squash practice, Walters came up to him and tried to thank him, but Campbell would never let the conversation get started. Finally, late one afternoon, when they were alone in the musty confines of the dingy squash courts, Walters blurted out, "Sir, thank you for sticking your neck out for me."

Campbell stared directly at him, penetrating him with his eyes. "Cadet Walters, nothing happened, do you hear me? Nothing happened. And as long as either of us is at the Academy, don't ever bring this up again."

"Sir, yes sir." And with that, the incident was closed. But what was not closed was Walters's loyalty to Campbell, a loyalty that was to sustain itself over decades as they both rose through the ranks to more and more important positions in the Army.

Now, as they enjoyed the warm sun on the clubhouse deck, the two men reminisced about their days at West Point. The cares and the day-to-day pressures of the Pentagon seemed to drift away. Their careers secure and their friendship firm, Campbell decided to stretch the limits of Walters's loyalty to him.

"Charlie, we sure as hell have watched things unravel over the past three years, haven't we?" Campbell looked not at Walters, but over the beautiful eighteenth fairway of Army-Navy's well-manicured golf course.

"I would say that we have, Mr. Chairman." Even though their friendship was deep, Walters insisted on using Campbell's official title and referring to him as chairman. It was an action designed to honor his colleague and his high position—as well as acknowledge their long and abiding friendship.

"Do you think that we are in a position to help put things back on track?"

"I don't know. I sure as hell don't feel comfortable just sitting back and watching things go to hell in a handbasket. I don't know exactly what we can do, though."

"Well, Charlie"—Campbell paused for dramatic effect—"perhaps we do have the power to do something."

"Mr. Chairman, I'm not really following you on this

one." Walters's body language told Campbell that he was interested and that he should go on.

"Charlie," continued Campbell, now leaning closer to his friend, "you see all of the changes that the Calhoun administration has brought to our military. Hell, we haven't really had a voice in many decisions over the past three years. We're heading toward a paramilitary at best, maybe something less if this continues. Can you imagine where we'll be as a fighting force with *five* more years of this administration?" Campbell had a mixture of alarm, frustration, and resignation in his voice.

"The good news is that the polls aren't real favorable for the President. Maybe next November the country will vote for a change," replied Walters with some forced optimism in his voice.

"We can't wait that long and we sure as hell can't take the chance that he'll be back for another term." Campbell leaned even closer to Walters and gazed intently into his eyes. In a barely audible whisper, he said, "Charlie, we've taken an oath to defend the Constitution, not to carry the Calhoun administration as it emasculates the military that we've worked so hard all our careers to build into the world's most potent fighting force. It's unconscionable, Charlie, *unconscionable,* for us not to act!"

Walters actually felt himself moving back in his chair, away from Campbell. He too was extremely dissatisfied with the Calhoun presidency, but until now he had never heard such thoughts uttered, especially not by the nation's highest-ranking military man. "But Mr. Chairman, surely you're not talking about taking any overt action against the President. I mean—my God—we can't, we—" Walters stammered.

"Charlie, of course not. We could never do that, would never do that. *We* won't take any action against the administration; it will take action against itself. We just need to present the opportunity—and maybe cause some other events to happen—and the American people will decide that they've had quite enough of the Calhoun presidency and particularly its meddling with military matters. I need your help, Charlie, yours above anyone else's. Are you with me?"

"Mr. Chairman, you have my undivided attention."

With that, Campbell began to lay out his plan.

CHAPTER 6

LIEUTENANT LAURA PETERS WAS HANDLING HER RE-
sponsibilities as assistant duty officer at the U.S. Southern
Command headquarters with the same professional dispatch that distinguished her service as an intel officer in
the Intelligence Directorate, or J-2 section, of this large
and complex staff.

Headquartered at Quarry Heights, near the Pacific entrance to the Panama Canal in the Republic of Panama,
SouthCom drew many of the best and brightest officers
from all the military services. Service on a Unified Command staff, especially one that was responsible for all U.S.
military activities in South America and Central America
south of Mexico, was a significant career milestone. Laura
Peters had eagerly sought assignment to this important
command, and she was already making her mark as a
bright, professional junior officer. She hadn't completed
all of her duty officer qualifications yet, but she was confident she could deal with anything that could come up
during her watch.

The SouthCom duty officer, Air Force Lieutenant Colonel George Beall, was near the end of his three-year tour
and was eager to pass the responsibilities to the younger,
talented, and strikingly attractive Navy lieutenant.

"Peters, have you made it through this evening's message traffic yet?" asked Beall.

"Not yet, Colonel, it's a bit heavier than usual. I'm moving through it, though."

"Need to have you start tending the bat phone too.
That goes with the territory," said Beall. Even after innumerable hours working with her, Beall had to keep
himself from staring at Laura. Even in those unflattering
Navy khakis and with her hair put up to comply with Navy

grooming standards, Laura Peters was a genuine beauty. Not a scrawny, half-starved type, but at a full five feet ten inches and a solid 120 pounds, she had the poise of the athlete and the grace of a dancer.

Lieutenant Peters looked at the bat phone, the most important piece of communications gear on the large, curved duty desk crammed with phones, screens, encoding equipment, and the like. The SouthCom watch officers had at their command a dazzling array of communications equipment, displays, and monitors that could connect them with literally any other military command center and display the disposition of forces anywhere within the millions of square miles that comprised their area of responsibility.

"No problem here, Colonel. I know you have some calls to make to set up your move back to the States."

While her growing duties on this watch team might have made others feel harried, Peters reflected on her good fortune. First, her assignment to SouthCom, one of the more important U.S. Unified Commands, put her at the forefront of her nation's military and diplomatic efforts. Her assignment to Watch Team Bravo, the most undermanned watch team on the staff, meant that she had far more responsibility than her fellow Navy lieutenants or Army and Air Force captains. Finally, her watch section posting with Lieutenant Colonel Beall, a competent officer but one who was already focused on his next assignment to Andrews Air Force Base, allowed her to become very involved in issues that officers with twice as much time in the service had only passing knowledge of. For Peters, it was an opportunity for professional growth that might not come her way again.

It was not surprising that Laura loved what she was doing. The daughter and only child of a Navy chief petty officer, Laura had been the apple of her parents' and particularly her father's eye. Master Chief Donald Peters had risen through the ranks as far as he could, but he always wanted to be an officer. That goal, unfortunately, had eluded him. When it was clear that his marriage would produce no sons, he regaled Laura with the opportunities that beckoned in the Navy. The master chief knew enough about how the Navy worked and what it looked

for in its officers—and particularly its need to recruit more
women officers—that he groomed his daughter throughout high school to make her a shoe-in for winning a Navy
ROTC scholarship. Laura had thrived at the University
of Virginia, earning top grades, serving as a class officer,
and lettering in cross-country, squash, and tennis at the
prestigious Charlottesville school. Sensing that the Navy
was still not enlightened enough to really accept women
as equal partners commanding ships and aircraft squadrons, she opted for the intelligence field upon graduation,
correctly surmising that it would provide a more level professional playing field and afford her the opportunity to
prove herself and advance through the ranks. She would
make retired Master Chief Peters proud indeed.

In her eight years since graduation she had sought out
only the toughest assignments, usually registering firsts,
breaking ground where female officers had not gone before. Her assignment at SouthCom was the best yet,
though. Now Lieutenant Colonel Beall was allowing her
to monitor the bat phone, the command's euphemism for
the direct line with the Joint Chiefs of Staff in the Pentagon. This line kept the SouthCom staff connected with
the Joint Chiefs twenty-four hours a day and was used for
only the most important matters. During the normal
working day it was forwarded directly into the offices of
the SouthCom commander and his deputy. After hours,
the duty watch team took the initial call from the Joint
Chiefs and then were responsible for locating the
SouthCom commander or deputy commander if the importance of the issue warranted his immediate attention.

Peters was observing the many Watch Team Bravo soldiers, sailors, and airmen update status and enter data into
various computer consoles. She was not thinking about
anything in particular when she was startled by a ringing.
It was the bat phone.

"SouthCom headquarters, staff watch officer, Lieutenant Peters. How may I help you?" answered Laura as she
picked up the bat phone on the first ring. Lieutenant Colonel Beall was out of the command center and she was in
charge.

"Please hold for Colonel Keating," said the voice at

the other end of the line, obviously a Pentagon secretary who was placing a call for her boss.

"Colonel Warren Keating here, executive assistant for General Campbell. The chairman wishes to speak with General Walters."

Peters was energized. She was one horse-holder and one intercom button away from talking to the chairman of the Joint Chiefs of Staff. General Walters was not in the headquarters; he was at that moment playing tennis with a very attractive and, as Laura had heard it told, very willing Army nurse. He had let the staff know in no uncertain terms that their games were not to be interrupted.

"Colonel, the general is, ah, not here at this exact moment. I believe that I can reach him if it's an emergency, though."

"Dammit, if it were an emergency I'd damn well tell you," replied Keating. "The chairman wants to talk to him now, period. Do you think you people have the technology to make that happen . . . *Lieutenant*?" He lingered on the word to punctuate the significant difference in their rank and position.

"Right away, sir." Peters tried not to sound like she was losing her composure. Just stay cool and sound professional, she told herself.

"How soon shall I tell the chairman he should be expecting the call?" Keating's tone had become icy.

"Within ten minutes, sir, you can count on it."

Laura's mind raced. Years of military education and a succession of tough assignments, but nothing really prepared you for moments like this. You had to go on instincts. I'm running the watch, she thought. I have to take the general the portable bat phone. As she was casting about for who was the next most junior watchstander to turn things over to, Lieutenant Colonel Beall returned to the command center. "Got to find General Walters. You got it back, Colonel," she said as she raced out into the parking lot and jumped in the closest staff vehicle she could get to, a white Cherokee four-by-four.

As she drove the short distance to the compound tennis courts, Laura thought the situation a bit odd. It was after normal working hours, Washington knew that. There was no crisis going on—as an intelligence officer, she more than anyone else would have been alerted to that sort of thing. Yet the chairman of the Joint Chiefs of Staff just had to talk with her boss and she had some mad dog colonel on the phone ready to bite her head off if she didn't make it happen immediately.

As Laura approached the lushly landscaped officers' tennis courts, she was met with a scene that she was all too familiar with. The tennis part of the game had evidently just finished and General Walters was going through some more affectionate moves with his partner. This was a well-known scenario at SouthCom. Those in the know on the staff had dubbed Walters the "affectionate commander." Laura recalled with some revulsion that the general had tried on more than one occasion to be more than just a boss with her after their friendly lunch-hour squash games, but thus far she had been successful at steering the conversation away from that area and in having to dash off somewhere. It was getting tougher, but Laura tried to look at this effort as just another professional challenge—elude the general but use enough diplomacy to not come off as some scared little bunny.

That problem paled in comparison to the immediacy of the current situation. She had to get the general on the phone with JCS in a hurry, but she didn't want to anger him by intruding in his romantic maneuverings. She couldn't slink around behind the bird of paradise plants and banana trees ringing the tennis courts, hoping against hope that the general would stop rubbing his partner's shoulders and begin playing tennis again. She decided in an instant that only a direct approach would work, and as she got within fifty feet of the courts she downshifted the Cherokee, revved the engine, and then slammed on the brakes, screeching to a halt only five feet from the fence around the courts. This noisy approach gave the general and his partner sufficient time to back away from each other and at least appear to be just changing sides of the net.

"Lieutenant Peters, is that you? You trying to destroy government property driving like that?"

"Evening, General; evening, *Major*," Peters said pointedly. "General, I just fielded a call from Colonel Keating, General Campbell's EA, and sir, he indicated that the chairman wanted to talk with you right now." She hoped her professionalism not only impressed her commander, but differentiated her from the other officer, who had not been fending off the general to Laura's satisfaction.

Walters seemed to take this in stride. "Well, Lieutenant, if the chairman wants to talk to one of his Unified Commanders, let's make it happen. Do you have the box?"

"Yes sir!" Peters, the picture of efficiency, was already holding the portable, secure phone and offered to place the call for the general.

"No need, Lieutenant, I'm a big boy. Just let me have it."

Generals never do this sort of stuff for themselves, thought Peters, as General Walters took the phone and turned the secure key. It just doesn't add up. And what added up even less was the snippet of conversation she overheard as General Walters moved to the far reaches of the tennis courts away from the two women.

"Great job, Howard ... We've got to make it move along ... I'll take point from here ... This is our operation."

As the sun eased down into the Pacific, igniting the ocean in a dazzling display of brilliant colors, Laura's curiosity was aroused by these strange actions. Was it all so strange, or was she just too new and naive to understand the nuances of this Unified Command? She hoped she would catch on soon.

CHAPTER 7

"ALL RIGHT, GENTLEMEN, ALL RIGHT! LET'S SIT DOWN and *GET STARTED!*" General Howard Campbell did not usually have to be this insistent to bring a meeting of the Joint Chiefs to order—but these were far from usual cir-

cumstances. As his fellow officers finally settled down into
their chairs in the JCS conference room, they all looked
directly at the chairman.

Had he been a lesser man, or one with a less well-
developed ego, Campbell would surely have withered in
the face of the enormity of his task. Everything he was
about to do would have to be done while lying to his five
colleagues so convincingly they would not only believe
him, but be enthused about the plan that he was about to
present. Furthermore, he had to be the bridge between
the President and General Charlie Walters, convincing the
President to throw his prestige behind an operation that
Charlie had predesigned to fail. No one else could pull
this off, he thought—no one but him.

General Ken Rainbow, commandant of the Marine
Corps, spoke first. Rainbow looked every bit the model
Marine. Ramrod straight, seemingly without an ounce of
fat on his tall, lanky frame, his extremely close-cropped
hair and crisp, starched uniform conveyed the perfect warrior image. "Mr. Chairman, how serious is the President
about really stopping this drug flow?"

"I have every indication that he is deadly serious and
that he's prepared to commit the right resources to do the
job," replied Campbell.

Admiral Boomer Curtis, chief of naval operations,
leaned forward to speak. Curtis was the tallest of the Joint
Chiefs, and the oldest. He was the scholar among them,
and his pale complexion and thick, horn-rimmed glasses
made him look more like a college professor than a four-
star officer.

"We've been fighting this drug war for a decade now,
but the commitment's not been there," said Curtis.
"Every ship I send down there I take out of hide, should
be off doing something more important, not chopped to
the JTF drug czar for months on end, only to come away
with absolutely zero to show for it."

"He's right, you know," said General Hank Paxton, Air
Force chief of staff. "We've been logging thousands of
AWACs hours each year out of our base at Howard with
virtually nothing to show for it. There's just no funding

stream—and I don't have to tell you it's not getting any easier to scrape up the assets."

Campbell anticipated their dissatisfaction, which provided him with just the opening he needed to present the plan.

"I know the President recognizes that the efforts in the past have been halfhearted at best. Remember, he campaigned to stop the flow of drugs, and after three years in office he recognizes that attacking the demand side doesn't work as well as all of the social engineers say it will . . . or at least doesn't work as fast as he'd like it to. Therefore, he's come back to us, but this time with a real commitment to win this fight. No halfway measures here. We should seize this opportunity and go into this in a big way. I've already turned Charlie Walters at SouthCom on to put plans in place for a big-impact operation that can let the drug cartels know the world's only superpower is not going to be nibbling around the edges anymore—we're going to win this one."

Campbell's pitch was winning over his fellow Joint Chiefs. They were all presiding over the most precipitous downsizing of the U.S. military since the end of World War II. The peace dividend had turned out to be fool's gold. With no more Soviet superpower to face and to drive military requirements, troops and equipment were being slashed. However, the new world order was anything but ordered, and very untidy regional crises, from revolutions to famines, required the response of the U.S. military. Forces were being stretched thinner than they had ever been. Soldiers, sailors, and airmen were enduring longer and more frequent deployments and equipment was wearing out. Then, perversely, when the distant crises had abated, the public either quickly forgot about them, or questioned the military for *its* decision to become engaged in such faraway places. Therefore, the opportunity to focus on a cause that had the strong backing of the administration, and presumably Congress, was something that should be a twenty-four-carat opportunity.

"I'm still a little skeptical myself," replied General Walt Prestridge, Army chief of staff. "This all sounds fine right now. But once we've gone into this in a big way, how do we ensure that the President will still put the power of his office behind us, and not move on to the next thing on his agenda, leaving us holding the bag again?"

His fellow Army officer had worked with Howard Campbell long enough to pick up the not-so-subtle hints that the chairman had been dropping over the past several weeks. Campbell had told Prestridge that he was going to present this plan today, and that, if Prestridge would raise this issue from the Army's point of view, then he would be able to nominate another Army officer to lead this important, high-visibility operation. Congress might legislate against interservice rivalry with laws like Goldwater-Nichols, but service ties ran deeper than a scrap of paper generated by congressmen with more and more tenuous ties to the military.

"Well, I think we should give the Commander in Chief the courtesy of assuming that he'll stay the course, but you're right, Walt, maybe if he had more of a personal stake in it—perhaps if we let him have some ownership in who the leader of whatever operation we come up with—he will be more inclined to stay the course once the operation gets under way," replied Campbell.

Howard Campbell had also planted the right seed with his vice chairman, who, in turn, moved Campbell's agenda forward exactly as he wanted it moved. Admiral Dan Bell—who, as the longest-serving member of the Joint Chiefs and as the Navy's former head of legislative affairs, had worked closely with then-Senator Taylor Calhoun for years and knew more about the President than any of the other Joint Chiefs—said, "Mr. Chairman, the President has always taken a keen interest in the career of Brigadier General Ashley Lovelace, always asking if he's being given important assignments. But hell, I don't even know where he's assigned now."

Smiling with satisfaction at the way his plan was coming together, Campbell looked at Walt Prestridge and asked the question he already knew the answer to. "I don't know either, Dan. Where is he, Walt?"

"He's heading up Defense Mapping Agency now, not a particularly high-vis job—not surprising that the Navy's lost track of him. Come to think of it, I don't think the

President was really pleased to see him assigned there, but hell, Mr. Chairman, Ashley's no Clausewitz and with DMA in Washington it kept him available for the White House social scene. The Army's been promising the President that we're looking for something better for him."

Prestridge knew his subordinates well. As Army chief of staff, he knew that Brigadier General Ashley Lovelace had been the President's college classmate at Washington and Lee University. Lovelace was from a fine southern family and Washington and Lee University was where the fine sons of these fine families were sent. Initially, Lovelace had no particular interest in a military career, but the ambience of a university that had been founded by the father of his country and that had had the revered General Robert E. Lee as its president had its effect on a southern gentleman with no other particular ambitions at the time. Perhaps more profoundly, his graduation at the height of the Vietnam conflict had ended his draft deferment and he surmised that Army life as an officer would be more tolerable than life as a ground soldier. He was commissioned a second lieutenant after OCS at Fort Bragg.

It wasn't that Lovelace was a bad officer; he just was a very unconventional one. He didn't fit the mold of his contemporaries, the majority of whom had attended one of the military's service academies, where one presumably was dedicated to a military career at entry as a teenager. Fluent in three languages, an accomplished pianist, his principal hobby was carving wooden duck decoys. He just didn't fit in that well with his fellow officers.

Lovelace saw brief service in Vietnam but no significant action. He experienced a routine rise through the ranks during the Cold War, when promotion opportunities were such that an officer with a good education who applied himself just a bit and avoided controversy could count on being promoted with some regularity. The Army offered a comfortable lifestyle and he particularly enjoyed working with the common soldiers, rough but honest and genuine men whom he had been insulated from during his formative years. He had no driving ambition to enter another line of work—so he let himself be carried along into a de facto career. He kept in contact with his friend Taylor Calhoun through the normal course of events, with the families often vacationing together. Just when Lovelace was reaching the point in his career where he had been promoted to a natural, non-Academy glass-ceiling and as far as his own intrinsic talents could take him, Calhoun was becoming a force on the Senate Armed Services Committee and could nudge the system a bit to keep his friend moving up the career ladder.

It was unsurprising, then, that Prestridge was not excited to see such a different kind of officer lead such an important mission, but the overriding importance of keeping the President interested in, and committed to, this operation was the more critical issue—and this seemed to be precisely what the chairman wanted too. If he languished at the dead-end assignment at DMA, he would be a one-star forever, which was certain to alienate the President. "Maybe with a strong staff, Lovelace could do a competent job," he said.

"So you're thinking that if we pulled him out of a dead-end job and picked him to lead a major anti-drug operation, even though he has no real experience in this area, it would get the President involved and keep him involved?" probed Campbell.

"Sure, and if we can get the President to *ask us* to pick him, so much the better," replied Prestridge.

The nodding acquiescence of the other Joint Chiefs to this idea reassured Campbell that he had pulled this one off just the way he had planned it. Now he needed to ensure that the President did exactly as Campbell wanted him to do. Howard Campbell was confident that he could pull this off.

CHAPTER 8

YES! CHIEF RICK HOLDEN SMILED WITH SATISFACTION at his handiwork. He had just spent over three hours repairing a delicate piece of crypto gear—the equipment that enabled the ship to code and decode classified radio transmissions—in *Coronado*'s radio shack. Repairing this antiquated gear would be a challenge in even the most modern and well-equipped industrial laboratory, but here in the crowded confines of *Coronado*'s tiny radio shack, with its small, cluttered workbench and dim lighting, and with the constant movement of the ship, this kind of sensitive repair—the Navy called it "micro-miniature repair"—was especially challenging. It was right for Rick Holden to smile with satisfaction.

Petty Officer Second Class Joe Reid walked back into the small shop to talk with Holden. "Hey Chief, looks like you've finished the job," said Reid.

"Sure have, Joe, and it checks out on the bench!" replied Holden with enthusiasm. It would be nice to just do his job, he thought, and blend in with everyone else, but that could never be. He could never forget about his past or about why he was sent here. For Commander Ben Malgrave and his crew; Rick's platoon leader, Ensign Bob Kemp; and all aboard *Coronado* naturally assumed that Chief Petty Officer Rick Holden had come up through the ranks as a Navy SEAL and was now at a normal career progression point as the assistant platoon leader for his unit. But there was nothing natural or normal about his situation. Rick had been wearing a Navy uniform for only two years and didn't know whether he would be wearing it for two more days, two more years, or twenty more years. It all depended on what the Agency wanted.

Rick reflected on the strange turn of events that had

brought him here. Growing up in Chicago, Rick was the son of hardworking, second-generation immigrants. His Polish father and Czech mother had instilled good, solid working-class values into their firstborn. Rick was the model for his two brothers and three sisters. Altar boy, Eagle Scout, all-star varsity tennis player at Bishop Francis High School, Rick had earned a scholarship to the prestigious University of Virginia.

At UVA Rick had been an outstanding student and superb tennis player. However, midway through his senior year, his father died of a massive heart attack. Thoughts of graduate school, even with a partial scholarship, went by the wayside as his mother struggled to make ends meet and still give his younger brothers and sisters a chance at college too. Rick started attending job fairs held regularly on campus.

The CIA had been the last thing on Rick's mind, but the recruiter, attracted by Rick's all-around performance— grades, athletics, student government—as well as the language proficiency he'd inherited from his parents, was persistent, and Rick agreed to take the placement test. He scored very well, and one thing led to another and soon he was off to Langley. Rick excelled in his training program—this type of work really seemed to be right up his alley. He had high grades going into the final phase of his program and was looking forward to having his pick of assignments.

The Agency already had a specific plan for him, though. Initially it bewildered him, but after some thought it made sense, and it sounded exciting.

The Cold War was winding down and Eastern Europe was breaking away from communism and the iron hand of the Soviet Union. Groups within many of those countries needed support from the West, but most importantly, they needed to communicate whenever they needed to. Could someone travel freely throughout those countries, someone who had a legitimate reason for being there and who was conversant in many of those languages?

Yes. The satellite tennis tour was becoming well-established in the former Warsaw Pact countries, and playing on the tour would provide a perfect cover for Rick. He was a good but not overpowering tennis player, so he would be invited to almost every tournament, but would probably lose in one of the early rounds, thus leaving him ample time for his missions before the tour pushed on to the next city the following week.

The Agency trained Rick thoroughly for his assignments, which were to carry in and set up communications gear for the various groups to talk to the West. Always encumbered with what looked like a half-dozen tennis rackets and bulky bags for many pairs of tennis shoes, warm-up gear, shorts, shirts, socks, and the like, Rick had ample opportunity to transport the equipment. He was successful—and in great demand—and the Agency trained him on increasingly sophisticated gear as he supplied more and more important groups. His tennis fortunes continued to improve too, and he actually started advancing further than expected in some tournaments. On one or two occasions he was doing so well he had to actually "tank" matches to avoid going too far in the tournament and not having enough time to accomplish his mission.

The Agency watched Rick become increasingly proficient at his craft; then, when they felt that the time was right, they assigned him his most difficult mission yet. He was to set up a communications network for a breakaway group in the Ukraine. The group was under intense surveillance by the government, but his handlers thought Rick and the local group could finesse it. They were wrong. Just as they were making their final connections for a primary transmission station, they were discovered. One of the group panicked and shot and killed a security policeman who had discovered them. The full force of the government tracked all of them down—including Rick—and considered executing the lot. Only through exceptional diplomacy—and a wealth of favors being called in—was Rick able to be quickly repatriated to the United States.

It hadn't been his fault, and he had performed admirably, but in this sort of business he was instantly too hot. He had to be moved underground immediately and kept there for some time. The Agency worked out a plan for a good cover and devised a way that he could keep his talents sharp for the time in the future when they might want to call on him again. He was too good to just cast off.

CHAPTER 9

CHRISTEN CHAMBERLAIN'S FUNERAL AT SAINT DUN-
stan's Episcopal Church in McLean, Virginia, was a subdued and somber affair. No celebration of her life. No
hopeful sermon about going on to a greater reward after
a life of accomplishment. Christen had simply died too
soon. Family, friends, and scores of schoolmates filled the
small church but those who loved her seemed to want to
get this untidy chore of burying her over and done with
as quickly as possible before resuming their very tidy lives.

But there were others who had a different agenda. Outside the church, the news media were gathered en masse.
Joe Hache's dramatic pictures of Christen had made it to
the front page of the *Washington Star* and had made her
death a rallying cry for the drug war, both inside and outside the Washington beltway. It was a compelling story.
Young, talented, bright, athletic, the daughter of upper-
class parents, dead of a crack cocaine overdose, and in her
cheerleader uniform! It was just too good a story to pass
up and now other reporters had dutifully come to the final
scene of her brief life, hoping to build on this tragic story.

Forbidden to enter the church, the reporters bandied
about their various ideas about how to follow up on the
Christen Chamberlain story. There were fruitful ways to
do the story and some not so fruitful ways. There was not
much leverage in pillorying the girl; with that sweet face
and that damned cheerleader outfit, she was definitely cast
as the victim in this one. Not worth going after the family
either, although there was definitely something missing if
the girl went off to a crack house. How did she get there?
Where did the parents think she was? There was certainly
no value added in bringing in any racial overtones, black
inner-city drug dealers luring upper-class white *children*

to their crack houses. That definitely wouldn't work. Blame the city of Washington? The public had grown tired of that—it was such an easy target. Who, then? Someone *had* to be blamed. They tossed ideas around on the lush green lawn outside the church as they had once tossed around Frisbees in school. It seemed only logical: Why not blame the Calhoun administration? They weren't doing nearly enough!

As the flower-laden casket of Christen Chamberlain was carried out the door of the church, eight strong young schoolmates carrying her, the media snapped picture after picture. The solemn youngsters, the weeping mother. The very upper-class mourners. The understanding reverend. The beautiful church in the background. The pictures would punctuate what the reporters would write in a most dramatic way. Individually and collectively, they could barely wait for the stream of mourners to pass by so that they could rush back to their papers to file their stories. Maybe some of the pictures would be carried in color!

John Carberry of the *Star* was following up on Joe Hache's original story and had some particularly good pictures taken by his camera crew. He looked at the copy he had just pounded out eight hours earlier and smiled in satisfaction. Set in the correct column and flanked by three pictures, left, right, and underneath—one of the flower-laden coffin, one of the slumped body against the crack house wall, and one of Christen taken at a recent Langley High football game, jumping high with her lithe body, perfect teeth, tousled hair, and cheerleader outfit— Carberry knew that he had an impact article. It read:

LANGLEY HIGH SCHOOL CHEERLEADER LATEST VICTIM OF ADMINISTRATION'S DO-NOTHING DRUG POLICY

MCLEAN: Young Christen Chamberlain was buried today, the victim not only of crack cocaine but of the Calhoun administration's toothless "war" on drugs. The victim, an honor student, varsity athlete, and co-captain of the school's award-

winning cheerleading squad, was found dead four
days ago in a crack house in the District, the victim
of an apparent overdose of crack cocaine.

Miss Chamberlain's death is just another in a
series of seemingly innumerable drug-related
deaths in the District and environs. In spite of
abundant campaign rhetoric, the Calhoun
administration has done virtually nothing to stop
the flow of drugs into the country and particularly
into our cities. Miss Chamberlain's death, less than
two miles from the White House, merely serves to
punctuate this lack of action, or even of an
effective game plan. Justice Department figures,
obtained under the Freedom of Information Act,
show that the flow of illegal drugs into the United
States has actually increased during each year of
the Calhoun presidency. When reached for
comment, administration spokesmen replied that
"the administration is doing everything that it can
to stop this scourge."

Two congressional subcommittees, one in the
Senate and the other in the House, will meet later
this month to evaluate all aspects of the
administration's efforts to stop the flow of drugs
into the U.S. It is expected that the subcommittees
will draft legislation requiring the administration
to add teeth to its program or risk losing funding
for various other projects. Further, a recently
released GAO report documents general
mismanagement and, in particular, interagency
conflicts in pursuing the war against drugs.

Carberry's article was just one of many, but the eye-
popping pictures of Christen Chamberlain, first in life and
then in death, made it the most prominent in all the clips
the next morning—clips that were on the most influential
desks in Washington before breakfast. Carberry was already writing follow-up stories and planned to make this
an ongoing series for the paper in the coming months.

In the White House press office, Ray Weaver read Carberry's article with a mixture of resignation and disgust:
resignation that the administration continued to get beat

up on the drug issue, and disgust that the *Star* reporter had used such sensational pictures in this piece. Weaver needed to impress upon the President just how badly such reporting was hurting him. More importantly, he needed the President to do something before it was too late.

CHAPTER 10

"NICE OF YOU TO SEE ME AGAIN, MR. PRESIDENT," SAID General Campbell as he stood rigidly at attention in the Oval Office, just inches from the President's desk. Crisp and sharp in his uniform, the general conveyed poise and confidence—which were exactly what the President was looking for at that moment.

"Sit down, General, sit down." Calhoun's smile and warm greeting were sincere as he motioned for Campbell to take the high-backed chair on the right-hand side of his desk. He was convinced that his chairman of the Joint Chiefs of Staff and his principal military advisor was a reasonable and malleable sort who would assist his President in using the U.S. military to secure his presidency. "Have you had a chance to think about what we talked about at Camp David—I mean, about getting our arms around this drug business? About coming up with a plan to perhaps take down one of these drug czars?"

"Yes, Mr. President, we have had time to revisit our plans after my initial meeting with you, and I think that we can engineer considerable successes in this area. I have been working closely with General Charlie Walters, the SouthCom commander. I'm sure you remember that when he was with the Joint Chiefs recently, the anti-drug war was one of his primary areas of responsibility. Unfortunately, Mr. President, as you know, the previous administration was niggardly with its funds to fight drugs at the source—and if I may say so, sir, your predecessor didn't have the personal commitment that you have displayed to stop this scourge."

"Well, General, you have my commitment. And you have the commitment of the American people. How any-one could have watched the news stories of the funeral of the young woman who died in that crack house in the District, or have seen the newspaper stories with the pic-tures of what she'd been, and not be committed to stop this scourge is completely beyond me. If I do say so, Gen-eral Campbell, this is the perfect time for our entire nation to mobilize behind us in this effort. Now, what does Gen-eral Walters think he can accomplish?"

"Seems that there's a major drug czar—Maradona's his name—who has garnered an awful lot of power and who has pulled together an incredible amount of resources. General Walters thinks we can make a surgical strike and take him out, destroy his headquarters and who knows how many weapons and how much drugs. The Ortiz gov-ernment wants to be rid of him and we've learned back-channel that they have given tacit approval and will move their government forces out of the area for the duration of this operation. We think it will accomplish several things. It will eliminate a top drug czar. It will put a major dent in the drug supply. It will also let the drug traffickers know that the U.S. military isn't going to stand around and put up with this." Tactical error with that last sen-tence, thought Campbell, and the President was quick to follow.

"It will tell them that the American people, and this administration, and this *President* won't stand for it, Gen-eral, that's what is most important."

"Of course, Mr. President, of course."

"Now, I know of General Walters, and I imagine he has a superb plan. But can he run such a dynamic operation from his headquarters in Rodman?"

"We don't think so, Mr. President. We currently have our Joint Task Force commander, JTF Eight, aboard one of our best command and control ships, USS *Coronado*. Admiral McDaniel has been JTF Eight for a little over two years and we'd like to move him to Europe to be the deputy NATO commander. We'd like to pick a new com-mander, subject to your approval, of course, Mr. Presi-dent, and put him aboard *Coronado* as soon as possible.

We can run the operation from *Coronado,* where the commander can be close to the action, direct it all, and also keep us—that is, the chiefs, NSC, and yourself—informed minute by minute. The JTF Commander has to have a great deal of autonomy and, Mr. President, given the extremely high visibility of this counter-narcotics business and the need to move very quickly to seize opportunities, we recognize that JTF Eight can't always be encumbered by operating within our traditional military chain of command."

"Sounds like an important assignment. Have you picked the new commander to replace Admiral McDaniel yet?"

Bingo! The President never dabbled in such low-level assignments on a routine basis, and Campbell knew he had taken the bait. He had hoped that General Lovelace—once he learned from Walt Prestridge that the JTF Eight job was coming open—would use his long-standing friendship with the President to lobby for this plum assignment. He had to struggle not to let a smile reveal his pleasure. "Not yet sir, we are looking at several candidates from each of the services, trying to find just the right leader to take this one on. I'm sure we'll come up with the right man."

"I'm sure you will, General. I know that one officer you are undoubtedly considering is Brigadier General Ashley Lovelace. I know he's quite a star and it seems like he's been at DMA for quite some time. Now, General, I certainly don't want to tell you all how to run the military. Lord knows, you're doing such a great job."

"As a matter of fact, Mr. President, Brigadier General Lovelace is one of our *leading* candidates. We are certainly giving him serious consideration."

"Well, I appreciate it General. I just had an inkling that you would be doing that and I appreciate it, I *really* appreciate it."

With that, the President rose, his well-known signal that he had given the visitor all of his time he intended to. As he did, he congratulated himself on how easily he had been able to manipulate the JCS chairman. The military had their talents, but mental dexterity wasn't one of them.

In just a few brief minutes he had secured their cooperation in his anti-drug efforts, had steered them to come up with a major operation that would get him back on track in the polls, and also helped his good friend Ashley Lovelace move out of a dark corner of the military world and into the national limelight. Not bad, not bad at all.

CHAPTER 11

As THE T-39 ROLLED ONTO A LONG FINAL AT HOWARD Air Force Base, Brigadier General Ashley Lovelace surveyed the rich tropical Panama landscape and the ships plying their way through the Panama Canal. This narrow slit, which carried such a huge portion of the world's oceanic traffic, seemed to intrude on the lush landscape, but like a human body healing an unwanted scar, the tropical foliage had healed right to the very edges of the canal, seeming to just tolerate the waterway and the locks that controlled it.

Lovelace reflected on the whirlwind events of the past few weeks: the call from the Army chief of staff informing him that he was selected to command Joint Task Force Eight, the busy days and nights at DMA as he prepared to turn that command over to his deputy, the meeting with the chairman of the Joint Chiefs of Staff who told him how important this assignment was, the seemingly endless briefings by the Joint Chiefs, CIA, NSC, DIA, DEA, and the rest of the alphabet soup of agencies that had some ownership in his new assignment. Regardless of his own opinion about the efficacy of the United States' counter-drug efforts aimed at the supply side, he was determined to do his absolute best in this assignment—for his country, for the Army, for himself, and perhaps most importantly, for his friend President Taylor Calhoun.

One evening shortly before Lovelace's departure for Panama, the President had sent for him. There, in the relaxed intimacy of the family quarters in the White

House, the President had mused at length about their long relationship. After mentioning obliquely that he had had a hand in Lovelace's assignment as the JTF Eight commander, the President wished him well and alluded to the fact that Lovelace's success in this assignment, and especially his ability to create positive media coverage for this success, was vitally important to the President and his presidency. Taylor Calhoun couldn't bring himself to come right out and say it, but Lovelace could read the polls as well as anyone else, and the unspoken understanding between the two old friends was that only a big win of some kind could rescue his fading presidency.

As he emerged from the T-39, Lovelace stretched to restore his muscles after the long flight. He wasn't a particularly large man or a very well-built one; he just looked rather ordinary. At five feet ten inches and 190 pounds, Lovelace looked like so many millions of other middle-aged men. With thinning brown hair, green eyes, and unremarkable features, had he not been in uniform it is unlikely that anyone would have guessed he was a military man—let alone a general. He squinted to accommodate the blazing tropical sun and felt the hot, moisture-laden air envelop his entire body. Not until he was several feet away from the T-39 did he notice the white sedan with the polished plate reading COMMANDER, UNITED STATES SOUTHERN COMMAND. Nice touch, thought Lovelace. Although the four-star Unified Command leader didn't come personally to pick him up, at least he sent his personal sedan and his duty officer.

"Good morning, General. Welcome to Panama. How was your flight from Andrews?" said Lieutenant Laura Peters, the SouthCom assistant duty officer for the day.

"Long, Lieutenant, long—thank you for asking," replied Lovelace. Lieutenant Peters was a strikingly attractive woman, especially in her crisp, starched white uniform, no doubt donned immediately before driving the short distance from SouthCom headquarters, and which stood out in stark contrast to his flight-rumpled green uniform. Lovelace did not know much about General Charles Walters, but he was aware of his reputation for having extremely attractive women of all ranks just happen to be assigned to his staff. He immediately wondered whether Peters was assigned to SouthCom for personal or professional reasons.

"General Walters is expecting you, General, wants to meet you right away and then get you briefed by the staff. I'm with the J-2 Intelligence Directorate and I'll be briefing you late this afternoon. I'm afraid it will be fast and furious during your short time here, sir. We have you billeted in the VIP suite at the Q. I'll have General Walters's driver take your things there as soon as we get to headquarters."

As Peters spoke in her clipped, efficient manner, the Air Force technical sergeant driving the sedan drove rapidly and skillfully across the taxiways of this sprawling base. At a time when the U.S. military presence was diminishing worldwide, Howard Air Force Base was one of the only places where there was actually a high level of activity. Huge C-5 Galaxys and smaller but more numerous C-141 Starlifters seemed to be jammed into every corner of the base, some starting engines, others taxiing, and one lining up for its takeoff roll. In one corner of the base, two squadrons of Air Force F-15s were lined up precisely in front of their hangar. In another corner sat a squadron of Army MH-60A Medical Evacuation, or Medevac, helicopters. Howard was an impressive base and an ideal focal point for orchestrating the war against the drug trade.

"Lieutenant, I'm about to meet a four-star general who'll be my boss for at least the next year or so. Sure would like to put on a fresh uniform first," said Lovelace as the sedan exited the runway mat area. He phrased it more as a request than an order, to see if the junior officer had a streak of reasonableness in her.

"Ah, sir—General Walters asked to see you as soon as you arrived," Laura replied.

"Well, I understand all that, Lieutenant. I guess I could have changed aboard the T-39 and only looked half as bad as I do now. Tell you what—let's just cruise by the Q and I'll change in a flash. It will just be our little secret—and the sergeant's here."

Laura found it hard not to like General Ashley Lovelace. He was a general officer and could have ordered her around, been downright abusive with her, but he was applying all his considerable southern charm to get her to agree to something that sounded eminently reasonable.

"Why, yes sir, General, we certainly have time to do that. I'll just have Sergeant Brooke here put the pedal to the metal a bit and we'll get you to headquarters in plenty of time—and looking sharp too, sir," offered Laura, surprising herself at how relaxed she felt with a senior officer she had met only minutes before.

Sergeant Brooke wheeled the white sedan right up to the front door of the BOQ, the Bachelor Officers' Quarters. As Laura raced to the front desk to get the key to the general's VIP suite, Sergeant Brooke was gathering his luggage and bringing it in. The general followed Laura and Sergeant Brooke to his room. The sergeant left immediately to return to the still-running sedan, but the general stopped Laura before she could leave.

"Tell you what, Lieutenant. While I change in the bedroom I'd appreciate you filling me in on what things are like down here. Just make yourself at home in the sitting room here."

After enduring the advances of General Walters, Laura might have felt uncomfortable with this arrangement, but General Lovelace was so unassuming and so charming that it felt like the most natural thing to do. "Certainly, General, though I'm pretty far down in the food chain. I'm not sure how much I can tell you."

"Well, I'll be working with your headquarters a great deal. This assignment to JTF Eight was a bit of a surprise to me. I'm delighted to have the job, of course, but my background in the anti-drug effort is a little sparse. I understand that your boss has been dealing with this anti-drug business intimately since his time with the Joint Chiefs."

"That's right, sir." Laura wanted to strike a fine line between being informative and overstepping her bounds as a junior officer, so she chose her words carefully. "General Walters is very knowledgeable about all aspects of the anti-drug business. He dialogues frequently with the chairman of the Joint Chiefs of Staff on the matter," said Laura loudly enough to be heard in the bedroom. Recal-

ling the strange after-hours conversation at the tennis
courts, she couldn't help but add, "And at all hours of the
day and night."

"Oh," said Lovelace, caught slightly off guard by that
response. "Somehow I thought that the Unified Command
leader would be given free rein to run things without too
much guidance from above."

"Well, I don't think it's that," replied Laura, afraid she
was revealing too much about her own internal staff matters, but finding it easy to talk with this likable general.
"I just think that the two of them consult a great deal on
our upcoming operation. This one is more closely held on
the staff than anything else that we've done in anyone's
memory."

"Well, it's nice to know that this effort has strong backing—all the way up to the President himself. I expect that
we'll be forcing some action really soon—but, of course,
you're with the intelligence directorate and you'll probably know things before I do," said Lovelace with a slight
chuckle.

"Yes sir, General, it seems like the level of activity on
the staff has been building. I think you arrived here at the
right time," replied Laura, significantly impressed that
General Lovelace had remembered what field she was in.

"Okay, Lieutenant, let's not keep General Walters
waiting," said Lovelace as he emerged from the bedroom
looking exceptionally crisp in his clean uniform. "And
thanks for your understanding about this little stop."

As they emerged from the Q, smiling as a result of their
successful dialogue, Sergeant Brooke made a mental note
of how long they had been in there together—General
Walters would want to know. For good measure, he took
a picture of them together. Some pictures just might come
in handy someday.

CHAPTER 12

HAROLD FRANKS TRIED NOT TO LOOK OR ACT NERVOUS as he toyed with his appetizer at Taverna Cretekov on King Street in Old Town Alexandria. He was just doing his job, but this was a little out of the ordinary. Across the small blue and white tile table from him, Juan Zubidar and Carlos Rios, "representatives" of the government of Costa Rica, appeared to be all business and not the least bit bothered about this most unusual way of doing things.

"Señor Franks, we must thank you for coming here to meet with us," said Zubidar, clearly the leader of the two. The two men had picked this small restaurant with its festive atmosphere in hopes of putting Franks at ease. It didn't appear to be working.

"Well, this is a bit unusual, you see. Normally these exchanges take place a little more formally, but my boss, Captain Vienna, assures me that this has absolute top priority and has been cleared through all the right channels," replied Franks, still nervous but gaining a little more confidence now that he had broken the ice.

"Yes, señor," continued Zubidar. "We do not understand all of the regulations of your government, but we are glad that your Captain Vienna has been empowered by your President to help us get the tools we need to stop this scourge of drugs in our nation."

"I know it's helpful that these are not newly manufactured weapons. With our forces downsizing we can sell you our used but still very functional weapons and not have to deal with the congressional oversight that we have to put up with for new weapons purchases. I understand you have been informed that we are funding this under the Patrol Craft account," said Franks.

"That is correct, Señor Franks. I think all should be in order."

All of Harold Franks's training as a twenty-year civil servant told him this was *not* the way business should be conducted, meeting furtively in a restaurant to conduct government-to-government weapons sales. But Captain Hank Vienna had told him how important it was and had reminded him this was a key element of the President's war against drugs. Captain Vienna, program manager for sale of the Navy's new Cyclone Class patrol craft, was handling the sale of these craft to Costa Rica and other nations and was also handling the small—and not so small—arms that were used by the crews who manned those boats. Costa Rica had bought its patrol craft without the extra weapons packages: heavy-caliber machine guns, powerful mortars, and, perhaps most importantly, the lethal Stinger missiles that had been used successfully by the Afghanistan Mujahedin against the Russians.

The damned congressional legislation that governed all of this was like a rat warren that made everything difficult. Vienna had told Franks he was just taking a shortcut and that this had the backing of the Joint Chiefs of Staff themselves.

Of course, there was also the matter of the captain setting up Franks's interview for that GS-14 job in the Naval Sea Systems Command's AEGIS program office. Franks had been working as a GS-13 far too long, and Vienna was only too happy to recommend him to his close colleague with whom Franks would be meeting, but he just wanted Franks to complete this assignment first.

"So, gentlemen, this will be covered under the contract: You wish us to ship the arms package for the two craft that you are already operating to our base at Rodman, Panama, and then your boats will journey there to pick them up."

"Yes, of course," said Zubidar. "They are still completing their shakedown cruises with the assistance of your Special Boat Unit trainers and Rodman is a routine place to stop. This will allow them to return to our base at Puntarenas fully outfitted. That will be a big morale boost for all of our forces."

"Then, gentlemen, we will take care of the rest. After all, you know that our government runs on paper."

"Thank you, Mr. Franks," said Zubidar as he shook his hand warmly.

"Thank you," replied Franks without enthusiasm.

As Howard Franks sat on the Washington metro en route to his office in Crystal City, he thought just how true his last statement was. Here he was, just one of thousands of nameless and faceless bureaucrats working for the government, yet he was about to move some of the most closely controlled weapons in the U.S. inventory between two countries—and do it all with just the stroke of a pen, merely filling out some forms—the same kind of forms that passed across his desk day in and day out. In a government where the simple could often be so complex, he was making something that should have been complex very simple. As he entered his office his secretary handed him a fistful of messages and told him that Captain Vienna wanted to see him.

As he entered the captain's office, Vienna rose to greet him. "Howard, welcome back. How did the meeting go?"

"Just great, Captain. I think it went off without a hitch. Both gentlemen seem to be genuinely appreciative of the extra efforts we are making to help their country. I'll get the paperwork started tomorrow."

"Howard, I think I'd like you to get it started right now," said Vienna in a very serious tone.

"Sure, Captain. Can I ask why?"

"Orders, Howard, orders."

CHAPTER 13

GENERAL ASHLEY LOVELACE EMERGED FROM THE SEdan in front of SouthCom headquarters at Quarry Heights and strode purposely toward the office of General Charles Walters. He had mentally rehearsed this meeting with his new boss and thought he was prepared.

Navy Captain Steve Gallic, executive assistant for General Walters, rose as Lovelace approached. "Welcome to

SouthCom, General Lovelace. The commander's expecting you. Please go right in."

As General Lovelace entered the large, impressive office, filled with the memorabilia of General Charles Walters's three-plus decades of military service and cooled to an agreeable seventy degrees to counter the sweltering Panama heat, he gathered himself together and sounded off, "Brigadier General Ashley Lovelace reporting. Good afternoon, General Walters."

General Walters was just finishing some paperwork and looked up for just a moment, motioning Lovelace to come in. He continued to write for a few moments, then got up slowly and extended his hand. "Well, good to see you, General. Please sit down."

Although they both were general officers, Walters seemed to be emphasizing, rather than downplaying, the difference in rank and importance between his four stars and Lovelace's one. It was done for a reason. Walters wanted to impress upon Lovelace the fact that he was his immediate superior, but that Lovelace would be expected to make his own decisions. If it created confusion in the junior general's mind, so much the better. "This is a big assignment," he said. "Sure you know what you're getting yourself into?"

"Yes I do, General. I've been preparing for this assignment all my life."

"Well, the drug trade's been going on at least that long, but we don't have that long to stop it. I understand that you've seen all the right people in Washington. Down here on the firing line we don't worry too much about the niceties of beltway politics. We're just here to get the job done. My staff will start briefing you this afternoon. I'm your operational commander so I expect that you'll listen to what I have to tell you. I'm bringing together an incredible number of assets and putting them at your disposal. I think that the operation we evolve will be a big success if you just follow the script we give you. Anything else, General?"

"Well, no ... that is, is that all, General?" Lovelace could not hide his surprise that the meeting was already over.

"That's it, General. Down here we don't believe in a lot of hand holding. You're a JTF—I'm sure you know what that entails. We expect you to execute the mission we give you and execute it smartly. You damn well better check everything through my staff, but I don't want you waiting for me to tell you what to do. You come up with a plan, chop it through us, and then if I okay it, you get to execute it. This is a lot different from the D.C. beltway social scene," he added, a touch of sarcasm in his voice. "You actually get to do something and be held accountable for your actions down here. Anything else on your mind?"

"No, sir, General Walters. Thank you, sir."

"My staff will take care of you now. Good luck."

Lovelace rose and departed, annoyed and a bit perplexed by the brisk treatment he had received from Walters, but perhaps more annoyed at himself at not having the right answers and not thinking more quickly on his feet. He knew he would show them his mettle in time.

Moments after Lovelace departed, General Walters quickly placed his own call to Howard Campbell. After relating the entirety of his conversation with the new JTF Eight commander to the chairman, Walters probed a bit, gently nudging Campbell for a bit more guidance and for some assurance that the Chairman had done everything possible to ensure the success of their plan. "Mr. Chairman, I think I sent General Lovelace off with the charter we discussed. I hope he does what we think he needs to do."

"It won't be what Lovelace does that makes our plan work and that seals his fate. It will be what it appears he could have done."

Captain Gallic met General Lovelace at the door as he walked out. "General, the staff is all assembled and ready to begin their briefings to you. We can get started right now—or later, if that's more convenient to you."

"Now's as good a time as any, Captain. Let's get started," responded Lovelace, happy to be out of Walters's office and glad to be treated with some degree of deference.

Lovelace was ushered into the huge SouthCom briefing room, where he sat at the end of a polished oak table with a glistening silver water pitcher in front of his seat. White-coated messmen stood by to fetch coffee or attend to any of his other needs. The various assistant chiefs of staff—the J-1 for personnel, the J-2 for intelligence, the J-3 for operations, the J-4 for logistics, the J-5 for plans, the J-6 for communications—as well as special staff assistants, legal, public affairs, and others, stood at attention arrayed around the table, their thick black briefing books uniformly in their left hands, all eager to brief Lovelace.

One by one, Captain Gallic had each of the principals give the general a concise brief on SouthCom command structure and on the basic plans for Operation Roundup. General Walters's senior staffers all reinforced what he had heard directly from SouthCom himself. Although Lovelace and his JTF Eight staff would be embarked in *Coronado* and near the action, General Walters did not intend to abdicate any of his authority to call the shots on any operation that went down. Finally, at about 2100, just after the J-4 for logistics had finished, Captain Gallic interrupted. "General, if it's all right with you, we'll stop now. I have a sedan standing by to take you back to your quarters. The general's orderly has already prepared a meal for you there."

Damned efficient, thought Lovelace, and damned detached too.

The next morning the sedan was waiting at his quarters at the appointed hour. Sergeant Brooke put his luggage in the trunk and then whisked General Lovelace directly to the SouthCom headquarters to continue his briefings. All very efficient. All very precise. It struck Lovelace that, although the SouthCom staff would provide help and assistance in many ways, the operation was his to conduct in the best way he knew how. Heady stuff indeed for a fairly junior brigadier. The briefings by the principals complete, Captain Gallic addressed Lovelace.

"General, we hope these briefings have been of some

value to you. We know that your staff is well up to speed on this operation. Ever since Admiral McDaniel's departure for NATO, General Walters and your chief of staff, Colonel Hicks, have dialogued frequently on the operation. I think you are arriving here at the perfect time, sir, if I may say so myself."

"Thank you, Captain. Your briefings were complete, as I expected they would be. Would you ask General Walters if he desires an outcall by me?"

"We already have, General, and he doesn't. The commander is just a terribly busy man."

"Yes," replied Lovelace. "It seems so. It certainly seems so."

As he stepped out of the SouthCom headquarters building, General Lovelace saw that General Walters's sedan was already running and the driver was holding the door open for him. Lieutenant Peters snapped to attention and saluted. "Afternoon, General. Hope that your briefings were successful. I'm to escort you to the air terminal. There's a helo already turning, ready to take you to *Coronado*."

"That's pretty efficient, Lieutenant. I'm anxious to get started. Let's go."

As the sedan sped away, Ashley Lovelace reflected on the day's rapid-fire events. He was still bothered by the abrupt treatment by Walters. Lieutenant Peters had been helpful before and he decided to venture a question.

"Lieutenant, the staff briefings were excellent. I feel most welcome, but my meeting with the general was a bit—ah—abrupt."

Laura hesitated a moment. General Lovelace was an extremely likable man—especially for a general officer. She decided to go out on a limb and tell a tale out of school.

"Well, General, General Walters has been a bit preoccupied with this operation. I think he just wants to go on with it."

"Well, I'll put it down to nervous tension. I guess that is not all bad before an important operation."

"No sir, General, I think it's probably a good thing," responded Laura, not understanding the situation completely herself, but wanting to be as accommodating as possible.

As the sedan approached the airfield, they could see the thick blades of the Blackhawk helicopter already whipping the air and stinging the face of the crew chief, who stood at attention to greet the general.

Before alighting from the sedan, Lovelace turned to Peters. "Lieutenant, thank you for all of your help during this visit."

"Thank you, General—enjoy your flight to *Coronado*."

Laura Peters motioned for the driver to stay seated as she jumped out of the sedan and grabbed General Lovelace's luggage. As they walked toward the crew chief and the waiting helicopter, she shouted over the noise, "Be careful, General."

"Thank you, Lieutenant," said Lovelace. Strange sendoff, he thought. Strange sendoff.

CHAPTER 14

"GENERAL LOVELACE ARRIVED IN-COUNTRY AS SCHEDuled," Campbell reported to the Joint Chiefs. "He received his briefings by General Walters and his staff, and is now aboard USS *Coronado*. Where's *Coronado* now, Boomer?"

"She's about two hundred miles west of Rodman, Mr. Chairman," replied the chief of naval operations.

"Good. I expect it will take them some time to get their staff planning going. We should pretty much leave them alone for a while."

"What's the word from General Walters, Mr. Chairman?" asked Admiral Dan Bell.

"General Walters may be able to present us with an even more outstanding opportunity than we had originally thought. Maradona has been consolidating more men, weapons, and drugs at his headquarters than even our most optimistic original intelligence estimates. As he's consolidated, he's had more people from other drug king-pins go over to him. General Walters and his folks think there may be several hundred men in and around the mesa and there are probably more coming all the time."

"How does this affect General Walters's concept of operations?" asked General Walt Prestridge.

"It's really up to General Lovelace. He's been briefed and, as a fully functioning JTF, it's his operation to run. SouthCom will, obviously, provide a great deal of support, everything from intelligence, to logistics, to air support. But the actual conduct of the operation will be under the direct control of General Lovelace."

"Mr. Chairman, I know General Lovelace is a very capable officer, but isn't this a pretty tall order for someone who's been out of the operational arena for so long, and especially for someone who'll have been in command for only a few weeks when we begin Operation Roundup?" asked General Hank Paxton.

The question provided Campbell with a lead-in he'd been preparing for.

"General Paxton! I do agree with you that General Lovelace is inexperienced in this type of operation. And I cannot disagree that he has been out of the operational arena for some time. But let's not forget that General Lovelace is a *most* capable commander who has had a distinguished career, and remember that our Commander in Chief personally picked him to lead this operation. The President has given very explicit guidance to General Lovelace regarding his expectations for this operation. The President has even asked this staff for background information regarding the drug trade in general and the Maradona cartel in particular. He has also told General Lovelace to speak frequently with the White House Situation Room during the operation. So, General Paxton, if our Commander in Chief has that kind of confidence in General Lovelace, then perhaps we can too."

The other Joint Chiefs had dealt with Howard Campbell's body language enough to know that he was not pleased. Whenever he addressed his fellow Joint Chiefs by starting with their military title, he was reminding them that he was the chairman and the individual who reported

directly to the President, while they were only there to
offer their individual expertise as it related to the service
they represented. Even Admiral Dan Bell, the vice chairman, was treated as a junior partner by General Campbell
during meetings of the Joint Chiefs. Howard Campbell
always chanted the familiar logic of Goldwater-Nichols as
requiring him to exercise this extreme authority, but, in
fact, the other Joint Chiefs knew he relished the power.

Indeed, had any of them been in his position, they
would surely relish it too.

CHAPTER 15

BRIGADIER GENERAL ASHLEY LOVELACE SURVEYED
the sea of faces arrayed around the staff conference table.
USS *Coronado* had been reconfigured as a flagship and
his plush cabin contained a huge conference table that
could accommodate over two dozen of his key staff members at the morning message meeting. This was his first
meeting as JTF Eight commander and his desire to get off
on the right foot was matched by the desire of his staff to
support their new leader.

JTF Eight was a joint task force—military jargon for a
staff composed of officers and noncoms from all of the
services. The military had learned that no one branch of
the service had the requisite assets to pull off any significant operation single-handedly, and joint task forces, controlled by a staff composed of representatives of all the
services, were the only way to get the job done. Staring
back at Lovelace, therefore, were not only Army officers
in their green uniforms, but Air Force officers in their
light blue uniforms, Navy officers in their traditional
khakis, and Marine Corps officers in their camouflage uniforms. The military had coined the term "purple" to describe this potpourri of uniforms, backgrounds, and skills,
and it struck Lovelace that the term was an apt one.

"Good morning, General—and welcome aboard," said

Colonel Conrad Hicks, the JTF Eight chief of staff and second in command. Hicks provided a striking contrast to his commander. He was tall and broad-shouldered, his six-foot three-inch, 210-pound frame hard and well-muscled. His hair was jet-black, his eyebrows thick and bushy, and his teeth straight and pearly white. His seemingly endless rows of ribbons looked impressive on his starched uniform. "I know you met everyone briefly when you flew aboard yesterday afternoon, but I'll have the key players introduce themselves as we go around the table. Ladies and gentlemen, let's keep our briefings this morning short and not send the general into information overload."

Briefing the new commander was a familiar ritual for everyone in the military—and a challenging one. Military commanders are given such a great deal of authority and latitude that a staff member is always keyed up to make the best impression on a new boss. Under the able tutelage of Colonel Hicks, the JTF Eight staff was well prepared for their new commander.

"Before you start, Colonel, let me make a few remarks," said Lovelace. He was going to establish his authority right up front. "I'm extremely pleased and proud to be your new commander. Admiral McDaniel did a superb job, but the nation needed his talents more as the NATO military deputy, so he's in Europe as we speak. I know you are far along in planning this upcoming operation, but I have been briefed by General Walters, General Campbell, and yes, even by the President. I can also assure you I'm a quick study and, working together, we shouldn't miss a beat."

Lovelace felt good about his opening salvo. The days when military leaders just dictated to their staffs had long since passed, and Lovelace was astute enough to sell himself to his staff, not merely command them. He reflected on his good fortune in securing this assignment. Heading a joint task force was a plum assignment for a one-star military officer. While officers who were years senior to him toiled in the bowels of the Pentagon carrying out the wishes of even more senior generals and admirals, a joint task force commander had almost complete autonomy and commanded an impressive array of forces from all the services. His predecessor had earned his second star here and had moved on to an assignment that was almost certainly going to get him his third star. He was on the fast track indeed.

Yet this pleasure with his career prospects was dampened somewhat by the timing of his assignment and the cool efficiency of the staff. The planning for Operation Roundup was already virtually complete and the staff in general, and the chief of staff in particular, did not seem to be waiting for him to make decisions before moving ahead. The conduct of the staff briefing confirmed this.

The J-2, intelligence director, began the morning briefing. "Good morning, General. Our intelligence updates tell us that Maradona now has a force of slightly more than four hundred men clustered around the Polara Mesa. Although they have all of the usual light weapons and seem well prepared to deal with interference from local competitors and the local constabulary, they don't have any of the heavier stuff and aren't in any kind of alert posture. Mostly they're working. Moving drugs and arms around, working on enlarging a small airstrip, and the like. We think they're just consolidating the gains they've made thus far."

. "How are we getting this information?" asked Lovelace.

"Satellite imagery, mainly, General, as far as the big picture is concerned. We have also been flying some Navy F-14 TARPS missions out of Howard. They have provided the really close-up work."

"Any chance that they might know we're putting this kind of surveillance on them?"

"Unlikely, General. We're being awfully circumspect about it."

The other briefers continued in turn. The J-3 for operations had a large role, going over the plan in some detail, from the movement of Marines, all of them special forces, onboard *Coronado,* to the shuttling of the Army Blackhawk helicopters from Howard Air Force Base, to the building of the fuel farm for the Apache attack helicopters providing shotgun coverage for the Blackhawks, down to the most minute details of the plan. Lovelace had few questions and the entire staff presented the plan with an air of assured self-confidence. More often than not, when he did ask a question that a junior staff briefer did not have an immediate answer for, Colonel Conrad Hicks jumped in with it. This was an efficient staff, if a bit detached. He was sure he could warm up to them—and them to him. After the briefings were completed he called Colonel Hicks into his small but well-appointed inner cabin. He had more selling to do but also some nagging questions for his chief of staff.

"Colonel, I want to commend you and the staff for such an outstanding in-brief. No commander could have asked for a better venue to hit the ground running. You have prepared these folks really well. It sounds like we have a good plan, but that's what troubles me—it's *a* plan. I'm sure you remember what they preached to all of us at National War College, that we devise alternate courses of action, present them to the commander, and then the commander chooses the preferred option." Lovelace kept his tone cordial but firm.

Lovelace could see he had hit a raw nerve with his chief of staff. Hicks bristled, seemed at a loss for words, then shot back, "General, we have done that and, if I may say so, have done that exhaustively with Admiral McDaniel before he departed. We presented six good options and this is the one that bubbled up as the best. *Your* staff, sir, has been working twenty hours a day to smooth out every detail of this plan. I must say, General, this is no time to turn back and start again. SouthCom could give the go order on this at any time." Colonel Hicks was bordering on insubordination, and he knew it, but there was a reason for his stridency.

Lovelace was taken aback by the colonel and tried to calm the situation. "Colonel, I have no doubt whatsoever that you all have planned magnificently for this operation. No staff could have planned better. As commander, I just need a little more ownership in it than just being presented with a fait accompli. I'm sure you can understand that, Colonel."

"Absolutely, General. And I apologize if I'm coming

on a little strong. But this plan will work, General. There will be decision points as we go along and we recognize that you will want and need to make a big input at each juncture. We'll be here to provide the best support we can."

There, thought Lovelace. I can bring this high-strung colonel to my way of thinking.

Colonel Conrad Hicks could read General Lovelace's thoughts in his face. He knew what the general was thinking—and he knew he had to allow him to continue to think that.

"Well, Colonel, I appreciate your understanding," said Lovelace as he rose to bid the colonel farewell. "I know that we'll make a fine team."

"Thank you, General. I know we will too."

After Colonel Hicks left General Lovelace's cabin, he passed through the compact staff spaces greeting officers and noncoms along the way. It appeared to most of them that the colonel looked to be in a particularly good mood, but that he was in a great hurry to get somewhere.

Two decks above, Chief Rick Holden was in the tiny maintenance shop in the far rear corner of Radio Central examining one of the many circuit cards for a piece of crypto equipment. This particular gear had stymied all of Commander Ben Malgrave's petty officers and, as usual, he had turned to Holden to make these sensitive—and unauthorized—repairs. The Navy was replete with thousands of rules and regulations; however, few were as draconian as those that dealt with secure communications equipment. The rules said that when any of this specialized crypto gear malfunctioned, it was to be returned to the issuing agency for repair or replacement. No organizational maintenance was permitted. This was a good theory, admitted Malgrave, but with a big operation coming up and a huge demand for secure—or covered—circuits, he faced the reality of producing for the staff. He did not want to let his new boss down and therefore was willing to take some unauthorized shortcuts. He trusted Rick Holden not only to make the repairs correctly, but also to be discreet enough not to mention it to anyone.

Rick was about to finish this part of his troubleshooting and test the card when he heard much shuffling around in the outer foyer of Radio Central. "Attention on deck," shouted the senior petty officer in charge of that watch team. All of the sailors in Radio Central snapped out of their chairs. "Good evening, Colonel Hicks," said the senior petty officer.

"Carry on, men," said Hicks. "Petty Officer, I need to get on the INMARSAT ASAP, and I'd appreciate a few minutes of privacy too."

"Yes sir, Colonel. I'll just have the men here get their cleaning gear. We were getting ready to do a field day this evening anyway."

"Fine, Petty Officer. Why don't you go with them too?"

"Well, Colonel, I'd be leaving the radio unmanned, and I—"

"I know how to answer the phone and answer the radio too. I'll just be a minute. Now, if you please, Petty Officer."

"Yes sir, Colonel." With that, the perplexed group of radiomen left Radio Central. Chief Rick Holden's instincts told him to stay put.

Colonel Hicks picked up the INMARSAT and dialed a number. After waiting a few moments he said, "This is Colonel Conrad Hicks. Put me through to General Walters—right now!"

Rick picked up one end of a conversation that both surprised and confused him.

CHAPTER 16

GENERAL HOWARD CAMPBELL WHEELED HIS DARK green BMW 325I convertible into the parking lot of the Richfield Sanitarium in suburban Maryland. Although he enjoyed all of the considerable trappings and accoutrements that went with his office, the sense of freedom he felt in driving his car, and the smell of the still-new sports sedan, was a tonic that temporarily relieved him of the stress of his office.

That brief relief was broken, however, as he took the short walk from the parking lot to the imposing facade of this former mansion, now converted to a sanitarium to care for the reasonably well-to-do who were suffering from various mental disorders. Even though the mansion was both beautiful and imposing, from its four impressive white columns, to its immaculately restored grillwork, to its high arching doorways and windows, to its perfectly kept outbuildings, Richfield's elegance could not make him forget what it stood for, and why his wife was there. Even the spectacularly landscaped grounds, with their azaleas and dogwoods, neatly kept lawns, and perfectly pruned shrubs, couldn't make him forget.

"Good morning, General. The misses had a comfortable night, I think," said Lucy Johnson, the always amiable receptionist.

"That's good," replied Campbell, choking back the lump that always came to his throat in the many, many times he had made this trip. "I know that Mrs. Campbell is in good hands with you all, Lucy."

As he walked down the long white corridor toward her room, General Campbell felt pangs of guilt. He had visited much more often in the past, hoping that his presence, that command presence that had influenced so many military men, would have some effect on his wife. It hadn't, and now his weekly visits were more pro forma than anything else. It would not do for him to fail to visit.

"Morning, Alice," said Campbell as he passed the attendants' station just outside his wife's room. He was always solicitous to everyone at Richfield, knowing that these people were the ones who did for his wife what he could no longer do.

"Morning, General," replied Alice Watkins, head nurse on this floor. "Mrs. Campbell been doin' real good, sir. She been doin' real good." General Howard Campbell had become used to their cheerful responses, although he knew that "doing good" meant things were just the same. Alice was assigned to the day shift on this wing and had gone out of her way to try to make his wife as comfortable as possible. He knew the value of that and appreciated her efforts. Every Christmas he had an envelope for Alice with a generous tip for her to buy something for her four young kids.

He hesitated before pushing open the door to Harriet Campbell's room, hoping against hope that it was all a bad dream and that the woman in the room would be the same woman who had captivated him almost four decades ago at West Point. As he pushed the heavy pine door open, the sounds of her regular but shallow breathing began to bring him back to reality. As he swung the door fully open and gazed at the thin, pale figure in the bed, with her eyes open but uncomprehending, the full magnitude of the hopelessness of the situation again assaulted him. The full spectrum of emotions—rage, sorrow, bewilderment, and a host of other feelings—overcame him. However, he still managed to muster a cheerful, "Hi sweetheart," hoping against hope that somehow she heard him.

CHAPTER 17

THE JOINT CHIEFS WERE MEETING MORE AND MORE regularly to discuss Operation Roundup. They were past the point where only the principals were involved. An operation of this magnitude, although classified as "compartmentalized," with very few having access to it, now needed the detailed planning expertise of many officers assigned to the Joint Chiefs. The JCS meeting room was packed, with the Joint Chiefs, their senior deputies, and an assortment of action officers crowding the room.

The immediacy of the operation was signaled by moving it from the J-5 Planning Directorate to the J-3 Current Operations Directorate. The vice chairman, Admiral Dan Bell, led off. "General Terry, please brief us where we stand with SouthCom's preps for this operation."

"Certainly, General," replied Lieutenant General Pete

Terry, the J-3 current operations director. "General Walters's operations people have put a plan in place that has thus far received a favorable review from my people. *Coronado* is going to serve both as flagship for JTF Eight and as the staging point for the Blackhawk helos transporting our Marine Corps Special Operations troops to the objective area."

General Campbell jumped in and directed the questioning in a way that suggested to the other Joint Chiefs that he wanted to retain oversight of the operation in spite of his frequent protestations that General Lovelace was in complete charge of it. "Do we have enough choppers for the job, General Terry?"

"Yes sir, and with adequate backup. We have the Blackhawk squadron at Howard with their twenty-four UH-60A Blackhawks as primary, with their sister squadron with their twelve Blackhawks as backup. With each helo accommodating eighteen troops each, we'll have more than enough lift for the four-hundred-fifty-plus Marine Corps Special Operations folks we have to move in."

"What about cover for the Blackhawks?" countered Campbell. "Even though this is a benign environment, I want to do this by the book with the right kind of protection for our troop carriers."

"We've arranged to have the Apache squadron out of Fort Huchyca, with their twelve AH-64A Apaches, at Howard for their annual training," replied Terry. "We've also billed it as a demonstration of our hardware for our southern neighbors so as not to arouse any suspicions. They'll stage out of Howard and refuel at the FARP site we'll build landward of the beach line and about a hundred miles southwest of the LZ. That will let them land with just enough reserve after their long flight from Panama. We already have the refueling bladders packed up and ready to go. Eighty thousand gallons of JP-4 fuel, all told—should be more than enough, even for multiple missions. It will be a small LZ, will only accommodate two Apaches at a time, but big enough for our purposes."

The operation was growing, perhaps more ambitious and complex, but the Joint Chiefs were impelled by strong memories of prior operations that had gone awry because of forces that were too austere or because of a lack of aggressiveness. They had been junior officers during the disaster in Vietnam when their comrades had died because the government did not have the political will to prosecute the war in a way these military officers knew it should be prosecuted. They had all been field-grade officers during the debacle at Desert One, when another administration had let a too-strong penchant for secrecy outweigh the advice of the military officers planning the operation and, by providing too few helos, had caused the abject failure of that effort to rescue our hostages in Iran. They had worn their general's and admiral's stars when hesitation by another administration had allowed the bulk of the Iraqi Republican Guard to escape sure annihilation by General Schwarzkopf's overwhelmingly powerful coalition forces. That would not happen again. They had gotten an administration known for inaction and vacillation to back Operation Roundup and they were not going to let it fail by committing niggardly forces.

"Are you saying, then, General Terry, that we have overwhelming superiority in all aspects of this operation?" continued General Campbell, clearly leading the three-star general.

"Yes sir, especially based on our intelligence regarding the dispersion of their men and especially the lack of firepower. We actually have quite a few more troops than we need to seize the objective area, but the numbers have been increased in order to provide ample troops to chase down as many of the fleeing druggies as possible and hold them for the local gendarmes."

"You've gone over this with General Walters and with General Lovelace? Each of them knows where his respective responsibilities begin and end?" asked Campbell.

"Yes Mr. Chairman, we approved the initial concept of ops. General Walters tells us that JTF Eight has added troops and helos incrementally based on updated intelligence, and that they're now satisfied they have the right force package to do the job, with enough redundancy and flexibility to ensure that the job gets done in any circumstance. It's General Lovelace's responsibility to let SouthCom know when he feels he has enough forces in place to get the job done, but General Walters will maintain tight control over the operation and give General Lovelace the go-ahead once we know we have the right correlation of forces in place."

General Howard Campbell was satisfied that *his* plan was going exactly as he had designed it. The false intelligence he and General Walters had passed along to the Joint Chiefs and General Lovelace alike had convinced all concerned that they had the right forces to do the job—when in fact they had just the right amount of men committed to make this upcoming debacle the beginning of the end for Taylor Calhoun and his presidency.

CHAPTER 18

THE UH-60A BLACKHAWK, THE ARMY'S PRIMARY UTILity and troop transport helicopter, turned on *Coronado*'s spot one, awaiting its passengers. The air boss in *Coronado*'s tower preferred this spot because he could keep a close eye on the helo and the deck around it. *Coronado*'s flight deck looked huge and inviting from a distance, but the air boss treated every square foot of it as sovereign, even sacred territory. No light, no pad eye, no safety net, no item large or small escaped his watchful eye. Nothing happened here that he did not will to happen.

The passengers getting dressed out in their cranials and float coats in the helo hangar enjoyed it less, as the powerful whirring blades of the Blackhawk rattled the hangar's thin aluminum doors with such force that it sounded and felt like the helo was going to drive right into the hangar. *Coronado* was launched over three decades earlier, and designed a decade before that, when helicopters were small and underpowered and when their whirling rotors delivered a fraction of the power the Blackhawk's rotor blades did.

Commander Ben Malgrave and Chief Rick Holden adjusted the Velcro straps on their white float coats as they listened to instructions from the Blackhawk crew chief. The all-too-familiar safety brief was a requirement before carrying passengers, but it should have been shortened, Holden thought, to, If you're in the back of a helo when it goes in the water—you're toast.

Malgrave was flying into Howard Air Force Base, Panama, a "short" 150-nautical-mile flight over water to pick up the next month's issue of Classified Material System, or CMS, codes. These codes, inserted manually into the radio systems aboard *Coronado,* allowed the ship to send and receive encrypted radio transmissions. However, Malgrave could not complete this alone. Largely as a result of the Walker-Whitworth spy scandal over a decade ago, federal agencies in general, and the Department of Defense in particular, had mandated "two person integrity," or TPI, on all CMS materials. This made it necessary for two people to handle this CMS material at all times and that each of these people have a special CMS clearance.

There were a limited number of JTF Eight staff members with the requisite clearance who were not deeply involved in detailed planning for Operation Roundup—and fewer still who relished a 150-mile over-water flight in a bouncing helicopter. His communications specialty had required Chief Rick Holden to maintain his CMS clearance and Commander Ben Malgrave had naturally turned to him for help in completing this minor administrative chore. Holden had welcomed the opportunity to get off the flagship. For a SEAL accustomed to action, being confined to a gray hull for almost two months threatened to dull his edge.

Passengers safely aboard, the Blackhawk pilot cycled his landing light as his signal that he was ready to take off.

"Nightstick 102, tower. Winds are forty-five degrees to port at ten knots, pitch one, roll three, green deck, cleared to lift on signal from the LSE," commanded *Coronado*'s air boss.

"Roger tower, Nightstick 102 cleared to lift on signal," replied the Blackhawk's pilot, Warrant Officer Second Class Frank Grassey.

The LSE—the Landing Signalman Enlisted—highly vis-

ible in his yellow flight deck float coat, signaled for the
flight deck crew to remove the chocks securing the Blackhawk's wheels—and the blue-shirted men moved crisply
under the arc of the Blackhawk's spinning blades, ducking
out of habit from hundreds of previous takeoffs of this
kind. As soon as the blue shirts had cleared the arc, the
LSE raised his arms over his head in quick pumping motions, signaling the Blackhawk to lift over the deck. Warrant Officer Grassey pulled the helo smartly over the deck
and, when the LSE gave the depart signal, applied power
and departed over the edge of the flight deck.

"Tower, 102, ops normal, five souls onboard, two plus
one-five to splash, request switch to control," said Grassey.

"Roger, ops normal," replied the air boss. "Cleared to
switch to control, 285.7, have a good flight 102," replied
Coronado's air boss.

"Control, 102, with you on 285.7."

"Roger 102. Have you a bit scratchy, but readable. Turn
ninety degrees to port for radar identification."

"Control, 102, wilco." Chief Rick Holden and Commander Ben Malgrave leaned hard and tried not to look
alarmed as the Army warrant officer jerked his craft into
a hard left turn, partially to make identification easier for
Coronado's controller, but also to give the Navy folks in
the back a jolt. Those squids deserved it, he thought, living
on that love boat with hot meals, hot showers, and the
like.

"One-oh-two, control, have you on my scope. Your vector, steer 078 for one four eight miles, Howard Control
should pick you up in about four five mikes. Contact them
on frequency 312.5."

"Roger control, copy vector, miles, and frequency."

As the Blackhawk roared across the wave tops at 150
knots, Rick Holden reflected on the events of the last several days. The level of activity aboard *Coronado*, the secrecy and intensity of the JTF Eight staff, the surprise
arrival of a new JTF commander, the unprecedented
amount of high-precedence message traffic, and, most disturbing of all, the furtive INMARSAT conversations be-

tween Colonel Hicks and General Walters. He couldn't put all of the pieces together, didn't even know if all of these pieces belonged to the same puzzle, but there might be more he'd learn ashore.

CHAPTER 19

HAROLD FRANKS WAS A BUREAUCRAT, BUT HE WAS also an ambitious man. The more involved he became in this special weapons transfer to Costa Rica, the more it didn't appear just right to him. But his boss, Captain Robert Henry "Hank" Vienna, was calling the shots—and controlling Frank's advancement opportunities—and those damned congressmen and particularly their staffers meddled too much with the Department of Defense orderly weapons procurement process. If Congress had bastardized the system anyway, why not bend the rules a little bit?

"Now, Harold, do we have all the paperwork in place?" inquired Captain Vienna.

"Yes sir," replied Franks. "The folks at Naval Coastal Systems Center in Panama City, Florida, are fitting the new Cyclone Class patrol craft out for delivery to Costa Rica. We'll 'buy' the upgraded weapons package for the third and fourth craft they're receiving, ship them to Panama City for installation on those craft, but then further ship the pallets on to the Special Boat Unit Twelve folks in Rodman. It's just really an internal accounting procedure within our Foreign Military Sales account in the Program Office."

Vienna swiveled around in his large brown leather chair, his fingers folded and his chin resting on the perch they made. He looked out his large window here on the eighth floor of one of Naval Sea System Command's— NAVSEA's—buildings in Arlington's Crystal City, hard by Route One, and idly watched the airplanes landing at Washington's National Airport. Watching the huge birds

silently descend into National seemed to put his mind at
ease and take the edge off the wringer he was really putting Harold Franks through and the risks he was causing
them both to take. It had all better be worth it, he mused.

Then, aloud, he said, "It sounds like you've got this one
all tied up with a neat bow, Harold."

"Yes sir, for now. But of course when Costa Rica takes
delivery of those new craft, they are going to wonder
where the associated weapons are. Are we planning on
playing this shell game indefinitely?"

"Of course not. By the time those two craft are ready
to be delivered, the funding stream for regular weapons
delivery will be opened up, the counter-drug operation
that their government is so anxious to have succeed will
be complete, and we can resume our normal way of doing
business."

Vienna could read the discomfiture in Franks's body
language. Fine. That was not his worry. Franks might even
be left holding the bag for this one after it was all over,
his job opportunity in the AEGIS office be damned, because unbeknownst to Franks and anyone else in the Program Office, Vienna's tour in this job was soon to end.
He was going to a plum assignment with the Joint Chiefs
at the request of the chairman himself, whom he had
worked for previously during Operation Desert Storm.
General Campbell wanted to bring him onto the Joint
Chiefs right away—but just needed him to attend to this
delicate matter before leaving the Program Office. The
general had said he greatly appreciated Vienna's candor
and Vienna was not going to disappoint him.

"I look forward to that, Captain, and I think that when
we finally get these weapons transfers back to a routine
basis we'll all feel a lot more comfortable," said Franks.
But he was enough of a bureaucrat to think first and foremost of insulating himself against any eventuality. He was
complying with Vienna's wishes, but he was also laying
out—in excruciating detail—the complete specifics of this
highly unusual arms transfer. Too important to even bring
into his office in Crystal City, Franks had the memo
tucked securely into his desk in his home in Great Falls
in suburban Virginia.

CHAPTER 20

WHAP! THE SQUASH BALL FLEW OFF THE FRONT WALL and rocketed down the side wall of squash court No. 1 at the Howard Air Force Base gymnasium, just out of reach of General Charles Walters. "Good shot," panted the general. "You're hitting the ball better than ever, Laura. I think that should be our last game. Duty calls, you know."

She'd just finished the part she liked, playing three tough games of squash at lunchtime and, incidentally, taking all three games from the general. Now Laura hoped they wouldn't move on to the part she didn't like, the general being just a little too "friendly." Actually, she would prefer that he call her Lieutenant Peters, just to keep it more professional, but hadn't yet found a diplomatic way of asking him to do that.

"They were all close games, General, could have gone either way, and I was lucky on some of those touch shots in the corners," said Laura, satisfied with her playing but trying to make it more palatable to Walters's senior—and male—ego.

"You're being too humble, Laura. You've got it all: brains, athletic ability, and you're an awfully attractive woman also," replied Walters as he toweled off outside the squash court.

Oh no, here it comes, thought Laura. Why couldn't this just be one game, not two? Lieutenant Laura Peters and General Charles Walters were two of only a very small handful of officers on the JTF Eight staff who played the game of squash. Laura had excelled at tennis and squash at UVA and a lunchtime game of squash in the air-conditioned courts at the gym was preferable to sets of tennis in the blistering noontime Panama sun. The general had been a top squash player at West Point and was the

best competition Laura could find. She and the general
had a standing match every other day at lunchtime and
she welcomed the competition, and the chance to get
some visibility with her boss. After a few weeks, though,
the general seemed to be more and more solicitous. She
wasn't going to turn out like his "tennis Major" she had
confronted at the tennis courts.

"Well, ah, thank you, General. We have a lot of good
players on the staff. There's Colonel Bayliss in J-4, then
Lieutenant Shaw, he played at Navy, in J-1, and—"

"Well, why don't we just keep our wonderful game going?" continued Walters as he dabbed some perspiration
off Laura's shoulder with his towel. She tried not to flinch,
drawing away slowly.

Walters persisted, "You know, Laura, we don't always
have to play at lunchtime. Perhaps an evening match after
work one day and we can follow that up with a quiet dinner."

Good Lord, he's really serious, thought Laura. "Well,
General, that's awfully nice of you, but you know I'm in
Watch Team Bravo, and that's the most undermanned
one, and I'm still working on my duty officer qualification,
and the intel traffic has been extra heavy over the past
months, and—"

Walters cut her off, moving ever so slightly closer to
her. "Well, you just remember who's in charge down here.
I can fix a little watch team problem if *we* want it fixed."

"He's not letting up, thought Laura. She would have to
turn this off, and soon. "General, I'm a little late getting
back. Got to run. Thanks so much for the squash game."

"Good-bye, and thank you, *dear.*"

Dear, now he's calling me *dear. Oh shit*!

CHAPTER 21

RICK HOLDEN AND BEN MALGRAVE HELD ON TO THEIR
gear as the Blackhawk that had transported them to Howard Air Force Base taxied away from the transient line.
Holden was struck by the same scene that had greeted

General Ashley Lovelace only weeks before, a jammed base with a high level of activity, aircraft everywhere and military men with a sense of purpose moving everywhere quickly. Was it always like this? Holden wondered. And if not, did it tie in to all the activity on *Coronado*?

"Follow me," shouted Malgrave, making himself heard over the sound of a C-5A Galaxy on its takeoff roll. "We've only got about four hours before the Blackhawk will be back for us. The Air Force comm tweets can make the process of getting our CMS gear painfully slow."

"Rog, Commander," replied Holden as he watched the helo disappear across threatening skies. "Feels good to be on something that doesn't move."

"Don't get too used to it, Chief." Malgrave chuckled. "Navy's missions at sea and that's where all of us belong."

"I'm with you, sir."

Malgrave and Holden encountered the usual amount of red tape at the Air Force communications center and the large number of folks clogging the center only exacerbated the problem. Commander Ben Malgrave was "lead" on this one and was unsuccessfully trying to use the fact that he *was* a Navy commander on the staff sergeant at the front desk, who was making it abundantly clear that *she* was singularly unimpressed by Malgrave's rank or by his sense of urgency. "We do have procedures, sir," she said with thinly disguised annoyance.

"And we do have a ship a hundred and fifty miles off the coast that can't go anywhere until we return, and if you haven't noticed, *Sergeant,* sky's looking pretty black already. Don't suppose you'd much enjoy a Blackhawk ride in that, would you?"

The sergeant sighed and continued her routine at her pace, causing the annoyed Commander Ben Malgrave to stalk off. Rick Holden confirmed Malgrave's weather observation—the sky was looking pretty bad—and the Blackhawk had only rudimentary over-water navigation equipment. This was not good. He thought he'd try some diplomacy.

"Hey Sarge, I know that you guys, ah, you all, are really strapped, but it'd be a big favor to this SEAL if you could get us back to our ship before the weather hits. Wouldn't want to miss out on that good Navy chow," said Holden, flashing his toothiest grin at the harried sergeant.

"You're one of those snake eaters, man. I tell you, this place has been Grand Central Station with your kind of crazy people, Recon Marines, our Special Forces guys, all sorts of those intel geeks going over to SouthCom head-quarters. What ya doing, playing some war game or some-thing?" replied the sergeant, interested in talking to Holden, but not making much progress in expediting their business.

"Tell ya, Sarge, this chief isn't cut into the big picture. Just doing my bit."

"You tell the commander there not to get his skivvies all in a flutter. We'll try to help you squids out," replied the sergeant. "Why don't you both go get some chow? Keep the caffeine away from him, though."

Holden detected a hint of a smile from this particularly disrespectful sergeant. "Yes ma'am, thanks for the help." Then he walked across the comm center lobby to get the still-fuming Malgrave.

CHAPTER 22

JUST A FEW MILES FROM WHERE MALGRAVE AND HOL-den paced, a U.S. Military Sealift Command—or MSC—ship was unloading its cargo at pier two at the Rodman Naval Station. Rodman was at the Pacific end of the Pan-ama Canal and was the major Navy port on the Pacific side. Any Navy ship transiting the canal from the Pacific side to the Atlantic side typically stopped at Rodman for fuel and stores. Rodman's piers were old—and showed the effects of not only age but years of pounding by the thousands of landings by ships that had called there. All along the piers, at every conceivable spot, Navy crews had painted their ships' names, logos, or nicknames with bright colors, marking the fact that they had visited there.

It was a ritual not replicated in many other ports, but Rodman was a unique port of call. It was the only place where a Navy ship's captain surrendered responsibility for his ship to a canal pilot, who then had total responsibility for his ship for the journey through the canal.

The usual contingent of military and civilian representatives from the Navy Supply Center were there to meet this MSC ship to ensure that its papers were in order, that it was unloaded properly, and that the right equipment was sent to the right warehouses. It didn't help that the darkening skies were now beginning to deposit the beginnings of a torrential downpour on them, and they were slightly annoyed by the attitude of Major Smith from SouthCom.

"Commander," said Smith to Lieutenant Commander Scott Flaherty, the Rodman Naval Station assistant supply officer, "we've got four high-priority pallets that are part of a delicate foreign military sales case that General Walters sent me to *personally* take custody of. We know you have procedures, but this is a very important government-to-government agreement and we don't want them getting lost somewhere."

Flaherty bristled, first at the major's overall attitude and then at the not at all subtle slam at the Navy Supply Corps. Had he not been being pelted by a downpour that showed no signs of abating, he might have decided to show him who was *really* in charge and put those pallets deep in the bowels of his most decrepit warehouse, but he just wanted to be rid of the annoying Air Force staff puke. "Fine, Major, just fine. Sign here and just get them and your truck the hell off my pier so we can get on with what we need to do."

Major Smith didn't even respond as he signaled his work detail to load the pallets on the five-ton stake truck. That done, the truck pulled off pier two, sending geysers of water up from the huge puddles that were rapidly building everywhere on the pier.

Lieutenant Commander Scott Flaherty thought it strange that the truck didn't have the usual military markings, but didn't hold the thought long as his people struggled to move the rest of the pallets off pier two, which was rapidly beginning to resemble a small lake.

Major Smith and his work detail drove off the pier and made the left-hand turn that took them out of the general wharf area. They headed out the main gate of the Rodman Naval Station, seemingly bound for Howard Air Force Base, but as they left the Bridge of the Americas behind them, they sped past the Howard cutoff road and continued north along the Interamerican Highway.

CHAPTER 23

COMMANDER BEN MALGRAVE HAD REACHED SUCH A point of frustration with the wait at the comm center that he had buried himself in a paperback novel. He had let Rick Holden, who had clearly set up a better rapport with the Air Force sergeant than he had, take lead on getting their CMS gear so that they could get back to *Coronado*. It didn't help that the tropical storm wasn't abating after an hour or so like such storms usually did.

Rick's fourth trip to the sergeant's desk in as many hours, twice with "gedunk," the military's term for any kind of fast food, as a subtle bribe, had finally gotten the desired results. "Okay, Chief, you can draw your gear. Just sign this and then you'd better go up to base ops to see about calling the helo to come pick you up. You sure you want to go flying in this muck?"

"Anything to get back to that good Navy chow, you know," said Holden cheerfully. "And I really appreciate your help ... ah ..."

"Charlene," she offered.

"Thanks, *Charlene,*" replied Holden, extending his hand. Yes, charm went a long way and, well, she was cute, if a bit of a smartass. "Hope to see you again, Charlene."

"Won't be on one of your squid ships, SEAL. Air Force is a great way of life, remember that."

"Yes ma'am," replied Holden.

Malgrave was waiting, and not at all patiently, for Holden to finish his schmoozing. "Well, can we pick it up now?" he asked.

"Yes sir, Commander, just have to arrange for our return flight with base ops," offered Holden as they took the short walk through the downpour to the base operations building.

"You fellas crazy?" Great, thought Holden and Malgrave simultaneously, another Air Force noncom with an attitude.

"Look, *Sergeant,* you don't understand. We have a high-priority mission for JTF Eight to get back to USS *Coronado*. You just call up our Blackhawk and we'll be gone."

"Commander"—there was an edge to the sergeant's voice somewhere between exasperation and contempt—*"you* don't understand. Howard's way below minimums, and predicted to be that way for the rest of the afternoon and into the early evening. Doesn't matter if it's a Blackhawk or Air Force One, it ain't gonna come in or outta here! You might want to get yourself a room at the Q before they're all gone. Gonna be lots of transients stuck here tonight."

Malgrave resigned himself to his fate. "Holden, better tell your sergeant friend in the comm center we won't be drawing that CMS gear tonight. Can't put it under our pillows or anything. First thing in the morning, though, we want to get it right away. Buy her breakfast if you have to."

The commander did recognize his talents, thought Holden, as he grabbed the nearest base telephone to call Charlene. Ben Malgrave was already on the phone to billeting to arrange for rooms at the BOQ and BEQ. Well, this was an unexpected night of liberty. It had to beat the movie on the ship. Why not make the best of it?

CHAPTER 24

GENERAL HOWARD CAMPBELL HAD COMMANDED MEN in combat, directed the fortunes of armies, and been a relentless bureaucratic infighter in the Pentagon. However, nothing in his past could properly steel him against the helplessness he felt as he sat in the antiseptically clean room of the Richfield Sanitarium and held the frail hand of his wife, Harriet. He could not even look at her, but stared at the pale yellow wallpaper covering the small but neat room. Acting according to his instructions, the staff maintained a crystal vase with a bouquet of yellow spring daisies on the table next to her bed. Harriet had always loved daisies, Campbell recalled. Maybe, just maybe, she knew that they were here.

Ordinarily it would have been hard for him to look at his wife of almost forty years in this state—but it was even more difficult because Harriet Campbell was, or had been, an extraordinary woman. Arguably the most beautiful woman, and one of the smartest, at classy Bennington College, she had first met Cadet Howard Campbell at a "tea fight," the cadets' euphemism for a mixer dance, at West Point. There had immediately been a strong mutual attraction, and Campbell had survived significant competition for her favors. He had bested the best the Corps of Cadets had to offer and had married Harriet in the West Point Chapel immediately after his graduation.

Beyond beauty and brains, Harriet possessed the social skills and subtle flair for Army politics that had made her a terrific asset to his career. Always able to entertain with class, even on a shoestring budget, Harriet achieved as much with charm and grace as he did with his driving, but sometimes transparent, ambition. They were the model couple and, as a couple, caught the attention of the Army hierarchy early on. Keep an eye on these up-and-comers, was the word.

Their marriage was blessed early with a son, and although they wished for more, they did not have other children. From the earliest age, Howard Campbell, Jr., appeared as if he would, at the very least, equal his father's considerable accomplishments. After he graduated first in his class at West Point, he received his pick of assignments: air cavalry. Things had all been going so well and according to plan—until the accident. That's what they had called it for public consumption, but Campbell knew the facts: the "extra" training mission, the maintenance problems with the unit's helicopters, the questionable weather, the inexperienced wingman, the fiery crash, and then, worst of all, the insensitive duty officer who, knowing that the general was at a conference in Europe, called his wife in the middle of the night to identify her son's body. Harriet Campbell had carried out her gruesome duties with dignity, but then, returning home alone to their large base quarters—the fools had left her alone!—she suffered a complete mental breakdown, the worst the doctors at Silas B. Hays Hospital at Ford Ord, California, had ever seen. Months, then years of therapy had not helped, and General Howard Campbell had suffered the final indignity of having this once beautiful and vibrant woman committed to a private sanitarium.

He allowed his eyes to wander as he continued to hold her hand, looking for some response but finding none. Everything was in place in this small room, just as it was in the Army; the illusion of order when the facts were something else indeed. He thought of the many Army friends who admired him for staying the course and continuing with his career; he thought of their overtures of sympathy when they could not begin to understand how this had unalterably changed his life.

Of course, there was an inquiry and an investigation. The system found some junior major who was the squadron operations officer and hung him out to dry, but the investigation covered up major problems with the unit's helicopters, gross deficiencies with squadron training, and the like. Howard Campbell was powerless to do anything—and beyond the loss of his son, that is what grieved him the most.

Howard Campbell had continued his military career. He had risen to command the Joint Chiefs and thus the most powerful military machine in this, the most powerful of nations. Outward appearances suggested it was business as usual for the successful career climb of General Howard Campbell. But things had changed. There was no more of what had begun as a nóble purpose. No more of the selfless devotion to duty. And he had shared this change of heart with no one—not his wife in the eternal quiet of her room at Richfield, not his son at his plot at Arlington, and certainly not his close friend and ally, General Walters.

CHAPTER 25

FROM ALL OUTSIDE APPEARANCES, BALBOA YACHT Club was a nondescript concrete building tucked in among the aging, weatherbeaten, warehouses in an out-of-the-way corner of the Rodman Naval Station. Few passing this building would ever give it a second look; fewer still would have the curiosity to enter. That was all right, for the regular patrons liked it that way. Perched on the water's edge, overlooking the long causeway marking the entrance to Rodman's harbor, it looked just as nondescript from the seaward side, and no one on the literally scores of ships that passed by every day on their way to or from the Panama Canal gave it a second look—no one, that is, except those who knew what this place was.

No one could quite remember how long Balboa Yacht Club had been there, or why it had come into existence in the first place. The hundreds of U.S. military bases worldwide had their very structured hierarchy of clubs; officers' clubs; E-7 through E-9 clubs, or "Chiefs Clubs," in the Navy parlance; and enlisted EM clubs for the more junior soldiers, sailors, airmen, and Marines. That structure had suited the military well for forever and helped to reinforce the unique military caste system whose central tenet was that a man or a woman was a better person the more lofty his or her rank. It was not an egalitarian approach by any means.

Balboa Yacht Club didn't care for either the rank or the stature of its patrons. In fact, those patrons who were military men or women seemed to go out of their way to downplay, if not totally disguise, their rank. Of course, military people were not the only ones to frequent this club—although they did so in such numbers that the established military clubs on base were affectionately known as "sleepy hollows"—and that is what gave the Yacht Club some of its particular appeal and even intrigue. Its patrons ranged from canal pilots, to military support people, to large numbers of women, both local and from nearby nations, who hoped to attract a man's attention for either the long term or an hour or less. The Yacht Club had an atmosphere somewhere between an opium den and a Hard Rock Café.

Laura Peters entered the club at about ten P.M. with a contingent of fellow junior officers from SouthCom headquarters. It was early yet and the Yacht Club was not at all full. They were in a particularly festive mood because they were "farewelling" an Army captain who had completed his two-year tour here and was transferring to the Army's Command and Staff College in Fort Leavenworth, Kansas. Laura was also particularly in need of the relaxed intimacy of her peer group, having had to work too hard to fend off the affections of General Walters that afternoon. Why her? she thought.

As Laura and her group walked down the cracked concrete steps into the interior of this club, she mused that it was a sight to behold. Even before peak time and on a weekday night, the Yacht Club was an amazing place. On the right, small tables lined the long, screened windows facing the small cove. Each table held one or two couples engaged in intimate conversations, with many, no doubt, making plans for later in the evening. On the left, the main bar was alive with activity, every stool around its periphery filled, with a line of patrons pressing against those seated demanding drinks from the harried bartenders, who, as always, gave first priority to the equally har-

ried waitresses pushing up to the bar to fetch drinks for
the tables. Many of the seats at the bar had been com-
mandeered early by canal pilots who were swapping stories, often bending the ear of some wide-eyed Navy junior
officer who was scheduled to pass through the canal for
the first time the next morning. Just beyond the bar, and
barely visible in the dim lighting, the dance floor was already filled to overflowing with couples. There were also
many of the local girls who danced in skimpy garb, mainly
short shorts and halter tops, designed, no doubt, to accen-
tuate their primary virtues—or lack thereof—to the Yacht
Club's male patrons. Around the room in small clusters
were other nondescript groups who appeared to value
their privacy, often above all else.

At the same time, Ben Malgrave and Rick Holden
alighted from their cab in front of the Balboa Yacht Club.
"So you've never been here before, Holden?" inquired
Malgrave.

"Never even heard of it, boss. You know, us SEALs
are usually just out in the woods, looking for a juicy snake
to chow down on," replied Holden. Sometimes, when he
got a little carried away with maintaining his cover as a
Navy chief petty officer and SEAL—although with two
years of it under his belt, his cover was becoming less and
less a fiction—Rick Holden wished he lived a more
straightforward existence that would allow him to be who
he really was: a highly educated son of hardworking,
upper-middle-class parents who had given a hundred percent to his career. Maybe sometime things would return
to normal, whatever normal was.

Malgrave chuckled. He was now in a festive mood,
having accepted the delay in returning to *Coronado* for
what it was—not his fault, and a great chance to pull a
night of liberty. Due to their rank difference, neither the
O-Club or the Chief's Club would have done for both, so
the Yacht Club provided the perfect compromise, and
Malgrave knew that this place was where the action was
anyway. He hoped Holden wouldn't be a drag, but SEALs
had a certain reputation and he was hoping for the best.

"You grab a table, Rick. I'll rustle us up a couple of
the local brews."

"Rog-oh, boss." Rick wasn't minding this either.

As Rick Holden drummed his fingers on the tabletop to the pulsating beat of the DJ's latest selection, he began to absorb the sights and sounds of the Yacht Club. Across the room he saw a group of about a dozen young people about his age, probably junior officers, from their haircuts, clothing, and body language. No doubt successful in their careers as he was once, and hoped to be again. Thank God for second chances. Even through the dim light and the hazy smoke, one of the young women looked awfully familiar. Pretty, really athletic build. He couldn't place her right away; it must have been someone from sometime years before. But who?

Just then, one of the young men from the table who had obviously been sent to get the next round yelled back to the table where she was sitting. "Hey Laura, what'd ya say you're having?"

It couldn't be, but maybe it could. Ben Malgrave was still trying to work his way to the bar, so as if pulled by some irresistible force he approached the table.

"Laura Peters?"

"Yes."

"UVA?"

"Yes?" she said, now looking up. "Rick? Rick Kapla?"

"The same."

Well, not exactly the same, thought Rick. There was the little matter of his new name. They'd have to deal with that, of course, but for now Rick was energized by the prospect of becoming reacquainted with this wonderfully attractive woman he had known in another place and at another time that now seemed so distant.

As the rest of the JOs in Laura's party looked on in bemused acceptance, Laura rose and began to get reacquainted with someone she had known long ago.

CHAPTER 26

THEY WERE GIVEN STRICT INSTRUCTIONS TO DRIVE straight through and stop only for gas, and so after twenty bumpy hours of traveling along the Interamerican Highway, Major Smith and his two companions pulled the stake truck off the road at the designated location and drove down a narrow, winding road that led to a small farmhouse. A truck of similar size, but much older and more road-weary, was parked next to the house. A few figures moved forward by way of welcoming them. Major Smith ordered his truck stopped and clambered down to meet his hosts.

"Good evening, gentlemen," offered the major.

"Buenos noches, señor," said Juan Zubidar. "We know that you have traveled a long way."

"Yes, we have, and through some very rough weather. I hope next time we can come up with a more standard way of transferring this equipment."

"Indeed, I hope so too, señor. The important thing, though, is that this will be a great aid in the drug war that both of our countries are determined to win. I am sure it is all here, but shall we examine it?"

With that, Major Smith and his crew began to muscle the pallets onto the hydraulic lift on the back of their truck and then lower them one by one to the ground. This completed, they began to open them in turn and pull out the carefully packed weapons. The smell of gun oil, applied liberally to preserve the weapons during storage and shipment, punctuated the tropical night. The first crate contained eight Stinger missiles, which were passed to Zubidar and Carlos Rios for their inspection. The admiring glances between and among them and the other half-dozen or so helpers assured the Americans that this was an important mission and that they were an integral part of the anti-drug war.

"These are very nice weapons," offered Zubidar, "though clearly they are not brand-new."

"Way we understand it," said Major Smith, "part of the transfer agreement meant that we had to take these from Army stock and not direct from the manufacturer. I'm sure that if our folks have used them in the field, then they're A-okay."

"I am certain that they are, señor."

"Makes me wonder a little bit, though. These aren't quite the types of weapons we figured you'd be using on your PCs."

"Ah," replied Zubidar, "you Americans are so well insulated from the front lines of this drug war that you don't understand the power of the drug cartels. Their armament is formidable indeed, some of it actually American made, but most of it the best that Europe can make. The international arms market, unfortunately, is even freer and, in some ways, more lucrative than the drug trade. These weapons will barely let us keep pace with our enemies, but they are a good start indeed."

Satisfied, Major Smith and his companions continued to unpack the cartons with dispatch, knowing that they had to face a brutal drive back to Rodman. Zubidar and Rios continued to examine each weapon and then pass it to the others, who loaded it onto their truck. The array of weapons was impressive. The Stinger missiles were the biggest-ticket items of the bunch, but almost equally impressive were the fifty-caliber light machine guns, the field mortars, and especially the twenty-five-millimeter chain guns. Their job completed, they mounted their Army truck.

"Señor Zubidar and Señor Rios, we hope these weapons are helpful to your government in its efforts. We will tell the appropriate people that they are in good hands now."

"And thank you, Major, for such an efficient delivery. Please tell your commander that we share a common goal."

Zubidar stepped up on the running board and reached up to the cabin of the truck. He shook hands warmly with the American and smiled with a look of true gratitude. That smile was the last thing the American remembered as a bullet exploded inside his skull and two more shots finished off his two companions.

Quickly, Zubidar, Rios, and the others dragged the three bodies into a deep trench they had dug earlier in the evening. Within minutes, the bodies were covered and the tropical landscape was moved about enough to totally obscure the site. To maintain the best possible cover, they would later run the Americans' truck off a cliff at a most dangerous curve along the highway. The authorities would report this unfortunate accident to the American Consulate and any trail to the weapons would be dried up.

Both trucks wheeled out onto the Interamerican Highway and began their journey north. They had to get to their destination in a hurry.

CHAPTER 27

THE FRAGRANT SMELL OF TROPICAL FOLIAGE, THE warm night air, the gentle Pacific breeze, the ships approaching the canal with their lights ablaze, the pulsating music of the DJ, all combined to provide a perfect backdrop to reminisce.

Rick began what soon became a barrage of exchanged questions. "Laura Peters, best tennis player out of UVA in a bunch of years. Not bad on a squash court either, as I can recall."

"You weren't bad on the courts yourself, Kapla. Seems we hit more drills together than either one of us probably cares to remember. I guess it helped our games, though." Rick seemed a lot more handsome and self-assured than the rather intense and almost skinny undergrad she had remembered.

"Don't know if it helped me, though you sure were a bright star. Thought you were going to go on the tour after graduation." Holden returned her admiring glance and thought that she was much more becoming than that uptight and sometimes downright bitchy tennis phenom he had worked out with in college.

"Oh, I did, played the U.S. satellite circuit in the summer," Laura said. "Lots of travel, met some nice folks, won more matches than I lost, but no way of life for the long term. Besides, I had to pay back my ROTC commitment. Don't you remember how cute we looked wearing those darling uniforms once a week?"

If he didn't know better, Rick would think that Laura was flirting just a little bit. He recalled that she did look cute in that uniform. "So are you still in the Navy?"

"That's what I'm doing here. Joined the intelligence community. Guess that makes me kind of a Navy spy." She chuckled. "Just been assigned to SouthCom headquarters, working in the J-2 Intelligence Directorate. Speaking of spies, weren't you looking at the CIA? I sort of had a vision of you stuck in the TV serial *I Spy*. Would have been great: Rick Kapla, tennis-playing spy."

Laura was radiant, and yes, she was flirting. Rick wanted to keep the dialogue rolling, but her reference to the CIA made him instinctively evasive.

When the Agency had wanted to hide him, special favors were called in from the Department of Defense and the record of Chief Petty Officer Richard Holden materialized in the Navy's Personnel Bureau as a member of the Navy's elite SEAL forces. The SEAL community was small enough that having him materialize as an officer was too risky, so he returned as a SEAL chief petty officer who had been with the reserves for enough years to erase the corporate memory of anyone who might have remembered him. Then he was inserted into a brand-new unit where virtually all of the men were strangers to one another. A generous CIA stipend supplemented the rather austere pay of a Navy chief petty officer. He had now been with them for several years, the CIA had not called, and he was enjoying his life with the SEALs. But he was still CIA at heart.

"Well, that didn't work out exactly as I wanted," began Rick. That part was true. "Tried it out, but running around in a trench coat and funny-looking hat wasn't my style. Wanted more of an outdoor job, so I joined the

SEALs. Actually, I'm assigned to SEAL Platoon Two. We're embarked in *Coronado,* right off the coast here. Just came in today to pick up some equipment, but the weather got to be too much for our helo. Goin' back tomorrow, though. But heck, you're in the spy business, you probably know everything that's going on. Oh, and, well"—might as well mention it now, so it seemed like no big deal—"there was a little identity problem when I left the CIA, so it became kinda convenient to pick up a new last name. Chief Petty Officer Rick Holden at your service, ma'am."

Laura didn't know how to ask the next question diplomatically, so she just blurted it out. "Rick, you're an enlisted man? With your education, maybe you should have stayed with being a tennis-playing spy."

"Well, don't knock it. You know, I barely graduated in the top ninety percent of our class. Maybe spent a little too much time on the courts. And, hey, I just might put in for an officer program. Then we could go to the O-Club together, right?" Rick was attracted to her. He longed to tell Laura the truth about his past as their camaraderie on the courts flashed back, but he just couldn't. And it gnawed at him.

Laura's group had sensed the attraction between the two of them and had left them alone, while Commander Ben Malgrave just nursed his beer at the bar, figuring that the much younger Rick had needed to jettison him. From the looks of things he was doing pretty well for himself. The DJ's next song was a current favorite and Malgrave watched Rick escort the attractive JO to the dance floor. She held his arm tightly.

As the music rose and as Rick held her close on the dance floor, Laura recalled the tacky harassment of General Walters and so welcomed the innocent closeness of a man who had no dishonorable intentions—and who was awfully cute.

"Rick, is what you do dangerous?" asked Laura, with a genuine note of concern in her voice.

"No ma'am—say, you must be a commander by now," Rick teased.

"I'm just a lieutenant, and if you say *ma'am* one more

time I'll take you out on the tennis court and show you a thing or two."

"Sorry, *Lieutenant ma'am.*" Rick chuckled.

They were still at the Yacht Club well after midnight, talking about everything yet talking about nothing: where they had been stationed, who they had kept in contact with, when they had last been back to UVA. Reminiscing at this place, with its sense of intrigue and in this faraway country, only made the good memories come back faster. There was an attraction here that neither one of them could deny. Laura's friends had left earlier, as had Malgrave. The voice of the bartender calling last round shook them out of their spell.

Rick knew it was supposed to be his move and didn't know which way to proceed, teetering on that brink of wanting to be with her that night and moving too fast— but Laura made the decision for them. "Rick, this has been wonderful, catching up and all, you look so great. I *think* your ship is going to be around for a while, and I'm going to get you out on that tennis court, you know." She said it in a way that was so encouraging. To Rick it seemed that she was saying: No, not this night, it would be too fast and not quite right, but there may be a night. . . .

"I'm all for that," Rick said. He hadn't really been ready for too much too soon and the feeling that now they had to get together again had its own special appeal. "I think there's some operation coming up soon, so I don't know how much longer we'll be down in this op area, but heck, we have to go through the canal to get back to Norfolk, so I guess I can say, you're on—better practice too!"

As they shared a taxi back to the main part of the base, Laura to her nicely furnished BOQ and Rick to the transient chiefs' barracks, she let her hand rest lightly in his. Words just didn't seem necessary as they drove along the waterfront and saw the dozens of ships massing in the roads, the seaway, for the morning's journey toward Miraflores Lock. As Rick helped her out of the car she kissed him—an impulsive, quick kiss—and then ran quickly up the steps to the BOQ. Rick rode back to the barracks to try to grab a few hours of sleep before his flight back to *Coronado* and he felt that all was right with the world.

CHAPTER 28

LAURA PETERS WOULD HAVE LIKED TO SIT AT HER DESK for just a short while remembering the wonderful evening with Rick Holden. She hadn't flirted with anyone like that in a while, and she was sure he was attracted to her too. This might not lead anywhere, but it was wonderful for now. She'd been working too hard anyway, so she hoped she'd see him again. Her reverie was broken by Commander Bob Fraser, assistant intelligence officer.

"Okay, Laura, up and at 'em. Looks like we may have an operation coming up. I&W"—the Navy parlance for intelligence and warning—"looks strong. We got lots of intel to decipher and fuse, and we have to brief the boss right after lunch," said Fraser.

"Sure, Commander," replied Laura, but her heart wasn't in this. She was sure of it now: Rick was attracted to her—and why shouldn't he be?

"Why don't you start with a review of the last week's message traffic, see what you can pull from that while I hit the back channel stuff?" offered Fraser, deciding to let the junior officer take care of the more mundane chores today.

"Will do, boss."

Laura sat in front of her computer and scanned the various message queues that let her access the huge volume of messages that poured into SouthCom every day. She had a wonderful, intuitive sense of separating the wheat from the chaff and making sense of the enormous volume of traffic. While other, more senior officers on the staff were comfortable only with locating and understanding the messages presorted for their particular code, Laura was adept at dropping in and out of directories, comparing a message for one officer with another a day later for another officer, drawing together the disparate portions of a jigsaw puzzle. Her first-class intellect, strong professional drive, dexterity on the computer keyboard, and curiosity sustained her and focused her as she made the connections and made the pieces of the puzzle fit together.

This complex puzzle was beginning to come together for Laura Peters. She noticed that there were actually a relatively small number of genser—general service—messages related to Operation Roundup. Most of those covered fairly routine and mundane administrative and logistics details of the operation. They only provided the skeleton for an operation such as this, not the flesh, the tendons, the muscles, and the heart. Scanning through these on the Local Area Network—or LAN—she noticed that the usually meticulous General Walters had not attached tasking notes to various staff members on any of the Operation Roundup messages, an interesting omission, since he typically used these messages as a de facto way of directing his staff.

Laura's curiosity would not let her quit. She sorted the messages regarding Operation Roundup by functional subject area, then noted how many had been routed to various staff members. A total of 226 messages were tagged with the Operation Roundup label. She had received only 183 of them. Now, even more curious, she entered Captain Fran Dawson's code. She was sure the captain wouldn't mind her doing this because it wasn't as if she had stolen the code; Captain Dawson had entered her computer many times with Laura standing there. To her surprise, Captain Dawson only had 185 messages routed to her. Back to the master file. Sort by type, genser, P-4, SPECAT. There, 185 gensers, 17 P-4s, and 24 SPECATs. Twenty-four SPECATs—an incredible number! Where had they gone? Sort again by code. General Walters, all the P-4s and all the SPECATs, and only to his code. Something secretive was in the works.

Where to go now? Phone conversations. Laura recalled that one of the techs had told her that the LAN had been adapted to log all phone calls as to place called and duration of call and from what extension. Seems the financial geeks had insisted on it to cut down on their massive phone bills. Here it was, phone calls. Sort by month. Sort by code. Yes, look at the volume of calls between General

Walters and the Pentagon. And to the same number almost three dozen times in the past several weeks. But whose number was it? Laura rifled through her disk and found the Department of Defense phone book. She had a hunch. She opened it to the Joint Chiefs, Office of the Chairman. It was the chairman's number—again and again.

Laura thought hard about what she had learned from all this. But now she was stuck. She'd learned all she could here. She didn't know why, but she felt she just had to find out more about what was going on. It wasn't going to happen here.

Late that afternoon, as the staff was wrapping up operations for the day, Laura approached Commander Bob Fraser with a proposal. She remembered the stories in the J-2 directorate about his terrible problem with airsickness. "Commander, I see from the general's schedule that he's flying out to *Coronado*. Air ops section says it's the usual loadout of staff assistants, you representing J-2 as usual."

"Looks like it—can't wait," replied Fraser with the voice of a doomed man.

"Well, the General is always telling me that I don't have enough shipboard time. Maybe this could be a chance for me to get that and look around. I've never been aboard *Coronado* before. Why don't we talk with Captain Dawson and see if she'd substitute me for you? Unless you'd really like to go," added Laura with just a hint of sarcasm.

"Pack your bags, Peters. You're as good as there," said Fraser.

CHAPTER 29

RICK HOLDEN AND BEN MALGRAVE STOICALLY ENdured the hour-plus Blackhawk flight back to *Coronado*. The worst of the storm had passed, but the winds were still gusty, making the flight a lot like Mr. Toad's Wild Ride.

Minutes after he and Ben Malgrave emerged from the Blackhawk helicopter back on *Coronado,* Rick Holden realized that all was not right with the world. In the twenty-four hours that they had been gone, the pace on *Coronado* had reached a new level of intensity. Commander Ben Malgrave was barely inside the helo hangar removing his cranial and float coat when the ship's 1 MC general-announcing system blared out, "Commander Malgrave, *lay to* Staff Communications." Malgrave was accustomed to the standard professional courtesy afforded an officer of having his presence "requested," but he moved quickly toward his communications office. Holden followed, carrying the CMS gear.

Colonel Hicks met them in the passageway before they could get to the office. "Malgrave, where have you been? I'll have your ass for this. Comms are in a shambles, your boys can't keep up with the load. I hope to hell you enjoyed your *vacation* on the beach."

Malgrave protested feebly, the effects of too many bottles of the local beer the night before still dulling his brain. "Colonel, the helo got weathered in last night. Caught the first—"

Hicks wouldn't let him finish and Holden could feel the stress level in the usually cold and calculating, but typically unflappable, chief of staff. "I don't give a shit what your excuse is. Get your ass in there and get your comm shack working right. We have got to get this operation moving now!"

Malgrave practically fell into the comm shack with Holden close behind him—anything to get away from the enraged chief of staff. As they did, the communications team gave them the resigned look that let them know things had not been pleasant aboard *Coronado.*

"Well, troops, what's happening?" offered Malgrave, collecting himself as best he could.

Chief Browne spoke first. "You wouldn't believe it sir. SPECATs have been pouring in too fast; they're way backlogged now. INMARSAT and STEL have been going like mad."

"General must be about maxed out with all that," said Malgrave.

"Well, kind of," replied Browne, "but quite a few of the SPECATs have been specifically for Colonel Hicks and, well, sir, you know what the rules say. Colonel's been in here about half a dozen times talking on the satellite channels."

"To who?" asked Malgrave.

"None of us around when he does," offered one of the junior radiomen. "He clears the place out, and quick."

"What about the messages for the general? What are they all saying?" asked Malgrave.

The radioman looked toward Holden, not sure if it was all right to discuss these sensitive matters in front of him, but a nod from Malgrave let them know that Holden was in this with him. "Well, sir," he began, "most of the traffic for the general is from SouthCom. Sounds like the operation we've all been suspecting is really heating up and is just about ready to go. Been choppers coming out all day with supplies and things. Word is a big bunch of troops are arriving tomorrow, the way they've been cleaning up troop berthing and all. Anyway, most of the traffic to the general has been pretty normal stuff, like saying when the ship departs this area, what frequencies we use. That sort of stuff."

"When's the last time Colonel Hicks has been here on INMARSAT?" asked Holden, now empowered by Malgrave to be a full part of the team.

"Just about two hours ago, which means he should be coming back soon. Never gives us enough time to even start a field day. Sorry the place is such a mess, Commander. As far as the gear goes, ship's company is working on it best they can, but the colonel won't let us shut it down long enough to do any decent troubleshooting or maintenance."

Malgrave could hear the frustration in the young man's voice and he was about to respond with something positive when Rick Holden asked the question he knew he must ask. "Commander, sure would like to know what these calls are all about. Maybe we could plan ahead a little better if we did."

Malgrave immediately grasped the full import of what Rick Holden was suggesting—nothing less than eavesdropping on highly classified phone conversations between their chief of staff and the SouthCom commander. He pulled Rick aside into a corner of Radio Central.

"I know things have seemed a little strange around here, but to go to that extent, I don't know," said Malgrave.

"Look, Commander, I don't like this any more than you do. If I'm wrong, well, you can hang me out to dry as some uppity chief with some half-baked, wild-assed idea. But if I'm right, and there's something strange going on with the chief of staff, don't you owe it to your boss to find out what's going on?"

"But there must be another way."

"Not one that I can figure right now. You know me well enough to know that I've thought this through, and you've seen part of it. What do you say?"

Ben Malgrave couldn't say anything. He was overwhelmed by the events of late. Rick was making sense to him, but he was nervous, extremely nervous. He couldn't bring himself to get out the word *yes* to Rick, but just nodded and walked away. Rick was on his own.

Rick set up shop and waited.

Colonel Hicks picked up the ship's internal phone in his cabin on the first ring. "Chief of staff," he said abruptly.

"Colonel, this is Petty Officer Deere in Radio Central. I have an INMARSAT call for you."

"I'll be right up," replied Hicks.

Hicks climbed the two decks to Radio Central, moving briskly past working sailors. He knocked loudly on the door of Radio Central and a petty officer immediately opened it. He strode rapidly to the INMARSAT terminal and picked up the headset. Then, turning to the radiomen assembled there, he hissed, "All right, move out. I want privacy on this call."

The radio shack crew needed no further urging and quickly cleared out. Only Rick Holden remained, crammed out of sight in a dark corner of Radio Central, with his own headset at his ear.

"Hicks here," said the colonel.

"Colonel, does your boss suspect anything?"

"No General, he doesn't."

"Are you *certain* of that?"

"Absolutely, sir. The volume of traffic and occasional calls that you have been feeding him have kept him and the rest of the staff fully loaded. They're ramping up for this operation just like all the OP-PLANS tell them to do."

"Then you think we should put our end of the operation in motion?"

"The sooner we go, the better, before someone gets cold feet. Are you sure the other side has the power to stop it? They're loading up pretty heavy over here."

"No cold feet here, Colonel, and I can assure you that our friend in JCS won't get them either, not with all he's been through, and not with all he has invested in this either. You just let us worry about the forces on the other side; we've got the handle on that."

"I don't want to be hanging out alone on this one, General."

"You won't, nor will I, nor will the chairman." General Charles Walters wished he hadn't said "chairman" to Colonel Hicks, but Hicks had always been expendable and now he was guaranteed to be.

Someone without his background might have gone into sensory overload, but Rick Holden was making sense of this conversation. Was Operation Roundup going to be sabotaged? Why were Colonel Hicks, the "general," and the "Chairman"—surely not the chairman of the Joint Chiefs of Staff?—talking about keeping General Lovelace out of the loop? Who would do such a thing and why would they do it? Holden had more questions than answers, but he knew he was in the middle of something he could not control.

CHAPTER 30

As his specially configured VH-60A Blackhawk landed on *Coronado*'s flight deck the ship's 1 MC blared, "SouthCom arriving," and sounded the appropriate eight bells. As General Charles Walters disembarked from the helicopter, "rainbow sideboys"—flight deck men in their green, blue, purple, yellow, red, and white flight deck jerseys—formed two lines for him to walk through as he left the arc of the helo blades, rendering a snappy salute as the bos'n pipe sounded off.

As he clambered up the ladder to the ship's boat deck, he was met by the ship's commanding officer, Captain Pete Howe, and the JTF Eight commander, General Ashley Lovelace. They strode quickly past working sailors and large numbers of Marines just getting settled in and went directly to the JTF commander's cabin. Following not too closely behind, Lieutenant Laura Peters and the rest of the general's entourage headed off in various directions to complete their business on *Coronado* quickly so as not to keep the general waiting when he was ready to depart.

The commander's cabin aboard *Coronado* rivaled any corporate boardroom for its imposing elegance. Running the full width of the ship, it boasted exquisite paneling, soft, indirect lighting, beautifully framed pictures, plush blue carpeting, and other appointments that gave it a rich, secure look. Save for the two portholes facing forward, it would be easy to forget that you were on a Navy ship at sea.

In the quiet surroundings of the cabin, General Charles Walters seemed like a different officer from the one that had treated Brigadier General Ashley Lovelace so abruptly at SouthCom. "General Lovelace, back at headquarters we can see that your planning and preparations are right on track. Doesn't look like you have any holes to speak of."

"Thank you, General. I think that we're in good shape," replied Lovelace, taken a bit off guard by the senior officer's softer approach. "We've been working hard getting prepared. We had more Marines than we expected show up over the last two days, but we're getting them settled in fine. Other than that, we've been getting all of the supplies that we asked for."

"Fine, General, that's fine. I do hope that you understand the importance of your mission."

"Without a doubt, sir. I have been well briefed, as you know."

"My visit to your flagship today is no coincidence, General Lovelace," said Walters as he leaned closer to the man, conveying the impression that what he was about to tell him was crucial—and top secret—information. "I expect that we will receive an execute order for this operation within the next twenty-four hours. I needn't tell you that this has the intense interest of our leadership—our *top leadership*. You may even receive the go-ahead to proceed in an unconventional manner. Just be flexible and do your duty, Ashley."

General Lovelace was so taken aback that the SouthCom commander had used his first name that all he could respond with was, "Yes sir."

"You know how important it is to keep my headquarters informed."

"Yes, of course, General."

"I'm sure that you do. However, you also know the public relations impact that we're trying to achieve and the importance of timely information flow. We want to tell the story before CNN does, don't we?"

"Of course, General." Lovelace wasn't sure where this was leading, but he continued to be attentive.

"Well, I expect you to keep my staff informed, but if you have great success, don't let one of my junior officer watchstanders delay your passing the good news up the chain of command, all the way up to the Joint Chiefs—and above—if you think it is appropriate."

"Thank you, General Walters, for that flexibility. Naturally I will make every effort to keep your staff fully informed, but I do understand the time-sensitive nature of passing the word on what we hope to accomplish."

"No, General, not *hope* to accomplish. We know you will accomplish everything you set out to do, and more. I know that you were hand-picked for the job and I endorsed that selection myself."

Lovelace was flattered by the confidence that one of the Army's senior commanders had placed in him. They were finally recognizing his talents. Surely this would be the jumping-off point for his next star.

As the generals were conferring in the luxury of the commander's cabin, Laura Peters was looking for Chief Petty Officer Rick Holden. After several wrong turns, she finally found the ship's SEAL platoon commander, and although he was surprised that a Navy intel officer was looking for his chief, he dutifully sent for Holden and introduced him to Laura Peters. "That will be all, thank you, Ensign," said Peters, dismissing the slightly bewildered SEAL.

"Certainly, ma'am," replied Ensign Bob Kemp. "Chief Holden, report to the well deck as soon as you are finished talking to the lieutenant. We *do* have an operation to prepare for," he continued, salvaging a little bit of his command authority.

As soon as his platoon leader had departed, Holden asked the obvious question. "Laura, ah, I mean Lieutenant, I mean . . . what are you doing here?"

"Rick, can the formality. I'm really worried. Nothing at SouthCom makes sense. There is an incredible amount of traffic to and from *Coronado,* but some important stuff is being left out and almost nothing is going to and from General Walters except P-4s and SPECATs. There are also a really large number of phone calls between General Walters and the chairman of the Joint Chiefs of Staff. They have talked up to a half-dozen times a day. I had to come out and see what was going on for myself. You work in communications, and you had said last night that things were busy." She paused as some other staff members came through the passageway.

"We can't talk here," offered Rick. "Follow me."

As casually as he could, he led Laura down ladder after ladder, six full decks to Lower Vehicle Stow, near the ship's weight room, and someplace he knew that they could talk more freely.

Laura was a bit taken aback over how fast he had hustled her out of the staff spaces, but her shock was soothed by the instinctive confidence she had in him. "Rick, I just needed to come out and look, but I really needed to talk to someone I felt I could trust. I don't even know why I'm telling you all of this. Maybe it's all nothing, but my instincts tell me something may be terribly wrong."

"You've always had great instincts on the court. No reason you shouldn't have 'em here too," offered Rick, sensing and sharing her alarm. "Things have been a little scary here too." He related the furtive conversations by Colonel Hicks and told her of his line-tapping the night before.

"You tapped into a secure INMARSAT call between your chief of staff and *General Walters*? Rick, you could be court-martialed."

"I'm having trouble making myself believe any of this, but—I mean—Colonel Hicks talking to General Walters, assuring him that General Lovelace doesn't know anything about the operation. Why would they be cutting the boss out of an operation like this? From the way this ship is getting loaded up, it looks like we'll be making a major insertion somewhere. But to cut the boss out ... Do you think that the operation is supposed to go in some direction or have some result that General Lovelace isn't supposed to know about?"

"I just don't know."

"Won't you know exactly what we'll be doing ahead of time as you get the intelligence on this operation?"

"Sometimes we lead events, Rick, sometimes we're behind events. It just kind of depends. I wish that I had a way of letting you know if I find something out."

"Maybe you do. Commander Malgrave has given me pretty much free rein of the staff comm shack. I can put up a discrete HF net anytime. Is there a way I can reach you at SouthCom?"

"There's an intel HF net that we don't use much anymore, what with satellites and all making our secure comms really secure. You could call me on that. But, Rick, please be careful."

"I will. And remember, this could all be nothing. I don't want you going out on a limb for this. I can handle it from this end."

Rick was thinking like a CIA agent again, but Laura took his cautious approach as some overprotective guy thing and snapped back, "Rick, no, you can't, you're on a *ship,* remember? Don't you put yourself in harm's way. I can tap into a lot more resources back on the beach and I, well, sort of see General Walters a great deal."

"Oh," said Rick.

Laura realized she was about to dent his male ego, so she added something she had not shared with him the night before. "All it is, Rick, is I'm his regular squash partner at lunch. I know how it looks, and his wife's not down here, so he's given me the 'big wink' once or twice too often, but I can handle myself."

"Laura, come on." Rick was definitely in big brother mode now. "If there's something fishy going on, you're right in his sights."

"Rick, let's just work together on this. We need to really think all of this through. You're going to have to call me if you discover anything."

Rick wasn't at all comfortable with putting so much on Laura, but he didn't have time to think about it. The sound of "Flight quarters, flight quarters" over the 1 MC signaled the arrival of the Blackhawk to take General Walters and his party back to SouthCom. "Be careful, Laura, okay?"

She took out a pen, jotted down the high-frequency number, and pressed it into Rick's hand. "You too, Rick Holden, you too." Then she followed him up the ladder and toward *Coronado*'s flight deck.

"About time you arrived here, Lieutenant," growled General Walters. "The rest of us are here and you almost bought yourself a long ride on this ship."

"Yes sir, I'm sorry, General," offered Laura weakly as she looked back at Rick one last time before boarding the Blackhawk. Was he in danger? Was she?

CHAPTER 31

THE JOINT CHIEFS SAT ASSEMBLED, WAITING FOR GEN-
eral Walters's call. The chairman had insisted on it, saying
he would like General Walters himself to brief them on
the full details of Operation Roundup. He wanted them
to have consensus on this important operation and he felt
that hearing the full plan directly from General Walters
would bring them to that consensus and do so quickly.

The general's executive assistant, Colonel Keating, announced that he had General Walters on the line. Admiral
Boomer Curtis picked up the phone. "Hello, General.
Yes, we're all here waiting for your brief. I'm putting you
on the speaker phone."

As the Joint Chiefs listened attentively, General Walters went over the broad concept for Operation Roundup
and followed it with more and more minute details: helo
movement, refueling plans, Recon Marine loadouts, communications nets, and the like. He held them spellbound,
relating the intricacies of the plan with the self-assurance
of a fully empowered Unified Commander who was the
master of all he surveyed. As his monologue continued,
his fellow four-star generals grew increasingly impressed.
The operation seemed foolproof.

General Campbell feigned interest in General Walters's
briefing, but he knew what the real plan was, the plan that
he and Walters had so carefully worked out. Campbell
and Walters had spoken earlier that day on his private
line. Walters would tell Lovelace to begin the operation,
but that conversation would soon be forgotten by the senior general. The weapons had been transferred and were
now in the right hands, General Lovelace and JTF Eight
were headed north, all other aspects of the operation were
in place, and those things that needed to fail were set to

do so. He was almost ready to give the word to begin. He would talk to the President tonight and formally get his permission. He was sure that Taylor Calhoun would be ready for his call.

CHAPTER 32

CORONADO MOVED GRACEFULLY THROUGH THE WATER as she headed north, the lights of Panama growing dimmer in the background. Her four hundred-plus sailors and almost five hundred Recon Marines worked purposefully at their tasks. The Air Department had been augmented with men from other divisions in expectation of extremely high-tempo flight operations and the air bos'n was running the new men through the proper flight deck procedures.

Inside *Coronado*'s huge well deck, dozens of fuel bladders were in readiness, available to be flown in to set up a FARP, or forward air refueling point, no doubt as part of a planned long-range helo mission. Six decks above, in his comfortable cabin, General Ashley Lovelace placed his call on the INMARSAT.

"White House switchboard," intoned the impersonal voice.

"General Lovelace for the President."

"Yes sir, General, we've been expecting your call. Let me put on the National Security Advisor first."

"Brian Stavridis here, General."

Lovelace had not expected to talk with anyone else except President Taylor Calhoun, but upon reflection, he supposed that not too many people ever talked directly to the President without first going through the staff.

"Yes, hello Mr. Stavridis, nice speaking with you again."

"The connection at this end is excellent, General. Our technology really is good, isn't it?"

"That it is, Mr. Stavridis. I believe the President is expecting a call from me regarding our preparations for Operation Roundup."

"Yes, and I'll put him on directly, General. I have to tell you, though, he's nervous about this operation. The closer it gets, the more he worries that it might not succeed. Do you think it will?"

It was Lovelace's time to move into the limelight and he could not look back or have second thoughts. "Sir, we have planned this out in excruciating detail. We will have battlespace dominance and overwhelming force. We are headed north to the objective area at flank speed. As long as all the other elements of this plan are in place I am going to tell the President we are ready in absolutely all respects to begin Operation Roundup."

"General, that's good to know, and when you speak with the President please be just as positive and upbeat as you can. We need to keep him on-line."

"I will, Mr. Stavridis, I will."

"Hold for the President, please, General."

After a few minutes, President Taylor Calhoun came on the line. "Hello General, how is the weather aboard *Coronado*?"

"Just wonderful down here, Mr. President. We are loaded up and moving north. I feel like we're fully ready for our mission, sir."

"I know. I expect that General Campbell will ask me formally this evening for permission to commence this operation. I want to say yes, but I want to know that we are really ready, and that we can engineer the success we want to achieve. But *Ashley,* I want to hear it from you, on the scene. Do you feel we can pull this one off correctly, and without any losses?"

"There are always risks in combat, Mr. President, but we have taken every possible precaution. I feel good about this operation, and if I may say so, sir, this will be a good boost for your anti-drug campaign."

"Ashley, I knew I could count on you. Go get us a win, a big win, and call me immediately with details as they occur. How we break this to the press is almost as important as how we actually conduct the operation."

"You'll know immediately, Mr. President."

"You're a good man, General Lovelace. The nation is counting on you and your task force. God go with you."

General Ashley Lovelace put down the radio handset and stared out the forward-facing porthole of his cabin. *Coronado* cut a wide, shimmering swath through the calm Pacific. There was a bright three-quarter moon out and not a cloud in the sky. Yes, even the weather was smiling on him tonight. This would be an excellent operation— no, a flawless one. He was about to make his mark as a superb military commander.

Far below the commander's cabin, Chief Rick Holden was in his familiar haunt, *Coronado*'s weight room. Lifting was usually a tonic for Rick, but the course of the last several days had been so intense that he was so worn down mentally even his workout didn't seem to help clear his mind. As he loaded even more weights on the bench press bar, he tried to make some sense of all he had heard. He worried, not about himself, but about the men who were about to be put at risk in Operation Roundup. And about Laura Peters.

CHAPTER 33

DARKNESS ENGULFED USS *CORONADO* AS SHE STEAMED steadily through the eastern Pacific. Although it was hours before sunrise, the level of activity aboard *Coronado* was as intense as it was elsewhere in the world where the day was already hours older.

Captain Howe sat in his bridge chair on the starboard side of *Coronado*'s wide bridge, watching his ship come alive with activity as first a few, then dozens, then scores of men, just shadowy figures on deck, moved purposefully through their preparations.

As the officer of the deck and conning officer directed the activities of the bridge watch team, Howe had a few moments to reflect on the circumstances that had brought him to this command—a major command and a joint task force flagship, at that. He had come up through the officer ranks as a helicopter pilot, first flying search-and-rescue choppers and then graduating into a warfare specialty, anti-submarine warfare, flying the bulky SH-3G Sea King from the decks of the Navy's aircraft carriers. A series of successful assignments, most of them in the cockpit, had eventually won him command of the Golden Falcons of HS-2, and he had commanded HS-2 aboard *Kitty Hawk* during Desert Storm. He had paid his dues as a "staff puke" with the Joint Chiefs after that, followed by a tour as executive officer aboard the aircraft carrier *Constellation.* A successful tour aboard *Coronado,* his deep-draft command, would pave the way for command of his own aircraft carrier, the career pinnacle for most aviators. The key word was *successful,* for one small miscue would be enough to derail his career ambitions—there were many more commanding officers who had had deep-draft command than there were aircraft carriers to go around. Though he had been mischievous enough as a junior officer that his aviation handle was Wild Man, Howe was the picture of caution now.

He leavened his excitement over the impending operation with a natural sense of "what if" that any commander would feel at this juncture. Usually the Navy's flagships served primarily as mobile command posts for the Navy's three-star fleet commanders. They rarely went anywhere, staying berthed in major naval ports such as Norfolk and San Diego as convenient floating offices for these senior officers to work in. When they did put out to sea it was usually to take the admiral and his staff to some major naval gathering or festival. The flagship commander's primary role was to have the ship looking sharp at all times, to make the staff comfortable, and to make the embarked admiral very comfortable. Howe had done that well, he mused, for the first year of his command tour, but then *Coronado* had been suddenly reassigned as flagship for JTF Eight.

Coronado no longer looked very sharp. Two months at sea in the hot, muggy, and rainy tropical seas had taken their toll and *Coronado* was showing her three decades of age. Even in the dim light, Howe could see where rust was gobbling up increasing portions of his ship. It was not something he liked, and his squadron commodore would not be pleased when they returned to pier six at the Norfolk Naval Station.

Howe's dissatisfaction with this turn of events was overtaken by the immediacy of the current situation and the need to have *Coronado* perform perfectly on this day. The JTF Eight staff had not given the ship much advance notice of this impending operation, although aboard a Navy ship, with men working and living in extremely tight confines, there were no real secrets. The word was out that they were going to be involved in a major anti-drug operation, that a force of Recon Marines were going to be flown into a friendly Central American country, and that the entire operation was to be completely controlled from aboard *Coronado*. Heady stuff for a chopper pilot whose main function in life had once been to drive around in endless circles off the starboard side of an aircraft carrier, waiting to pick up a pilot who had punched out of his aircraft due to some emergency.

He had briefed his wardroom the previous evening, once the staff had revealed their full plan to him. The SouthCom alert order delivered that evening by naval message, loaded with ponderous minutiae, authorized JTF Eight to begin loading Blackhawks with Marines and launching those helos toward preapproved way points, as well as setting other portions of the attack in motion. The SouthCom execute order, authorizing the attack to actually begin once the aircraft were airborne and all systems were go, would be delivered via secure radio from General Walters to General Lovelace. While some staff members, particularly those well schooled in proper staffing, noted that this single call between two general officers was not the normally prescribed procedure, no one wanted to question General Walters's specific instructions. Those who had done so in the past had had their careers irrevocably derailed.

His crew was ready and now were in the initial stages of executing the plan. Down in *Coronado*'s cavernous well deck, his Deck Department ATOs, short for air transport officers, had almost five hundred Recon Marines, and all their equipment, organized into "sticks," military jargon for a group of just the right number of Marines to *stick* into a helicopter. The Marines were passing the time re-adjusting their gear, mentally preparing for their mission, or just bitching the way only sailors and Marines can about anything and everything, from the lack of ventilation in the well deck, to the poor quality of the breakfast the Navy had fed them that morning, to the flying skills of the Army pilots who would soon lift them off *Coronado*'s deck.

Above decks, *Coronado*'s sailors were busy with their tasks. At various stations, sailors positioned their twenty-five-millimeter chain guns, the ship's primary defensive weapon, ready for surface action that few thought would come. Inside their deck-mounted stations, fire control technicians set the parameters into their Vulcan/Phalanx Close-In Weapons System—CIWS, for short—ready to take out any hostile air target should it approach. Inside the skin of the ship operations specialists in *Coronado*'s Combat Information Center sat poised in front of their radar consoles, electronic countermeasures gear, and radio circuit boards. *Coronado* at general quarters was a different ship from the fleet commander "show ship" that Howe had at first commanded.

It was on *Coronado*'s flight deck that tension was the highest. The air boss and his assistant, the mini-boss, manned an array of radios and other communications gear that taxed their dexterity just to handle, let alone make useful in a coherent fashion. Seeming to talk simultaneously to the bridge, CIC, the flight deck, control, and the first wave of Blackhawk helos now only thirty miles out, the air boss had his hands full. This is where the front end of the operation would either succeed or fail. The JTF Eight staff had demanded precise, fail-safe timing for this operation, and *Coronado* was to receive two Blackhawks at a time, starting just before sunrise, load each with its stick of Marines, and then launch them in rapid enough fashion to recover the next two Blackhawks just three minutes after that. A total of at least twenty-four Blackhawks had to be moved through in just over one-half hour, something that *Coronado* had little experience in doing. During her service as a Navy fleet commander's flagship, the main activity on *Coronado*'s flight deck had been the constant cleaning necessary to keep it looking sharp for the admiral's visitors.

But Howe and his Air Department officers had drilled his men as best he could in the short time they had. Now the young flight deck crew was poised for action. Yellow-shirted LSEs tested their lit red and green wands to ensure that they worked. Blue-shirted chock and chain runners hefted their chocks and chains, ready to use them to secure the Blackhawks to the rolling deck long enough to embark their Marines. The red-shirted "crash and smash" crew shifted uneasily around on their P-16 Mobile Firefighting Cart—the crash cart, for short—while the silver-suited rescue men, whose job it was to actually enter a crashed helicopter and pull the pilots out of the flames, held the hoods of their suits in their hands, not wanting to don them too early in the already sultry tropical morning.

The air boss moved to pick up the ringing phone that mattered the most, the direct line to the bridge, right at the captain's chair.

"How's it looking back there, Boss?" queried Howe, although the TV monitor just above his chair gave him a perfect picture of *Coronado*'s flight deck.

"Looking good back here, Captain. My folks are ready. Just talked with the lead Blackhawk flight. They're just a little less than thirty miles out, good comms. Recommend we come to Fox Corpen now," replied the air boss, pleased with his preparations and confident that his crew would perform well in this demanding environment.

"Okay, Boss, we'll do that; 330 should get us good winds."

"I concur, Captain. I'll let you know how it looks from here."

Fox Corpen, or flight corpen, was the course *Coronado* needed to come to in order to provide the proper winds for landing and launching helicopters. Although the Blackhawk was a sturdy aircraft and had been used by the hundreds in Desert Storm and elsewhere, as with any helicopter, it had a well-defined wind envelope that it could safely operate in. Land or launch the helo outside of that envelope and you stood a very real chance of having the pilot lose control of his craft. As fellow helo pilots, both Howe and the air boss were intimately familiar with these requirements and there was never a question as to whether or not *Coronado* would provide good winds.

"Officer of the deck, come right to course 330, sound flight quarters," said Howe to Lieutenant Mike Walsh.

"Aye, aye, Captain," replied Walsh. Just a look toward the conning officer, Lieutenant Junior Grade Josh Cole, was enough to move the junior officer to issue the correct commands.

"Helmsman, right standard rudder, come to course 330."

"Aye, aye, right standard rudder, come to course 330." Navy rules had the helmsman repeat back the command exactly as it was given. "My rudder is right standard, coming to course 330."

"Very well," replied Cole. "Bos'n mate, sound flight quarters."

"Aye, aye, sir," replied the bos'n with his bos'n pipe already at his lips. He pushed down the button, activating the 1 MC general announcing system. After a long wail of the pipe, he intoned, "Flight quarters, flight quarters, all hands man your flight quarters stations. The smoking lamp is out on all weather decks. Wear no hats topside. Now, flight quarters."

The familiar chant made *Coronado* come even more alive. Those flight deck men who had been lounging just the least bit stood erect at their stations. The motor whaleboat crew mustered at their stations, ready to go after any downed helo and its crew. Men walking topside on the weather decks who did not have a direct role in the flight ops moved quickly inside the skin of the ship. As *Coronado* steadied out on Fox Corpen, Captain Howe picked up the E phone and buzzed the JTF commander on the flag bridge. "General, we're all ready up here."

"Very well, Captain, let's bring in those Blackhawks."

CHAPTER 34

AT THE FORWARD AIR REFUELING POINT—OR FARP site, in Marine parlance—Captain Scott Rivas surveyed his handiwork. He still admired this masterpiece of Marine technology and ingenuity that he and his men had carved out of what had been dense jungle less than forty-eight hours before.

The Marines, as well as their Army brethren, had honed the FARP process to a science during Desert Storm. Military helicopters are notoriously thirsty "fuel hogs" and the only way to sustain an operation in the field for any length of time was to build a refueling site completely from scratch. Site Dagger had been built in the jungle ten miles from the coast and approximately one hundred miles from the objective area in order to provide fuel to the notoriously gas-guzzling AH-64 Army Apache helicopters that were going to ride shotgun for the Blackhawks transporting the Recon Marines into the LZ in Operation Roundup. The decision had been made not to operate the huge Apache helicopters from *Coronado*'s flight deck because it would overcrowd the deck and slow down the loading of Marines into the Blackhawks, and because it would take too long to rearm them on *Coronado*. Only the first two Apaches would accompany the Blackhawks to *Coronado*. As for the rest, they didn't have enough fuel to fly all the way from Panama to the Operation Roundup LZ, and the operation planners did not want to get permission from some host country to refuel them there for fear of tipping off the operation, therefore this FARP site was an operational necessity and a critical part of the operation. Rivas's satisfaction was well deserved.

Now that the small site had been completed, Captain

Rivas busied himself by posting assignments for his platoon that would maintain the site until it was needed for the operation. "Sergeant Clark, have we checked the fuel tight integrity on bladders Alpha through Hotel?"

"Yes, Captain, all of the fittings have been torqued to specs and we have no leakage to speak of," replied Clark.

"Not supposed to have any, Sergeant. None to speak of is second best."

"Yes sir, what I mean is, well, first we made all the fittings hand tight to get the setup laid out just right, and now I've got Graves and Laird making the rounds torquing each one to specs."

"They're our most senior troops. Have you gotten any productivity out of the two new wanabees we inherited last week . . . what are their names?"

"Corporal Abraham and Corporal Solberg, Captain. No sir, seems they had some snafu with their MOSs, not really trained as fuelies. Best I can do with 'em is have 'em walk perimeter. Don't think they're ready yet to get into any of the technical side of things. We'll teach 'em in time, not on this op though."

Rivas was mildly annoyed that the unit integrity of his small platoon had been broken up by the unexpected reassignment of two of his most experienced technicians and the arrival of two fresh-faced "boot" corporals to fill the gaps. He would just as soon have done without them, but his place as a captain wasn't to question orders, just to get the job done, and he was using all of his men the best way he could.

It was a sight to behold, thought Rivas. After Navy SEEBEEs—the familiar acronym for the Navy's construction battalions—had carved a small clearing out of the dense jungle, huge CH-53Es had lifted scores of five-hundred-gallon fuel bladders and their associated piping from *Coronado* to this jungle site. Though challenged by oppressive heat and torrential downpours, his men had speedily connected all of the piping, gauges, monitors, check valves, and other various and sundry equipment needed to bring this site alive. Although dwarfed by the enormous black fuel bladders, the piping and connections had a functional but somewhat Rube Goldberg look to them. Important thing is that I know they work, mused Rivas.

Then, two by two, other specially adapted Superstallions, with huge internal and external fuel tanks, had made sortie after sortie to fill the bladders. While the pilots kept the helicopters turning on the deck, Rivas's men quickly inserted hoses that drained all but a few hundred gallons of the fuel from each helo, leaving just enough for each to return to *Coronado* to pick up another load of fuel. Though his men were nearing exhaustion, they completed the transfer in near-record time, validating his pride in them. By the time the final CH-53E departed last night, Rivas calculated that he had just under eighty thousand gallons of JP-4 jet fuel, more than enough to keep the thirsty Apaches gassed and going for almost any conceivable operation. About the only thing that displeased Rivas was that at the completion of the operation, he would be ordered to destroy this engineering masterpiece. Small price to pay, though, for the satisfaction of playing such an important part in the operation.

"Sergeant, let's get *Coronado* on secure HF and report that Site Dagger is up and ready to go," said Rivas.

"Roger, Captain, I'll have the major on the line in just a shake."

As Sergeant Clark powered up the radio circuit, Rivas noticed that Corporals Abraham and Solberg were not just aimlessly patrolling the perimeter of the site but were looking closely at the maze of complex piping and fittings and apparently asking one of the more senior men in the platoon some questions. Maybe they'll be quick studies, thought Rivas. Things may work out even better than I expected.

Late that evening, the majority of the exhausted platoon at Site Dagger bedded down, as Sergeant Clark assigned the first watches. "Mason, Scott, you have the 2200-to-0200; Abraham, Solberg, you have the 0200-to-0600. Let's see all of you keep on your toes."

CHAPTER 35

PRESIDENT TAYLOR CALHOUN DID NOT WAIT WELL. He felt the crescendo building for Operation Roundup. He had spoken with General Lovelace, who had assured him the operation was all set to go and that he would be receiving a call from the chairman of the Joint Chiefs of Staff very soon. But General Campbell had not called yet. Damn! What was taking him so long? Was he going to get cold feet and come up with some half-assed reason why they couldn't proceed with the mission? Just like the military, thought Calhoun. They want to plan everything to death, and then when it comes time to execute, if everything isn't just perfect they drop back and punt.

As Calhoun paced back and forth across the Oval Office, Brian Stavridis, the National Security Advisor, paced with him. Stavridis was much more patient with the system, but paced along nonetheless, if for no other reason than to give his boss moral support. "Mr. President, I'm sure we'll hear from General Campbell anytime now."

"I'm sure we will, Brian. I just want to get on with it, you know. Once we've made the decision I want the folks in the field to execute it, not stand around like tailor's dummies."

"Sir, I'm sure the chairman will be calling you soon. There don't seem to be any more loose ends to tie up."

"I hope not, Brian. I hope not. Come on, now. Just what in the hell is taking him so damn long?"

Stavridis could hear the frustration in the President's voice. He had staked a lot on the success of Operation Roundup, and waiting was the worst possible torture he could be put through.

Trouble was, General Howard Campbell had sensed this and was using it to his great advantage.

* * *

In his large Pentagon office, the chairman of the Joint Chiefs of Staff waited. He was ready to start Operation Roundup, had made all the proper preparations, had talked with the theater commander, and had satisfied himself that all was ready to go—his way. All that remained was to get the President to give the go-ahead. He knew Brigadier General Ashley Lovelace had talked with him already—he had monitored the entire conversation and, in fact, had it all on tape. General Walters had seen to that, once Colonel Hicks had fed him the correct radio frequency, setting up a monitoring station to intercept all of the calls the JTF Eight commander made to anyone off his ship on his command net. Just need to let the President twist in the wind a while longer, Campbell thought.

After satisfying himself that he had waited long enough, General Howard Campbell picked up the direct line to the White House.

"Good evening. General Howard Campbell. May I speak with the President, please?"

Within seconds, Taylor Calhoun was on the phone. "Yes, General Campbell, nice to hear from you. Go ahead, please."

Campbell could hear the tension in the President's voice. He would make the most of it. "Good evening, Mr. President. The field commander tells me that we're ready to commence Operation Roundup—with your permission, that is, sir."

"Well, yes, General, if you think that you are ready."

"We do, Mr. President. Of course, we need to empower the theater commander to commence when he is ready. Then, on his signal and his signal alone, he will give the joint task force commander, JTF Eight, the go-ahead to commence the operation. The timing has to be precise, Mr. President, and it's a deliberate, step-by-step process."

Calhoun was impatient with this military minutiae. Was the general ready to start the operation or wasn't he? "General, you have my go-ahead. Make the process as deliberate as you want to, but let's get on with it."

"Of course, Mr. President. I'll inform General Walters at SouthCom that he has clearance to begin, and then once he gets his last intelligence updates, he'll authorize General Lovelace to put the operation in motion."

The President was tiring of this ponderous military ritual. *Just get on with the damn thing,* he wanted to say—but didn't. "Yes, General. Why, just proceed with the plan. I think we have gone over it in detail, thank you."

"Certainly, sir. I can't tell you precisely when it will kick off. I'll put that in General Walters's hands and then he will tell General Lovelace precisely when the intelligence is right to begin."

Let's go! thought Calhoun. This wasn't the goddamned Normandy invasion. These damn military officers could make even the most simple things seem difficult. No wonder none of them ever amounted to much in politics. "Yes, General, I understand completely, yes. You will tell General Walters, then he will tell General Lovelace, then we will begin the operation that has been in planning for all this time. Have I got it about right?" President Taylor Calhoun was trying to rein in his sarcasm while he hid his frustration—but was not doing a very good job in either case.

"Yes, Mr. President, that's exactly right," replied General Campbell.

"Thank you, General," said the President as he hung up the phone, more relieved now that things were in motion.

CHAPTER 36

LOCATED ON THE 0-3 LEVEL JUST AFT OF THE BRIDGE, *Coronado*'s Combat Information Center, or CIC, was alive with activity just before dawn. Every radar scope was manned by the most senior petty officer qualified to operate it, every supervisory position was held down by the most experienced watchstander, and the ship's executive officer, Commander Don Quintong, was serving as the TAO—Navy shorthand for tactical action officer—responsible to the captain for fighting the ship. Each of Combat's sensor and weapons stations were manned and ready and the tension was palpable.

While their shipmates remained ready for anything, the real action in the early hours of the morning were on the two SPS-40 air search radar consoles, which were tracking the inbound Army Blackhawk helicopters. Faintly at first, at the periphery of the screen, and then more well defined as they moved inexorably closer, the inbound helos would have presented a challenging puzzle to even the most experienced OSs, or operations specialists, manning the scopes. However, by using their IFF Mode Three transponder they were able to interrogate the unique code set in by each Blackhawk and thus had a digitized display of the exact location of each bird. Operations Specialist First Class Bob Peck carefully tracked each Blackhawk to within five miles of *Coronado,* when he handed each one in turn off to the air boss, who brought them on deck.

The first Blackhawk crossed *Coronado*'s fantail and, following the LSE's commands, moved up smartly until it was over spot one and ready to set down. As the helo approached ever closer, the LSE leaned hard into the wind created by its whirling blades in order to steady himself and remain on his feet. He had seen too many of his shipmates bowled over, or at least set embarrassingly off balance, if they didn't give this whirlwind the right amount of respect.

Sticks 101 and 102 of Recon Marines were already staged inside the helo hangar and as the second Blackhawk landed on spot two, the 5 MC flight deck announcing system blared out, "Stick 101, stick 102, away. Stick 103, stick 104, muster in the helo hangar, on the double. Sticks 105, 106, 107, and 108, muster on the mess decks."

It took less than two minutes to load each stick of Marines on their respective Blackhawk, and when both Blackhawks on deck were fully loaded, the air boss turned the annunciator light on the tower from red to green and keyed his radio to the preset land/launch frequency. "Pacer 208, Pacer 214, winds are 35 to port at ten knots, pitch and roll negligible, green deck, lift on LSE signal."

The level of intensity remained high as the CIC team

brought each pair of Blackhawks into *Coronado*'s airspace, the air boss brought them on deck, and the sticks of Marines embarked. The sky on *Coronado*'s port side continued to fill with more and more Blackhawks as the Pacer squadron awaited the loading of their remaining aircraft before pushing off toward the beach.

At SouthCom headquarters, sequestered in his imposing office with the door shut and with instructions to his aides that he did not want to be disturbed under any circumstances, General Walters set the final segment of his plan in motion. Speaking firmly but in hushed tones so as not to be overheard outside of his office, he dialed the direct command line to General Lovelace himself. Walters was brief. "I don't really have the time to hand-hold, General Lovelace," he hissed. "Things are heating up here. You're just going to have to make it happen when you're ready. That's all from this end. Get on with your mission."

Back aboard *Coronado,* one deck above the flight deck where the Blackhawks were continuing to load combat Marines, General Ashley Lovelace put his secure phone back in its cradle. He reviewed the rather cryptic call he had just received from General Walters. He had just been given the execute order for Operation Roundup—hadn't he? The SouthCom commander was elliptical, saying so much—but conveying a mixed message. Lovelace held the sides of his head with the palms of his hands, as if urging his brain to work harder. Snippets of his first meeting with General Walters rushed into his head: ". . . I don't want you waiting for me to tell you what to do"; ". . . If I okay it, you get to execute it." Yes, Walters had given him the go-ahead. What else could "make it happen" mean? He had been given the go-ahead—just as the President had said he would. He was certain of it. He bounded out of his cabin and raced up the steps to *Coronado*'s flag bridge two rungs at a time.

At SouthCom headquarters, General Walters was a blur as he whisked past his puzzled staff members. "I've spoken with General Lovelace again. He knows what he has to do. It's pretty much out of our hands now," he shouted to his aide as he left the building. "I'm going back to my quarters for a while. Have the duty officer contact me if there is any breaking information."

CHAPTER 37

THE SOUTHCOM COMMAND CENTER WAS A MADHOUSE as Watch Team Bravo saw Operation Roundup evolve, and as they tracked the activity aboard *Coronado*. The operational plan for the exercise had been rehearsed thoroughly and they all knew their respective roles and responsibilities.

Lieutenant Colonel George Beall, the watch team leader, was directing the efforts of the team from his command console. "Air ops, status of Blackhawk launches."

"Twenty-three of twenty-four Blackhawks launched, Colonel. One had to return to the line with a tail gear box chip light. Still have enough helos to lift," replied the somewhat harried air ops supervisor.

"Status of backup squadron?"

"All twelve helos preflighted, systems checked and ready to go on fifteen-minute standby."

"Roger. Where are our Apaches now?"

"Two are airborne, en route to *Coronado*. They'll get gas right after the Blackhawks all clear her deck. The next wave of four Apaches will proceed directly from Howard to the FARP site soon after that so they arrive at the LZ at H+30. The next two flights of four will go via the FARP at one-hour intervals and relieve on station over the LZ. Should give us continuous coverage for the entire operation."

"Let's bring up the surface picture and see exactly where *Coronado* is."

"Roger," replied the surface picture coordinator, and with the push of a few buttons the massive large-screen display in front of the command console displayed a geographic presentation of the objective area, with *Coronado*'s position exactly plotted. Overlaid on the map was the objective area, as well as the ingress and egress flight corridors for the Blackhawks and the Apaches.

Lieutenant Laura Peters walked into the command center carrying the latest intelligence reports. She was determined to carry out her duties as normally as possible, so as not to cast suspicion on herself, but the events of the past several days had given her cause for concern. However, now that the operation was off and running, she began to think that perhaps her concerns had been for naught. Certainly the operation appeared to have gotten under way smoothly and seemed to be running without a hitch thus far. Maybe she didn't know as much as she thought she knew, and she had no wish to commit professional suicide by coming across with some half-baked idea about a plot to sandbag a major operation.

"Lieutenant Peters, anything of significance in your latest intel traffic?" asked Colonel Beall.

"No sir, just standard stuff. Haven't received the satellite imagery of the LZ yet, though. Could be the normal processing delays with the satellite."

"I'm sure it is," replied Beall. "You intel spooks tell me that's normal, though. What about the latest TARPs mission?"

"F-14 should be returning to Howard in about twenty minutes. We'll have the tape over here at headquarters ten minutes after that. Should give us a good infrared look at activity levels and all, but I'm not sure how useful that info will be. We know there are a lot of folks there; kind of stands to reason that there will be some level of activity no matter what."

"Make sure I see it immediately after it arrives."

It was almost surreal, thought Laura a half-hour later. The SouthCom staff had been intimately involved in the planning of Operation Roundup. They were the Unified Command with ultimate responsibility for this area of the globe. They had liaisoned extensively with the Joint Chiefs to ensure that they executed the operation according to their desires, and they had in-briefed the JTF commander, giving him very specific guidance on the objectives of the operation as well as an extremely detailed alert order. Now General Walters had retired to his office almost hourly, presumably to call General Lovelace—but without volunteering the specifics of those conversations. The staff was certain he would inform them when he gave the JTF Eight commander the execute order—he had to—they knew that—but the general had been acting preoccupied during the past several days.

Yet as the warning order actions continued to unfold, setting the stage for what they presumed was the imminent execute order, they sat in their command center as virtual spectators. One thing that did strike Laura as odd: General Walters abruptly left the command center after making one phone call in his office. The general had a reputation as a micro-manager and all of the staff thought it odd that he left the command center at a time when they thought the operation would be moving into the execution phase. Maybe there was some delay up the chain of command. Wasn't that just like the military—hurry up and wait? But with aircraft already in the air and scores of other details taking shape, something had to happen soon.

Her thoughts were broken by the voice of one of her fellow watchstanders, Major John Coutere. "Lieutenant Peters, phone call. Staff J-2."

CHAPTER 38

SKIMMING JUST TWO HUNDRED FEET ABOVE THE SURface of the blue Pacific, Major Pete Holian stole quick glances at the rest of the formation in the side mirror of his UH-60A Blackhawk helicopter. Concentrating on keeping the heavily loaded Sikorsky level as he blasted forward at 160 knots, he left it to his controllers in the back of the lead Blackhawk to monitor the remainder of the flight.

"Captain Bills, have we got the entire formation on your scope?" asked Holian of the young communicator in the rear of this specially equipped command ship.

"Yes sir, Major. Four flights of four, left echelon, two flights of three, also left echelon, holding good line abreast," replied Bills.

Major Pete Holian reflected on his good fortune in drawing this assignment. Choosing Air Cavalry out of West Point, he had performed solidly in flight training at Fort Rucker and had been assigned to Blackhawk squadrons immediately. He had risen quickly, demonstrating a good mix of leadership and flying skills. Now, as a brand-new major, he had command of a squadron of twenty-four Blackhawk helicopters. This mission was enormously important, and if his squadron performed well it would suggest that his latest promotion should not be his last.

"Beach line five miles ahead," said Bills, reminding the command pilot that they were about to move into the most challenging phase of their flight profile. "Each flight will be spreading out to double standard distance as we move into nap of the earth."

"Roger," replied Holian. "Let's go dark in the cockpits now. Transition to night-vision goggles."

Captain Bills sent the short, prebriefed transmission: "Checkpoint Corvette, spread formation, goggles on, execute . . . now."

In a well-choreographed motion, each Blackhawk responded to Bills's command. The green, red, and white position lights, as well as the rotating red anti-collision lights on each Blackhawk, went dark. Each helo activated its ALQ-144 countermeasures systems to defeat anti-air missiles, infrared suppressors to mitigate the hot exhaust gases of the two General Electric gas turbine engines, and readied chaff and flare dispensers to further confuse and throw off any missiles fired at the aircraft. Even though this was briefed as a benign insertion, Holian knew that it was prudent to utilize all of the aircraft's defensive systems.

As the formation of Blackhawks crossed the beach line, their crews tensed and the embarked Recon Marines shifted uneasily, ready for their mission, which they now knew was only about thirty minutes away. Major Holian ordered Captain Bills to make the short, prearranged transmission to *Coronado*: "control, Pacer flight, feet dry, out."

Chief Petty Officer Rick Holden was aboard Pacer 236, one of the last helos in the formation. He and the other five SEALs aboard his aircraft, along with the six SEALs in Pacer 238, had a vital role in this mission. They were the combat rescue element—TRAP, or tactical recovery of aircraft and personnel. TRAP was specifically assigned to be prepared to extricate any Marines who were either pinned down by enemy forces or were actually about to be taken captive by the enemy. They had well-rehearsed procedures to accomplish this critical and dangerous mission. While Holden and the rest of the SEALs hungered for action, they realized that they would not be called upon unless one of their comrades found himself in dire trouble. On balance, then, Holden really hoped this would be a mission where he would do no more than observe the action that was taking place on the ground.

Bills keyed his intercom and gave Holian the call he wanted to hear. "Major, two contacts on radar. Coming from bearing 145, twelve miles, closing at good speed, looks like the Apaches, sir."

"Good," replied Holian. "Track 'em inbound."

As Holian continued to fly his Blackhawk formation forward, he spotted in his peripheral vision first one, then the other Apache, forming up on his flanks. Each flashed its anti-collision lights once as a prebriefed greeting signal, maintaining the radio silence that was dictated for this mission. Holian let himself relax just a bit. The mission was tracking beautifully.

CHAPTER 39

"LIEUTENANT PETERS SPEAKING, SIR."

"Laura, this is Captain Dawson. I'm over at Air Ops. TARPs squadron insisted on looking at this film before sending it over to headquarters. We looked at the film together and damned if it doesn't raise more questions than it answers. Think that you need to have Lieutenant Colonel Beall call the general on this one."

"Captain, I can't. I mean, what are you saying? What is the film saying? Are you sure this is an important enough matter to necessitate calling the general?" asked Laura.

"Look, it's hard to really pinpoint, but the level of activity there seems to be really high, especially for the middle of the night. Trucks moving, large groups of men out in the bush. It doesn't add up. We don't really have any analysts over here who can make much sense of it. I'll be bringing the film over to you as soon as we copy it and have the pilots who flew the TARPs mission come with me. The bottom line is that this isn't shaping up as something we briefed." The usually calm captain was worried, and that bothered Laura, for Captain Fran Dawson had a reputation of being totally unflappable under pressure.

"I'll talk to the colonel right away, but get that film over here in a hurry," commanded Laura, surprised she was now giving orders to her superior, but determined to take control of what could be a deteriorating situation. What could this mean? Why was there such a high level of activity at a place where their intelligence had told them Maradona was merely retrenching and consolidating his gains? Was it just a coincidence that a secret, well-planned and -coordinated mission was only a half-hour away from landing at this site? They couldn't have been alerted to this mission—or could they?

It took a few moments to fully sink in—and then Laura's call was almost a shout. "Colonel Beall!"

CHAPTER 40

NOE—OR NAP OF THE EARTH—FLYING WAS THE MOST challenging flight regime imaginable for the Blackhawk pilots. As the formations of Blackhawks roared across the dense tropical forest in the predawn sky, they flew so close to the ground that the entire forest seemed to bend with the powerful force of the helos' blades. Heavy with a full load of fuel and with the weight of their fully loaded Recon Marines, each Blackhawk was being operated at the limits of its envelope and the sluggishness of the controls reminded each pilot that his margin for error was almost nonexistent if he was to keep his aircraft from colliding with the earth.

Each bird continued to press inexorably forward, each pilot following the lead aircraft in turns as each checkpoint was passed, each crewman remaining tense as the minutes ticked away before they arrived at their LZ. There was no more easy banter, just the steely-eyed stare of professionals who knew they were the point on a critical mission.

In the lead Blackhawk, Major Pete Holian's confidence grew with every passing minute. The Blackhawks were perfectly arrayed in their formation, the two Apaches riding shotgun were formed up on their flanks, and he could see the payoff of the seemingly endless training his pilots had gone through. This was going to be the perfect mission.

"Control, Pacer flight, checkpoint Audi, over," said Captain Bills as the Blackhawks reached the first of the overland checkpoints.

"Pacer flight, control, roger, out," replied *Coronado*'s

air controller with his prearranged burst transmission.

As the Blackhawks pressed onward, Holian rehearsed the assault scenario in his mind. Even though this was going to be a surprise assault against a lightly armed and totally ragtag bunch of druggies, he was determined to handle the mission totally professionally and sting them with the armed might of his airborne armada. It was a good plan. The first two echelons would land on the northwest and southeast corners of the mesa, right at the foot of the steep hills, and set their Marines out in blocking positions to prevent any of Maradona's men from escaping into the hills once the attack began. The second two flights would land to the south, between the mesa and the river, and proceed upslope, fanning out in a manner that would let them cover all routes of escape in that direction. The last two echelons of three aircraft each, with the Apaches riding shotgun, would head directly for the compound, where the Marines would fast-rope down and surprise what was sure to be several hundred sleeping druggies. It was a simple and straightforward plan, and in Holian's mind, that was the best kind.

"Bills, how long to checkpoint Saab?" asked Holian

"Seven minutes, Major. We turn to course 082 at that time, next to final leg," replied Bills.

"Rog, sounds good. How about to the next checkpoint?"

"Four minutes to that, then three to the next. Gonna be some tight turns through the next two, Major."

"No problem, Bills. This bird can hack it." Holian loved his Blackhawk. He had over twenty-five hundred flight hours in these ships; the sturdy Sikorsky aircraft had never let him down.

"Updating nav now," said Bills.

"Roger. How have our GPS posits been?"

"All right on, plus or minus forty yards. Major, we could find this place in the bottom of a black-ass inkwell."

"Let's hope we don't have to, Captain, let's hope we don't have to."

CHAPTER 41

CARRYING THE TARPs FILM, CAPTAIN FRAN DAWSON entered a SouthCom command center that bore no resemblance to the usually calm place, especially in the hours before dawn, she was accustomed to. Lieutenant Colonel George Beall and his entire watch team stood in breathless anticipation as Dawson spread out the large package of pictures the F-14A Tomcat had taken only hours before.

"Captain, why don't you lead this and tell us what you think you've seen?" suggested Beall. He didn't like the way this was going and desperately wanted it all to just go away. Although he was in charge of the watch team, he was eager for someone else to take the lead in deciding what to do next.

"Right," replied Dawson. "It's more than just 'a think,' Colonel. This is not what we expected we'd be seeing by a long stretch. The whole equation has changed. What we thought we'd be seeing now is not what we're getting from these pictures. There's a major change here, a major change!"

As Dawson laid out the pictures of the entire hacienda on the Polara Mesa, Lieutenant Colonel Beall, Laura Peters, and the rest of the watch team pressed closer to the large metal briefing table that dominated the middle of the command center. Most of the rest of the SouthCom intelligence staff had been hastily summoned, as well as two Army intelligence specialists stationed at Howard Air Force Base that Beall had known from Fort Monroe. There were a few moments of anxious anticipation; none of the senior intelligence officers present wanted to commit to an opinion and risk being wrong in front of their colleagues. Then, unhampered by such pretensions, one of the Army intel specs spoke up.

"That's not right," blurted out the young tech sergeant, pointing at one of the pictures. "Look at the woods surrounding it, here, here, and over here. Have to be groups of men, and look at that, vehicle exhaust for sure, here, and here too. And look at the building itself. There is supposed to be a large group of men sleeping there, but this photo was taken at about 0330 and there is barely enough heat being generated to make out the outline of the building. Nothing going on in there, that's for sure."

A Navy IS, or intelligence specialist, petty officer from the staff backed him up. "I agree, Colonel. Got to be people; in all our previous photo recon of the site we saw absolutely nothing at these spots."

"I see it too," offered Laura. "There, there, this one seems to be growing in sequential photos. The jungle cover is pretty thick all along the periphery, so heat's all we'll pick up, but it's certainly not normal. Do you agree, Captain Dawson?"

Not accustomed to being put on the spot by one of her junior officers, Captain Fran Dawson replied tersely, "I see the evidence, Lieutenant." Turning to Lieutenant Colonel Beall, she asked, "What's our plan now, George? It's your watch team. You need to act on this information. What's the plan?"

Instinctively, Beall asked the assistant watch officer, "How far are the Blackhawks from the LZ?"

"Just eighteen miles out. Should be on top in eight minutes, maybe ten, as they slow down a bit for the approach. Should be right on schedule," replied the watchstander.

Beall stood frozen for a moment, the enormity of the situation seemingly overwhelming him. The remainder of the command center was absolutely silent, as if in mute respect for the colonel's need to think through his next move. He ran his hand through his thinning hair. Lieutenant Colonel Beall had a thin frame, but now he looked positively gaunt. His normally moderately tan complexion now looked totally pale, almost ghostly. He looked like a character from the grave.

Finally, Captain Fran Dawson, the most senior officer present, though not a line officer qualified to command a watch team, could wait no more. *"Colonel,* we need to do something, and we need to do it now."

"Do what, Captain? What is it you want me to do?" Beall literally hissed the reply. He was clearly breaking down under the pressure.

"We need to abort the mission, don't you see? This is not going to be a surprise attack. The men at the mesa, the ones we think are all sleeping, they're not in the hacienda at all. They're deployed in perfect defensive positions in the jungle all around the hacienda. That much heat at each position tells me there are a few dozen men at each spot. The truck exhaust all up and down the slope—clearly they're deploying more men every minute. And look here, Sergeant, this picture here, I missed these before. What are these large metal cases, kind of coffin-shaped, but not a size I'm familiar with?"

The tech sergeant stared at the picture as if trying to bring it into focus, then said what Dawson had feared but had hoped would not be the case. "Ma'am, those look an awful lot like Stinger carrying cases. Picture's a bit small, but size and shape are about right, and they've got . . . looks like about seven or eight of 'em, about right for a battery. Look, here next to this clearing. Same thing, can you make it out?"

Everyone in the room pressed closer to the table, drawn by the sergeant's ominous words. Yes, the imagery wasn't perfect, but Dawson and the rest saw it more clearly now.

"Colonel, you've got to call General Walters now! This is an ambush. We've got to stop this operation now!" Dawson's response was somewhere between a command and a scream.

Lieutenant Colonel George Beall's face was contorted, something between fear and incomprehension. Twenty-two years of sitting in missile silos during the Cold War, ready to push "the button"—but never having to—had left him ill-prepared for a crisis decision like this. Though it didn't seem possible, his color turned even whiter. The man was clearly on the verge of coming completely apart.

"Colonel, please!"

Reluctantly, Beall picked up the bat phone and within seconds had General Walters on the line at his quarters.

General Walters answered the phone in a crisp tone, immediately making the shaken Beall wonder whether he had done the right thing in calling the general.

"General, uh, Colonel Beall here, sir, Watch Team Bravo, sir. Well . . ."

"Get on with it, Colonel. What the hell is important enough for you to bother me? You the watch officer?"

"Yes, General," replied Beall, his confidence now almost totally shaken.

"Well, what is it, then?"

"Well, General," Beall managed, as every man and woman in the command center stared at him, offering neither hope nor encouragement, "sir, ah, we've just received some rather disturbing photos from the F-14 TARPs mission over the Operation Roundup LZ. It looks like there are men deployed in the hills, and, well, we have indications that they may have Stingers and other weapons. We think we may have a mission abort, sir." Beall breathed heavily after the final "sir," obviously relieved he had managed to say all of this without coming unglued.

"How far are the Blackhawks from the LZ?" asked Walters tersely.

"About seven, no, about six minutes out, General."

"And you call me now, you jackass? I'll have your oak leaves for this, Colonel. 'You think,' 'maybe,' 'perhaps'— you want me to call off this entire operation because of some half-assed, last-minute intelligence that you 'think' you have?" Walters seemed to literally come through the phone at the broken Beall, and those standing anywhere near the colonel could hear every word of the general's tirade.

Captain Fran Dawson grabbed the phone away from Beall. "General, Fran Dawson here, sir. This is pretty convincing stuff. I have no doubt that there is an ambush waiting and our men will take casualties," offered Dawson, pleased that she had stepped in and taken charge.

The pleasure lasted only a microsecond. *"Casualties, casualties! What the hell do you know about casualties, Captain? You haven't ever heard a shot fired in anger. Have you all lost your minds? Put Beall back on the line."*

Colonel Beall meekly picked up the phone. "Yes, General."

"Beall, is that you?"

"Yes sir, General."

"Well, speak up, dammit, man. You in charge or what?"

"Yes sir."

"You take charge, Colonel. I will not abort this mission based on some guess-and-by-golly by some goddamned Navy intelligence pukes. This mission is still a go. Have Sergeant Brooke bring my staff car over here immediately."

The entire Watch Team Bravo stood in shocked silence, knowing that by the time General Walters arrived at the command center, Americans would be on the ground in this "friendly" country, fighting for their lives. For Laura Peters, it was a nightmare come true.

CHAPTER 42

"LZ AT TWELVE O'CLOCK, THREE THOUSAND YARDS, Pacer flight, land now, now, now." The command from Major Pete Holian was given at precisely the time anticipated by the other Blackhawk section leaders and led immediately to well-rehearsed action by each helicopter.

As the dim first morning light was breaking in the eastern sky beyond the highest mountain peaks, the American forces swooped down on the Polara Mesa. The mission was sure to be a rather pedestrian roundup of unsuspecting druggies, but their training impelled them to conduct this mission like all others, and professional discharge was the order of the day.

Several hundred yards to the northwest and southeast of the hacienda, a total of eight Blackhawks flared in quick sequence and scores of Marines clambered out of the craft and took up their prebriefed static positions. Moments later, the same scene was repeated to the south, the

Marines from these eight helos dropping down on the wet grass and beginning their push up the slope toward the hacienda. The remaining Blackhawks were bunched in a tight formation that would have terrified most pilots, but which was standard operating procedure for the veteran Blackhawk aircrews. Led by Major Holian's aircraft, and now closely escorted by the two Apaches, they headed directly for the main compound, now clearly visible as the Marines aboard completed their preparations to fast-rope directly down into the compound.

The flash of light from one Apache immediately blinded the pilots aboard all of the aircraft as their sensitive night-vision goggles, designed to bring in even the faintest ambient light, now brought in the incredibly bright, pyrotechnic explosion of something hitting the aircraft. Years of training and practice caused the Blackhawk pilots to immediately push aside their goggles and slow their aircraft down to regain their orientation and situational awareness as their aching eyes attempted to readjust after that massive overdose of light. Out of his remaining peripheral vision, Major Pete Holian saw the second Apache explode and tumble toward the earth.

By now the Blackhawk pilots knew they were in a free fire zone and that each one was incredibly vulnerable in their high-hover positions, with Marines on ropes sliding toward the ground below them. The enemy on the ground took advantage of that vulnerability and launched more Stinger missiles at the hovering Blackhawks. First one, then another, then another was hit. One exploded in mid-air, sending shrapnel flying toward other craft. A second Blackhawk, on fire from hits in both engine compartments, started toward the ground in some degree of control but then exploded as fire reached its fuel tanks.

On the ground, those Marines who had already fast-roped to the deck were completely disoriented by the aircraft exploding above them and crashing around them. Most instinctively moved outward to set up some sort of a perimeter, but the majority were killed by the fireballs from the crashing helos or from the shrapnel that was everywhere. The remaining men clung to the ground, trying to get their bearings and sort out the chaos surrounding them.

Major Pete Holian's Marines had not yet begun to fast-rope down and he was about to push off and get away from the carnage, but the yellow lights that began to appear in rapid succession on his warning panel let him know that he was about to lose that option. He had escaped any Stinger hits, but exploding shrapnel had penetrated the skin of his chopper and had severed his tail rotor drive shaft. As the anti-torque tail rotor, now deprived of its drive, began to windmill down, Holian applied more and more left pedal to try to keep his aircraft from spinning. It was not to be. As more and more warning lights came on, as if to insist that he really had a problem, Holian did what his training and instincts told him he must do with his mortally wounded aircraft. He lowered the collective and headed for the deck 150 feet below. Working now on instincts, his adrenaline taking over, Holian did a credible job of landing his wounded craft in an almost level attitude, albeit hard enough to collapse the landing gear. There was just enough of a slope to destabilize the helo and it rolled over, its main rotor blades destroying themselves and sending deadly metal fragments everywhere as they chopped into the unyielding earth.

All of the Marines on the ground around the periphery of the compound saw the explosions and knew instantly that their mission had been ambushed. They were still forming up into their company units and did not have long to consider their next move. From well-entrenched and well-concealed positions in the hills around them, heavy-caliber machine gun fire rained down on them. Instinctively returning fire, Marine after Marine was hit as the machine gunners targeted the muzzle flashes of their rifles. As they were absorbing this withering fire, trying to form up into at least squad-sized units, the Marines were totally confused as to which way to move—outward toward the surrounding hills where the intense fire was coming from, or inward toward the hacienda where crashed helicopters were still giving off secondary explosions.

At the hacienda site, amid burning and still-exploding helicopters, the shrieks and screams of wounded and dying men provided a horrifying din. It appeared that the enemy had totally vacated all of the hacienda buildings and all of the fire directed at the Marines on the ground was coming from the surrounding hills. Amid this confusion and chaos, Major Pete Holian managed to crawl from his wrecked aircraft. Unable to stand on his shattered ankle, he dragged himself around the periphery of the helo, checking for signs of life among any of his crew or the embarked Marines who may also have survived the crash. His copilot looked like he might be alive but was trapped in his seat when the aircraft had rolled onto its left side. Holian had his sidearm drawn, but could see no enemy to fire at.

From one of the rescue birds, Rick Holden stared at the carnage ahead of him in utter disbelief. There had been much debate as to whether to even have these two aircraft on such a benign mission, but training, doctrine, and the insistence of the SEAL Platoon Commander, Ensign Kemp, had won out. Now Kemp and his group of six SEALs in Pacer 238 and Holden and his group in Pacer 236 watched in horror, wanting to act but not knowing where to go or what to do.

The radio transmissions among the surviving Blackhawks gave some sense of the utter confusion on the battlefield.

"Pacer 208, Pacer 302. That you on my wing?"

"Roger 302. Need to go in and get our guys out."

"208, 302, this is Pacer 205 and playmate 207. We're in a tight circle, thousand feet above you. What's the status? Can't raise the command aircraft."

"Uh, 205, this is 302, remain at altitude. I say again, remain at altitude."

"This is 201 and flight of four to the northwest, fifteen hundred feet. All my Marines are on the ground taking heavy fire. Going to send one bird back into the LZ to extricate 'em."

"Negative 201, negative. This is 302. Stingers in the area, I repeat, Stingers in the area. We need to call for Apache backup."

"Can't just let our troops get slaughtered, 302. We'll go on command of Major Holian."

"All Pacer aircraft, this is Pacer 302, Captain McGrath speaking. Can't raise Major Holian. His bird must have been hit over the compound. I'm in command of Pacer aircraft now. I say again, do not land, active Stinger missiles in and around LZ. Continue to circle outside of range. Stand by for further instructions, out."

On the ground some Marines had formed up into small squad-sized units and were bravely returning fires toward the hills as first light began to gobble up more and more of the night sky. With their small weapons they were clearly outgunned by the enemy in the hills. Their return fire became increasingly feeble as more and more men were hit. Disorganized, disoriented, only their training and pure guts kept the Marines firing back at all.

The silence on the radios that was the result of McGrath's "out" call was broken by a call on VHF guard, the emergency distress frequency. "Any Pacer aircraft, this is Holian, over."

McGrath responded immediately. "Major, this is Captain McGrath, Pacer 302. I hear you weak but readable. Say your position, sir."

"I'm on the deck inside the compound. Bird's totaled, lying on its side. Don't have a complete picture, but most of our men here have been killed, may be a few wounded remaining. My copilot looks like he's alive but trapped inside the aircraft. Have you called in the Apaches yet?"

In the confusion and the carnage, McGrath had forgotten to communicate with the relay Blackhawk, a bird that had stopped about twenty miles from the objective area to serve as a communications relay platform to call for additional Apache aircraft to join the battle and to keep the flagship informed of the progress of Operation Roundup. "Not yet, Major. Making the call right now," replied the shaken McGrath.

"Pacer 408, Pacer 302, over."

"Three-oh-two, this is 408, read you loud and clear."

"Four-oh-eight, we need Apache backup. Pacer flight has been ambushed, at least four Blackhawks down, both Apaches shot down, numerous wounded, all the Marines on the ground under intense fire. Get those birds in here now."

Warrant Officer John Pierre was stunned by what he was hearing, but his training took over. On his HF command net, he called the first group of four Apaches, which were now approaching the FARP site just over a hundred miles away, ready to refuel and close the LZ only if needed.

"Vanguard flight, Pacer 408, buster to my posit, ambush in progress, repeat, ambush in progress."

"Pacer 408, Vanguard lead, say again." The lead Apache pilot had heard the words clearly but, in disbelief, needed to hear them again.

"I say again, Vanguard, I relay from Pacer leader, at the LZ. Pacer flight has been ambushed, several helos down, Marines under heavy fire. Need your guns and rockets in here now."

"Pacer, Vanguard. What about the two Apaches at the LZ? Are they returning fire now? Over."

"Vanguard, Pacer. Both, repeat both Apaches shot down. Many Blackhawks down. We're losing men as we speak. We need you here *now*!"

The Apaches were closing the coast at maximum speed, low on fuel from their long flight from Panama but headed directly for the FARP site and a quick refueling. "Pacer, Vanguard, estimate ten mikes to the FARP site, less than ten more mikes to hot refuel, then another forty-five minutes to the LZ. Hold on."

"Roger Vanguard. I'll pass that to 302 at the LZ." Then he added what was unnecessary to say: "But hurry, please hurry."

Back in Pacer 236, Rick Holden leaned forward into the cockpit and turned first left, then right, giving each of the two pilots a long, knowing look. Just the barest nod from each told Rick they knew what they had to do.

CHAPTER 43

SERGEANT CLARK AWOKE EARLY AND PREPARED TO make his morning rounds. Dressing quickly, he pulled his gear together and prepared to walk the perimeter to check on his sentries. The two new men, Abraham and Solberg, had the 0200-to-0600 watch. The predawn one was always the toughest, he recalled—he'd probably catch them loafing around and would have the pleasure of giving them a good ass-chewing.

It had been faint inside of the cramped tent, so full of the body smells of six sleeping soldiers, but as he emerged from the tent it overwhelmed him—the strong, pungent, and unmistakable smell of aviation fuel. As he walked upslope a few steps to clear his head and get his bearings, his heart sank as the dim predawn light revealed enormous puddles of fuel, fuel from his fuel farm, all around him. *No, NO!* What had gone wrong, and where was his watch? He'd have their asses for this.

Instinctively, Clark began to move toward the captain's tent to tell him while he began to shout the alarm to roust out the rest of his men. *"Troop, everyone up, everyone up, we've got a huge leak somewhere, let's go, let's go, on the double, on the double."*

As he reached the captain's tent, Captain Rivas was already emerging, as were the rest of his men from their tents. They emerged just in time to see the huge fireball from one of the exploding bladders, feel the shock and the heat wave, and then see the flames engulf the now seemingly continuous puddle of fuel that spread everywhere.

Although the tents where the soldiers were sleeping were not in the middle of any of the puddles and were spared the immediate inferno, many of the Marines were hit by the flying debris of the FARP site as the lethal mixture of aviation fuel continued to blow apart in a series of secondary explosions, sending pieces of bladders, lines, pipes, and other material flying hundreds of yards.

As the stunned Marines hugged the ground, waiting for the inferno to pass and hoping that they would not be engulfed, Corporals Abraham and Solberg watched from a nearby bluff. They did not know why they had been told to blow up this site.

Sure, they had murdered the Panamanian national—but she was a prostitute and hadn't delivered what they'd paid her to. After all, she'd drawn a knife on them, and they had hit her pretty hard—hadn't really meant to kill her—but she collapsed in a pool of blood. Their military lawyer hadn't tried hard enough in their general court-martial at Howard Air Force Base—rumor was the United States convicted them of murder and sentenced them to die just to placate the Panamanians. But just before their transfer to Leavenworth he—never did give his name—said they had been given a pardon—by the general, he said—if they would take a secret mission, no questions asked. They would be transferred to this unit and on an appointed day they would blow up this site—$10,000, false IDs and passports would be waiting for them in a safe house in Panama City. Yes they could trust him—no they didn't have to go through with this. They could stay on death row and the general would order their executions in a speedy fashion. Abraham and Solberg—their new assumed names—were not the most trusting souls, but in this case their options were pretty straightforward. Now they had only to wait for the carnage to become final, return to the FARP site and mingle with the survivors— if there were any—then return to Panama after the operation, and they were free men. As they looked down at the site, it appeared that they would be among the few survivors.

CHAPTER 44

WAR SOMETIMES MAKES HEROES OUT OF THE MOST UN-
likely candidates. Pitched battles tend to make those heroics stand out even more. Losing battles, in which a
group, a force, or even an army is totally decimated, have
on occasion brought out incredible heroics in the most
ordinary men.

Lance Corporal Phil Bernstein was one of those men.
He never was really sure why he joined the Marine Corps.
Like many young men of the so-called X generation, he
had virtually sleepwalked through high school, not distin-
guishing himself academically, athletically, socially, or in
any other way. He tried a local community college for a
while but kept dropping courses just when they would become even the least bit difficult. Finally, he walked into a
recruiter's office after a particularly disastrous exam—English, as he recalled—and was swept up with the prospect
of adventure. He actually did quite well in recruit training—perhaps the Marine Corps had tapped into some
deep reservoir of interest and enthusiasm—and was offered the opportunity to "go Recon"—that is, join the
elite Reconnaissance Marines, who comprised the special
force of that branch of the military. He'd been with Second Company, First Marines, for a little over a year, and
was coming up for advancement when his unit got the call
for this multi-service, high-visibility mission.

The thoughts of how he had gotten to this place had
plenty of time to come back to him as Bernstein lay facedown on the warm dirt this morning. He was in the group
that had landed south of the hacienda and had just started
the push uphill when all hell broke loose and withering
fire had rained down on them from behind. One by one,
his comrades had been hit and most now lay dead or dying

around him. Bernstein was on a particularly well-exposed piece of ground and probably only escaped death because the enemy assumed anyone in that exposed a position had already been hit enough times and so no longer fired at him. For his part, he continued to lie perfectly still.

Bernstein surveyed the devastation around him. He saw the dead, silent and unmoving, and the dying, moaning or crying, moving ever so slightly and more and more slowly. He pondered his own fate, afraid to move but feeling that some action, any action, might be better than waiting on this hellish piece of earth for something to happen. It might never happen. He would make it happen.

Bernstein heard a low moaning to his left, about twenty yards away. He raised his head ever so slightly to look and saw Sergeant Josh Bingham, his platoon sergeant, trying to drag himself up the hill, away from the now-sporadic but well-directed fire from below them and toward what might be the relative safety of the hacienda. From the sergeant's movements, Bernstein could tell Bingham was dragging his leg—the right one, he thought—and was never going to make it. As he raised his head just a bit higher, he heard the staccato *whump, whump, whump* of a twenty-five-millimeter chain gun and actually heard the shells whistling by. Well, at least the mystery was over; they knew he was alive now. No sense playing possum forever. It was time to make his move.

Propelled by some force that he could neither understand nor describe, Bernstein hopped up into a low crouch and sprinted toward Bingham. The staccato of the twenty-five-millimeter chain gun became more insistent now and he felt himself flinching with every sound, running and flinching, covering the distance quickly now, finally diving down next to the wounded Bingham.

"Corporal, fancy meeting you here," said Bingham, mustering the battlefield humor that often defies explanation.

"Sergeant, you hit?"

"Yeah, Bernstein, think I took a piece of a shell in the leg. Hurts like hell and ain't real mobile, as you can tell. Looks like we've been totally wiped out here. Any Marines left where you came over from?"

"Doesn't look like it, Sarge. Can't really tell. Everyone

was so spread out and not formed up when we started taking fire. Sarge, what happened?"

"Got ambushed, Bernstein, pure and simple. From the looks of things these people knew exactly when we were coming and what we were coming with and were armed to the teeth. Looks like our big boys really blew this one. Hope there's hell to pay somewhere."

"So what's our next move?"

"Think you need to get up to the house up there. Looks like all the fire's coming from the jungle. Just get up there and lay low for a while. You'll be halfway safe until they send in the cavalry."

"Package deal, Sarge, we're doing this together."

"No way, Bernstein. I'm not mobile. I'll just hunker down here and wait it out. Can't be long is my guess."

"Package deal, Sarge. Recon, let's go."

With that, the thin and wiry Bernstein hoisted all 185 pounds of Sergeant Josh Bingham on his hip, and like two men in a three-legged race at the company picnic, they began hopping up the hill toward the hacienda. For a few moments there was no fire. Maradona's men must have been so astounded by the sight of the two Marines that they had to collect their thoughts before zeroing in on their sights, moving the barrels of their guns toward the pair, and then squeezing off rounds.

Bernstein half-dragged and half-carried Sergeant Bingham up the hill, zigzagging as he did, ducking and weaving, not as the result of any particular training but working on pure instincts and adrenaline. The hacienda, and the relative safety of its low stucco walls, was only a few score yards away now. He was just picking up momentum when he felt the first shell hit his boot. He flinched but kept moving. More twenty-five-millimeter shells hit the ground around him and now the sound of smaller-caliber bullets punctuated the air too. He continued to pull and drag the clearly exhausted Bingham with him, instinctively pushing him ahead now to protect him from the fire coming from behind. He felt the whap of a small-caliber bullet in his left arm. Little shits, need something bigger to stop him.

Moving faster now, just twenty-five yards away from the stucco wall, Bernstein drew new energy with every step and Bingham tried mightily to hop along on his one good leg to at least contribute something to their progress. Bernstein was half-yelling, half-cheering as they neared the top. "We got it, Sarge, we're there, we—" Just yards from the wall, the twenty-five-millimeter chain gunner finally found the range. The steady stream of shells walked their way up the hill, then onto his right leg, then up his torso, each one tearing flesh and shattering bones. With a last lunge, Bernstein pushed the horrified Bingham ahead of him. Bingham dragged himself through a small opening in the stucco wall, not letting himself look back at the shattered body of the man who had given his life for him.

As Bingham lay writhing on the ground, he looked back at the shattered body of Lance Corporal Bernstein. He felt gratitude, then remorse. As he tried to raise himself on his elbows to get his bearings, he felt some long cylindrical tubes underneath his back. He rose even further to get a look, but then the pain and shock overcame him and he passed out.

CHAPTER 45

As the sun continued to rise, the Recon Marines on the ground at the mesa saw their plight become more desperate. The enemy positions were so well concealed that the only indication of their location came when they poured their unrelenting fire on the Americans. Their fire was completely controlled and held in check until one of the Marines moved or attempted to return fire. Then he was quickly hit.

High overhead, the remaining Blackhawks flew in endless circles, not wanting to abandon their comrades on the ground, but daring not return too closely in the face of the Stinger threat. If they returned, the best they could do was evacuate the wounded survivors, because the fight that had begun as a routine roundup was now clearly unwinnable. The only hope of rescuing a number of their comrades lay in massing the firepower of the Apaches against the enemy manning the heavy-caliber weapons long enough to extricate as many Americans as possible.

The carnage on the ground was unbelievable. Two Apaches had been blown out of the air and were barely recognizable burning hulks. A total of seven Blackhawks had been shot out of the air, either by direct Stinger hits or by flying shrapnel. Inside the compound, the destruction was worse, most of the Marines who had been hit in the helos dying quickly, but those who had fast-roped into the compound being systematically wiped out by the fire from the hills surrounding them. Time, position, firepower, and numbers were on the enemy's side. It was not a battle. It was methodical slaughter of brave men.

Just then, screaming only feet over the ground and roaring ahead at red-line speed close to 170 knots, a Blackhawk sped straight at the hacienda house. The pilots ignored the burning wreckage of the helos on the ground and the still-billowing smoke and fires all around. They were intent on their purpose.

In the back of Pacer 236, Chief Rick Holden stood perched in the cabin doorway of the helo. Only the gunner's belt still attached him to the aircraft and his finger twitched nervously on the release, ready to jump as soon as the aircraft was on the ground.

"There! There!" shouted Rick into the intercom, his voice partially obscured by the wind rushing by his head.

Both pilots looked all over as if their heads were on swivels. "Where, Chief? I don't see his aircraft."

"*There,* two o'clock, really low. Start your flare now or we'll overshoot the spot for sure!"

With smooth precision learned from years of flying this aircraft, the pilots pulled the aircraft up slightly to gain about thirty feet of altitude, then pulled the nose up high, really high, executing an extreme flare. Airspeed bled off abruptly. In the back, Rick grabbed the cabin door with both hands to steady himself and saw only sky. Surely the helo must be going straight up, he thought.

"Get ready," said the pilot, before and dropping the nose of the Blackhawk to the horizon. With that, he bot-

tomed the collective and the Blackhawk landed—hard—
just twenty yards away from Major Holian, who was
weakly waving one arm.

"I'm out," yelled Rick, who had already released his
gunner's belt and now jumped out of the helo. Crouching
low, he dashed toward Major Holian.

"You okay, Major?"

"Yeah, fine, good to see ya. You a SEAL?"

"You got it, sir. Can you walk?"

"Can if you prop me up a bit. One ankle's messed."

As Rick tended to Major Holian, the remainder of the
SEALs in Pacer 236 poured out a withering fire toward
the muzzle flashes coming from the surrounding hills. It
was just enough to keep the enemy from zeroing in on
Rick and Major Holian.

Rick looked directly at the major. He was dazed.

"Let's go, then, Major."

"Wait. Just a little while ago I heard gunfire over by
that wall. Think there may be one of our troops still over
there."

"Major, are you sure?"

"Not sure, but we need to help him if he's there."

"I'm putting you in the Blackhawk first, Major." Rick
propped Holian on his hip and hopped with him toward
the Blackhawk. He had ordered the rest of his platoon to
stay in the aircraft, and now outstretched arms grabbed
Holian and pulled him as gently as they could into the
helo's cabin. Rick gave the pilots a clenched fist, indicating
that they should continue to hold on the ground. He
needn't have. They weren't going anywhere without him,
and continued to pour fire out of the Blackhawk to cover
Rick.

Still crouching low, Rick ran toward the wall where Major Holian had told him he thought he heard one of the
injured troops. So many dead bodies. Rick tried to stay
focused on what he was doing, but the smoke and the
stench almost overcame him. Looking, looking, no sign of
life yet. Wait, there.

Sergeant Bingham waved at Rick and Rick ran right to
him.

"You're a sight for sore eyes. Let's get into that flying taxi you brought and get out of here," said Bingham.

"You got it, Sarge," said Rick.

As Bingham got up, Rick noticed he was lying on a number of long, cylindrical fiberglass tubes. These tubes were almost five feet long and Rick knew exactly what they were—expended Stinger missile launch tubes. Instinctively, he grabbed several of them and held them to his side with his right arm as he supported Bingham with his left arm and helped the wounded man toward the Blackhawk. At the cabin door, outstretched arms helped them in, and as Rick jumped in, he shouted to the pilots, "Go, go, go!"

"Chief, I think we still have some wounded men around the periphery of the LZ," said Major Holian.

"We know, sir. Pacer 238 is right behind us. They're grabbing all those men. We're taking care of your troops. Just try to rest, Major."

At that, the Blackhawk lifted up and, as her nose dipped way below the horizon, roared off toward the coast.

CHAPTER 46

"STOP IT!" LAURA PETERS SAID TO HERSELF. SHE caught herself chewing her nails, almost down to the quick by now, sitting at her watch console in the SouthCom command center. Things had not gone well and now they were awaiting the arrival of a clearly enraged General Charles Walters. It was not going to be a pretty sight. The staff all busied themselves with various watch chores—making entries into logbooks, checking various frequencies, updating displays, moving paper on top of desks and consoles, even sharpening pencils—but it was not enough to cut the tension. Every so often, one or another of the Watch Team Bravo members stole a look at Lieutenant Colonel George Beall, who was staring blankly at the multicolored large screen that dominated this room, looking

like a man on death row whose time had come. They
wished they could do something to help him, but none
went so far as wanting to trade places with him.

Beyond the immediacy of the angry General Walters
arriving at any moment, Laura Peters felt a full range of
emotions. Less than two hours before, with the operation
in full swing and things seeming to be going well, she had
convinced herself that her fears—and those of Rick Holden—were unfounded and that all was right with the operation. Now those fears resurfaced with a vengeance and
she tried to pull it all together. All she'd discovered wasn't
making sense, though. What more did she need to find
out?

CHAPTER 47

RICK HOLDEN SAT IN THE BACK OF PACER 236 IN
stunned silence, supporting Major Pete Holian and Sergeant Bingham as they flew toward the coast. He also kept
the parachute bag—in which he had tossed the long, fiberglass cylinders he had collected—firmly secured between his legs. How, thought Rick, could these tightly
controlled weapons have wound up in the hands of druggies in some third-rate Latin American country? Something just didn't add up.

His thoughts were broken by a sudden weight on his
shoulder. Major Pete Holian had slumped onto him, no
doubt collapsing from shock and loss of blood. He had to
help and help fast. Warrant Officer Fred Jacobson was
flying the Blackhawk at redline and headed straight for
Coronado. It was up to Holden to keep the Major alive
until then.

· "Come on, Major, stay with me," shouted Holden,
knowing that keeping Holian awake was a key to his survival.

"Got ya," mumbled Holian.

"That's it, Major. We're almost there." Holden had

broken out the helo's field medical kit and was applying bandages as quickly as he could to Holian's multiple wounds, cuts, and abrasions. He had cut himself to shreds getting out of his stricken Blackhawk and Holden worked furiously to stem blood loss. The wound in Holian's left shoulder was the most worrisome and Rick loaded on the bandages, pushing down with the heel of his hand, trying to keep as much pressure on it as possible.

Holian groaned as Rick moved him to check out his other wounds. He wanted to lay him down, but there was no room in the cramped Blackhawk cabin.

As they crossed the shoreline, Warrant Officer Fred Jacobson called, "Feet wet," more to encourage his passengers in the Blackhawk's cabin to hang on than to pass along any particularly useful information.

Rick Holden's thoughts turned back to his suspicions and to the Stinger parts in his parachute bag. Had the drug cartel found out about the U.S. assault and decided to lash back? Why had they done this and not just moved their base if they knew they were going to be attacked? If someone in the U.S. government had a hand in this ambush, why? For money? To embarrass the U.S. government? To embarrass the government of Costa Rica? None of it made sense to Rick. But what stood out foremost in his mind was the unbelievable carnage on the battlefield, the scores of his fellow warriors who had already been slain and the rest who were hopelessly pinned down as the ambush played out. The enemy had been too well armed and too well prepared to counter their assault. That perhaps is what bothered him the most and he vowed to get to the bottom of it.

CHAPTER 48

BUILDING 1468 WAS JUST ANOTHER NONDESCRIPT CONcrete structure on the far reaches of Howard Air Force Base. The number assigned had no meaning to anyone, save whatever civil servant in the Public Works Department who invented it to serve some bureaucratic need to number things. It sat about halfway between the approach end of Runway 18 and the perimeter road ringing the entire airfield.

Had anyone taken the time to really look at Building 1468, he would have noticed that it looked ever so slightly different than it had in previous years. Recently, a single HF antenna had appeared on its roof. Many buildings on military bases carry antennas of various sorts, but an onlooker might have questioned this one, since the building itself was so unimposing. Antennas were typically used for communicating with the outside world.

Inside the building, Lieutenant Commander Andy Wilson stared intently at his watch, waiting for the appointed hour to begin his scripted transmissions. Crouching in this bare, dank building, which he had furtively sneaked into at 0400 hours, he was obeying the orders of his general as the only hope of extricating himself from an otherwise hopeless situation. As he looked around the stark sandstone-colored walls of the small building, waiting for the minutes to pass, he reflected on the unpleasant chain of events that had led to his crouching in this dank place.

Lieutenant Commander Andy Wilson had arrived in Panama six months ago as an officer on the fast track. An honor graduate of the Naval Academy, he had chosen jets upon graduation. He married Laurie O'Leary, a beautiful girl and, not inconveniently, the daughter of Vice Admiral Ben O'Leary, commander of all naval air forces in the Atlantic Fleet. Following a blissful honeymoon in Martinique, he was assigned to the Fists of VFA-25, flying the F/A-18 strike fighter. Andy had been such a crackerjack pilot that he had then gone on to be an instructor pilot at Top Gun, the Navy's fighter weapons school. Returning to a squadron, the Stingers of VFA-113, as a department head, with the additional plum of Carrier Air Group LSO, or landing signal officer, he continued to excel. His performance earned him a subsequent assignment as aide to Admiral "Bingo" Jenkins, head of the Aviation Division on the staff of the chief of naval operations. Andy was bright, talented, and ambitious, and he was making all the right moves and moving himself and Laurie ever upward on the fast track.

He had taken the assignment in Panama, a one-year unaccompanied tour as the assistant Air Ops officer on SouthCom staff, because it offered the fastest way of getting his "joint ticket" punched, making him eligible for even more career-enhancing assignments. But Andy had taken a shine to an Air Force colonel's wife and when caught in the act by the colonel had further complicated things by assaulting the husband, sending him to the emergency room, where he lingered in a coma for days before finally recovering. General Walters had moved quickly to dispose of the case at a private hearing so as to avert any negative publicity for SouthCom. Walters recognized Andy for exactly what he was—a totally ambitious young man who would do anything not to have his career derailed. Therefore, he offered him the option of completing this "minor mission" in return for brushing his case under the rug with only a nonpunitive letter of caution, the mildest possible form of official rebuke—and one which would not even find its way into his permanent service record.

The general's explanation of why Andy was to do this and what was at stake—it was part of an elaborate operational deception exercise which had to be conducted in utmost secrecy—did not make complete sense to him. The general, however, had made it clear that he held Andy's career in his hands, he was to do just as he was told or the general could take Andy to a general courts-martial for his crimes and find someone else to perform this small mission.

Andy held his script in his hands, along with some anticipated likely responses from the other end. Just follow the script, he told himself, just follow the script and we're back on track. Finally, the time had arrived. Andy began:

"Control, this is Pacer 408, over."

"Pacer 408, control, have you a little weak, but readable. Go ahead with your transmission," replied Operations Specialist Senior Chief Clarence Williams, the senior OS on the JTF Eight staff and the one selected to monitor the control frequency with the comm relay bird during

Operation Roundup. With a frantic motion of his arm, Williams signaled for one of the other watchstanders to go get General Lovelace, who had insisted on being notified as soon as Pacer 408 had a report from the scene.

"Pacer 408 with a report from the LZ, relay from Bullet One," continued Wilson. Bullet One was the code name for Major Pete Holian, leading the operation.

"Go ahead with your report," continued Williams.

"Bullet One reports complete control of the LZ. No, repeat, no friendly casualties. Complete surprise achieved. At least one hundred twenty enemy in custody now, rounding up the remainder at a rapid pace. All, repeat, all escape routes cut off. Blackhawks and Apaches sweeping the hills to pick up any possible escapees."

"What about drugs and weapons?" asked General Lovelace, and Senior Chief Williams dutifully repeated this on the circuit.

"Pacer 408, control, what about drugs and weapons?"

Wilson scanned down his sheet for the properly scripted response. "Control, 408, Bullet One reports an extremely large cache of both, still searching some buildings for a full accounting, but thus far at least twenty to thirty tons, repeat tons, of pure cocaine. Weapons are plentiful but light and of poor quality."

"What about resistance?" asked Lovelace.

"Four-oh-eight, control, indicate amount of resistance encountered."

"Again Wilson scanned his script, but didn't find an exact answer. He took the closest one and ad-libbed a bit. "Most of the men on the mesa surrendered immediately. A few tried to run but ran into our blocking positions. Thus far, have captured Maradona and one of his key lieutenants and we are searching for several others."

General Lovelace found it difficult to contain his glee. The operation was succeeding beyond his wildest expectations. He forced himself to maintain a professional demeanor and continue asking questions through Senior Chief Williams.

"Do we expect any difficulties in rounding up all of these druggies?"

Wilson didn't even look at his sheet. "Negative. We have all escape routes sealed off."

"Well, how many of them do we think there are?"

"Bullet One reports between two hundred and two-fifty," replied Wilson, returning to his script. He was in a groove now and sounding convincing—even to himself. Whatever exercise this was, it sure sounded important. It didn't really track exactly for him, but it was going so fast that he didn't have time to think about it right now.

General Lovelace continued the questioning for a bit, wanting to squeeze every bit of information out of Pacer 408, because he knew how important the next several hours would be.

But of course it was not Pacer 408. . . .

In his cabin, Colonel Conrad Hicks listened in on the conversation General Lovelace thought he was having with Pacer 408, but which he was really having with Lieutenant Commander Andy Wilson. Hicks had capitalized on the privacy he had always insisted on in radio and had installed a simple switching unit. Just prior to the beginning of Wilson's transmissions on a discrete frequency, he had patched that frequency into the net that General Lovelace was using. With all the checks and balances in military communications, nothing prevented such a simple switching. It was critical to the plan that he and General Walters had set up and he had done his part and done it brilliantly. Surely Walters would take care of him now.

Conrad Hicks did not think of himself as an evil man. He had been Walters's aide-de-camp in Europe years before. Then they had served together during Desert Storm. Hicks had done a credible job, but not a superb one, yet Walters's loyalty to him carried him through the war and made him a hero. He had just been selected for his brigadier's star, but didn't want to be a general officer in a military that the President was trying to destroy. General Walters had told him this was the only way to rescue their country from certain disaster. There had been no arm-twisting. The general had told him this was necessary and he had responded instantly that he would do it.

Hicks was broken out of his reverie by the buzz of the E phone on the bulkhead next to his desk.

"Hicks here."

"Chief of staff," said General Lovelace, "we've got wonderful news. You should come up here and hear this for yourself."

"On the way up, General," said Hicks.

CHAPTER 49

GENERAL ASHLEY LOVELACE ROSE FROM HIS CHAIR AT *Coronado*'s command console with the air of a victorious warrior. The report from Pacer 408 had been excellent— no, superb! Operation Roundup had exceeded even his most optimistic expectations. The men in the field had performed wonderfully and they had made him proud. Most importantly, this sting had accomplished just what his good friend President Taylor Calhoun wanted it to: put the power and prestige of his administration behind a successful assault against the drug cartels. Lovelace had accomplished the first part of his mission, and now came the equally important second part: letting the media, and by extension the American public, know that their operation, his and President Calhoun's, had been a smashing success.

General Lovelace and his key public relations and communications experts sprang into action. Based on the radio report, he had Commander Ben Malgrave draft the following message and send it "flash" priority directly to the Joint Chiefs:

QUOTE—Joint Task Force EIGHT: Today, at approximately 6:30 A.M. Eastern Standard Time, elements of Joint Task Force EIGHT, supported by other units under the command of COMMANDER, SOUTHERN COMMAND, and in cooperation with the government of Costa Rica, captured the leader of the largest drug cartel in that nation along with hundreds of his men, and an extremely large cache of drugs and weapons. This completely successful sting operation was conducted without the loss of a single American life. Planning for this extraordinarily successful operation has been in works for several months and was initiated by the President himself as part of his ongoing initiative to end the scourge of drugs on America's streets. President Calhoun personally planned many aspects of the operation, personally selected the JTF Commander, and gave the final go-ahead for the operation. JTF EIGHT will continue to operate in the littoral waters of Central and South America in order to totally stop the scourge of drugs in our nation.—END QUOTE

Satisfied that he had properly informed the Joint Chiefs, Lovelace now made the transmission he wanted most to make, to call his friend Taylor Calhoun and tell him personally. After the obligatory protocol with the White House switchboard, Lovelace was connected with the President. "Good morning Mr. President," began Lovelace, barely able to contain his glee.

"Good morning, General. How are things at the scene?" asked Calhoun. The bit of formality in his voice suggested that he had a group assembled, timed, no doubt, to capture the moment with the proper degree of fanfare.

"Mr. President, I have just released a flash message to the Joint Chiefs reporting that Operation Roundup is a complete success. We have more than met our objectives, captured the drug king Maradona and hundreds of his men, and seized large quantities of weapons and drugs. And, Mr. President"—here Lovelace paused to heighten the drama—"we did so without the loss of a single American life." Lovelace paused again, and taking poetic license to further give his friend the biggest possible boost, he continued, "And if I may say so, Mr. President, Operation Roundup would not have been nearly as complete a success had it not been for your active planning, your key suggestions, and your total support for this operation. I thank you, sir."

Calhoun beamed at the large crowd assembled in the Oval Office and exercised, as best he could, some degree of mock humility. "Well, General, I had only a minor role. You brave men in the field have done your nation's work and done it well. My congratulations to each and every one of you. Your nation is truly proud of you this day."

"Thank you, Mr. President. It is our pleasure to serve our nation this way and to validate your confidence in us."

Those favored reporters who had been invited by Calhoun to be around the Oval Office this morning "just in case something came up" rushed out to file their stories. Calhoun was now fairly bubbling. "Great job, General, I mean, *great job.* I can see a Presidential Unit Citation for your forces for this magnificent job."

"Thank you again, Mr. President. I'll sign off for now."

That task complete, Lovelace wanted to assemble his staff and make sure that even those not near the command console when he had heard the news from Pacer 408 had the full picture of the successful operation.

"Colonel Hicks, please assemble the staff on the flag bridge," ordered Lovelace.

"Roger, General," replied Hicks, but he had already anticipated Lovelace's request, and flag plot and the flag bridge were already filling with JTF Eight staff members.

Still smiling with satisfaction and even as the last few remaining staff members were cramming into the back of the flag bridge, Lovelace began. "Ladies and gentlemen, I have just had a wonderful report from the field. Because of your superb planning and flawless execution, Operation Roundup has been a complete success. Our men have captured hundreds of druggies on the mesa, including the cartel kingpin himself, Maradona, and at least one of his key lieutenants, and are holding them until the local authorities can pick them up. They have secured an incredibly large cache of drugs and weapons and, most importantly since they are all our shipmates, have suffered absolutely no casualties. Congratulations to each and every one of you. You have so much to be proud of."

The JTF Eight staff shared their commander's satisfaction. Many of the junior men and women began exchanging high fives and a few staff members actually embraced. It was the culminating event of many arduous weeks of planning, and the relief in pulling this one off was palpable. So joyous was the celebration that not everyone heard the 1 MC intone, "Flight quarters, flight quarters. All hands man your flight quarters stations. The smoking lamp is out on all weatherdecks. Wear no hats topside. Helos inbound at thirty-five miles. Prepare to receive wounded. I say again, prepare to receive wounded."

CHAPTER 50

GENERAL WALTERS BURST INTO THE SOUTHCOM command center almost bowling over the Navy petty officer who attempted to open the door for him. Barely controlling his rage, and looking well put together in his uniform for someone who had just raced to the command center from his quarters, he strode directly up to Colonel Beall, his eyes flaring and his body language conveying the message that the colonel had better have a good explanation for insisting that he come to the command center.

"Good morning, General. I have the photos we discussed right here," began Beall.

"Let's see 'em," said Walters. "Who's going to explain this spook stuff to me?"

"I will, General," volunteered Captain Fran Dawson. This was not only her responsibility as the staff J-2, but she felt the need to take control from the wilting Beall. "General, we've annotated these photos with time references that show the various TARPs missions over the past forty-eight hours. Here, in an early photo, you see clear indications of a large group of men inside buildings throughout the compound. These are consistent with similar photos of like types of buildings with the same environmental conditions. These later photos show almost no heat signature in the buildings, yet in the surrounding jun-

gle there are numerous pockets of heat, here, here, here—
really in about a dozen places that you can see, General.
These dark lines here, here, and yes, here, we're quite
sure that these are vehicles moving through the jungle—
no doubt some sort of four-wheel drive vehicles—moving
men and equipment around. Additionally—''

General Walters's outstretched hand indicated to Dawson that she should pause. The entire command center
was silent as a tomb. Every man and woman stared intently at the general, waiting for his response now that he
had seen this evidence.

"Colonel Beall, you're the team leader. Do you agree
with this assessment?"

"Yes, General, the evidence seems compelling," replied
Beall.

"Captain, what about your other intelligence people
here? Do they concur with this?"

"Yes, General, Tech Sergeant Dolan and Specialist
O'Connor here are from the 802 Intelligence Group at
Howard. They have a lot of background in this imagery
and they have provided the fine-grain analysis. Lieutenant
Gaylord, who flew the TARPs flight, is here too and he
definitely concurs, and—''

Walters raised his hand again. He noticed Lieutenant
Laura Peters in the group. "What about you, Lieutenant
Peters? I'm told that you've been to all the right schools
to figure this out. Do you agree with all of this?"

"Yes, General, I think Captain Dawson has called it just
right. This is very convincing imagery and, well, General,
we think we're at a critical juncture here and need to stop
the mission."

Memories of the phone call to General Walters were
still fresh in the minds of the entire staff assembled in the
command center and they all waited for the explosion
from the general at Peters's suggestion that the mission
be scrubbed. Walters stared intently at Peters and said,
"Lieutenant, you're making sense of this situation. I think
there are some serious questions here. We may need to
rethink this. I think you have done your homework and I
agree with your analysis."

"Yes, General, thank you, but sir, we, well, I think it may be too late."

"*What do you mean, too late?*" But Walters had turned away from Peters and was now staring at the hapless Beall. "*Colonel, did you let this operation continue when it clearly ought to have been aborted?*"

"General, sir, I, ah, we . . . when I called we told you, yes, our indicators are that the aircraft were approaching the LZ, sir, as you recall. . . ." The colonel was stammering, barely able to get the words out of his mouth as the general edged closer to him. "Since then, they've arrived."

"*Excuses, excuses, you incompetent—*" As he moved still closer to Beall, who now had his back pressed up against the command console and could move no further back, he began to raise his hand.

"General, we must call JTF Eight now, before it's too late," said the chief of staff, Colonel Fargo, breaking the tension momentarily and causing the general to take a step back from the now-terrified Beall.

"Someone raise JTF Eight on the command net," said Walters, now seemingly in control again.

CHAPTER 51

GENERAL LOVELACE SAT IN HIS HIGH-BACKED COM-mand chair in *Coronado*'s flag plot, reflecting on his good fortune. Although the 1 MC had announced some wounded being brought back, the chief of staff had suggested that it was probably just some lightly wounded men—no operation could be totally risk-free—and *Coronado* had superb medical facilities. It was a great way to start his tour in this high-visibility job and he anticipated nothing but glowing praise from his entire chain of command.

Lovelace was snapped out of his reverie by the voice of the JTF Eight duty officer, Lieutenant Commander Harry

Adams. "General, call from General Walters on the command net."

"Thank you, Commander, I'll take it right here," replied Lovelace. "General Lovelace here, General. Good morning."

"Lovelace, I'll come right to the point. We've got some updated intelligence that impacts on your operation. We need to take a hard look at this before we proceed."

Lovelace was caught off guard by General Walters's statement. It took him a moment to regain his composure and reply.

"General, we're already in full swing and, well, we laid it all out in our OPREP."

"What do you mean, full swing? What OPREP?"

"General, we're on the way to a smashing victory. It's all in our—"

"I never received any damned OPREP, and what do you mean, full swing?"

"Yes sir, we're fully engaged and—"

"What do you mean, fully engaged? You never had my permission to start this operation."

"General, when we met aboard the flagship, you said—"

"I cannot believe you have started this operation. Stop it now!"

"General, we can't stop it, and if I may say so, it's a great success thus far, and sir, I distinctly recall our conversation aboard my flagship where you told me that I would be given the go-ahead and your subsequent call from your headquarters telling me to 'make it happen' when I was ready . . ."

It sounded as if General Walters were going to come through the phone. "*Are you calling me a liar,* Brigadier General *Lovelace. You did not have permission to start this operation. We have intelligence that there is an ambush. You do not have permission. You do not!*"

Nothing he had ever encountered before had prepared General Ashley Lovelace for something like this. Why was General Walters saying this? He couldn't have forgotten what he had told him. What intelligence reports? What ambush? Everything in the field was perfect, wasn't it? There were a few wounded inbound on the choppers, but probably only minor casualties. He did the best he could to fend off the general. "General Walters, sir, I'll evaluate the situation and get back to you immediately."

Two decks below, Colonel Conrad Hicks listened to this conversation the way he had listened to the others. Of course, there had been no OPREP. Though *Coronado*'s radiomen had dutifully put the message "on the wires"— Navy parlance for sending the message out—unbeknownst to them, Colonel Hicks had disabled that particular comm circuit, so that the message went exactly nowhere, for now. Later, when he set the circuit back up again, all of the messages queued up would go out. But by then it would be too late—much too late.

CHAPTER 52

Lieutenant Colonel Beall mustered all of the intestinal fortitude he possessed as he stood before General Walters in the SouthCom command center. Every staff member there stared at Beall with looks that were a combination of pity and support, somehow hoping against hope that they could deliver some kind of physical fortitude to him to help him withstand the withering attack by General Walters. To his credit, Beall stood his ground and, to the best of his ability, continued to look toward the general.

"Well, *Colonel*," began Walters, "let's see if we can begin to take this in bite-sized chunks, if that's all right with you." Walters's patronizing tone and the measured cadence of his voice added to the tension in the command center.

"Yes sir, General."

"First of all, have we received any OPREP report from JTF Eight?" Walters knew the answer to that one, but needed to ask it to protect the ruse.

"No sir, General, nothing at all from their staff."

"Are you sure, *Colonel*? After all, things have not been going all that well in command center this morning. Are you absolutely sure you might not have missed it?"

"No sir, General, we're quite sure. All of our message traffic to and from JTF Eight comes through on satellite channel ST804Z1 and is backed up on channel ST804Z4. Additionally, for all OPREPs there's the requirement for a receipt acknowledge back from the receiving command, so if they sent one and we didn't acknowledge it, they'd keep sending it until we did."

"All right, then, *Colonel,* we'll assume that the commander on the scene has a little problem, but he thinks his operation is going well—let's talk about your watch team, shall we?"

"Certainly, General."

"You have this evidence of an ambush that you all seem to think is ironclad, yet we proceeded on with the operation. Why?"

"General, your instructions when we called you in your quarters—"

"Colonel, colonel, you disturbed me in my quarters when I was attempting to relax and collect my thoughts. You dazzled me with some gobbledygook about some photos and expected me to come up with an instantaneous decision?"

"Well, yes sir, General, I mean—"

"Beall, you were on watch. You had command oversight. Every standing order that I have signed out in my tenure here directs my watch officers to act with my full authority in my absence. What you're telling me now is that you had clear evidence of reason to stop this operation, but you elected not to. Instead, you called me in my quarters and wanted me to make a decision based on evidence that I hadn't seen and couldn't possibly evaluate. Is that about right, *Colonel*?"

Beall was at a loss for words. As much as they all supported him, the other staff members knew that the general was right on this point. He had taken pains to train his staff to do just the kind of things he was chastising Beall for failing to do. It was all in the standing orders, those often obscure instructions that everyone is supposed to read—but often doesn't. Nothing really prevented him from communicating directly with JTF Eight, even if just to pass the information along to General Lovelace and let him decide what to do with it. But he had elected not to do that. As much as his fellow officers hated to admit it, ever since he had received his orders to Virginia, Colonel Beall had pretty much mentally detached from the staff already. It was now coming home to roost.

"Yes, General, you are right. Your standing orders are quite clear."

"Yes, they are, Colonel." Walters's tone now turned just slightly more conciliatory. "But the JTF Eight commander tells me that things in the field have gone well, that he's sent me an OPREP telling me that—I'm sure we'll find that somewhere, *won't we*?" shouted Walters as he glared at his communications people. "And so, Colonel, we've managed to recoup rather nicely, don't you think?"

"Yes sir, General," was all that Beall could offer.

"Well, yes, I think you all have offered me enough excitement for this morning. I think I need a little fresh air and a drive to clear my thoughts a bit. Sergeant Brooke, I won't be needing you. I'll just take the staff car myself."

The SouthCom staff breathed a collective sigh of relief as General Walters strode purposely from the command center. They had escaped the general's wrath relatively unscathed. Now, as was his habit when he tried to cool down, he was going to drive alone in his staff car, probably at high speed to some little-used road in some out-of-the-way corner of Howard Air Force Base, and run the rims off the car. The staff welcomed having the car take the abuse rather than them.

Lieutenant Laura Peters turned to Captain Fran Dawson with the TARPs photos in her hand. "Captain, it still doesn't add up, what we're seeing here and what the general says General Lovelace told him. I just don't get it."

"Neither do I, Lieutenant. Neither do I. We'll just have to wait and see where this one takes us."

General Walters was indeed going to an out-of-the-way corner of Howard Air Force Base. He wheeled his staff car directly up to building 1468. Inside the building, Lieutenant Commander Andy Wilson had been waiting just as General Walters had told him to do. But he had also been thinking. This hadn't turned out exactly as the general had told him it would. It sure didn't sound like an exercise. It had sounded very real. After finishing his conversation, Andy's curiosity got the best of him. Although General Walters had instructed him to talk to no one about what he was doing, he thought that he needed to, in a roundabout way. He occasionally played pickup basketball with Major Jerry Young, one of the midlevel ops types on the SouthCom staff. He called Jerry from Building 1468.

"Jerry, Andy here. How's your game? You got a jump shot yet?"

"Not yet, Andy. What ya need?"

"Hey, I've got a little tasker," Andy lied. "I'm supposed to be helping out with some big exercise, but it's one I never heard about before. What's going on, exercise-wise, with your staff?"

"Nothing, Andy, absolutely nothing. We're all tied up with an actual op. Really can't talk about any specifics."

"Real op, no exercise?"

"Listen, Andy, I really can't say much. But hey, you haven't seen me at the courts lately, have you? That should tell you something. We're doing the biggest op we've had in the two years that I've been down here. Exercise? Hell, we're so strapped now, if we were doing an exercise we'd have to have the janitor run it."

Andy wasn't much placated by Jerry's humor. Now he was worried. Had General Walters misled him? Come to think of it, with the hot water that he had gotten himself into, why would the general let him off the hook with such a simple task? Andy couldn't stand it. He picked up the phone and dialed again.

"Good morning, Squadron Duty Office. Corporal Maxwell speaking, sir."

"This is *Commander* Wilson," said Andy, stretching his rank just a little bit to convey an extra sense of importance to the enlisted man. Let me speak with First Lieutenant Finley."

"Yes sir. Wait, please," responded the corporal.

After a short pause, Andy heard a familiar voice on the line. "First Lieutenant Finley. How may I help you, sir?"

"Scott, it's Andy."

"Andy, hey, what you need? We're real busy here."

"Busy? You guys in an exercise or something?"

"Exercise! Andy, you on Mars or something? There's a big op going on up north. Scattered reports, but looks like lots of our birds shot up. We're all rushing around trying to get some backup birds ready in case we have to go."

"But Scott—"

"Andy, look, I gotta go."

"Okay, sorry, but just tell me this. What's your squadron call sign?"

"It's Pacer, Andy, Pacer."

"Scott, tell me one more thing. Do you have a call number 408?"

"Yeah, we do, Andy, if it hasn't been shot down too. Hey, I really gotta go. Call me some other time."

"Okay, pal, thanks."

Andy's mind was swimming. What had he done? What had he been trapped into being part of? His thoughts of self-preservation were overwhelmed by his rage. He wasn't going to sit here and wait. He pushed at the door of the building—it was locked from the outside! Andy threw himself against it repeatedly until he slumped down, weeping, then fell asleep.

His sleep was broken by the sound of the padlock being taken off the door and the voice of General Charles Walters. "Well, Mr. Wilson, I think our work here is over."

"General, I want to talk to you about—"

"Nothing to talk about, son. You've done what I told you to do. Your record's clear now."

"But my conscience isn't. You haven't leveled with me, General."

"Now, son, don't trouble yourself with things that don't concern you. You just take some leave. Go back stateside to visit that pretty wife of yours and tell her that everything is okay with your career again."

"Not so fast, General. This was no exercise. What have I done? Why have we done this?"

"Enough, mister. I told you, your job is over."

"No, it's not, General. I'm not just keeping this under my hat."

"You'll do what I tell you to do."

"Not on your life, General. We'll see how this plays up the chain of command, *sir!*"

"No, we won't, Wilson. I *order* you to never talk about this!"

"Your orders don't carry weight with me, General."

"Stay right here, that's an order," replied Walters as he started toward the door, intending to leave Andy Wilson in that building for . . . how long?

"No chance," screamed Andy, and he rushed toward the general and tried to push his way past him. Walters resisted and managed to force his bulk against Andy. Andy tumbled onto a broken-down couch, surprised that the older man had pushed him down.

General Walters realized the gravity of this situation. Wilson could blow this whole thing. He wasn't listening to him. He needed to make him know that he was serious.

"Wilson, don't get up."

"What's to stop me, General?" said Andy as he started to come off the couch, glaring at General Walters.

"Stop! Stop, dammit, or I'll shoot!"

As if guided by some sixth sense, General Walters had drawn his sidearm and pointed it straight at Andy Wilson. The SouthCom staff had always been slightly amused that the General carried a sidearm—thought that he was overdoing the warrior image. But now, here he was, pointing it right at Andy Wilson.

"General, are you crazy? You won't; you can't." But as Andy talked, he kept moving toward the general. Closer and closer he came, now shouting, *"You can't! You won't. Don't do it!"*

Blam! The gun went off and Andy Wilson collapsed at General Walters's feet. Andy was a victim of his philandering, a victim of General Walters's plotting, and now a victim of the strange turn of events that Operation Roundup had brought with it.

CHAPTER 53

PRESIDENT TAYLOR CALHOUN HAD NOT GOTTEN TO the Oval Office without having some well-honed political instincts. Those instincts were going full throttle now, telling him to secure the maximum amount of political capital from the events of the last few hours. The reporters who had been present an hour earlier had rushed out to file their stories, and information about the success of the operation had undoubtedly leaked out—if you could call the well-orchestrated efforts of his staff leaking. One of the major networks had even teased their audience with an allusion to the operation's success when they pre-empted their regularly scheduled programming to announce the imminent presidential report.

He sat in the Oval Office in a subdued suit but with a white shirt and a bright red tie, better to signal aggressiveness and the ability to take charge. The intense bright lights wheeled into the Oval Office to make the television images bright and sharp put out incredible heat, but the air-conditioning more than compensated for them, leaving Calhoun looking, literally, cool, calm, and collected as he prepared for what could be the most important address of his presidency.

Calhoun was fairly beaming as the director counted down, "Three, two, one—and—rolling, Mr. President."

My fellow Americans. Good morning. As you know, my administration came into office dedicated in part to ending the scourge of drugs that is debilitating this country, particularly our young men and women. As you know, I have been vigorous in attacking the demand side of this problem. We have begun key educational initiatives on a scale unprecedented in previous administrations and have taken our message directly to our youth, especially in the inner cities. All this is ongoing, and we are already seeing good results.

As you know, I am sure, we must attack both sides of this problem, not only demand, but supply too. In cooperation with our partners in this hemisphere we have undertaken many counterdrug initiatives. Most of these have been low-key and have primarily involved our support of initiatives by the host government. These efforts have been successful to some extent. However, some particularly large drug traffickers have continued to operate with impunity, having power far beyond the ability of the local governments to deal with. As a result, they have continued to push tons of drugs across the southern borders of this nation.

Early this morning, with the cooperation of the government of Costa Rica, we moved against one of these drug lords. At approximately 0730 Eastern Standard time, elements of Joint Task Force Eight, embarked in the command ship USS Coronado *and, supported by the full forces of the United States Southern Command, conducted a lightning assault against the drug lord Diego Maradona. This operation, which was months in planning, was a resounding success, capturing Maradona and hundreds of his men, and seizing a large amount of drugs and weapons. This victory was achieved without significant American casualties and not only broke the back of a key drug kingpin, but also served notice that the United States will not sit idly back as drugs are funneled into our country. We will strike anytime, anywhere, to end this scourge, and I pledge to you to continue this fight.*

Finished, Calhoun smiled and stared intently at the cameras until the director said, "Cut. Thank you, Mr. President."

Taylor Calhoun leaned back in his chair, secure in the knowledge that he had turned his presidency around.

CHAPTER 54

GENERAL HOWARD CAMPBELL HAD A FACILITY FOR dealing with the media. Although all people who had risen to such high positions had acquired this ability, Campbell's seemed to come naturally. His instinctive feel for how to court the right reporters had stood him in good stead throughout his career and was now about to pay great dividends.

Liz Kennedy was not an unattractive women. Petite, with a good figure, deep brown eyes, short, perky black hair, and a winning smile, she had that girl-next-door look that appealed to men—in most places. But this was not most places; this was Washington, D.C., and with a female-to-male ratio of about three to one, and with power the name of the game, a mid-thirties woman with a demanding reporter's job who offered nothing more than girl-next-door looks was not exactly fending off suitors left and right.

It had started off innocently enough—a round of doubles in a charity benefit tennis tournament on the well-maintained clay courts at the Army-Navy Country Club. The general was in his fifties, but he was so fit and so attentive . . .

"So, Ms. Kennedy, do you cover your beat for the *Washington Post* as aggressively as you pound that tennis ball?" inquired General Howard Campbell as they finished three sets of doubles. Together they had bested a good club team that had been favored to win the tournament.

"Only when there's a good story there," replied Liz. The chairman might just be a source for such stories.

"Do many pieces on our military?" asked Campbell, although he knew the answer to that question.

"Occasionally, General. My main area is business, but when there's something there like base closings or defense conversion that makes a good tie-in between the military and business, I usually go for it. We have a pretty big military readership, as you know."

"Oh, I do know," answered Campbell agreeably, "and I think we have a responsibility to provide you with the information that enables you to do that, don't you?"

"That's music to my ears, General."

"Howard. Please. Howard."

And so it had started. Howard Campbell would provide Liz Kennedy with bits of information—nothing that compromised military security, just information about military contracts, base conversions, that sort of thing. Things that would shortly be released officially, but Kennedy was always out in front on those stories. Campbell always insisted that they meet for an early dinner so he could share the information in person. No place terribly romantic, just a little bistro in Old Town or Georgetown. She was saddened to learn about his wife—but wasn't he a wonderful man for visiting her so often. Then one evening it just happened. They'd gone back to her apartment to go over the mundane details of the latest round of base closings— it would be an important scoop for her—and she'd decided that she needed him and wanted him. He was a patient and gentle lover and their relationship continued in both ways.

As was her habit, Liz Kennedy listened now to the answering machine after her phone had rung the programmed four times, but picked it up abruptly as soon as she heard Howard Campbell's voice. "Hello. I didn't expect it would be you. It's early yet by Pentagon standards, isn't it?" Liz and her lover had a running joke about who worked harder, Pentagon generals or reporters on the way up. She happily decided that a reporter's life wasn't that bad after all.

"Liz, I can't talk for long, but I have some *very interesting* information for you. Can you meet me for dinner at Cate's Bistro?"

"Oh, I was going to a baby shower for Ann McGrath—

she's our assistant local sports editor. Starts in about an hour. I was just freshening up—"

"I don't think you want to miss this one."

"Howard, I know, but Ann is a dear, dear friend. Most of the things we talk about aren't that time-sensitive and—"

"Liz, this is time-sensitive. We *need* to meet, tonight, and soon."

Howard Campbell had never pressed this hard to meet with her plus he had been so solicitous to her last weekend. Even if it weren't as important as he seemed to think it was, she owed it to him to meet anyway.

"I'm sure Ann will understand. I can be at Cate's in less than an hour."

"I'll be waiting for you. You won't be disappointed."

"You never disappoint me, Howard."

Liz Kennedy was excited enough about the prospects of what Howard Campbell might share with her that she wheeled her light blue Mazda Miata up to the front of Cate's Bistro on King Street in Old Town Alexandria and sprung for valet parking. She strode purposely past the hostess at the door of the bistro and straight toward the back of the place, near where the piano player was playing a slow Gershwin tune. Cate's was one of their favorite meeting places. Its small tables, recessed lights, exposed beam ceilings, brass overhead fans, and eclectic collection of pictures appealed to both of them. As he said he would, Howard Campbell had already secured a small table in the most out-of-the-way corner. None of the twentyish crowd gave a second glance at the late fiftyish man and his younger companion sitting at their small table with the tiny glass of fresh flowers and solid-looking captain's chairs. Although he was the chairman of the Joint Chiefs of Staff, Howard Campbell had such ordinary looks that, out of uniform, he looked like just a businessman or bureaucrat. Even if he were recognized, military officers, even the highest-ranking ones, didn't have the star appeal that would cause any but the most patriotic citizen to acknowledge their presence.

"Hello, Howard, great table. I rushed over as fast as I

could. Hope I didn't keep you waiting too long." Liz
brushed his cheek with her lips. Though they were lovers,
Liz still didn't feel comfortable with too much affection in
public.

"Not at all, dear," said Howard Campbell. "Just long
enough to get settled in."

"Well, what's this all about that can't wait? They find
Elvis on some base they're closing down?"

"Liz, this is big. So big I haven't even figured out exactly how you'll handle it. This has to be in absolute confidence."

"Howard, we've been doing this for over six months.
It's always in confidence. You seem really spooked by this
one."

"Never a word about the source?"

"Of course not, Howard."

Howard Campbell genuinely liked, perhaps even loved
Liz Kennedy. The sex was, well, incredible. He'd forgotten how good it could be and he had rediscovered passion
that he thought he would never find again. And she was
an exciting and vivacious companion. He hated to use her
in this way, but she was such an important link in his
bringing down the Calhoun presidency.

"Liz, this has nothing to do with base closings or procurement or conversions or anything like that. It has to
do with national security and reaches to the highest levels
of our government. All the way to the top."

Liz wasn't making any sense of this. Howard actually
seemed a bit nervous, which was so unlike him.

"I really don't quite know where to start, Liz."

"Why don't you just try to give it to me step by step?"

"All right. You know that we conduct ongoing counterdrug operations in this hemisphere. Run them out of
our SouthCom headquarters down in Panama."

"Sure. Seems that it comes up every year during budget
reviews. The Department of Defense wants to get out of
that business—or at least have someone else pay for it—
but Congress likes to keep it going. Seems like President
Calhoun made combating drugs a big part of his platform
and, oh yeah, just as I was leaving, he was on CNN talking
about some operation that they just did somewhere in

Central America. I figured that his press secretary must have been desperate to get him some air time. Didn't sound like a very newsy item: 'Found some drug guys and captured them. Operation was a success.' Is that what this is about?"

"I'm getting to that. We, the Joint Chiefs and SouthCom, have been working to make this mission a little more viable for a while. You know, adding to our forces, enhancing our contacts with the right Latin American folks, and the like. We've worked hard to sell the President on doing the smart thing there. We even put our most knowledgeable counterdrug officer, General Charlie Walters, at SouthCom so he could oversee operations there."

"Howard, this is all very interesting, but I don't see many newspapers being scooped up so far."

"Liz, the operation wasn't a success. The President lied."

"Well, his details were pretty specific. What did he do, stretch the numbers a bit?"

"Liz, *listen to me*!" said Howard Campbell, feigning frustration but wanting her to work her way into becoming more and more incredulous. "The operation was a complete disaster. We're still getting reports in, but over a hundred Marines have been killed. This could be worse than the Marine barracks in Beirut."

"But how . . . why would he lie?"

"We don't know yet. But he personally bumbled this one. When they pull the string on this one, Liz, they'll find out several things. Calhoun put his own man, General Ashley Lovelace, in charge of the operation. Gave him specific instructions about what to do and how to do it. General Walters, the SouthCom commander, paid a special visit to Lovelace's flagship to tell him not to start any operation without getting his permission first. Then General Walters learned about a planned ambush and got the info directly to Lovelace, but Lovelace had, on his own—after talking *directly* with the President and bypassing all of us—started the operation with some half-assed planning and now we're getting reports on men dying in this third world shithole."

"But why would the President bypass all of you, all of his experts, and kind of do this on the fly?"

"Liz, don't you see? You read the polls. He's at best a long shot to get reelected. Maybe he thought a big splash would help put him back in the good graces of the voters."

"Yeah, but he couldn't possibly think he could keep it a secret forever."

"Of course not. That's part of it. He's got to be losing it. Maybe Lovelace panicked and sent a fouled-up report. Maybe there's enough blame to spread around. The point is, Liz, the President picked the commander. He directed exactly how the operation would be run. We, the Joint Chiefs, were told to stay out of it and then *his man* gooned up the entire operation. This isn't the man we want as our Commander in Chief."

"Howard, I'm not sure I know where to start on a story like this."

"Liz, you're too good a reporter to believe that. This will all come out in the investigations we've started already. I thought you'd be happy to have lead on a story like this."

"Oh, Howard, don't misunderstand me. I am grateful. This is so complex, though, I'm not sure where to begin."

"How about: PRESIDENT DIRECTS COUNTERDRUG OPERATION FROM OVAL OFFICE—HUNDREDS OF MARINES AMBUSHED—U.S. DISHONORED AND DISGRACED! I think that would just about capture the moment."

"I think it would, Howard. It could also be the end of his presidency."

"Indeed it might be, Liz, and here, take this; the background may be helpful. I've got to get back to the Pentagon now and I think that we can't have any more communications about this operation for a while. As you might imagine, I'm in a bit of an awkward position, since I serve at the President's pleasure. I'll wait with you while they bring your car around."

Liz took the small manila envelope that General Howard Campbell passed to her, not yet fully comprehending that she was about to become the agent who would accelerate the fall of the President. "Yes, Howard, thank you."

As they walked out of Cate's Bistro together, Liz thought about Howard Campbell, and she thought about the disaster in the field. But mostly she thought about being a reporter—a very well-known reporter.

They waited while the attendant brought her Miata around, standing between Cate's and Murphy's Irish Pub. Howard had her momentarily baffled on this one, but she hoped that whatever was in the envelope would help her put together a good story.

Her car arrived. Liz got in, turned around, and said, "Good night, Howard."

"Good night, Liz," he replied. But she was already speeding back toward her office.

CHAPTER 55

"PACER 236, WINDS TWENTY-FIVE TO STARBOARD, TEN knots, pitch and roll negligible, green deck, spot one. Playmate 238, take loose trail, you'll be cleared to spot two as soon as he's on deck, acknowledge." *Coronado*'s air boss was moving the process along rapidly, knowing that both birds contained wounded Marines.

"Pacer 236, copy the numbers."

"Pacer 238, roger."

The wind generated by both Blackhawks pushed hard at the LSE, who leaned into it as best he could while signaling first Pacer 236, than Pacer 238, to land on spots one and two, respectively. *Coronado*'s medical response team moved toward the aircraft as soon as the Blackhawks were secured on deck with chocks and chains. Rick Holden was the first to jump out of Pacer 236.

"Take him first—he's the one in the worst shape," said Rick to the first corpsman on the scene. He was yelling at the top of his lungs, but he wasn't sure the corpsman heard him above the din of the helo's whirling blades, so he all but thrust Major Pete Holian into the man's arms.

"We've got him now," responded the corpsman, yelling back at Rick and putting an extra-tight grip on the major.

One by one, *Coronado*'s medical crew assisted the other wounded Marines from each of the Blackhawks and led them along the port side of the hangar, through the mess decks, and down to the ship's sick bay. Once they knew their comrades were taken care of, Rick and Ensign Kemp ran up and forward on *Coronado*'s starboard side directly to the bridge and reported to Captain Howe. The captain was out of his bridge chair and on the bridge wing watching them race up the ladders.

"What is it, men? We heard your call about wounded. But the staff had a call that the mission was a total success with no casualties," said Howe, his look incredulous.

"Captain, I don't know anything about any call, but it's a slaughterhouse out there," said Ensign Kemp. He was clearly agitated but trying to keep his composure in front of his commanding officer. "We walked into an ambush, plain and simple. Never had a chance. Lost both Apaches to Stingers right away and then the Blackhawks started taking hits. Must be over a hundred men dead or dying, Captain. The follow-on waves of Apaches never showed up. Captain, we need help to get our guys out of there."

Captain Howe could not conceal his shock. "But you had firepower, numbers, everything. How did a rabble of druggies pull this off? You said Stinger missiles took out our helos? They're some of the most closely guarded weapons in our inventory. Are you certain?"

As the captain finished his sentence, Rick Holden opened the duffel bag he was carrying and pulled out several Stinger casings. "Captain, I've worked with these weapons before. These are the genuine article. That's not all. They had heavy-caliber weapons well entrenched in the hills. Those things didn't fall off a truck either. They had a major supplier somewhere and must have had intel about when we were coming too."

"We need to tell General Lovelace and the JTF Eight staff and then they need to get us the help to extricate our Marines," said Howe, as he moved into the bridge and down the starboard side ladder that took them directly to General Lovelace's cabin. Captain Howe didn't need to tell the Marine orderly stationed there that he had to see the general immediately.

General Lovelace met them at the door. "Captain, men—I saw the plat shots of the wounded being taken out of the Blackhawks. That doesn't jibe with the report I got from Pacer 408. Did these men get wounded in some after-action accident or something?"

"General, it's much worse than that. We ran into an ambush," said Captain Howe.

"An ambush—no, that's *not* the report I got. There must be some mistake!"

Captain Howe spoke quickly because he could see that both SEALs were ready to leap at General Lovelace out of frustration over the loss of their comrades. How could their leader be so out of touch? "General, these men were there. We've lost over a hundred men in a well-coordinated ambush. Marines are dying on the ground. We can worry about the details later, but we've got to help these men now!" Howe was surprised that he was so forthright with the JTF commander, but the urgency of the situation dictated it.

"Captain, you have certainly confused me with this info. And General Walters has called me and told me that we should not have even started this operation. What about my report from Pacer 408? Can I not get any valid information about this operation I'm supposed to be running? Ensign, Chief, what is going on out there?"

Ensign Kemp and Rick related the same tale they told Captain Howe, sparing neither detail nor emotion. General Lovelace seemed almost uncomprehending. They tried to provide him with as much detail as necessary but truncated their story as much as possible so that he would move out on extricating the men still alive on the ground. Just as they were completing their story, the E phone at General Lovelace's desk rang, signaling a call from the JTF Eight staff watch officer.

"Lovelace here."

"General, Major Blose, staff watch officer. We've just received a hicom call from Vanguard 202, the lead Apache in the assault wave. He's orbiting the FARP site and reports that it's apparently blown up. He says there's an incredible amount of smoke and flame. They don't have enough fuel to return to base; they're just going to try to find a clearing and set their aircraft down. They'll tell the other Vanguard aircraft to do the same."

"No. Tell them to go to the field. We need them there!" Lovelace was almost screaming now that he understood the gravity of the situation and realized that the Apaches were vitally needed to stem the slaughter.

"Sir, they don't have enough fuel to get there," responded Major Blose, hearing the General's near-panic and trying to inject some rationality into the situation.

Captain Howe jumped in. "General, if I may, I've heard the full report from these men. Let me sit down with your staff and prepare a concise, verbal OPREP, and then we can give it to you to transmit to General Walters. He may have the assets to help these men. We need to move quickly, General. Time really is of the essence."

"I agree, Captain, yes. Do it, but do it quickly!"

CHAPTER 56

GENERAL WALTERS RETURNED TO HIS QUARTERS AFter disposing of Lieutenant Wilson. He looked at this as just one small bit of untidy business that he had to finish up. Remorse was not a word that occurred to him at all. Now all he had to do was wait. It was good that he was out of reach for a while, better to give the tormented Lovelace more time to stew and fret before making the call he knew he would have to make.

As expected, the red light on the phone by his bedside table was flashing, telling him that the command duty officer needed to get in touch with him. Normally, his driver, Sergeant Brooke, carried the bat phone everywhere they drove, but by storming out of the command center and insisting on driving alone, he had conveniently departed without giving his staff the wherewithal to contact him.

He picked up the receiver, ready to begin a conversation whose script he already knew.

"General Walters here," he said after Commander Harry Pagano, the duty officer who had relieved the hapless Lieutenant Colonel Beall, picked up the phone on the first ring.

"General, Commander Harry Pagano here, sir. Sir, General Lovelace has urgently been trying to contact you."

"Has he?" queried Walters, feigning surprise.

"Yes sir. He is standing by for your call. Shall I patch you through to *Coronado*, General?"

Walters still marveled at the electronic wizardry that allowed him to connect with virtually any location on earth right from his bedroom. He had made good use of it to pull this off; now he was in the home stretch. "Certainly, Captain. Get him on the line and buzz me right back."

This moment would be too good to savor without a drink. Walters strode confidently to the wet bar in the far nook of his large bedroom and poured himself a scotch. He was just settling into his large black leather recliner with the bat phone in his lap when it rang again.

"Walters here."

"General, this is Commander Pagano. I'm ready to patch General Lovelace through."

"Please go ahead, Commander, seeing as that's why I'm sitting here waiting."

Within seconds, General Ashley Lovelace was on the line. "Good morning, General Walters. I have a report from the field that is ... well, that is ... what I mean is, quite a shock."

General Walters didn't get to this position without being a good student of human nature, and from just this sentence he could tell that Lovelace was a defeated man. His voice betrayed him: He just could not come to grips with what was happening let alone imagine that Walters had a hand in the operation's failure. He decided to play the straight man as much as possible.

"Well, General, let's have it. Bad news doesn't get any better with age."

"I've just had two Blackhawks return from the field with wounded. Our men were ambushed by a well-coordinated enemy action. We lost at least a half-dozen aircraft. God knows how many men have been killed already. All the others are pinned down. General, I need help getting the rest of the men out of there."

"General, what about your OPREP—which, by the way, I still haven't seen—and your report to me that everything is going well? General, do you really have a picture of what's going on?"

"Yes sir, now I do."

"Thought you had told me the Pacer relay helo had given you a report of a successful operation."

"Yes sir, they had. I listened to it myself. We're still trying to figure that one out."

"Think the enemy might have made a false transmission to you?"

"I know that is theoretically possible, but this was supposed to be a benign operation and there were supposed to be only a ragtag bunch of—"

"General, how long have you been involved in this anti-drug business?"

"Well, sir, you know when I reported down here—"

"Damn right I do. I've been at this for *years,* General Lovelace, *years*! You can't underestimate these people. I thought we made that clear in our briefings to you at my headquarters, but evidently it didn't take. Sounds like you've been the victim of some serious operational deception. Are you now more inclined to believe what my staff has been trying to tell you based on air analysis of the TARP's photos shot by the F-14?"

"Absolutely, General, it all tracks now. But my main concern now is with our men. We need help extricating them from this hopeless situation."

"General, I've given you an entire squadron of Apaches. I assume you're using their firepower."

"No sir. You see, the first two Apaches were hit by Stingers—"

"What about the backups? We set up an entire refueling scheme just for this operation."

"Yes sir, but, well, you see, the FARP site suffered a

casualty and we can't refuel them and can't get them to the scene."

"What kind of casualty?"

"It appears that it blew up."

"*Blew up?* General, has anything gone right with this operation? You start it without permission. You don't take what would seem to be ordinary, prudent precautions. You ignore the advice of me and my staff. You get duped by some amateurish operational deception. You clearly don't have much of a backup plan. Now you want me to bail you out. What do you think I have down here, the entire base on strip alert?" Walters was on a roll now, leavening his sarcasm with just enough sympathy to make Lovelace think that at least at some level he empathized with him.

"General, you mean there's nothing you can do?"

" 'Fraid not. It's in your hands. We have to put the best spin on this and do damage control and tell the chain of command immediately. Now I need some more information from you, and—"

Lovelace interrupted, "But General, I've already told the Joint Chiefs that this was a success, and—"

"*You've told who, what? With the half-assed bit of information you had, you told my boss that this was a success, fed him totally false information? Who else have you told?*"

"The President," offered Lovelace meekly.

"*My God, man have you lost your mind?*" But of course Walters knew it all. That very moment, President Taylor Calhoun's muted image was on CNN and was piped directly into his quarters.

"Well, General, you've made a fool of yourself and a fool of your President. Looks like the two of you have bypassed the entire chain of command in concocting this failed operation. The blood of all of those brave men is on your hands, Lovelace. It's on your hands."

General Ashley Lovelace almost jumped as the sound of the phone slamming down on General Walters's end of the line jarred him. He had never felt more alone or more confused in his life. How could this have happened? Was he really responsible for fouling up this operation? Where had he gone wrong?

CHAPTER 57

BRIAN STAVRIDIS, THE PRESIDENT'S NATIONAL SECU-
rity Advisor, got the call from General Campbell just
minutes after the President's address to the nation ended.

"Stavridis here."

"Mr. Stavridis, General Howard Campbell here. I just
saw the President's address. I don't know where he has
gotten his information, but what he just announced to the
American public bears no semblance to reality."

"What are you talking about, General? I was in the
Oval Office with the President when he got the word directly from General Lovelace at the scene. Is there some
minor detail or some sort of military semantics that we
didn't get quite right, General?" Stavridis's tone was icy.
He had little patience with military officers and barely suffered high-ranking ones. Hired legions, he was fond of
calling them.

"Mr. Stavridis, I'll say this again. I have *direct* communications with the SouthCom commander, General
Walters. *He* has spoken with General Lovelace. *He* has
spoken with the pilots who have flown over the battlefield.
He has spoken with the Apache pilots who flew over a
decimated FARP site. *He* has a full picture of what is
really happening. I don't know where the President got
his information. Now, Mr. Stavridis, I can see the administration trying to do a little spin control on a bad situation, but—"

That was as far as he got. Stavridis nearly leaped
through the phone. "Are you suggesting that the President was not *completely* forthright with the American people? Are you suggesting that, General? Do you recall that
you serve at the pleasure of the President?"

"Just as we all do, Mr. Stavridis, just as we all do."

194

Campbell was clearly enjoying Stavridis's discomfiture but was taking great pains not to reveal it. "The fact remains, Mr. Stavridis, that the President needs to level with the American people, and my sense of it is that the sooner, the better."

"Perhaps you'd better get over to the White House and brief the President personally," said Stavridis, attempting to exercise his authority over Campbell, but not succeeding.

"I don't think so, Mr. Stavridis. I'm needed here in the Pentagon to try to mitigate this disaster," said Campbell. Then, almost as an afterthought, he added, "I may have to immediately relieve General Lovelace, even though he was the President's personal pick for this assignment."

"What do you mean, his personal pick? What has that got to do with anything?"

"Surely you recall that the President *directed* me to put General Lovelace in charge of the operation? I voiced my opinion that he had neither the experience or the temperament for the assignment. It's well-known in this building that the President coached him on how to conduct the operation. General Walters, a man I have served with for decades and who I trust completely, tells me that Lovelace commenced the operation without his permission, but shortly after talking with the President. General Walters had indications of an ambush but could not get General Lovelace to buy it or even consult him. Then Lovelace sends a totally false report to the President, which the President buys, or so you tell me, without question. I don't think I have a choice but to replace him. But of course, Mr. Stavridis, you're directing everything else from the White House, so you might want to override me on this issue too." The sarcasm in Campbell's voice was palpable.

Brian Stavridis was going on pure political instinct now, logic having apparently been stripped from the situation. General Campbell demonstrated neither rage nor concern for this horrific military disaster but seemed detached from the entire episode. Was he remaining calm to mask his own incompetence? Surely this wasn't the President's *fault*, he thought. The military had fouled this up, just like they did everything else, and now they would have to stand up and be counted. Stand up next to their President and take the blame for this failed operation. Yes, that was it: the President had authorized the mission at the military's urgings, he had given them the green light, but they had dropped the baton and really gooned it. They had let the President down.

"Well, General, I hear what you're saying, but I *really* think that you need to come over here, perhaps with the other chiefs."

"I don't think so, *Brian.* You all are on your own on this."

Stavridis recognized how desperate their plight had become. He needed to rouse President Taylor Calhoun to action before his administration began a downward spiral on this one.

CHAPTER 58

THERE WAS SOMETHING ABOUT THE WHITE HOUSE West Wing Cabinet Room, just twenty feet from his Oval Office, that conveyed an air of solidness and stability. Perhaps it was the marble busts of George Washington and Benjamin Franklin flanking the fireplace. Perhaps it was the Edouard Armand oil painting *Signing of the Declaration of Independence* that dominated the room. Perhaps it was the portraits of George Washington, Thomas Jefferson, Abraham Lincoln, and Teddy Roosevelt that graced the walls. So although the Oval Office had the literal seat of power, President Taylor Calhoun felt a larger sense of control in the Cabinet Room. Surrounded by his closest advisors, all sitting in chairs with brass plates indicating their Cabinet position: National Security Advisor Brian Stavridis, Vice President Alex Paul, the Secretary of State, the Secretary of Defense, Press Secretary Ray Weaver, and a handful of others—he pondered his next move.

"Brian, do I understand correctly that the Chairman feels he can't leave the Pentagon right now?" queried Calhoun.

"That's what he *says* Mr. President. I don't quite understand why he can't make a half-hour to come over and personally brief his Commander in Chief," responded Stavridis, clearly annoyed that the President wasn't keeping the recalcitrant general on a shorter leash.

"Alex, this has certainly gone to hell in a handbasket. What are our options?"

"Mr. President, we have a catastrophe here, there's no two ways about it. I think that we need a clearer picture of exactly what has happened, and we need to find out why General Lovelace gave us such a glowing report that now appears to be so totally detached from reality. We may need to set up a conference call with all the parties."

"Mr. President," said Weaver, "whatever we do, we must do it quickly. The public relations aspects of this are absolutely disastrous. You need to show the American people that you know what is happening and that you are leveling with them—and, most importantly, that you will take action to correct whatever military mistakes the Pentagon has made."

"I agree with you, Ray. We have to move quickly. The Vice President's idea of a conference call is a good one. Let's get all the principals on the line. I want General Campbell, General Walters, and General Lovelace all linked up ASAP. Let's ensure that we get the real story."

The White House Communications Agency was a little-known but absolutely essential element of the operations of the White House. Possessing state-of-the-art equipment and manned by the brightest technicians the federal government could find, their role was to link the President instantaneously with anyone in the world. It was only a short amount of time before Brian Stavridis announced that he had all three military men on the line and on the speaker phone, ready to talk with the President.

"Gentlemen, Mr. Stavridis has briefly told you what this call is all about. I need to learn exactly what went on with Operation Roundup. General Campbell?"

"Mr. President, as I've already related to you, this was a disaster. Our forces walked into a well-planned ambush, pure and simple. Obviously, the cartel had prior and, from the looks of it, comprehensive knowledge of what we were going to try to do. We had late-breaking intelligence that led us to want to stop the operation, but the field commander had moved too soon."

"Yes, Mr. President," began General Walters, "we have already started an investigation at my headquarters. We have checks and balances, Mr. President, but those were violated. Those are the key things that I think you need to know now."

"Mr. President, clearly we are still gathering all of the facts. General Walters's next priority is to try to extricate survivors from the mesa. I think that we need to let him and his staff continue with those efforts," said General Campbell, clearly taking charge in this conversation.

"Mr. President, yes, my priority is on getting any survivors out. I must say, though, Mr. President, there shouldn't have been any casualties. I never authorized the operation—"

"*What?* General, are you saying you never gave the word for this to start even after I gave you the green light?" said the President. "General Lovelace, we haven't heard from you and I still don't know how we came up with a report that this was all a smashing success."

Clearly wounded by the words of his superiors, General Ashley Lovelace didn't exactly know where to begin. "Mr. President, General Lovelace here. We did have a complete disaster, Mr. President. I take full responsibility as the officer in charge of the operation. As for the report of success, we suspect now that that was a well-planned deception by the enemy, perhaps to keep us from having reinforcements ready. I apologize for any embarrassment that may have caused you, Mr. President."

"More than embarrassment, General," said Taylor Calhoun, now barely able to control his rage.

"Yes sir, Mr. President. We will dig into that and—"

General Walters cut off the junior brigadier. "Mr. President, General Campbell, it would seem to me that we're a little overfocused on what was just a crude but effective bit of operational deception by the enemy. The real issue is why this operation got going in the first place. General Lovelace did *not* have my permission to begin this operation. Had General Lovelace followed my *explicit* instructions not to go beyond the actions spelled out in our alert order until he received the final go-ahead from me, none of this would have happened. Under that fairly robust alert order, our forces were to proceed toward the objective area and remain poised to strike, but were to stay outside of a ten-mile radius of the objective until I gave the final execute order to General Lovelace. I had the late-breaking intelligence that the enemy had learned of our plans, but General Lovelace had taken matters into his own hands and I was powerless to stop him. Now we've lost a lot of brave boys because of it."

"I'm afraid that's the long and the short of it, Mr. President," chimed in General Campbell. "We have a lot of checks and balances in the military, particularly for an operation of this importance. Clearly, General Lovelace circumvented those checks and balances."

"General Lovelace?" queried the President.

His character and upbringing compelled General Ashley Lovelace to assume the blame for this failed operation. Mustering all of his courage, he began. "Mr. President, I take full responsibility. I must have misunderstood General Walters. I thought I had the authority to begin on my own. If I had seen the TARPs photos that General Walters had, I wouldn't have gone ahead. So much has gone wrong that we didn't anticipate."

"I know, General," offered the President, trying to take some of the sting away from his noble friend.

"Mr. President," said General Campbell in a somber tone, "perhaps there was a little too much pressure on General Lovelace right from the start. The Joint Chiefs had questioned this operation from the beginning. Your interest, Mr. President, is what kept this going and we all knew that General Lovelace was your personal pick for the operation—"

"Well, General," shot back the President, "as I recall, you proposed General Lovelace and I accepted your recommendation."

"Well, Mr. President, you hinted rather broadly that he was your man. We also know that you gave him very explicit instructions, without my input or that of the theater commander, General Walters, that ran counter to sound military practice. If I may say so, sir, I think we really could have avoided this one if we had let the chain of command work the way it's supposed to and not direct the operation from the White House—"

President Calhoun cut him off. "You may say what you like, General, but this was not directed from the White House—"

Amazingly, General Walters cut the President off. "Mr. President, I'm no longer working inside the Washington beltway, so I don't feel like I have to be politically correct. But sir, General Campbell is right. Every time I consulted him on this operation my advice was overridden because of the direction that you had provided regarding the operation. It's all here in my notes. Additionally, I track the communications to and from the flagship and we saw a lot of comms between General Lovelace and yourself right before the operation commenced."

The President could barely control his rage. *"Your notes . . . and you're monitoring my conversations?"*

"No, sir, Mr. President. Not monitoring, just noting when calls are made to and from military units. It's all standard procedure, sir."

General Campbell continued, "Mr. President, General Walters is just doing his job the best way he knows how. Neither he nor I ever advised playing politics with the lives of American boys—"

"No one, do you hear me, no one was playing politics with anyone. I approved of this operation that you all sold me and now all of a sudden it's my operation. Damned if I'll stand for that!" The Vice President and Brian Stavridis both backed away from the President, as he was now standing and shouting at the speaker phone and pounding the console in the situation room.

"Mr. President, we serve at your pleasure and have tried to give you our best military advice. But when you choose to ignore it, we can't be responsible," continued Campbell, clearly unfazed by the President's outburst.

"You damn well are responsible and I'll have your stars for this, General. Just who in the hell do you think you're screwing with? You'll be out on your ass so fast you won't know what hit you!"

"Perhaps the American people need to decide who's responsible, sir. And now, if you'll excuse me, sir, I'm needed back at the National Military Command Center. We have work to do. You have enough people here who can keep you informed. Maybe we can still save some of our boys. Good-bye, Mr. President."

With that the line went dead as the President, Vice President, National Security Advisor, and the few other principals gathered in the West Wing Cabinet Room sat in shocked disbelief. Not only had the country just absorbed its worst military disaster in over a decade, but the military commanders were now pointing directly at the President as the reason for its failure. Brian Stavridis finally had the presence of mind to break the silence. "Mr. President, I recommend we gather all of your principal advisors immediately and plan our strategy."

"I agree, Brian. What is happening?"

"Mr. President, they can't challenge your authority like that. They just can't. We'll wipe them out."

"But they are challenging my authority, Brian. They are challenging it to the core. What's more, at this point, I don't know if we have the power to stop them."

CHAPTER 59

LIZ KENNEDY TRIED NOT TO LET HER THOUGHTS WANder as she worked furiously to tie together the details for her story on Operation Roundup. Not only was there a deadline to worry about, but also the formidable task of pitching the story to her editor, Joe Abramowitz. Still, she had to wonder about the musty smell and the seemingly total disorder of the *Washington Post* editorial offices. Partitions had been set up in rather haphazard manner to try to divide the room into some semblance of sections, but most who worked there had long since forgotten what went with what. Now desks were grabbed in rough order of seniority. When someone left the *Post,* his or her desk went to the next most senior reporter or editor, with everyone who wanted to moving up in daisy-chain fashion. Because of that, there was little value added in tidying up one's particular little alcove, only to have to tear it down and move to a more prestigious desk at a moment's notice.

Liz's desk was no worse and no better than any of the others in this chaotic place. Word processors were the only commonality among the desks, with IBM being the tool of choice and of necessity, as all the computers were tied together on a local area network, or LAN, allowing reporters and editors to send stories from screen to screen to review, change, edit, and finally publish. The endless cables that ran from the back of these computers into various overloaded surge protectors on the floor would have, by themselves, defeated any attempt to bring order out of this chaos. Liz tried to stay focused in spite of the ambience.

It was a good story. The contents of the envelope had provided the details of the story that Howard Campbell had sketched out for her. She kept coming back to the headline he had suggested to her. It would be quite a scoop if the wire services or that damned CNN didn't grab it first. But it was already after the network evening news and if no one picked the story up before the late evening news, the *Washington Post* would be on the front doorstep of thousands of the most important homes in America the next morning before anyone had a chance to beat them to the punch. But she was less worried about details at this point than about selling the story to Abramowitz.

Finally she banged out a first draft and sent it directly to Abramowitz, bypassing two junior editors in the process. *Post* protocol allowed this leap if the story was a hot one (damned if the burden of proof for that wasn't always left to the reporter, though). She thought it was hot enough, never had second thoughts about it at all. She was so sure that she tagged it with the *Post*'s alert cue that would flash on Abramowitz's screen no matter what he was doing. As she sent it, Liz rose from her desk and looked toward Abramowitz's corner office. He was on the phone and she saw him wheel his well-worn high-backed black leather chair around to look at his screen. Soon the phone went back on the receiver as Abramowitz stared at his screen. As he reached for his intercom, Liz was already headed for his office.

"Liz, where did you come up with this? Does anyone else know about this yet?"

"I don't think so, Joe." Abramowitz was at least as old as her father and "Joe" never did trip off her tongue very naturally, but Abramowitz insisted on a first-name informality among all of his editors, reporters, and assistants.

"Well, where did you get it?"

"I have a highly placed source; he just broke this to me less than two hours ago. He's been my source on most of my military pieces before," added Liz, sure that this would give Abramowitz confidence that she knew what she was talking about.

"You've written a good story in that short a time, Liz, and I know you know your stuff vis-à-vis the military, but this is a *big* story. We can't be wrong on this. Any chance you want to tell me who the source is?"

"Afraid I can't, Joe. I learned from a pro," Liz said with a smile. Abramowitz was her mentor and she endured endless ribbing by her fellow reporters about being "Abramowitz's girl Friday." "But, Joe, he is an unimpeachable source."

"I believe you. But we've got to think about the paper. If we flub this one, no matter how good your source, we're the laughingstock øf the industry, to say nothing about lawsuits. Sometimes people trip off the line. Can you get a second source?"

"There's just no time, and, well, my source is so highly placed that no one under him would lend any additional credence."

"Maybe not in his organization, or even in this town, but I need something more, Liz. I want to go with this one, but you've just got to tie it up in a neater bow for me."

Liz Kennedy walked out of Joe Abramowitz's office feeling a mixture of elation and frustration. She *had* latched on to a good story and had, if she did say so herself, written it with just the right amount of flair to make it a potential prizewinner. But, oh, this second source crap, it was all so unnecessary. How did you ever really get anything done? What to do? Who would she ask? Clearly, she couldn't ask anyone highly placed in the Pentagon without betraying Howard Campbell's confidence. No one outside of Defense probably even knew about it yet. She sat down heavily at her cluttered desk and started flipping idly through her Rolodex, as if that would spontaneously bring up some name who would be the perfect second source. No such luck. *Think, Liz.* A military operation goes bad in Latin America. Somebody got bad information. Somebody pressed ahead in spite of it. Wait. Doubles league, Army-Navy Country Club. That cute Navy girl. Worked at the Pentagon—intelligence, wasn't it? She was getting transferred. . . .

Liz dialed the Navy locator, where the low-level GS clerks at the Bureau of Naval Personnel dutifully provided the duty station of every officer, noncom, and sailor in the U.S. Navy. She thanked the operator and placed her next call. After four rings a tired voice answered: "Lieutenant Peters speaking, sir, how may I help you?"

CHAPTER 60

RICK HOLDEN AND ENSIGN BOB KEMP EMERGED FROM Captain Howe's cabin unsure of what to do next. They had told their stories to their commanding officer and what seemed like an army of yeomen who had dutifully copied down everything they had said. Captain Howe had assured them that a rescue effort would be mounted at once, but, they would not be a part of it; they had seen enough action for one day and night. "Just go get cleaned up, men, and thanks for coming forward with this," had been Captain Howe's parting words to them.

Holden and Kemp went directly down the port side ladders three decks to the second deck sick bay. There they found Major Pete Holian and the other Marines they had pulled out of the LZ, all weak but all recovering. Holian gazed up at the two SEALs.

"You snake eaters earned your keep today. You've both got first-class accommodations in my helo anytime," said Holian, forcing a smile through the pain and the pain-killers.

"No problem, Major," said Ensign Bob Kemp. "Holden here did all the hard stuff. Pulled two badly injured men to safety."

"We just got wiped out. Didn't know what hit us."

"What knocked down the helos, Major?"

"SAMs, good ones too. Came from all over the jungle. Our IR suppressors and other gear is supposed to be good against almost anything in the inventory, certainly anything these third world druggies could come up with."

"You said 'almost anything,' Major. What won't it deal with?"

"Well, we know that our Stinger missile is the best shoulder-fired weapon in the world. Tests the Navy's done at China Lake confirm it time after time. No helo can avoid the Stinger, no way, nohow. I don't think we even have countermeasures for it on the drawing board. From the way our two Apaches and our Blackhawks went down, I'd have to say they were Stingers."

"How many people were you fighting?" asked Ensign Kemp.

"Fellas, I have no idea. Could have been fifty, could have been five hundred. They were all concealed in that thick jungle. Just blew us out of the sky, then rained fire at our guys from the hills all around the hacienda. I don't know how many of our men could have survived that. Have they gotten them out yet?"

"SouthCom's working on that, Major. I know that they're going to give it their best shot," said Ensign Bob Kemp as reassuringly as he could. He dared not tell the major about the disaster at the FARP site, at least until he recovered a bit more.

After leaving sick bay, Rick Holden went back to his berthing compartment. By now, all of his fellow SEALs were asleep, exhausted by the day's efforts. He took off his fatigues and headed for the shower. There Rick allowed himself the luxury of a "Hollywood shower," Navy slang for what civilians considered a normal: You turn the water on when you get in and turn it off when you get out. It was a forbidden joy because it wasted precious water that had to be made in the ship's evaporators—the Navy required you to drench yourself quickly, turn the water off while soaping up, then turn it back on briefly to rinse—but Rick figured he owed it to himself. As he let the hot water beat down on him, he tried to make sense of the day's events.

It was all coming together with frightening clarity. Furtive calls aboard *Coronado* and at SouthCom headquarters. A JTF commander who was clearly in the dark about the operation. A devastating ambush that was astonishingly well planned. Evidence now in his duffel bag that American weapons had been used in the attack. All that was missing was the why, and at this stage Rick Holden was totally baffled as to what was behind all of this. He'd been involved in some strange occurrences at the Agency, but this seemed even more convoluted than anything he had encountered before. Instinctively he knew that he needed to tell Laura Peters, who might put herself in more danger than she realized if she followed up her own suspicions. But how could he reach her?

Rick dressed quickly, donning a fresh set of fatigues, and raced to the radio shack. The action there was frantic as Ben Malgrave and his crew attempted to keep up with the inevitable after-action reports to the plethora of requests for details of this disaster. Only a few more Blackhawks had arrived with survivors, an ominous sign, and the mood in Radio Central was somber. It would undoubtedly get worse once the level of intensity died down and his shipmates had a chance to really dwell on the fate of their Marine brethren.

"Holden, you back from the field?" asked Malgrave.

"Just finished debriefing the captain and the general, Commander. By way of a shower, that is."

"Was it as bad as these reports are saying?" Malgrave had read every one of the reports going out and had a complete written record of what had happened, but Holden had *been there.*

"Worse, I'm afraid, Commander. Our guys never had a chance," replied Holden. Then, telling himself to stay focused on his reason for being in Radio Central, he continued, "Probably why I can't sleep, Commander. Just going to work on some of my gear, take my mind off the field, if that's okay with you."

"No problem, Holden. You can tell we're keeping busy too. I'll holler if we need your help."

Rick worked his way past the radiomen jammed into this small space and toward the far port side of Radio Central, into the area called the "closet." The actual hardware was there and it was where the men did their periodic checks of the equipment. The level of operations going on right now ensured that no one would be back here doing maintenance on the gear. Rick was alone for now.

Using a small tool kit he kept in the large pocket of his fatigues, Rick attached the right cables and then a small mike to one of the HF radios inside the closet. He dialed in the right frequency, then hesitated. He was calling SouthCom headquarters. What if Laura wasn't the one who picked up the radio? Did he tell them who he was? As Rick turned up the frequency in the secure HF radio, he seized upon the idea of going "command to command," just identifying himself as part of the JTF Eight staff and making contact with the SouthCom staff. If things got sticky he could just break off the transmission. HF nets were notoriously vulnerable to atmospheric and other interferences. Quickly he looked through the appropriate publication for the standard military, daily changing call signs for each command.

"Kilo four xray, kilo four xray, this is hotel eight tango, hotel eight tango, over."

"Hotel eight tango, this is kilo four xray, have you weak but readable, go ahead with your transmission, over."

"Kilo four xray, this is hotel eight. Staff intel wishes to speak with one of your assistant staff intel officers, Lieutenant Peters, over." Rick didn't think this slight stretch would burn him.

"Hotel eight, this is kilo four, stand by."

After waiting for what seemed like an eternity, Rick

finally heard the voice he wanted to hear on the other end of the line. "Lieutenant Peters, SouthCom intel. How may I help you, sir, over?" There was surprise in Laura's voice, since she was fairly far down the food chain to have the JTF Eight staff calling and asking for her specifically.

"Am I speaking with Lieutenant Peters, over?" offered Rick, emboldened now that he had made initial contact.

"Affirmative. Request to know whom I'm speaking with, over."

Rick had to break it now. "Laura, this is Rick. I'm calling on the net you gave me. Can you talk?"

"Yes. Wait." Laura turned to the Navy petty officer who had been guarding the net near the "intel vault" at SouthCom. "I've got it, Petty Officer. This will probably be a long transmission from JTF Eight. Why don't you take a break for a while? I'll come find you when I'm done."

The petty officer had been sitting fruitlessly at this desk for his eight-hour watch and welcomed the chance to walk outside and stretch his legs a bit. He happily complied with Laura's request.

"Are you on the flagship? What's going on? Why are you calling me?"

"Laura, Operation Roundup has been a complete disaster. You know that, don't you?"

"Yes, it's awful. I mean, all those men slaughtered. We're still piecing together all of the information, but this is worse than the Beirut marine barracks and Desert One combined. And then there's the press interest."

"I imagine they'll jump on this eventually."

"Not eventually, they've got it now. I got a call last night from a friend from Washington, Liz Kennedy. She covers military affairs for the *Washington Post.* I don't know how she tracked me down, but she heard the whole story, stuff even I didn't know yet, from what she called 'a very highly placed source in the Pentagon.' She needed a second source for confirmation, off the record and background only, of course. I didn't want to say much, but I couldn't outright lie to Liz. I read her columns when I was stationed in D.C. and played some tennis with her. She gives a pretty balanced perspective, maybe even goes out of her way a little bit to make the military look better—that's rare in this climate."

"Does anyone at SouthCom know that you've talked to her?"

"No, Rick, of course not. But for her to have this info this soon and to be prepared to break a story in tomorrow's paper, I can't believe that anyone in Washington could have that complete and detailed a story yet. I mean, we're still churning out our SITREPS and she had details we haven't even gotten to yet."

"Laura, there's more. I was out in the field, part of the backup rescue birds. Brought some wounded folks back, but there weren't many of them. You're right, the devastation was complete. Lots of brave men died for no reason. The ambush wasn't a pickup game either. It was planned with military precision and was well coordinated. The FARP site to refuel the Apaches blew up just as the operation commenced. A coincidence? Wiped out any chance we had to turn the tide in the field. Are you sure no one else is on this net?"

"I'm sure. Why?"

"Out in the field, when I was picking up our wounded guys, I came up with some Stinger missile casings. These are some of the most closely guarded weapons in our inventory. Remember the flap when some of them found their way to the Mujahedin in Afghanistan? Talking to the Blackhawk pilots who were shot down, they're sure they were hit by Stingers. Now I've got the parts to back that up. Someone sold or gave Stingers to the cartel."

"What are you saying? Do you think someone in our government knew about this?"

"Don't you see? The operation fails miserably. Tightly controlled weapons from our inventory are used in the enemy ambush. The President is fed false information and goes on national TV with it. The press knows about it immediately. . . ."

"But Rick, the false report, they know about that in headquarters here. They don't know where General Lovelace came up with that, and General Walters is irate. He'll probably relieve him for cause and put it in a new JTF Eight commander."

"Do you think General Lovelace made that up? It has to be part of an elaborate deception." He thought she should know that. It was not dissimilar to the types of deceptions he had been involved with at the Agency, but he couldn't reveal anything from those days. "Do you think a drug cartel really has that kind of capability?"

"If not them, then who?" Laura was tracking with Rick's logic but she still wasn't ready to buy fully into the big picture he was presenting.

"Laura, someone wanted very badly for this mission to fail and worked very hard for that to happen. I can't see this all coming together without some inside help from the U.S. Question is, why? I haven't figured that out yet. Maybe someone's in cahoots with the cartel and sharing the drug profits. Maybe someone is disgruntled with the military. There are probably possibilities I haven't thought of yet."

"What are you going to do?"

"I don't know yet, I just don't know. You just keep your head down at your end. Call me on this frequency if things get sticky for you."

"I will, Rick, but you be careful too."

Rick unkeyed the transmitter, his head still swimming with possibilities as he pondered his next move. He returned all of the radio gear to its original configuration and walked back into the heart of Radio Central ostentatiously fumbling with his MRC deck, the maintenance cards that described what work had to be performed on various equipment. "Well, that's done. Think I'll hit the rack," he announced to no one in particular as he left Radio Central, nodding to the still-harried Ben Malgrave as he left, secure that he had communicated with Laura and done so without being noticed. He couldn't know that one of the staff radiomen was now doing exactly what he had been ordered to do as the phone rang at Colonel Conrad Hicks's desk.

"Yes, chief of staff here . . . Who? . . . . How long? . . . . What net was he on? . . . Do you know who he communicated with? . . . Got it. Keep me informed."

Meanwhile, at SouthCom, inside a little-used storage

room, a secure military computer was recording all radio and telephone transmissions to and from the JTF Eight staff, a small "precaution" that General Walters had ordered just that morning.

CHAPTER 61

COMPARED WITH THE EVENTS OF THE LAST SEVERAL days, this day broke fairly calmly for the SouthCom staff. Operation Roundup was complete—a complete failure. The druggies had faded back into the jungle, no doubt to prepared locations where they were again conducting a brisk business. SouthCom had managed to extricate several score more wounded Marines and pick up all of the dead, a total of 136 good men, and if there was a silver lining, all of the Marines who went into the field were accounted for. The last thing they were prepared to deal with was a hostage situation. Now it was back to routine, making follow-up reports, planning future operations, and the like. General Walters had been quiet and a bit distant at the morning staff meeting, asking few questions of any of the staff briefers.

But it was *not* normal, thought Laura, nor should it be. An operation that was designed to be no more than a simple roundup of druggies had turned into a total military disaster and it didn't seem to faze anyone. Laura couldn't be the only one who was surprised by all of this. She had to run this to the ground. Her boss had always been a good sounding board. She hoped she would be again.

Laura hesitated for only a moment, then knocked confidently on Captain Fran Dawson's door. "Captain, do you have a minute?"

"Sure, Lieutenant, come in." Captain Dawson was "old school" and didn't encourage any familiarity among staff members of different ranks, least of all in her own department. "What's on your mind?"

"Captain, I'm not exactly sure where to start. Today it's just business as usual on the staff. We're just moving along like Operation Roundup never happened. But there are a lot of questions that haven't been answered. I just don't get it," said Laura, a great degree of frustration coming through in her voice.

"Well, Lieutenant, there are some things we still don't know and many things we do know. We know the druggies ambushed our guys, plain and simple. Seems to me they'd have a vested interest in doing that. We know they had some good weapons, but those must be fairly easy to come up with on the black market. We know we were plagued by really bad luck with the FARP site blowing up. We know our people did a good job getting as many Marines medical treatment as soon as they did. Finally, we know General Lovelace started this operation on his own, without permission, in direct violation of General Walters's orders and the result is over a hundred dead Marines. I'm not sure there's too much mystery here, Lieutenant. Perhaps the only remaining question is why Lovelace acted so irrationally. Maybe he had a different agenda."

Laura was staggered. If anyone should be trying to analyze what had happened it was the intelligence community, yet Captain Dawson was accepting all of these events at face value without questioning any of them. Laura knew she wouldn't find answers here. "Well, thanks for clearing things up a little bit, Captain. I guess I'm still new at this business. Sorry to bother you with this."

"No bother at all, Lieutenant. Glad I could be of help."

Laura strode out of Fran Dawson's office determined to get to the bottom of this. Her concerns—and those of Rick Holden—couldn't be that unfounded, could they? She wanted to do this soon, since she was scheduled to attend the Joint Intelligence Officers' Conference at Colorado Springs the next week.

General Walters was pensive when his executive assistant announced that his 1300 appointment was ready. His chief of staff entered with Colonel George Miller, the staff communicator.

"Good morning, gentlemen. What do you have to tell me this afternoon?"

"General," began Colonel Miller, "in accordance with your orders we initiated a monitoring program for all incoming and outgoing communications to the staff. I've put my best team on it with strict instructions not to reveal their activities to anyone else on the staff."

"How many people do you have on it, Colonel?"

"Four of my top noncoms and petty officers. I've briefed them that there may be a security leak on the staff. They were to screen all communications and pass anything even remotely suspicious to either Commander Bud Howser or myself."

"Anything interesting yet, Colonel?"

"Yes sir. Seems one of the lieutenants on the staff received a call in quarters last night from Washington, D.C. At first my techs thought it was from the Pentagon. I know that with the hours all of our officers keep they often make and take calls from their Q rooms. This wasn't the Pentagon, though, General. It was a *Washington Post* reporter, asking about the failure of the operation. I've provided a transcript of the conversation to the chief of staff. I don't think she made any security breeches or anything, but still, the officer shouldn't have been talking to a reporter, at least without letting us know about it. And there's more."

"Go ahead, Colonel."

"This same officer also had communications with JTF Eight staff aboard *Coronado* on a little-used HF net. Had a rather lengthy conversation with a chief petty officer at the other end where they discussed their speculations as to why Operation Roundup failed. I've provided that transcript to the chief of staff also."

"Was it just the normal postmortum, Monday morning quarterbacking?"

"No sir, General, they sounded like they had come into information no one else had and were speculating that the operation was designed to fail."

"*Designed to fail!* By whom?" replied Walters, now clearly much more interested in the colonel's report.

"They didn't seem to have an idea, just speculating."

"And who is this lieutenant, Colonel?"

"Lieutenant Peters, in the J-2 Directorate."

"Well, ah, good, Colonel. You've done a fine job. Continue to monitor all circuits as before and report back to the chief of staff whenever you have something worthwhile."

As Colonel Miller departed, General Walters tried to sort out his emotions. Laura Peters? Involved in this? He had figured that in just a short while he would have swayed her with his considerable charms—the squash games leading to dinner, then to an outing on his sailboat, then maybe a weekend away in Curaçao. He had pursued women like her before, the young, ambitious ones, and many had seen it his way eventually. But now had she put herself in a position where she could find out his part in the failure of Operation Roundup. Could she do him in? Would she?

Walters pressed the intercom. "Get Captain Dawson in here ASAP." The general's secretary made the appropriate call and within minutes she appeared, a little breathless from the unexpected summons.

"Captain Dawson reporting as ordered, General."

"Ah, Captain, good afternoon. I trust that things have gone pretty much back to normal in the Intelligence Directorate."

"Yes sir, General. We are getting back to pretty much our regular routine."

"Captain, what can you tell me about Lieutenant Peters? She works for you, doesn't she?"

Captain Fran Dawson's mind raced. How should she handle this one? She knew Lieutenant Peters was the general's regular lunchtime squash partner, but she didn't know whether the relationship went beyond squash. She had a certain loyalty to Laura, as her officer. She had a definite loyalty to General Walters, as her commander. She decided to keep it strictly professional.

"General, Lieutenant Peters is a fine officer. Came to us with a superb record. She was personally recommended to me by several people in our intelligence community. She's done a fine job here, probably has performed better than any O-3 on the staff. . . ."

"There's a hesitation in your voice, Captain."

"Well, General. She's been a little adrift about Operation Roundup. Just today she came by my office and had some strange questions. Didn't think we were doing enough to follow up on why the operation failed, that sort of thing."

"Do you think our follow-up is lacking, Captain?"

"No, General, not at all. But I don't believe I persuaded Lieutenant Peters. She left unconvinced, I think. Perhaps next week will do her some good."

"Next week?"

"Yes, General. She and Major Fitzgerald are attending the Joint Intelligence Officers' Conference at Colorado Springs. I've attended the last two and thought that it would be good if I let some of my junior officers attend."

"That's good thinking on your part, Captain, but, ah, for now at least, let's back Lieutenant Peters out of that trip. You can attend yourself or send someone else."

"Well, yes, General, but, well . . ."

"Will there be anything else, Captain?" said Walters as he rose. Fran Dawson knew it was time to leave. Now she was even more puzzled than when she had entered.

CHAPTER 62

BRIAN STAVRIDIS BELIEVED IN PRESIDENT TAYLOR Calhoun, believed in him fervently. He believed in him so much that on matters of national security he knew that he had to take the lead rather than just advise because the President's ponderous style and desire for details often put him behind the decision-making power curve. Now he clearly saw the runaway train aimed at the President and his administration and he needed to stop it. He had convinced the President that the situation was grave. The challenge left was to convince him to take effective action.

Here in the West Wing Cabinet Room, the President had gathered his advisors around him. That it was evening conveyed an additional sense of importance to the moment. "Brian, why don't you recap to bring everyone up to speed on what we have right now?" said the President.

"Certainly, Mr. President. Gentlemen, as you all know, Operation Roundup was a complete disaster. We lost 136 Marines and had about the same number wounded, many seriously. We've gotten all of our boys out of there. Thank God there were no hostages taken. The druggies have faded back into the jungle. From an operational perspective, that's about the long and the short of it.

"Obviously, this puts a crimp—a big crimp—in our counterdrug operations. Naturally, there will be an investigation as to why this all went awry. Clearly we need everyone in this room to stand behind the President on this one. No strategy is perfect and the President would have had to be clairvoyant to envision the Pentagon blowing this one." Heads nodded around the room. The appointees gazed intently on President Taylor Calhoun in an unspoken show of support.

"There seems to be a problem with the Pentagon, although not with your office, of course, Mr. Secretary," continued Stavridis, now speaking directly to Secretary of Defense Elliott Higginson, "but with the Joint Chiefs, particularly the chairman himself. He has made some outrageous accusations regarding the President's personal direction of the operation. Claims that the President directed the operation completely from the White House and made the operational commander, Brigadier General Lovelace, ignore orders from both SouthCom and JCS. We don't know where General Campbell is coming from on this one, but while we get to the bottom of this we need each and every one of you to support the boss on this matter."

The President leaned forward and spoke. "Yes, gentlemen, the National Security Advisor is right, as usual. I don't know what's gotten into the Joint Chiefs on this one. The chairman seems to have turned into a loose cannon, don't you think, Mr. Secretary?" Calhoun stared at the Secretary of Defense.

"I'm not sure exactly what is going on with the Joint

Chiefs either, Mr. President, but I'll certainly find out," replied the Secretary of Defense.

And so the President and Brian Stavridis continued, sounding out all of the President's closest advisors, both hearing what they had to say on the major issues and also measuring the depth of their support for their President. Stavridis's read was that indeed they were all lined up firmly behind Taylor Calhoun.

Finally, Press Secretary Ray Weaver spoke up. "Mr. President, we obviously need to devise a strategy for dealing with the press on this one. They leap on disasters like this with both feet. Sure would like to get out in front to tell our story."

"I knew you would be on top of this one, Ray," said the President. "The good news is that we're way out in front on it and I know the press will hear our side of the story first." Smiling broadly, Calhoun rose to conclude the meeting. Had he been standing in the editorial offices at the *Washington Post,* his smile would have melted away quickly.

CHAPTER 63

LIZ KENNEDY LEANED BACK IN HER CHAIR AND twisted her neck from left to right, trying to work the kinks out of her tight muscles. It had been a long, exhausting night, writing and rewriting her story. To his credit, Joe Abramowitz had been there with her every step of the way, lending his decades of experience and expertise and a great deal of moral support to boot. She had really gotten into sync on this story. Howard Campbell had, of course, been right in all the details of this story. With any luck, there would be multiple follow-ups to this one, and her byline would appear again and again in the *Post*—with any luck, on the front page. Who knows, Pulitzer Prizes had been garnered with much less than she had right now, and she had the right sources for even

more. The shadows of Woodward and Bernstein hovered
at the edges of her imagination.

Alone at her desk for a moment, for now Liz contented
herself with reading the last proof of her piece, which was
being printed in Tuesday morning's *Post* and which would
be on people's doorsteps and at newsstands in a matter
of hours:

U.S. COUNTERDRUG OPERATION FAILS—
136 MARINES KILLED
WHITE HOUSE INTERFERENCE ALLEGED

COSTA RICA—Details are still being gathered, but
veteran observers are calling a failed U.S.
counterdrug operation in this small Central
American nation the worst U.S. military disaster in
over a decade. Yesterday, a Joint Task Force
controlled from the U.S. Navy command ship USS
Coronado put hundreds of Recon Marines on the
ground in an attempt to capture drug kingpin Diego
Maradona and a large cache of drugs and weapons.

The predawn assault had just gotten under way
when the Marines were ambushed in what was
apparently a well-coordinated attack by the drug
cartel. Using advanced weapons, the drug cartel
shot down a number of U.S. helicopters, killing 136
Marines and wounding scores of others. The
wounded Marines were taken to the *Coronado,*
where they are receiving medical treatment. The
names of the servicemen killed are being withheld
pending notification of next of kin.

A full investigation of this disaster is under way.
Informed Pentagon sources indicated that the
operational commander, Commander, Joint Task
Force Eight, General Ashley Lovelace, may have
commenced the operation without permission of his
immediate superior, Commander, U.S. Southern
Command, General Charles Walters. These same
sources also suggest that General Lovelace, known
to be a close personal friend of the President, may

have been pressured to begin the operation prematurely for reasons unknown.

Liz was already mentally laying out a series of follow-up stories: official commentary from the Pentagon regarding what the mission had hoped to accomplish, details about why the on-scene commander had acted without authority, human interest stories on some of the slain Marines, speculation into what direction the President gave to General Lovelace and why, follow-up regarding where the cartel had evaporated to, speculation regarding why the military couldn't carry out such a seemingly simple operation, and many more. The possibilities were virtually limitless and Liz thought how truly fortunate she was to be so close to General Howard Campbell.

Even while she basked in her good fortune for the moment, Liz could not stifle her natural reporter's instincts. The deeper she delved into the details, the more bizarre the entire story seemed. Certainly drug cartels were powerful, but until now none had been known to have the kind of weapons that were used against the Marines. And druggies deployed to the jungle just as the Americans struck—that said they had incredibly good intelligence, almost complete knowledge, of the operation. How could they have come up with that? And how could the President have received such an incredibly incorrect report regarding events in the field? And how could the U.S. forces be the victims of such an awful coincidence as having the FARP site blow up just at the critical juncture of the operation? Finally, her unfailing source, General Howard Campbell, certainly had all the facts at hand in an amazingly short time, plus he seemed awfully detached from the dilemma the President now found himself in. It just wasn't adding up for her. She'd ride this story for all it was worth, but she had to know more. And from a secondary source in case Campbell hadn't been entirely forthcoming. To hell with the hour. She picked up the phone and dialed the number.

CHAPTER 64

THE WHITE HOUSE PRESS ROOM WAS FILLED TO OVER-flowing at the hastily convened press conference. Press Secretary Ray Weaver had received a call from a friend at the *Post* warning him that the Operation Roundup story would break in the morning. After a few hasty pre-dawn phone calls to his key staff members, he had briefed the President at seven A.M. and had received the go-ahead to convene the press conference at ten Eastern Standard Time. Details were provided by the Pentagon; Weaver noted that the Joint Chiefs, the regular source for this type of information, were not rapidly forthcoming with the in-itial notification of the disaster, nor with timely details, but he did not have time to ponder this peculiarity for long. The immediate task was to deal with the information he did have.

Weaver shifted uneasily on the balls of his feet, scan-ning the sea of faces of the scores of reporters and news-casters filling the room, men and women whose names were household words across America. He looked for an understanding face to gaze at, convinced that this would buoy his badly shaken confidence. It would not be easy to put a positive spin on this disaster, but Weaver was de-termined to give it his best shot.

"Ladies and gentlemen," he began, attempting to look as cool and confident as possible, "I have a prepared state-ment to give you regarding a counterdrug operation re-cently attempted by our military forces. Some information on this event has already appeared in the national media, but my briefing will be a comprehensive recounting of the events leading up to this tragedy and the events that oc-curred in the country of Costa Rica as we know them thus far. I want to emphasize that details are still rather sketchy this soon after the event and we will continue to keep you informed as we develop further information. I will be happy to answer questions after the prepared statement."

Satisfied that he had set the stage properly, Weaver began a methodical accounting of the events leading up to Operation Roundup, carefully crafting the administration's version of events into an eminently plausible tale. Ray Weaver was in his element now, speaking in his down-home, folksy style, portraying the President as the sage Commander in Chief who had only consented to the operation at the virtual insistence of the Joint Chiefs of Staff, who had continuously assured him this would be no more than an administrative roundup of some poorly armed and completely disorganized druggies. The military was very capable at some things, Weaver explained, but they had bungled this one. Naturally, the President had called for a full investigation by the Defense Department's Inspector General's Office and this review would undoubtedly point to serious flaws in the nation's military leadership, requiring the President to exercise even more control over what had been, to be candid, a recalcitrant senior leadership within the military services.

Weaver was good and felt he was convincing. He paused and raised a glass of water to his lips, confident that most of the questions would be the kind he could readily answer. He put down the water glass and pointed to the first questioner, *Wall Street Journal* reporter Rachel Pedrotty.

"Ray, there have been suggestions in the *Post* that the administration interfered with the military commanders in this operation, and that the President directed the on-scene commander to commence the operation without authority of his immediate chain of command."

"Well," began Weaver, a bit startled by the directness of the question, "I think you know of the President's extensive experience with military matters. I can assure you that he, probably above all others, knows the value of the military's chain of command and would be the last person to jeopardize that. I'm not sure where such an idea generated." He pointed again. "Yes, Fred."

"Mr. Weaver, following up on that just a little bit, if you don't mind." Fred Baxter reported for the *L.A. Times* and was one of the most gracious members of the press corps. "We have heard that the Pentagon insists that the President had constant, direct contact with Brigadier General Lovelace and that he overrode the orders of the SouthCom commander, who had hard intelligence that an ambush was waiting."

"Fred, now, just a minute. That's a little off base. Don't you think that it's a real stretch to think the President would give stick and rudder to a junior general, overriding the advice of one of the most senior generals in the military?" Weaver felt himself losing some of the veneer of charm that he was so well known for.

"It may be a stretch, but that's how it appears to us," responded Baxter, now shouting and ignoring the fact that Weaver was pointing and nodding to another raised hand. "What's more, the Pentagon says so. They seemed really miffed that they were cut out of the pattern on this one."

"Look," said Weaver, coming ever so close to losing his cool, "the chairman of the Joint Chiefs of Staff personally briefed the President on this operation and was the one who said it would be completely benign. As to presidential interference with the operation, hell, I couldn't even tell you right off hand that the President ever talked with Brigadier General Lovelace once he left Washington."

"The Pentagon says he did, and"—Baxter paused for a dramatic moment—"they have tapes of the radio transmissions between the President and General Lovelace."

"Tapes!" yelled Weaver, now coming close to a full rage. "The chairman of the Joint Chiefs, who serves at the *pleasure* of the President, is taping his conversations?"

"Says it's for national security purposes, Ray. Suppose he would know. Also says he has tapes of General Walters telling Lovelace not to begin the operation. Can't seem to figure why he ignored his direct orders. Thought that's something you might tell us." Baxter was outfolksying Weaver and it was having an impact on the rest of the assembled press.

"Another thing, Ray," shot ABC news anchor Alex Taylor, without waiting for Weaver to call on him. "We've also heard that there were some real irregularities in some foreign military sales—albeit with administration approval—and that these may have led to the cartel coming into possession of some of the high-tech weapons that they used. Any truth to that one?"

"No, of course not. Next question." Weaver was reeling now, like a punch-drunk fighter, trying to field questions he had not even vaguely anticipated. These were not leaks that they were peppering him with. The whole goddamned dam had burst and he was standing in front of a torrent of water. He had to make some sense of all this and recover gracefully the best he could. The usually amicable group of reporters and newscasters—hell, they were *supposed* to be his friends—were making him the whipping boy for something Taylor Calhoun *had* obviously gooned up. Finally, he could stand it no more.

"Okay, let's hold the damn questions for a minute. We had an operation go bad. The Pentagon let this one get away from them, pure and simple. The President is *not* meddling in military matters. If he did, maybe things would have turned out differently." He wished he had those words back, because even as he spoke them, a number of reporters were already rushing out of the room, and the President's chief of staff, Carter Thomas, turned and walked away, disgusted.

CHAPTER 65

"GODDAMNED PRESS! *GODDAMNED PRESS!*" PRESIDENT Taylor Calhoun stormed around the Oval Office like a caged tiger, looking as if he would grab the first loose object and hurl it through the television, which had just carried Ray Weaver's press conference into tens of millions of American living rooms. Just outside the door to the office, his secretary, Debbie Van Pelt, cringed with every expletive and waved off anyone who approached. The President rarely flew into rages like this, but when he did the entire White House staff knew it was prudent—no, essential—to keep their distance from the President.

These outbursts always died down quickly and afterward the President always returned to his amiable, folksy self.

This outburst was lasting longer than any that anyone could remember, but with good reason. Taylor Calhoun now knew that his entire presidency was in mortal danger.

The range of emotions he felt—grief for the Marines killed in Operation Roundup, anger at the intransigence of his top general, disappointment that the *Post* had run the story this way, resignation that Ray Weaver's press conference had run downhill so fast, bewilderment that all this was even happening—was so broad that they would have overwhelmed most any other man. However, there was one emotion that was stronger than all of the others, so strong that it became his single focus, an emotion that had been an integral part of his psyche since his first days in politics: survival. Taylor Calhoun was going to weather this attack on him and on his office. Damned if he'd let these bastards, these military marionettes that served at *his* pleasure, ruin him. It would not stand. It would not stand!

He began to think with blissful clarity. As the President leaned back in his chair and gazed out the window onto the White House lawn, he realized there was one consistent thread that tied the debacle together. It had all come together much too conveniently. The seemingly urgent need to do something about the drug problem. The way *he* had *convinced* the Pentagon to come up with a major drug interdiction. The way they had agreed to put his friend, General Ashley Lovelace, in charge of the operation as the on-scene commander. The appalling slaughter in the jungle. The totally erroneous information General Lovelace had initially provided him. The surprising way that the press had the details of the failed operation almost instantaneously. Then, most egregiously of all, the way that, in an almost perfectly choreographed motion, they had stepped away from him. No, this was no coincidence. They were after him, Taylor Calhoun—state representative, member of the House, senator, *President*— they were after him. Fucking ingrates. Didn't they know he wielded the power, he doled out favors, he decided who would continue to serve and who would go out to pasture? He wasn't going to be hung out for this one, not by some two-bit cabal of tinhorn generals. Shit, didn't they know who they were fucking with?

Despite this assessment, he was still baffled as to why they were after him. Unfortunately, a man with his considerable ego couldn't believe that he wasn't the most beloved and revered President to ever inhabit this office, what the polls said be damned. Fortunately, he recognized this blind spot and knew he needed help seeing through it. He leaned back over to his desk and pressed the intercom: "Debbie . . ."

They all rose as the President entered the West Wing Cabinet Room. This had, by now, become a familiar routine and his closest advisors knew that Taylor Calhoun felt most comfortable here, dealing with a crisis. Although many of his predecessors had used the Situation Room in the West Wing basement, this smallish room could not accommodate the numbers of his key advisors that Taylor Calhoun wanted to be surrounded by during times of crisis. In the wake of Ray Weaver's press conference earlier that day, some of the President's closest friends, those very few that the White House operators knew to put through to him, had called to express their concern with the gravity of the situation. Yes, they were behind him one hundred percent. Yes, they would do everything they could to influence everyone they could to stand behind the President. No, they couldn't be sure where this would all lead. Taylor Calhoun tried to put those calls behind him as he surveyed the sea of faces arrayed around him as he entered the Cabinet Room: Vice President Alex Paul, Secretary of Defense Elliott Higginson, Secretary of State Trevor Gaylord, National Security Advisor Brian Stavridis, Chief of Staff Carter Thomas, and, of course, Ray Weaver. The President began by trying to lift Ray's spirits.

"Ray, you acquitted yourself well in there with those jackals. Don't know if I could have showed the restraint you did. You made us all proud and I think you put the best spin on a bad situation. We'll sure as hell remember who our friends in the press are and who they aren't when it comes to priming the pump with this administration."

"I'm not sure we have any friends left, Mr. President," replied Weaver. "They sure as hell turned on us. It was a regular feeding frenzy in there."

"Why you reckon they're so hell bent for leather to run so hard with this one, Ray? I mean, yeah, it was a fuckup, a major fuckup, but why are they trying to pin this one on me? You'd think the military and the press had thought this one up together!"

"Perhaps they have, Mr. President," offered National Security Advisor Brian Stavridis. "I mean, the press has been getting details awfully quickly. They seemed to know things as soon as the military brass did—and maybe before you did."

"Are you suggesting that the military knew what was going to happen in advance and were all prepped to tell the press?" asked the Vice President.

Taylor Calhoun was actually enjoying the interchange. He had his own suspicions and his own theory of what had gone wrong and why, but he needed the validation of having his closest advisors hash it out among themselves, if only to clarify it in his own mind. He would play devil's advocate and let them run with it.

"I'm not sure I'm prepared to go quite that far," replied Stavridis. "I just think the chairman of the Joint Chiefs and General Walters were awfully quick to jump to the conclusion that the President was directing all aspects of this operation. It just seems fantastic to think they could assume the President would do that."

"Could be they didn't believe it themselves because only they knew it wasn't true, but they wanted everyone else to believe it," replied the Vice President.

"Hold on," said Secretary of Defense Elliott Higginson. "I don't like where this is going. You're making it sound like there's a conspiracy here."

"Well, isn't there, Elliott?" shot back the Vice President. Alex Paul was an average-sized man but had the build of an athlete—the yuppie look, Calhoun had been heard to say in private, one that appealed to younger voters and helped to round out his ticket—and as Paul tensed, he stared directly at Higginson as if measuring the man. He'd better not be defending the generals. "Seems like they have their stories lined up just a little too well and are much too quick to criticize the President—"

"Whoa, I'm telling you," said Higginson. "These men took an oath to support and defend the Constitution—"

"But not their President," answered Paul. "Maybe that's the problem. It's well known that both General Campbell and General Walters have not been fans of the changes the President is making and proposes to make to the military."

"Now, fellas, slow down," said Taylor Calhoun, wanting to probe a bit to see just how strong their feelings were, to see if they saw the same picture he did. It was critical that they all be on board, really on board, if and when this came to a full-blown fight. "I know the Pentagon isn't too happy with some of my programs, but they're all good soldiers. Soldiers follow orders, don't they?"

"That's just it, don't you see, Mr. President—they don't want to follow you. They want to do it their way. If they could do something to have you—well—out of office . . ." Alex Paul rose to his feet as he spoke, making his point with a passion he rarely showed.

"Are you talking about their having the President impeached?" Now even Secretary of State Trevor Gaylord, a thin, sallow man with an almost ghostly demeanor, was on his feet. "My God, this is an attack on the Republic. We've got to put a stop to it and now!"

"They're right, Mr. President," said Brian Stavridis. "The military leaders want to go back to doing things the way they have always done it. They don't really care how that is accomplished. I think they'd welcome it if you were impeached."

"Now, Brian, wait just a minute," said the President, now assuming his most fatherly and conciliatory tone. "I think it's a little far-fetched to think that some generals would try to—hell, even think that they could—affect the political process. Congress has the last word on that and we have too many friends there that wouldn't let that happen."

"But Mr. President . . ." protested the National Security Advisor.

And so the discussions continued, each of his key advisors painting a grave picture of the situation, but the President, playing the innocent, continuing to suggest that their fears were unjustified. Yes, they were worked up, and yes, he could count on them. Their discussions had clarified it all for him, though. He was convinced now that the military wanted him out and he was beginning to understand why. Wait until they tried anything with Congress, he thought. He had too many friends there, and had doled out too many favors to key Congressmen and senators. There was no problem there, that he was sure of, and he'd turn it right around and have them out on the street. He had been pushed too hard and now he was going to push back even harder.

CHAPTER 66

HOWARD CAMPBELL HAD ALWAYS BEEN AN AMBITIOUS man. That quality had propelled him to the pinnacle of his career. It also helped him to identify other ambitious men. Senator Jay Lindsey, junior Senator from the State of South Dakota, was one of those men. Just forty-two years old, he had crafted a meteoric rise in South Dakota politics and was just beginning his second term in the Senate. As the junior senator, his senior counterpart being a decades-long incumbent, and with the added handicap of being in the minority party, he saw his career plateauing and membership on key committees eluding him. The only committee of any note that he had managed to secure a seat on was the Senate Intelligence Oversight Committee, not the place for an up-and-comer.

General Campbell had met Senator Lindsey at a charity fund-raiser at the Kennedy Center. The two men had hit it off instantly, each admiring in the other the qualities he admired in himself. They had kept in touch periodically, the general inviting the senator for an occasional game of tennis at the Army-Navy Country Club, the senator reciprocating with a round of golf at his club. Neither had a specific agenda about how the other would be of use someday, but in the unspoken understanding of Washington politics, there was always value added in courting friends that were, or would be, at or near the seat of power. It was a scenario played out literally thousands of times a day in a city whose name had become synonymous with power. Campbell and Lindsey were among countless players in that city; they were just better at the game than most.

Senator Lindsey had just bade farewell to a large group of 4-H students and was about to get back to the mound of paper on his desk on the second floor of the Sam Rayburn Office Building when his executive assistant, Fred Robertson, told him that the chairman of the Joint Chiefs of Staff was trying to reach him. Lindsey's secretary was astute enough to put him on the line with General Campbell's executive assistant and, in that strange Washington ritual of always knowing what a phone conversation was about before it took place, Robertson had learned that the general wanted to speak with him about a matter for the Intelligence Oversight Committee. A quick flurry of activity throughout the staff determined that there were currently no military issues of any import before, or scheduled to be before, the Committee, so Lindsey and his key staffers surmised that the chairman would raise a new issue. Comfortable that he was up to speed on what to expect, he had the call returned to Campbell. Soon he was on the line with the chairman.

"Good afternoon, General. It's a pleasure to hear your voice again. I've been working hard renovating my backhand since our last encounter at Army-Navy," said Lindsey.

"Well, your strokes have always been A-okay, Senator. We just have to get you used to our slow Har-Tru courts, that's all. Need to have you come out more often."

"I'd like to do that, General. Let's make a day of it."

"You're on, Senator."

The pleasantries complete, Lindsey wanted to know

why the general had called him out of the blue. "Well, general, what can I—or should I say, what can the Intelligence Oversight Committee—do for you today?"

"Well, Senator, that's exactly why I called. I do think that a situation has arisen where you—that is, the committee—can get out in front of an issue."

"What would that be, General? Do we want to hold off another one of those moves to consolidate all of the military's intelligence agencies?" Lindsey was fencing, maybe even baiting Campbell a bit, wanting to get to the point quickly. Not knowing exactly where he stood did not sit well with him.

Campbell sensed his uneasiness. "No, Senator, this is a more important—and I think a much more pressing issue."

"Go ahead, General."

"You know about our horrible debacle in Costa Rica, Senator."

"Of course, General. The unfortunate loss of those men was a national tragedy."

"Yes, it was, Senator, indeed it was." Campbell was speaking in empty sentences now, clearly drawing the younger man out.

"Well, yes, General. I'm not sure I see yet what all this has to do with intelligence—with me and the committee, I mean."

"It has everything to do with intelligence, Senator. We knew at the highest levels that those men would be ambushed."

"We? Who knew, General?"

"At the highest levels, Senator. Now, I'm speaking off the record, of course. But I think that if your committee would investigate this tragedy, they would find out exactly who was to blame and where the order to begin the operation came from."

"Well, it came from the commander on the scene, didn't it?"

"Not entirely, Senator."

"Wait! I remember the press reports about direction from the White House. They were unsubstantiated, of course. I didn't put any stock in them."

"You should have, Senator."

"Are you telling me that the operation *was* directed from the White House?"

"I'm not asking you to jump to any conclusions, Senator. But if you investigate, you may find out that, yes, the White House was involved, and also that the intelligence apparatus was in place to let us know to call off the operation, but that the White House pressed on in spite of that."

"I think I'm following you, General, but of course that begs the question of why they would do that."

"You read the polls, don't you, Senator?"

"The polls."

"Yes, Senator, the polls and the press. The polls that show the President at a low ebb in approval rating and the press that shows young Christen Chamberlain of Langley High School dead of a crack-cocaine overdose."

"You're saying the President was pushing so hard on this anti-drug campaign that he went into this operation in spite of intelligence that it could fail?"

"I don't want to make anyone jump to any conclusions, Senator, but then, ah ... well ... your committee would be the correct one to investigate this, I would think, and then, well, a man of your stature, and especially future, would, of course, want to look into the President's fitness to continue to serve, and, well ..." Campbell was being elliptical, but Lindsey knew exactly where this was going.

"Fitness to serve, General. Are you talking about what I think you are—impeaching the President of the United States?"

"That's certainly not for me to say as a military man, Senator. Of course, if you feel uncomfortable with this, perhaps one of your colleagues in the Senate would be better suited to deal with—"

The younger man interrupted. "General, whatever needs to be done will be done. No one is going to shirk any duty here. It's just that, well, this all comes as a complete shock to me."

"I'm sure it does, Senator. But few men have the opportunity to make a difference. Men of destiny ..." The general paused, as if collecting his thoughts, purposely leaving an opening for the senator.

"Of course, General. We understand each other perfectly." Jay Lindsey was on his way. He needed no further urging, no further coaching. He knew what to do with this. Laboring in relative obscurity as the junior senator from South Dakota would not be his highest calling. It was not his destiny.

"Good day, General . . . and thank you."

"No need for thanks, Senator. Just a simple patriot doing his duty."

Believe that and you'll believe anything, thought Lindsey. He was sure he and General Howard Campbell would be talking again soon.

Howard Campbell leaned back in his chair in his Pentagon office, easily one of the most well-appointed offices in this building of well-appointed offices. He allowed himself a smile. The next calls he made he placed himself, without the help of the army of secretaries or assistants who usually performed such chores for him. After speaking briefly first with Charlie Walters and then with Liz Kennedy, he allowed himself an even broader smile. Yes, it was all falling into place, even better than expected.

CHAPTER 67

THE USS *CORONADO* CUT A WIDE SWATH THROUGH THE sea as her two 600-pound steam boilers pushed her toward Rodman, Panama, at her max speed of just over twenty knots. On her broad fo'c'sle and all around her weather decks, sailors worked furiously to try to recapture their ship from the recent ravages of the sea. They worked away with grinding tools, chipping hammers, primer, and steel gray paint, trying to put back some of her looks that the sea had taken away. She might not be beautiful when they reached Rodman, but at least she'd be presentable. Beautiful would have to wait for Norfolk.

Throughout the ship her crew was finally settling down after enduring the roller coaster of emotions over the past several weeks. The boredom of the endless, seemingly meaningless patrols. The tension as rumors of their impending mission began to circulate. The excitement of hearing that they were embarking on an important mission. The flurry of activity as they embarked their Recon Marines and supplies. The exhilaration as the Blackhawks arrived and pushed off for their mission with the Marines. The anxiety waiting for word of the mission's outcome. The shock of seeing wounded Marines return to their ship. The despair when no more came back after the first few score wounded arrived. Accustomed and proud to be part of the world's finest military, its only superpower, they were overwhelmed and incredulous that this could have happened.

Their incredulity was surpassed only by that of the JTF Eight staff. They had been in on all the planning, they had asked for and received the go order, they had followed the progress of the helos to and from the landing zones. They knew it couldn't have happened. They couldn't have sent men to their deaths like this. Their mood was more than somber. It was as if they all were ghosts, only going through the motions of their duties.

Among the staff, their leader, General Ashley Lovelace, was easily the most subdued of all. Lovelace would sit for hours in his bridge chair and say almost nothing. Taking a page from the most famous president of his alma mater, General Robert E. Lee, when the subject of Operation Roundup came up, he would say, again and again, "It was all my fault. It was all my fault." Nothing any of his staff members did or said seemed to be able to shake him out of his gloom.

But Lovelace's facile mind was racing, organizing, sorting, asking, answering. It had all been too perfect, then it had all gone to pieces with almost blinding speed. General Walters's changes in mood, up, down, uncommitted. The conference call with the President. He had nobly shouldered the blame. The chairman and General Walters had not only allowed him to do this, but had heaped it on. He knew he could not have misunderstood his instructions so badly. He knew there was more here than met the eye. How could a drug cartel, powerful as they were, acquire such weapons and, more importantly, the intelligence to ambush the Marines as they did? He had confided all of this to his chief of staff, Colonel Conrad Hicks, but the colonel had just been fatalistic, and while empathizing with General Lovelace, he seemed to be fully prepared to let their staff take all the blame, as the leader, General Lovelace, certainly had to shoulder it. Talking to his chief of staff was not a mollifying or a positive experience, it just plunged him deeper into the depths of depression.

While General Lovelace had trouble putting together all of the pieces of the puzzle, deep inside *Coronado,* Chief Rick Holden had figured out another piece. If a setup of this magnitude were to work logistically, then General Walters, the SouthCom commander who oversaw it all, had to be involved. The only piece that was still missing was why. But the why now became less important that the what—what to do. Everything had returned to normal too quickly. *Coronado* was returning to Rodman. She would soon transit the Panama Canal en route back to Norfolk. The newspapers would stop carrying reports of this disaster and everything would return to normal. But it would not be normal; it could not be normal. If this could happen, what did it say about the military, about the nation? And if something like this could happen once, it could happen again.

This was beyond the realm of understanding for a Navy chief petty officer, what Rick was ordered to be, but not what he was. Langley had given him strict orders to go underground and stay underground, not to surface, not even to check in unless he was contacted. However, these were extraordinary circumstances. Duty went beyond instructions, beyond orders. He needed to make a move, and he needed to contact the Agency. But first he had to get to the one person so clearly implicated in the disaster that, if this *was* the result of a conspiracy, he wouldn't be involved. And he could be trusted. He needed to talk to General Lovelace.

The general's orderly showed him into the commander's cabin. As Rick entered, the general and the chief of staff rose to greet him.

"Good evening, Chief Holden," said General Lovelace. "It's good to see you again. Your brave actions in the field will be remembered for a long time. You've met Colonel Hicks, I assume?"

"No, not officially, General," said Rick. Then, turning to Hicks, he said, "Good evening, Colonel, how do you do?"

"Evening, Chief," said Hicks. "I'm sure the general appreciates your coming by. We're scheduled to pull into Rodman early in the morning. I think the general might have only a minute or two for you."

"Yes sir, Colonel. Ah, General, what I really asked to see you about . . . well, sir, it's really a very private matter."

"Surely not something you can't also share with the chief of staff, is it? We don't really have any secrets on the staff, you know."

"Well, General, you see, it really would be . . ." Rick was wobbly now. He hadn't really counted on Colonel Hicks being there. He could be part of the plot. Rick couldn't reveal anything in front of him. He was about to beat a hasty retreat, but unexpectedly, Hicks spoke.

"Well, General, I'm sure the chief would be more comfortable just talking to you alone. I've got to see the captain about preps for entering port tomorrow anyway. Good night, General. *Good night, Chief.*"

As the chief of staff left and the door closed behind him, the general turned to Rick. "Well, Chief Holden, what's on your mind?" The General was clearly a little impatient.

Rick began talking and General Ashley Lovelace never stopped listening.

CHAPTER 68

GENERAL CHARLES BIGELOW WALTERS SAT AT HIS large desk at Quarry Heights, looking out at the lush Panama landscape and the Pacific Ocean beyond. He allowed himself a small smile. It had all gone so perfectly. He had done his part and he knew the chairman had already set the wheels in motion to do the rest. Charlie Walters had his network, and it never let him drop out of the loop.

There would likely be the small matter of Mrs. Wilson, Andy Wilson's soon-to-be grieving wife back in Virginia Beach, Virginia. Once they found Andy's body—they would find it soon, he was confident of that—he would use the man's death to his great advantage. He had a plan for dealing with Wilson's death. But first he needed to clear his head. He pushed the intercom: "Sergeant Brooke, bring the sedan around."

Far from General Walters's imposing office, in another wing of the sprawling SouthCom compound, Lieutenant Laura Peters was going through her daily routine of reading messages, reviewing publications, attending to her division officer duties, and taking care of the seemingly endless chores that Navy junior officers were responsible for. Operation Roundup still bothered her deeply, but she didn't know where to go or what to do. She had run into a dead end here at SouthCom and her boss, Captain Fran Dawson, whom she trusted, had insisted that this disaster had just been the result of a number of errors, none in and of themselves a critical path, but collectively enough to derail the operation. And then there was Rick Holden. He really seemed hell-bent-for-leather to do something, but she didn't know what. She was in over her head and really didn't know how to handle all of this. She consoled herself with the fact that perhaps this trip to Colorado, and maybe some extracurricular time on the ski slopes, would be just the tonic she needed and she would forget all about Operation Roundup, about SouthCom, and about Panama.

Laura was about halfway through her burgeoning in-basket when she found the temporary additional duty—TAD—package for her trip to the Joint Intelligence Officers' Conference at Colorado Springs. Laura had been looking forward to this conference for the past several months. She had not been to a professional conference of this magnitude before, nor had she ever been to Colorado Springs. As she pulled out the folder that had contained her original request to attend the course, she expected to find a set of orders, an itinerary, airplane tickets, all of the usual items. Instead, she found her original request sheet returned to her. Her immediate superiors had all checked the "approved" block in the "approved/disapproved" column, but when she got to Captain Fran Dawson's name, "approved" had been crossed out and a large X was placed in the "disapproved" block, which didn't make sense. Captain Dawson was the one who wanted her to go to this conference.

Laura sat in her worn chair in her cramped office, and for the first time she could remember, she let her emotions overrun her professionalism. She leaped up and stormed purposely out of her office and down the bright corridor, right past the staff sergeant in the captain's office, and directly into Fran Dawson's inner office.

Dawson looked up in complete surprise. "Lieutenant Peters, I'm in the middle of reading some reports. What is it that can't wait?"

"I need to talk with you, Captain," replied Laura, trying to remain as calm as possible but hearing the edge in her own voice.

"Well, that's all well and good, Lieutenant, but we have procedures in the Intelligence Directorate and those procedures don't usually include lieutenants storming into captains' offices," replied Dawson, now raising her voice and sounding genuinely annoyed.

"No ma'am—I mean, I know that we have procedures, but . . . I . . ." Laura felt herself wavering. She knew she had come on too strong, but there was no way of backing down gracefully now. "I just was, well, surprised, that's all, by my TAD request that was turned down. I was looking forward to that conference." She was trying a more conciliatory tone and she hoped it was working.

It wasn't. Captain Dawson shot back, "Well, Lieutenant, yes, I know you wanted that conference, but I'm afraid we have had a change in priorities and, well . . . I mean, it's not possible to send you there anymore."

Laura now detected that the captain wasn't on really firm footing herself and pressed her argument. "Captain, you had recommended to me that I put in for that conference some time ago. I would have thought that you wanted me to go."

Dawson tried to collect her thoughts and maintain her composure and command presence while fending off this clearly angered young officer whom she truly liked. "Lieutenant, there are a lot of factors that go into the planning for who makes what trips. You have to understand that I don't have the final say on all decisions. We'll try to send you another time."

"Captain, are you sure you won't reconsider?"

"Lieutenant, I told you, I don't have the final decision in these matters."

"Who does, then?" Laura was surprised by her own boldness.

"The commander always has the final say on such decisions."

"General Walters?"

"Look, Lieutenant, you don't really get a vote in this. Why don't you just go back to work? I'm sure it will all work out in the long run."

Laura could sense Dawson's mounting discomfiture. She believed her. But the commander? "Captain, I don't know why General Walters would cancel my trip," she said. "Did you recommend that I go?"

Captain Fran Dawson was too good an officer and too honest a person to outright lie to Laura. "Lieutenant, I had planned to let you go. Now, I am telling you this in confidence. General Walters directed me to take you off this trip."

"But why?"

"You see, the general called me in to inquire about your performance lately. I just told him that you seemed upset about Operation Roundup and he just spontaneously said to take you off this trip, that's all. You know, Lieutenant, maybe he's just concerned about you. You know, seeing that you're his regular squash partner and all." Dawson was sounding less and less professional and authoritative, as if she too were searching for the answer to the same question.

"Captain, I beg your pardon," protested Laura. She did not like where this was going. "Are you suggesting that General Walters has more than just a professional relationship with me?" She was raising her voice now and she knew it.

"Well, of course not, Lieutenant," replied Dawson, now clearly put off balance by the tenor of Laura's outburst. "Only that, well, the talk around the office—of course, I'm not a party to any of those discussions—is that you and the general are quite regular partners, and that, well, one thing can lead to another."

"*Captain!*"

"Now calm down, Lieutenant!" This was getting bad very quickly, thought Dawson. She wished she hadn't said anything now. "I'm only telling you this for your own good. I'm not suggesting anything."

Laura was dazed. She'd always been professional, but now she was being toyed with and her boss—another woman, no less—was all but accusing her of the worst. She couldn't control herself anymore.

"I've had it, Captain. I want to see General Walters and I want to see him now." Laura was screaming loud enough to turn heads outside of Fran Dawson's office.

"Just a minute, Lieutenant—"

But Laura wheeled and stormed out of Fran Dawson's office and headed back down the corridor, through several wings of the compound, and directly toward General Walters's suite of offices.

"Lieutenant Peters, hold on," shouted Captain Fran Dawson, now outside her office and looking dazed herself. But Fran Dawson's words were lost on Laura as she almost ran toward her destination.

As Laura approached the general's outer office, she slowed down long enough to collect herself and smooth down her hair and her uniform. She brushed right past the petty officer in the outer office and right up to the general's civilian secretary. "Lieutenant Peters here to see General Walters."

"Lieutenant, do you have an appointment?"

Gathering all of her courage, Laura responded, "No, I don't. But it's very important that I see him right away."

"Well, unfortunately, Lieutenant, the general left just a bit ago. I expect him back within the hour. Perhaps I can call your office when he gets back and set up an appointment for you via your division head?"

"No, no, forget it. . . ."

Laura ran from the compound and then the short distance to her BOQ room, slamming the door behind her. She paced the small room for a moment. She felt trapped. She couldn't just sit here. She all but ripped off her uniform, put on her jogging clothes, and went out for one of the longest runs of her life.

CHAPTER 69

ASHLEY LOVELACE SAT IN HIS BRIDGE CHAIR ON THE flag bridge as *Coronado* wove its way carefully through the crowded roads just west of Rodman, Panama. The flag bridge was a curious place. Set one deck below the ship's bridge, it had no helm, no engine order telegraph, no radar repeaters, no chart table, no GPS receivers, and only a few radios. It was merely a place for the embarked flag or general officer to sit, designed, no doubt, by former ship's captains who recognized full well that if a place were not provided for the senior officer to sit with a commanding view, then he would be on the "real bridge" bothering the ship's captain. Thus, this virtually useless place directly below the ship's bridge—but with a commanding view—served its primary purpose of containing the embarked commander. As he scanned the horizon, Ashley Lovelace saw the lights of scores of other ships, large oil tankers, smaller coastal freighters, huge container ships, sleek cruise liners and the others, most of which were at anchor, all awaiting their turn to pass through the Panama Canal early the next morning.

He had been in the bridge chair for hours, going there to seek solace and solitude after spending almost an hour listening to Chief Rick Holden. He had waved away staff members and even his orderly, making it abundantly clear that he needed to be alone with his thoughts. Throughout his long career he had usually found that the more information he had, the better equipped he was to make a decision and the clearer the picture became for him. After listening to Chief Holden's story, though, the additional information left him staggered.

It all made sense, but it made no sense. What the chief had presented to him was nothing less than well-founded speculation that a conspiracy was in action to completely discredit the President of the United States. Although Holden had phrased it with the most temperate terminology, the bottom line was that he, General Ashley Lovelace, had been the fall guy. Lovelace was wrestling with his emotions and it was interfering with his ability to think rationally. He didn't want to believe he was a pawn in their hands. Even less did he want to believe that his fellow Army officers could be behind this betrayal of him, of their President, and of their nation. It was just too overwhelming to consider, and he found himself playing devil's advocate, questioning his own assumptions, trying to prove, at least in his own mind, that this couldn't be true.

The chief had emphasized continuously that he was baffled as to why such a thing would happen. The general had said that he shared his bewilderment, but it didn't take long for his agile mind to work up a plausible motive. He knew what the President's policies were and knew that some of the highest-ranking officers in the military—including, in particular, the chairman—held the President in disdain and had groused, sometimes too openly, that they thought his presidency would mortally wound the military. He knew of the chairman's service reputation of being an outspoken maverick at times and had heard stories of his not being a team player if the team was going off in a direction he didn't like. It *could* happen, but such a bold move, such a strong stroke? Why would he dare, how could he dare?

However, the more he thought about it, the more Ashley Lovelace realized how well the chairman of the Joint Chiefs of Staff—the most powerful military man in the nation, the man who had the most to lose from the radical changes the President was making to the military—had both put this plan in motion and covered his tracks. Campbell hadn't done anything. Insulated in the Pentagon, the only part Campbell had played in the operation was to relay the President's execute order to the SouthCom commander. He, in turn, had everyone believing that Lovelace executed the final phase of the mission without permission—ostensibly with some strong coaching by the President. He, Ashley Lovelace, had let it fail, had disobeyed orders, had done in the President. Oh, and how quickly his seniors had left him to twist in the wind, virtually forced him to admit his incompetence to the President.

A man of less intestinal fortitude might have come completely unglued under this kind of strain. In fact, that may have been part of the traitors' plans. But they had misjudged him. Somewhere deep inside Lovelace roiled a depth of fortitude and courage that surprised even him. He would overcome this obstacle. He would save his President. He had to talk to his friend and he had to talk to him now.

Debbie Van Pelt took the call from the White House switchboard. It was only seven A.M. and the President was not yet awake. Staffers had told her he had been up late and was exhausted. She did not want to disturb him in quarters, but the general was insistent, almost frantic. Even years of dealing with—and disposing of—"very important callers" had not prepared her for this eventuality, and at the general's persistence and insistence, she put him through to the President in his personal quarters.

"Ashley, good morning. It's awfully early here. What

time is it there aboard *Coronado*?" The President was barely able to hide the annoyance in his voice for having been awakened earlier than he had planned.

"It's the same time here, Mr. President," said Ashley Lovelace, realizing that the President did not yet share the same sense of urgency he did and now wishing he had waited until just a bit later to call.

"Well, of course it's good to hear from you. Things have taken a pretty bad turn, haven't they?"

"They have, Mr. President, and I know I have let you down terribly, but Mr. President, I initially found this hard to believe myself, but now I'm sure."

"Sure of what, Ashley?"

"That it's a conspiracy, Mr. President, a conspiracy to discredit you, to see you taken out of office."

"Ashley, are you sure?" But now it was Ashley Lovelace's turn to talk and Taylor Calhoun's turn to listen.

CHAPTER 70

DEBBIE VAN PELT HAD NEVER BARGAINED FOR THIS, but her loyalty to her President was absolute. She had to help the President somehow, but she was not sure how. As the crisis deepened, she knew he depended on her more and more. She was becoming, for all intents and purposes, his conduit with the outside world, deciding on her own which calls to put through to the President and which ones to put off, which calls to immediately place for him and which ones to slow down just a bit, perhaps not being as insistent with the secretary, aide, or executive assistant of the principal that the President wanted to reach if she did not think it would be good to reach him right away.

It was an extraordinary amount of power for someone with the title of secretary to have, but if the truth be known, Debbie's power exceeded that of many heads of state and many captains of industry. She knew the President's likes and dislikes, the people he trusted and the people he loathed, his hopes, his fears, his foibles, and his strengths. In some ways she felt she knew the President better than he knew himself. Surely she knew him better than the First Lady, Beverly Calhoun, knew him. Maybe if she'd spend less of her life at charity fund-raisers and more with the President . . .

Before the buzz on the intercom had stopped, Debbie knew what the President was going to say.

"Debbie, you got General Campbell on the line yet?" said the President, trying not to raise his voice or sound anxious, but not doing a very good job of either.

"No sir, not yet. He's in transit at the moment," replied Debbie, stretching the truth just a bit.

"Dammit, with what I've fed into the Pentagon budget, you'd think they'd have goddamn car phones."

"We're trying just about everything. They tell me he'll be in his office in less than ten minutes. I know we'll get a call back immediately," offered Debbie in her most soothing voice.

The President didn't bother to reply, as the intercom just went dead. Debbie had been holding off the call to General Campbell, hoping Taylor Calhoun would calm down. She wanted him to be composed when he talked with the general, who was always the picture of composure himself. She had overheard the entire exchange the last time the general talked to the President and she fully recognized the disadvantage of Taylor Calhoun losing it. When she finally felt she could delay no longer, she placed the call.

An hour later, General Howard Campbell was ushered into the Oval Office. The President received him alone, without any of the advisors who might normally have been there. That was not a good sign. Some time had passed since his last heated exchange with the President, and the chairman assumed that he had this figured out well enough. The President was going to enlist his help to "put the best spin on things" and present a united front. "Stop the bleeding," as they were fond of saying. He'd feign concern, then indicate that of course he would do everything he could—after all, he was on the team. But then he would let things continue to go downhill for the President.

"Well, General," began the President, "I'm glad you could carve out some time in your busy schedule to come see your Commander in Chief."

Campbell instantly knew this wasn't going to be the collegial conversation he had anticipated. *Commander in Chief*—oh, this was going to be a show. "Why, I'm sorry I was so hard to reach, Mr. President. How may I help you?"

Taylor Calhoun let loose. "You can help me, *General Campbell,* by telling me just what went on with Operation Roundup. How did it fail so miserably?"

Howard Campbell wanted to proceed cautiously. He had had one confrontation with the President the last time this came up—he had played the "blame game" that time—but his instincts told him that this time a more conciliatory approach might work better. "Mr. President, I know we exchanged some rather harsh words last time we talked. I think all of us were just so upset with the loss of all of those brave men that we didn't keep a cool head. It was a tragedy, to be sure, but we must incur risks in military operations. I just wish we had all been on the same page on this one."

"I'm not sure I follow you, General."

"Well, Mr. President," continued Howard Campbell, his mind racing to try to react to the President's confrontation, "we—that is, General Walters and I—thought we had a good plan worked out. We didn't know that you and General Lovelace would move out the way you did. Now, I know we disagree on this, Mr. President, and I think you acted on your—and General Lovelace's—best instincts and intentions based on the knowledge you had, but the plan had no chance of success. We just shouldn't have moved forward." The chairman was actually quite pleased with himself and thought he was turning this his way.

Taylor Calhoun pressed. "So, General, what you're saying is that this operation didn't have a chance to succeed."

They were fencing now. Two quick and agile minds,

probing, trying to get to the heart of the matter, trying to read not just the other man's thoughts but his intentions, his feelings, his very soul. It had gone beyond their positions as President and as chairman of the Joint Chiefs. It was now a battle of wills.

"Why, looking at it in hindsight, yes, Mr. President, I think what you are saying is accurate."

"That it didn't have a chance to succeed?"

"Yes, I think you could say that." Campbell wasn't sure where this was going now.

"And why would that be so, General?" Calhoun was probing now and Campbell could sense it.

"Why, the correlation of forces just wasn't there, Mr. President. As I was—"

Calhoun cut him off. "They weren't there because you saw to it that they weren't there. Isn't that more like it, General?"

"I don't know what you mean, Mr. President."

"I think you do, *General.*" Calhoun had a way of almost snarling out the word that made his feelings most clear. "You and your cronies didn't want this operation to succeed in the first place. You let this fail disastrously and let those poor boys die. For what? So you could prove your superiority? So you could prove that you knew more about how to run the military than anyone else? So you could make fools of us? Well, I'll tell you what, *mister.* It won't stand here. You got that? It won't stand *here.*" Calhoun pounded on his desk with each word. For a politician of his demonstrated finesse to be slapping down all his cards on the table was, well, extraordinary. But this was an extraordinary juncture in his presidency and he needed the release of confronting the man he thought was responsible for this debacle, this mortal wounding of his presidency.

Howard Campbell was surprised and shocked by the tactic. Had he thrown the President that much off balance with his actions? Had he made a tactical error with his outburst? "Mr. President, surely you can't think that we in any way let this go on because of some . . . some . . . grudge! Mr. President, the American people would be shocked that their leader, their Commander in Chief, would even think of something like this. How, sir, if I may ask, could you come to such a conclusion?" Campbell was doing all he could to sound indignant now, for he now began to fear that the President really did know what was going on.

"I've got my connection to people on the scene, if you'll recall, General. They've told me some very interesting things about this operation, about what has happened, and about what they've found. Seems that the druggies knew an awful lot and *had* an awful lot in the way of U.S. weapons. You wouldn't know anything about that, would you, General?"

"Of course not, Mr. President. Do you mean some notion about U.S. moves? Access to weapons like ours?"

"I mean precise knowledge of our forces' intentions and movements, and possession of the most advanced American weapons. Stinger missiles, to be exact."

"Well, Mr. President, of course I find this shocking. I'll certainly look into it. I'll have General Walters look into it. Obviously we need to get to the bottom of it." Campbell sounded almost relieved now. The accusations had been more general in nature than he had expected from the early tenor of their conversation. He was almost home free.

"Seems my highest-ranking military man would have known of such activities. The American people would seem to deserve more from the chairman of the Joint Chiefs of Staff!" shouted the President, now going for the jugular.

Campbell was wounded by the blow. "Perhaps those same American people deserve not to have their civilian leaders meddle in military business," he shot back, but then wished he hadn't.

"Meddling? Is that it, General, *meddling*? I won't stand this outrage another minute. Get out of my office, *get out, get out*!"

"As you say, Mr. President." Howard Campbell left quickly, for he knew he had much to do.

CHAPTER 71

HOWARD CAMPBELL CONSIDERED THIS EVENTUALITY, but had always dismissed it as unlikely. The President might suspect something—hell, he might even know something, though Campbell didn't see how—but he sure as hell wouldn't be able to prove anything and trace it back to Campbell. No, Campbell was not worried about being caught holding a smoking gun. That was for cowards, not for men of destiny.

What he did fear was failure: failure of a plan *he* had given birth to, *he* had developed to the *n*th detail, *he* had put into motion, and he would be damned if he'd see it collapse just because the President had gotten a notion that he thought he could derail it. He needed to move and he needed to move quickly.

If Howard Campbell had a blind spot, this was it. His plan *was* going the way he wanted it to. Yes, Calhoun would protest and say that there was this plot or that, but there would be too many questions, and the country would have had enough of him. He would be gone, and with him the devastating changes that he was making. Campbell already knew how he would work the succession. He had it planned to that level of detail. But the presence of a loose end, any loose end, drove him to distraction. He would close this loose end with great finality. There would be nothing left to chance. He would definitely see to that.

The staff sergeant buzzed the intercom on General Charles Walters's desk and announced that he had General Campbell's office on the line. General Walters grinned as he waited to be connected. He and General Campbell had pulled this off perfectly, and for a man of his considerable ego, a little Monday morning self-congratulation never hurt anyone. His smile disappeared quickly, though, as he was forced to hold the phone away from his ear to keep from being deafened by an irate Howard Campbell.

"Charlie, I'll skip the pleasantries and come right to the point. Can't you keep a lid on things down there? I thought Lovelace was taking this on as his bust. Now he's feeding the President this crap about a goddamned conspiracy."

General Walters spoke in his most conciliatory voice. "Mr. Chairman, I'm not sure precisely what you're talking about, but we never figured them for complete dupes. The possibility always existed that they might begin to suspect that all of this didn't just happen. But they'd never have proof."

"Well, they think they do now," shot back Campbell. Clearly, Walters's words did not have the desired calming effect.

"But Mr. Chairman, if we've got some kind of speed bump in our plan, some sort of leak, I'm sure we can plug it."

"You're damn right, and you're the one who's going to do it." Campbell was starting to calm down a bit—Walters could tell, he'd known him that long—and that was good because the SouthCom commander didn't know how long he would have been willing to endure this ranting.

"Of course, Mr. Chairman, of course."

"Look, Charlie, Lovelace has talked to the President and gotten him all stirred up. Told him that the druggies had intelligence on the movement of our forces and had modern American weapons. He mentioned Stinger missiles specifically."

"Sounds like Lovelace got wind of some pretty good specifics."

"I *know that*," hissed Campbell. "The question is what are we going to do about it?" There was an unmistakable cautionary tone in his voice, and had both men not been certain that their phone line was absolutely secure, they would not have dared to discuss these matters.

"Did you say he focused on the druggies having good intelligence of the operation?"

"That's exactly what I said." Campbell was getting agitated again. It was fine for Walters to be so calm and so smug down there in Panama he thought. He wasn't the one being summoned to the White House and accused. He wasn't the one with it all hanging out.

"That's interesting," replied Charlie Walters. "I've had some unusual developments in my Intelligence Directorate. I may be able to come up with something down here that will deflect some of the heat."

"Okay, Charlie, that's more like it. What about the weapons? They can't be traced, can they?"

"That's your end of the bargain. Let me work this intelligence angle and I'll get back to you."

"Good-bye Charlie. You keep me in the loop, you hear?"

Howard Campbell put down the phone, somewhat relieved that Charlie Walters shared at least some of his concerns regarding the seriousness of the situation confronting them. He wasn't out of the woods yet, though.

"Kennedy." Liz always answered her phone at the *Post* with the same short, jablike response. She wasn't sure why, it just made her feel like a more efficient reporter.

"Liz, Howard Campbell here. How are you?" He spoke in his smoothest and most accommodating voice.

Actually Liz wasn't doing too well. The story Howard Campbell had started her on had dried up. After the first burst of information, and especially that package he had given her, nothing else had really come her way. She had done the usual digging, but none of her sources had panned out and Howard had been, well, a bit aloof.

That wasn't the worst of it. What had once been an exclusive scoop for her was now being picked up by other media and was getting wide play across the board. Television had reached the saturation point. Several former chairmen of the Joint Chiefs of Staff had discussed the situation on *Face the Nation*. The issue of civilian control of the military was the topic for discussion for *The McLaughlin Group*. That senator from South Dakota, what was his name—Lindsey—had gotten major visibility with David Brinkley on *This Week*. Ted Koppel had done his usual routine on *Nightline*. Bill Safire, George Will, David

Broder, and the rest had moved the issue into their syndicated columns. Others were developing their own spins on the story. The general consensus seemed to be that the President had interfered with the military for all the wrong reasons and that he had gone too far this time—far exceeding the prerogatives of his office. Liz would have to find a novel approach once she turned up some new information—assuming that she ever did. Howard certainly hadn't been much help lately. She really *was* pissed off at him.

"I'm fine Howard. Just a bit busy, that's all. Actually, I'm on deadline now." Liz was not doing a very good job of hiding her annoyance.

"An important story, no doubt?" responded Howard Campbell, sensing instantly that he was not on the best ground.

"No, nothing that you'd be interested in. Just the usual stuff I write about."

Yes, he could tell, he'd have to go a ways to mollify her. "I've called to try to help fix that. I know I haven't been much help on your big story lately, but I've had to wait for some details to get worked out. I just spent almost an hour with the President, and—"

Liz cut him off. "Listen, Howard, I want to follow along on this, but *I am* on deadline."

"Fine. Just call me, okay? I have some very interesting information that I know you'll want to hear."

"I will, Howard. I will."

The chairman wasn't accustomed to getting this kind of brush-off. She'd want to talk to him soon, he was sure. He had to be.

CHAPTER 72

GENERAL WALTERS HAD PREPARED FOR THIS EVENTUALITY, although he hadn't thought that it would present itself in quite this fashion. His mind had been racing after his conversation with Howard Campbell and now he needed to throw his backup plan into motion. But first he needed some more facts.

Captain Fran Dawson knocked firmly but politely and entered his office. "You wanted to see me, General?" She was never really comfortable in his presence. His reputation with women was well established and Dawson wanted no part of it. She was one hundred percent professional and angling for her own star. The last thing she needed was some horny general after her. Even the hint of any of that would drop her name from any promotion list.

"Yes, Captain, come in, come in." Walters was being overly solicitous. She knew that she didn't like this already. "I suppose you'd like to know why I called you in."

"Well, yes, General. I assume it's got something to do with the Intelligence Directorate. Has everything been functioning to your satisfaction?"

"Why, yes, of course, of course. Actually, it involves your Lieutenant Peters."

Dawson had suspected this and was ready. She really felt she needed to go to bat for her officer. "Well, General, I assume you are referring to the incident yesterday. I'm sure Lieutenant Peters was just reacting to the stress of the last week or so. There's really no problem."

"A junior officer comes *running* into my office unannounced, *demanding* to see me, and you tell me it's no problem. I'm not sure what your expectations for *your* junior officers are, but *mine* are obviously a bit higher."

Fran Dawson felt herself stiffen a bit with the criticism, but she held her ground and continued. "General, Lieutenant Peters was genuinely disappointed that she was scrubbed from the trip to Colorado. For professional reasons, of course," she was quick to add. "I wasn't able to really give her a completely satisfactory answer as to why she was dropped out."

"So you told her, of course, that I had made the decision."

"Not explicitly, General. Just that it was made above my level."

"Quit fencing, Captain. Would you be interested in knowing just why *your* lieutenant was taken off this trip?"

"Yes, I would, General."

"You're sure you're not emotionally caught up in this? You *can* look at this dispassionately, can't you?"

Dawson was stung by the intimation that she wasn't totally professional. "General, *of course* I can look at it that way. Lieutenant Peters has just been a good officer and I was just trying to give her the benefit of the doubt—"

Walters did not let her finish. "Well, Captain, it seems that your good officer has had some very interesting activities of late. Do you know anything about her numerous calls to USS *Coronado*?"

"No sir."

"Or perhaps she told you about her calls from the newsroom at the *Washington Post*?"

"The *Washington Post*? No, of course not, General!"

"I see. You're sure, now?"

"Yes, General, absolutely!" Dawson was off balance now. First Walters had questioned her professionalism. Now he was hinting that she might be hiding something.

Walters was allowing her to twist in the wind, pausing for what seemed to Dawson like an eternity between sentences.

"And you wouldn't know anything about this torrid little affair with Lieutenant Commander Wilson, either, would you?"

"Andy—I mean, Lieutenant Commander Wilson—and Lieutenant Peters? But he's married. I mean, I would never think that Lieutenant Peters would . . . Well, I'm shocked, General."

"I'm afraid you might not know Lieutenant Peters very well at all, Captain. Did she have any financial difficulties that you knew about?"

"No, General, not that I knew about."

"But clearly you didn't know her all that well if what I'm telling you is such a big surprise to you."

"Well, no General, I suppose that there's a lot that I didn't know."

This is where Walters wanted her: surprised and

shocked and now part of the plan that would make Laura Peters the foil for the failure of Operation Roundup.

On the one hand, he didn't want to do it. Their squash games were regular and for a while he was certain he could bed her. They were his favorite conquests, the young ambitious ones who slept with him at least partly because of the power he held over their careers. It was one of the best rewards for the sacrifices he'd made during his career. On the other hand, this one was fending him off too vigorously. Much as he hated to admit it, it didn't look like she was going to give in. He had too much power to waste any more time on her. There were others. Plenty of others.

"I see, Captain. Well, I suspect that we'll need to work together closely in the next several days. I assume I have your full cooperation and your full confidentiality."

"Of course, General, of course."

"By the way, Captain, where is Lieutenant Peters now?"

"She's in her quarters, General?"

"Odd place to be at this time of day. Perhaps you should bring her in here and have her do the work we pay her to do."

"Yes, General, right away."

As Captain Fran Dawson left, her head was spinning. She didn't want to believe all the things General Walters was telling her about Lieutenant Peters, but the general obviously had his sources and now it was her job to help him get to the bottom of this. As she strode back into her large office, she almost barked at the yeoman, "Petty Officer Sanders, call Lieutenant Peters in her quarters immediately and have her report here."

CHAPTER 73

OUTSIDE THE OVAL OFFICE, DEBBIE VAN PELT WAS DO-
ing a masterful job of obeying the President's orders to
the letter and holding off all visitors. He had told her in
no uncertain terms that he did not want to be disturbed—
by anyone. So there he stayed, pacing his office like a
caged tiger. Beyond anyone else's help. His key advisors
had set up their own crisis action center in the Executive
Office Building, sorting through the possibilities, working
with what they knew, but recognizing that events were
moving so fast that the President had not yet shared
everything he knew with them. They longed for a meeting
with him, to compare notes, to bring their collective
thoughts and energy to bear to get through this crisis, but
they knew that when the President said he wanted to be
alone, he meant it. Debbie Van Pelt was sure they received that message loud and clear.

The President's confrontation with General Howard
Campbell had had a clarifying effect on him. Every instinct he had, told him that he had at best been allowed
to fail, and at worst been set up for failure by the chairman, and perhaps by other unknown conspirators. How
had he let it all come to this? Was he that much of a threat
to the military and to their way of doing business? Wasn't
he really the most beloved President who had ever served
the nation?

Debbie Van Pelt finally ushered the President's key advisors into the Oval Office. They were a haggard-looking
lot, all of them having spent most of the last several days
together. Bathing, sleep, exercise, anything in the way of
normal human functioning had been seen as an obstacle

to their strategizing. That none of them had yet come to blows had been a miracle.

They were still settling into their chairs when the President began. "Gentlemen, I am now more convinced than ever that our *uniformed* leaders in the Pentagon are not part of the solution to our present crisis but are part of the problem." Looking directly at the Secretary of Defense, he continued, "Elliott, do you think you can rein in these generals and admirals and get them to stand behind their President, or do I have to fire the lot of them?"

Elliott Higginson was a careful man and he paused before answering. The President's remark had confused him. On the one hand, the President was suggesting that the chairman of the Joint Chiefs of Staff, and perhaps other senior officers, had let Operation Roundup fail and were out to wound his administration, perhaps mortally. On the other hand, the President seemed to be saying that the chairman and the others had only misbehaved slightly and that they should now be brought back into the fold and become full members of the team again. Was the President asking him to decide which route they should take? It was a position that made him extremely uncomfortable and he shifted in his chair as he groped for an answer.

"Mr. President," he began, "clearly I am disappointed with the behavior of our senior military officers. The entire premise of military service is to be accountable for one's actions and I haven't seen much of that from the chairman or from any of his subordinate officers—with the possible exception of General Lovelace. I'm really not prepared to jump to the conclusion that there is a plot or anything untoward actually going on. We simply don't know at this point."

The President liked Elliott—hell, he had to do some pretty good arm-twisting to get him to give up his $750,000-plus-a-year job as Bechtel's CEO and join his administration—but decisiveness was not one of his strong suits and the President felt he needed decisiveness now.

"Okay, Elliott, fine, but are they with us or are they agin' us?" Maybe the folksy approach would break through.

"Mr. President, on the one hand we can conjure up all sorts of conspiracy theories if we let ourselves, and I know that the chairman and General Walters in particular have said some pretty strong things. On the other hand, in my association with them over the past several years I have found both of them to be exceptionally professional. I know that the Pentagon and SouthCom took extraordinary efforts to develop plans for this operation and that they thought it would help to boost their image with the American public. Perhaps they just overreacted when it failed. We really have to look at both sides of this, sir."

Well, thought Taylor Calhoun, that was about as decisive as oatmeal. This wasn't getting anywhere. He would have to drive it himself. "Okay, Elliott. Here's the deal. They stand up and stand behind me or they're gone. Now, you talk to 'em and get 'em on board and do it quickly."

"Yes sir, Mr. President."

"Good."

The President's pause gave Secretary of State Trevor Gaylord a chance to chime in. Gaylord had served in the House for two terms and the Senate for one term, and he still had a reliable network on the Hill. "Mr. President, we may have a problem with Congress that could require your intervention."

"What problem, Trevor?"

"The Senate Intelligence Oversight Committee has announced that it intends to hold hearings on Operation Roundup. Senator Lindsey has already held one press conference to talk about why he is calling for hearings."

"And why is he?" said the President.

"The word our sources have is that he supposedly has come into some information that there was an intelligence leak within the Department of Defense that may have tipped the Maradona cartel to the fact that Operation Roundup was about to begin. I've already talked to Elliott about it and we're following one or two leads."

"That's why we think the cartel had such an accurate picture about when and where the operation was about to commence, Mr. President," added Brian Stavridis.

"And just where do we think that this leak is?" asked the President.

"We're working twenty-four hours a day to try to determine that," added Elliott Higginson. The Pentagon is cooperating fully and has one particularly promising lead—actually, an officer at SouthCom headquarters."

"One of our officers? That's unbelievable," said Ray Weaver. "Oh, the press will really have a field day with that one."

"Well, who is this officer?" asked the President.

"We're not positive yet. The Joint Chiefs are working closely with SouthCom and may have a name for us in the next day or two," said Elliott Higginson.

"I really find it incredible that one officer could have caused an entire operation to go south," said the President, a bit incredulous and almost overwhelmed by the idea.

"Well, Mr. President," said Brian Stavridis, "you recall, I'm sure, the incredible damage that the Walker spy ring did to national security. You recall too the power that one Colonel Oliver North wielded in the Iran-Contra mess. These things can happen in any big bureaucracy where enough controls and checks and balances don't exist."

Elliott Higginson bristled. "Brian, I think maybe we ought to reserve judgment before casting too many stones, don't you think?"

"Certainly, Elliott, certainly."

"All right, then, enough," said the President, clearly in no mood for bickering. "This doesn't do a damn thing to insulate us from what the committee may or may not find. Ray, tap into your network and get to the bottom of this."

With that, the President rose and saw his advisors out. Then he started pacing again.

CHAPTER 74

RICK HOLDEN FELT RELIEVED THAT HE HAD BEEN ABLE to relate his story to General Lovelace, and he felt validated because the general had freely shared what he also knew, ignoring the huge difference in their ranks. But the strongest emotion he felt was fear. If what their stories were starting to point to was true, then they were dealing with something far more serious than just one military debacle. It involved more than just their operations with USS *Coronado,* or with SouthCom, or with the drug war. They were now dealing with an assault on the Republic itself. They were dealing with men who, for whatever reason or motivation, had orchestrated a major military operation to fail and who were now pointing the finger directly at the Commander in Chief, directly at the President of the United States.

Now that Holden and Lovelace knew this, though, what could they do with it? Would the President recognize that he was in mortal danger? Could Rick warn him, and do so while still maintaining his cover as a Navy chief petty officer? He hoped General Ashley Lovelace would continue to work with him and keep him in his confidence. He was certain he could trust the general but uncertain about anyone else.

Rick fought his fear by realizing he had done all he could here. They were heading toward Rodman and there they would be able to regroup, and by that time General Lovelace would be able to get to the bottom of what was going on.

But some sixth sense told Rick he didn't want to wait to get to Rodman to contact Laura. He needed to keep her in the loop right now. He returned to his familiar haunt in Radio Central.

"Hi ya, Chief. What's the good word?" said Radioman First Class Rodriquez, one of Rick's best friends in the shack.

"Nothing much, bud. Looking forward to that great liberty in Rodman?"

"You betcha. Got some pent-up demand I need some help with."

"I know that it's there, buddy, I know you can find it," replied Rick. "Gonna work on some of my gear, if I'm not gonna be in your way."

"Never in the way, Chief. We're outta here for chow. Be seeing you."

Rick rounded the corner and moved into the closet, the out-of-the-way cubbyhole where he hooked up to the HF radio he used to call Laura. After the usual sync problems he got through to her office, but when he asked for her, the petty officer who answered was not very helpful. Rick pressed.

"This is the JTF Eight staff tactical action officer. I need to speak with Lieutenant Peters on your staff."

"Yes sir! As I said, sir, she isn't here and I don't know her whereabouts."

"Let me talk to your supervisor," ventured Rick, wanting an answer but cautious not to press too hard or too far.

"Yes sir. Hold, please." Soon another voice came on the line.

"This is Major Pearson. How may I help you?"

"This is the JTF Eight TAO. I'm trying to reach Lieutenant Peters."

"Lieutenant Peters is not at the headquarters. Perhaps I can help you."

"No, I really need to speak with her." Rick was confused now. The tone of the major's voice was curt at best, defensive at worst.

"Perhaps if I knew the nature of your business, we could return your call. Now, you said your name was . . . ?"

Rick decided to go for it. "This is Lieutenant Colonel Hastings, Major. I'm not at liberty to discuss the nature of my business with Lieutenant Peters. Now, I insist that you reach her now and put my call through." He was really going out on a limb, but he hoped that he had the major off guard.

"Well, Colonel, I'm sorry, but the lieutenant cannot be reached at all at this time," offered the major.

"And why not?" shot back Rick, now having to go with his bold plan.

"She's indisposed, Colonel."

"Indisposed! Where?"

"I believe at her quarters, Colonel, and that is all I'm at liberty to say. Would you like to speak with my branch head, Captain Dawson?"

"No, thank you anyway, Major. We'll be seeing you soon enough when we return to Rodman."

"Oh, Colonel. I don't think that will be for a while. New orders for *Coronado*. Can't really talk about it on this net—top secret—the orders should already be there."

"What . . ." But Rick knew that he had to truncate this conversation. "Good day, Major."

"Good day, Colonel."

As soon as Major Pearson finished talking with Rick, he went immediately to Captain Dawson's office as he was instructed to do. "Captain, I just took a call on Lieutenant Peters's line from a 'Lieutenant Colonel Hastings' on the JTF Eight staff. I assume that radio control has taped it. Shall I have it brought to you, Captain?"

"Yes, Major, and tell them to hurry. Did you say Lieutenant Colonel Hastings?"

"Yes ma'am."

"Funny, never heard of him."

Back aboard *Coronado,* Rick knew Laura was in some sort of danger. And why was *Coronado* now not going to Rodman? He had to find out about that first.

He didn't even put on his gym gear, but sprinted down ladder after ladder to Lower Vehicle Stow to find Commander Ben Malgrave. It was his usual workout time and Rick hoped to find him there. He was not disappointed. Malgrave was surprised to find Rick in his khakis.

"What's up, Chief? Not gonna work out in uniform, are you?"

"Commander, word's going around that we're not heading into Rodman anymore."

"That's right. Top-secret message just came in from SouthCom an hour ago. Something very hush-hush. Message was SPECAT for just the general, the colonel, and Captain Howe. They just briefed the staff and the wardroom a half-hour ago, not a lot of details. Supposedly some short, super-secret mission. Down the coast a day's sail. We're just loitering in Rodman Roads for a few hours while they bring the duty barge out to refuel us. It's a lot faster than going pierside at night, and then we're off. Oh, and you can bet that my guys are excited. This entire operation is supposed to be done in a total communications blackout. No radios, no messages, no INMARSAT, no nothing. We've just been given a latitude and longitude to go to and told to stay there in complete silence for five days or until we are somehow signaled to begin receiving and transmitting again. We may actually get Radio Central painted out." Malgrave hadn't stopped pumping at the lateral press machine and was breathless.

"You mean no communication of any kind, with anyone?"

"That's it. Kinda like the days of sailing ships of old. Just us and the ever-lovin' deep blue sea."

Rick couldn't believe it. He retraced his steps, sprinting up ladders even faster than he had come down them. He reached *Coronado*'s flight deck and looked toward Rodman. He could see the lights begin coming on as night began to fall, and in the distance he could see the fuel barge coming out toward them. This "secret mission," and especially the radio silence, was just too much of a coincidence. He didn't like it. He felt cut off. It was time to take control of his situation.

CHAPTER 75

RICK THOUGHT HE'D GIVE THE CHAIN OF COMMAND ONE more chance. After spending some time in chief's berthing changing into his best-looking khaki uniform, he bounded up several ladders to the blue tile area that marked flag country, home to the JTF Eight staff. He knew he could trust General Ashley Lovelace and if he could talk with him he would find out if indeed some higher powers—he was certain he knew who they were—were purposely taking them out of the picture.

As he approached the door to the general's cabin and the inevitable Marine sentry posted outside of it, he knew exactly how he was going to approach the general. He didn't know, however, how to approach the imposing figure of Colonel Conrad Hicks just coming out of the general's cabin. He hoped the colonel wouldn't remember him. He did, all too well.

"Well, *Chief,* what brings you up to flag country? Get lost on your way somewhere?"

"No, Colonel, I have some brief business here," replied Rick, trying to keep his composure.

"Tell you what, *Chief Holden,* I put up with your insolence and with your barging in on the general once. Hell, E-7s on this staff don't get to see the general as often as you have. Now, if you haven't figured it out yet, we're a bit busy around here and the general sure as hell doesn't have time to see you . . . oh, that's why you're here, isn't it?" Hicks was on a roll. Rick was sure he knew something that he wasn't saying. Did he know what Rick and the general had been talking about?

"Why, yes, Colonel, but I only needed, I mean wanted, to take a minute of the general's time, and—"

Hicks ripped into him. "You just don't get it, do you, mister? The general's busy. I'm the chief of staff. You're in flag country, where you don't belong. Now, would you like to move along or should I have the master at arms help you move along?"

"Colonel, I only—"

"Sentry," said Hicks, looking directly at the Marine orderly. "Pick up that phone and call the master at arms now and have *Chief* Holden removed from the flag spaces," growled Hicks. The sentry moved menacingly toward Rick, ready to comply with the colonel's order.

Rick shouted, "That won't be necessary, Corporal. I'm leaving. Thank you anyway, Colonel!"

"Watch yourself, Chief. You're on very thin ice here."

Rick wheeled away and strode directly aft through the blue tile area. As he stepped out of the hatch and onto the port weather deck, he wondered why the colonel was so hell-bent-for-leather to keep him away from the general. As he approached Radio Central it hit him. Colonel Hicks. Radio Central. All of those furtive calls. And now a surprise mission and radio silence. Hicks was orchestrating this whole thing. No doubt he was behind keeping the general a virtual prisoner on his own flagship, cut off from communicating with the outside world. Rick grasped the rail, now needing the support more than ever.

Rick was staggered, but was undaunted in his desire to do what he knew needed to be done. Where to turn now? It didn't look like he could get to the general; the colonel would see to that. He could almost feel the forces conspiring to throw a blanket over any investigation into the failure of Operation Roundup. But he had been there. He had seen the dead and dying. He had cradled the wounded in his own arms. Those brave men will not have died in vain if he could do anything about it.

It all became clear in his mind in an instant. He had to surface. He had to contact the Agency and get them into the game. The very existence of the Republic was at stake. They would understand. If they didn't, Rick decided in that instant that he would absorb any criticism that came his way. Criticism was no match for knowing you had no honor left by *not* acting.

He ran the rest of way to Radio Central, but a Marine sentry stood right in front of the door. Strange. There was never a sentry here. Rick moved toward him, giving him an opportunity to pick up on his body language and considerably higher rank to move aside.

He didn't move.

"Hello, Corporal. Not sure what you're doing here, but I need to get into Radio," said Rick as authoritatively as he could.

"Sorry, Chief. No one goes into Radio without permission," replied the Marine, clearly not impressed with Rick's rank or position.

"Look, mister. I work here. If you're here to keep excess folks from coming in here, that's great. But for now, just step aside."

"Look, Chief, no one comes or goes without permission. Okay?"

"Well, I'm *Chief Holden*. I'm sure you must know that I have permission."

"Chief, you're one of the people I'm supposed to specifically keep out. If you don't move—"

Rick saw where this was going. "Okay, Corporal, no need to get all in a flurry. I'm moving along."

Rick was trapped and he knew it.

CHAPTER 76

As THEIR JEEP BOUNCED ALONG THE PERIMETER ROAD of Howard Air Force Base, Captain Gary Malzone and Major Fred Hong made an unlikely pair. Malzone was a member of the Marine security squad at Howard and was in charge of orchestrating the monthly IHR—in extremis hostage rescue—drill every month. At six foot four inches tall and a muscular 220 pounds, Malzone looked every bit the Marine, with muscles bulging from his starched camouflage uniform. He had that perpetual look of a man who was just looking for someone to kill. Hong, the base's public works officer, was a member of the Army Corps of Engineers—"civilians in uniform," their more warriorlike brethren were fond of calling them—and he could not have looked more different. Short, thin, with thick Coke-bottle glasses, he didn't look like he belonged in a uniform of any kind at all.

They were looking for a building—any building, really. Malzone's drill every month involved having his men "rescue" several "hostages" from one building or another on the base. Hong was responsible for finding an appropriate building, one that would be unharmed by the brief, violent activities that Malzone's boys inflicted on it. No, the Air Force base commander sure as hell didn't want a bill for building repairs for the silly games the Marines were playing.

Usually their search was brief and resulted in finding a suitable building—there were a good number of vacant ones at this sprawling base—but today they were having a tough time. Hong groused to Malzone that there were exercises going on elsewhere on the base and they couldn't use this sector or that, leaving them with just a small part of the base to actually look at to use. He had gotten the word that some particular buildings could not be used at all, but he had gotten a tip from someone connected with SouthCom headquarters that there was a really remote building that might do—building Number 1468, out on the perimeter road. Hong couldn't recall ever seeing it—it must be remote—but he'd do anything to avoid searching aimlessly around the base forever.

"We there yet, Fred?" yelled Malzone over the roar of the jeep. Although he was one pay grade junior, Malzone just couldn't bear to address Hong as "Major"—hell, this guy didn't even look like he belonged in the military.

"Almost, Gary. This map isn't the best. But I think it's over this way."

"Hey, over there," said Malzone. He could spot things a lot farther off than Hong could.

"Yeah, that's it. Whadda you think?" asked Hong.

"Size looks good. Let's open 'er up and see what kind of setup it's got. Want my boys to have a challenge when they turn it into a shooting gallery."

As Malzone braked the jeep to a stop, Hong got out a little unsteadily—God, he hated how this damn Marine drove—and fumbled with his key chain, looking for the key to Building 1468. Let's see, it's here somewhere. Yes, here it is. As he walked to the front door of the building, he looked back to call to Malzone, but Gary was trotting around the outside of the building, no doubt already planning for the takedown. As he pushed open the door, Fred stopped dead in his tracks. He couldn't get a word out for what seemed like an eternity, but then finally screamed, "Gary!"

Malzone rushed in to find Hong gaping at the body of Andy Wilson. Quite dead, it could only gape back.

CHAPTER 77

THE OTHER JOINT CHIEFS WERE GATHERED ONCE AGAIN in their large conference room waiting for General Campbell to appear. The chairman was usually prompt as a matter of professional courtesy to his colleagues, but as of late, in the wake of Operation Roundup, he seemed pre-occupied and often kept them waiting for interminable periods.

They didn't need to speculate too long as to why he had asked them to meet today. They knew full well that he had been summoned to the White House a number of times in the past forty-eight hours. They had their own network and had learned that his encounters with the President had been stormy. All of them had been assigned inside the Washington beltway enough times to know that when a disaster of the magnitude of Operation Roundup hit, political survival was the order of the day and that those with real responsibility for the debacle would work night and day to shift the blame to others, and not be terribly concerned about who might stop the bullet. The trick was to be agile enough to stay out of the line of fire. They knew their roles well.

Army Chief of Staff General Walt Prestridge broke the ice. "I have an inkling of what the chairman wants to talk about. I assume all of you have the same inkling too?"

"Sure do," replied Boomer Curtis. "The Navy doesn't miss a trick. I don't know precisely what went on at the White House between the President and the chairman, but all indications are that it was quite a scene."

"I think we've all heard that," Prestridge said, "but are we missing something here? It seems pretty clear that General Lovelace was taking stick and rudder from the President and that he ignored almost every basic tenet of good military operations in doing so. I didn't think bringing a guy out of DMA to take such a high-profile assignment was a good idea from the get-go."

"Well," replied General Hank Paxton, "you had a chance to voice your objections then. You're not trying to dodge this one, are you?"

"Absolutely not! All I'm suggesting is that we have a united front and make sure that this shit-storm that's swirling around the President doesn't get dumped on us," replied Prestridge.

"I don't see how anyone could possibly think we would direct such a botched operation from the Joint Chiefs," interjected Admiral Dan Bell. "The public has got to know that this was out of our hands and out of the hands of the Unified Commander."

"They won't know it unless someone tells them," offered Prestridge, now clearly taking a leadership role in getting all of the Joint Chiefs on the same page on this issue.

"He's right," said General Paxton. "I'll be damned if I'll have my thirty-six years serving this country capped by being part of the group that gets whipped by a royal screwup in some third world shithole."

General Ken Rainbow, Marine Corps Commandant, joined the fray. "He's right, you know. What's done is done. We can't bring those boys back. I think we all know why this operation failed. We couldn't have saved it no matter what. Why should we stand in front of an impending train wreck when it's not our fault?"

"I can't argue with that," replied Prestridge. "We need to get the chairman on board so he sees our point of view."

The collective murmurs around the table signaled agreement with this assessment. General Walt Prestridge had accomplished the task that the chairman had given him. General Campbell had been sharing just enough information with his fellow Army officer to enable him to serve as a perfect foil to energize the other Joint Chiefs with just the right mixture of self-preservation, anger at the President and General Lovelace for causing this debacle, and urgency to deflect the criticism that he wanted to be sure they felt was barreling toward them. As they stirred themselves into righteousness, Howard Campbell entered, as if on cue.

"Sorry to keep you gentlemen waiting," he began most graciously. "I know you all have important responsibilities and I don't like keeping you waiting. Admiral Bell, what's on the agenda for this afternoon?"

The vice chief looked surprised and a bit perplexed, because it was the chairman who had called this meeting. But he had learned long ago that even mildly criticizing General Campbell was not at all wise. So he called an audible. "Mr. Chairman, there are a number of things on the plate, but perhaps one matter of critical importance deserves our, and particularly your, attention first."

"What's that?" asked Campbell innocently.

"Operation Roundup, Mr. Chairman, and more specifically, the issue of who really caused this operation to go south and who, well, is going to take the blame for it." He was choosing his words carefully, walking a fine line between seeming to whine and making sure the chairman fully understood the particulars of their concerns.

Campbell began his well-rehearsed monologue, but tried to make it sound as spontaneous as possible. "Gentlemen, you all know that our Commander in Chief has summoned me to the White House several times during the past several days. Obviously, the subject each time has been Operation Roundup. I have to be quite candid with you that none of those sessions have been at all pleasant. It seems that the President is incredibly misinformed—or at least wants to appear to be that way—regarding this debacle. I'm not sure how to really phrase this"—he was really straining credulity now—"but I am so baffled that I am wondering if he has full command of his faculties." Campbell paused for dramatic effect and the other Joint Chiefs—as he knew they would—chimed in.

"Mr. Chairman," said Boomer Curtis, "you're not suggesting that the President is not fit to make decisions, are you?"

"No, I don't really believe I am," offered Campbell, playing the innocent.

"Mr. Chairman, what are you basing this on?" asked General Jamison.

Campbell continued, knowing he had the perfect follow-up. "Gentlemen, you are aware of the reality of recent events. Let's not forget the hasty press conference with the results of this "successful" operation. The President's staff will tell you of his ranting both toward me, and toward General Walters—and by extension all of you—literally screaming that he wouldn't take the blame for something *we* had fouled up. Really denying that he gave General Lovelace explicit stick and rudder on how to conduct the operation and ordering him to start it in spite of the crystal-clear orders of the Unified Theater

Commander, General Walters. Gentlemen, I owe it to you as my colleagues and brothers in arms to tell you that our President has no intention of taking even one scintilla of responsibility for this debacle that he created. Now, we really have to ask ourselves, if he isn't gong to 'take the fall' for this, to use his words, who do you think he's going to select? Don't you think we are all in a perfect position to find ourselves out on the street?"

"Surely he's not thinking along those lines?" said Walt Prestridge, now clearly alarmed for the first time.

"You gentlemen forget," continued Campbell in his most fatherly and collegial terms. "First, we serve at the pleasure of the President. Second, we are political neophytes in comparison to the President and his advisors. They know how to survive and are determined to survive. Third, you know that next year is an election year and the President isn't exactly knocking them dead in the polls. There's no way his administration can survive even the hint of blame for this. No, gentlemen, stand by for heavy rolls. To borrow one of Boomer's terms, this train wreck is headed straight for our station!"

Campbell paused, pleased with his masterful performance. He had appealed to their most basic instincts: survival, pride, and fair play. They were ready for what he would drop on them next. Now let *them* stir him to action.

"Mr. Chairman," said Admiral Bell—now asserting his position as vice chief—"unquestionably we are behind you. We signed on to support and defend the Constitution. If the President has 'lost it,' as you say, we must take action. But how should we proceed?"

"The good news is that I don't think we need to do anything overt right this minute. The Constitution has clear procedures for dealing with these sorts of issues. The most important thing for us is to present a united front. We must speak with one voice, so I'd ask all of you to check through me before making any statements at all about this operation. That way we'll have a coordinated response."

"We can certainly do that, Mr. Chairman," said Admiral Boomer Curtis, "but this all seems so very passive."

"Gentlemen, just let the system work. I can tell you right now that our Congress is looking at this matter very seriously, very seriously indeed."

CHAPTER 78

Liz Kennedy smiled at her good fortune. Just when she thought she was going to have to return to writing about the mundane subjects assigned a reporter far from favor, her story had been rejuvenated, not just with more military stuff but with some dirt as well. And how her readership responded to dirt! No one—not Bill Safire and not *This Week*—was going to beat her to the punch on this one.

Granted, the information was a little elliptical thus far, not heavy on specifics, but her source had guaranteed her more in short order and that had been enough to convince her editors to let her run with it. She was being careful about how she proceeded, but the payoff down the pike seemed exceptionally promising. Things were seemingly on automatic. White House denials, well, that was expected. Pentagon statements as to the importance of maintaining control of military operations. Vague, but increasingly frequent hints that someone inside of U.S. military, someone with access to important information, might have sold or bartered this information to drug lords for a substantial amount of money. And the dirt—it looked like it was going to be the darkest, wettest mud.

"Liz!"

She looked up, startled. "Huh?"

"Hey, you look like you're in a trance." It was summer intern Frank Michels, a good kid from Georgetown University, eager, polite. "Phone call."

"Who is it?"

"Someone named Howard, wouldn't give his last name."

"Oh sure, thanks Frank. Put him through."

Liz picked up the phone. "Howard, nice to hear from

you. You hardly ever call me here. What's up?"

"Liz, things are happening very quickly. Now, I can tell you that there are some very strange things happening with respect to the aftermath of Operation Roundup. I don't know how quickly it will break in other media and, well, dear, I always want to give you first crack at it." Howard Campbell was being as smooth as he possibly could be. He was even surprising himself.

"I know you have always been a dear and I appreciate it. But you've been promising me this for a while and my story has been running on fumes for too long. I've had to promise Joe Abramowitz a bunch just to get him to let me keep it alive."

"Now, have I ever let you down?" said Campbell.

"Not yet, Howard, not yet."

"Liz, dear. We think we may have a break in how this operation failed."

"I'm listening."

"I'm sure you are. Seems that it all revolves around those all too familiar themes of love and money."

She knew he wanted to toy with her. As much as he meant to her as a source, she had no patience for it. "I'm still listening, Howard."

"Liz, I'm not prepared to give you names just yet— soon, though—but we think we have nailed this down to a little love triangle that has played out in the worst possible way."

"How so?"

"It seems that General Walters, the SouthCom Commander, had a bright, ambitious young naval officer on his staff. This fella was really going places and had acquired the lifestyle to go with it. You know, entertaining beyond what he could really afford, joining all the right clubs so he could suck up to the heavies, just the right Old Town neighborhood, just the right car, that sort of thing."

"And how is he any different from the rest of the officers in the military?"

"But there's more. It seems that beyond blind ambition, this gent had a few bad habits too. One was gambling. Big sports bettor, and not always with the most amicable people, if you gather what I'm saying. Fell quite a bit behind and was leveraging everything, second mortgage, all his assets really, but not catching up. Even though he left a nice little wife behind in Norfolk, he had an eye for the ladies. Got rather attached to a female naval officer, and an intelligence specialist at that, down on Charlie's—General Walters's, that is—staff. Seems that she liked him lots more than the other way around and he co-opted her to some intelligence gathering for him—the story goes—so he could have enough money to dump his wife and they could live happily ever after. Word is that she was pretty much the innocent, thought that what she was doing was little more than industrial espionage, but when she learned what was done with the info she provided, she freaked out and turned on him—"

Liz was spellbound, but interrupted. "Turned on him?"

"Well, yes. Seems like they had quite a noisy argument and then both disappeared for a bit, but, well, you see, he's still missing."

"Do they think she did something to him?"

"We're not sure, Liz."

"Well, are they looking for her?"

"As we speak."

"Howard, does this change anything about what's going on between the White House and the Pentagon? After all, it's an open secret that you and the President are not exactly in the most cordial terms."

"Oh, we've had some tiffs, but under the circumstances—he's trying to wash his hands of the entire debacle—that's not surprising. I can take care of my end of things. But to answer your question, all this changes is that it answers the *how* behind the failure of this operation. If an intelligence officer on the SouthCom staff was feeding information on Operation Roundup to this traitor, and he in turn fed it to the druggies, it's easy to see how they could achieve a spectacular ambush."

"Yes, Howard, but one ambush. Surely they'd recognize that they couldn't do anything but slow down our counterdrug efforts."

"Ah, Liz, Liz, my dear." Now Campbell was sounding patronizing. "You forget that this country has no stomach for casualties to American boys. What do you think finally made us get out of Vietnam? And look at Lebanon. We turned tail and ran immediately after the Marines barracks were bombed. There's little enough public support for the drug war as it is. Most of the liberal bleeding hearts say that stopping it at the source doesn't work anyway, we just ought to concentrate on the demand side."

"Howard, you make it sound like a conspiracy."

"Isn't it, Liz? Big drug lord, big enough for us to mobilize this kind of operation to take on. Making huge profits. Even if he derails our efforts to stop him for a year, that's tens of millions of dollars of pure profits just in that country alone. And what is he risking? All of his workers and lieutenants are clearly expendable."

"Is the President still to blame for Operation Roundup's failure, then?"

"Of course he is, Liz. In spite of how the drug lords got the information about our operation and turned it into their ambush, we still knew they were mobilizing for their attack. We could have stopped, we would have stopped. But the President pushed Lovelace into it over the orders of the entire chain of command. Oh yes, he's still the one who needs to be held accountable."

"Fine, Howard, now just how do you want me to run with this story?"

"I may be able to give you names soon, Liz, but for now just give it your best shot."

"You can count on that, Howard."

After she hung up, Liz stared at the screen of her computer for a long time, trying to conjure up just the right way to approach this new twist to this story. After what seemed like an almost interminable time, the words started to flow together:

WASHINGTON—Informed sources close to the Pentagon indicate the failure of Operation Roundup may be tied to intelligence leaks from the military's SouthCom headquarters. An investigation is now ongoing into the activities of two naval officers, known to be linked romantically, who may have conspired to, and actually succeeded in, passing top-secret information regarding this operation to Costa Rican drug lords. One of these officers is currently missing. The Pentagon is conducting a full investigation. Officials emphasize that the fact that the drug lords had this detailed information about Operation Roundup and were planning an ambush was discovered by military intelligence prior to the beginning of the operation, but that a decision was made by the White House to go forward with the operation anyway.

The rest of the story was short on specific details but contained good, factual background data on how much money the drug lords controlled, the resources they had at their command, the ineffectiveness of the local constabulary in dealing with them, and other unremarkable information. But Liz had broken the story first, and she looked forward to more to run with.

Howard Campbell kept his promises—at least to people he wanted to keep his promises to. He looked at the pictures that Charlie Walters had sent to him, those an alert Sergeant Brooke had snapped, "just in case." Pictures of General Ashley Lovelace and Lieutenant Laura Peters, both smiling, both looking like they felt awfully good, coming out of the BOQ in Panama. So innocent, so meaningless, of no consequence to anyone, just another of the billions of meaningless events that go on the world on any given day—when taken without context. But Howard Campbell was about to put them in context.

CHAPTER 79

LAURA PETERS APPROACHED CAPTAIN FRAN DAWSON'S office trying to look as composed as possible. She must have slept for almost fifteen hours—a result of exhaustion, frustration, bewilderment, and a whole panoply of emotions. She still was not thinking entirely clearly, but the rest had given her some measure of focus. She no longer cared about Operation Roundup. She was only concerned about her professional survival.

She knocked and Captain Dawson motioned her in. "Lieutenant Peters reporting, Captain. You wanted to see me?"

"Awfully late in the day to be showing up for work, Peters. Any particular problems I should know about?" This wasn't going to be a pleasant exchange.

"No ma'am . . . Captain. I've had a rough couple of days and, frankly, I just overslept, that's all," replied Laura, trying to keep her composure but feeling the sting of the captain's hostility.

"Well, we're a little concerned about you, Lieutenant. I mean, your activities of late have given us cause for some concern."

"I'm not sure what you mean, Captain."

"Well, for starters, you rush out of here like some hysterical child, try to barge in on General Walters, and then disappear—you say to your quarters."

Laura bristled. "Captain, I was in my quarters."

"Well, we called your quarters—several times, in fact. I made two of the calls myself, and no one answered the phone. Does that strike you as odd?"

"Oh, well, Captain. I was there most of the time. Actually, I went out for a run. I guess I was so stressed I forgot to mention that."

Dawson continued, now playing the role of the inquisitor, "Well, Lieutenant, there are some activities that you have been involved in that really bear some explaining. Would you like anyone to be here to represent you?"

This was coming at Laura far too fast. "Represent me? Captain, am I being accused of something?"

"I really don't know yet, Lieutenant. But as your boss I just want you to be accountable to me for your actions. Can we keep it on that level?" Dawson's tone was becoming more and more hostile.

Laura could tell that the captain was uncomfortable with this entire process but had no intention of backing off. "Certainly, Captain, I think all our dealings have always been on a professional basis."

"Good," continued Dawson. "Well, then, Lieutenant

Peters, could you please explain the fact that you have had several HF radio conversations with someone aboard USS *Coronado*?"

How did she know about that? Laura stared mutely at her.

Fran Dawson wasn't a trained interrogator and rather than wait for Laura to respond, she played all her cards. "And there seem to have been several phone calls between you and someone at the *Washington Post,* conversations that took place very close to the time information was being published in that paper about Operation Roundup."

Laura's eyes grew wide. As unaccustomed as Fran Dawson was with conducting an interrogation, Laura was even less adept at fielding questions like this and thinking quickly on her feet. She decided no response was better than a foolish one.

The captain continued, now looking genuinely uncomfortable, "And finally, Lieutenant, I need to ask you . . . I mean . . . it has a bearing on . . ."

Laura knew this wouldn't be good.

"Lieutenant, it has come to my attention—that is, our attention—that you have been seeing Lieutenant Commander Wilson and that there may be an inappropriate relationship between you two." Dawson slumped a bit in her chair, seemingly relieved that she had gotten this out.

Laura continued to stare at her, a mixture of shock, rage, and incredulity overwhelming her.

"Well, Lieutenant. I know this is a lot to deal with. Is there anything you would like to tell me?"

Tell? For a moment, Laura felt incapable of speech. Even a scream would have caught in her throat. Nothing in her entire life had prepared her for how to deal with this. Where were they coming up with this? Where should she start in her explanations to Dawson? Should she explain anything to her at all? The captain was her boss and had her best interest at heart, didn't she?

Something clicked inside Laura. Maybe it was courage. Maybe it was anger. But she decided in an instant that this was all wrong. There was to be no reasoning with the captain. She didn't think all of this up herself. She simply did her job and brought it to her superiors' attention. Laura straightened up in her chair, she looked directly at Fran Dawson, and found her voice. "Captain, I don't know where you all are coming up with this. It's unbelievable. How long have I worked for you? Has there ever been any indication that anything about my performance has been less than totally professional? And now you just come out and accuse me of . . . of . . . this!"

Dawson was taken aback by Laura's anger. She backpedaled. "Now, Lieutenant, no one is *accusing* you of anything."

"That's crap, Captain. You may just be the messenger, but I'm being accused of all this falsely, and you know it!"

"Well, there are these tapes," continued Dawson.

"Tapes!" shouted Laura. "Tapes of what?"

"Of your conversations."

"You've been tapping my phone?"

"Well, I haven't, but—"

"This is unbelievable. What else, Captain? What else!"

"Well, this issue with Lieutenant Commander Wilson is particularly bothersome." Dawson was now on the defensive.

"Wilson? I'm not up to anything with Andy Wilson! I may have met him at work once or twice. I don't even know what he looks like in civilian clothes!" Laura was on her feet now.

There was a loud knock on Dawson's door. She got up to tell whoever it was that she didn't want to be disturbed, but as she opened it she saw the command duty officer standing there with two MPs.

"Yes, Colonel."

"Ma'am, I am Colonel Jerry Moore, SouthCom duty officer."

"Yes, I can see that you are, Colonel," said Captain Dawson. "What can I do for you?"

"Captain, is Lieutenant Peters in your office?"

"Yes. Why?"

"May I enter, ma'am?"

Without really waiting for her response, he brushed past her with the two MPs in tow and walked directly toward Laura.

"Lieutenant Laura Peters?"

"Yes."

"Lieutenant Laura Peters, I am Colonel Jerry Moore, the SouthCom duty officer. I am placing you under military arrest for the murder of Lieutenant Commander Andrew Wilson."

CHAPTER 80

RICK HAD RUN OUT OF OPTIONS. HE KNEW HE COULDN'T do anything more on *Coronado,* and because he was clearly a threat to the chief of staff, it was only a matter of time before some pretense was found to take him into custody. He had to make his escape. He ran from the communications office and out to the aft weather decks.

Rick had surveyed his options. *Coronado* wasn't going to pull into Rodman—no—that option had been conveniently precluded. He couldn't contrive a way to get off via helo; there was nothing coming or going from the ship in the near-term. They were anchored in Rodman Roads several miles from land, a possible swim, but not likely with the heavy currents in these waters. There must be a way.

As Rick stared forlornly looking at the twinkling lights of the Panama coast, a long, low, gray rectangular shape appeared. In busy roads where ships took great pains to steer well clear of one another, this low craft looked almost menacing as it continued to slowly approach the ship. He peered out into the mist, trying to make out what it was.

He heard voices, first one, then another, then a chorus of shouts and commands, getting louder. He looked down decks below and saw that several sailors had opened the portside after-side-port doors and were heaving on several lines and fueling hoses. The men at the side port became more and more animated. Orders were now being shouted.

"Stand by your lines," said a chief.

"Signal him to come inbound," said the officer in charge of the detail.

"Aye, aye," said the petty officer holding the signal light.

The fueling barge. That was his way off *Coronado*—probably his only way off. But he didn't have much time. He slipped inside the skin of the ship again and made his way quickly down toward the chief's berthing. Finally he reached his rack and locker.

Rick paused a moment to think. What if he did get off of *Coronado*? Where would he go once ashore in Panama? Rick had been reconstituted as a Navy chief long enough to know that the Navy had rules and regulations, procedures and policies, expectations regarding what was done and what was not done. He couldn't simply disappear without impelling a search for him. At best, this search would treat his disappearance as a hazard of the sea, a sailor falling overboard. But at worst, given his confrontations with Colonel Hicks and the suspicions that they were sure to have aroused, his disappearance would be looked on with great suspicion and would likely provoke a manhunt. However, he couldn't worry about that now if he was going to go.

He was starting to gather a few essential things that he had hidden on board and now needed to take with him, when suddenly a voice startled him. He spun around and saw he was only feet from the imposing figure of Bosn' Mate Chief Willie Hudson. At six-foot-four and a hefty 250 pounds, Hudson's bulk, scowl, and multiple tattoos gave pause to everyone who encountered him up close.

"What's up, Holden? You decide to tidy up that grip of yours?" said Hudson.

"No, Willie, just got a lot on my mind. Just really fiddling with my stuff, that's all," replied Rick, trying to look as normal as possible but not doing a very good job of it.

"Hey, your ensign, what's his name, Kemp, was down here just a little while ago looking for you."

"For me?"

"Well, sure as hell wasn't for me. Don't want you fucking snake-eaters getting hold of my trim body. Yeah, and he had some uptight master at arms brothers with him."

"Did he say what he wanted?"

"No, just told me to call him if I saw you. Told him nice as I could to a college-boy ensign that he could call up here just anytime and if you were here you sure could talk to him."

Hudson wasn't a big fan of officers—especially not ensigns—and he was doing a particularly good number on Rick's platoon leader. But Hudson had good street smarts. His body language was unambiguous. This visit wasn't a pleasure trip.

"Yeah, looked like he was gonna run off and look 'round somewhere else for you. The MAAs"—Navy parlance for the master at arms, the ship's police force—"yeah, they looked kinda pissed that you weren't right here. Shit, Rick, you in some kinda trouble?"

"No. Must be some kind of damn misunderstanding."

"Yeah, well, with you being a hero and all, maybe they were gonna take you up to the captain for meritorious mast, get you a medal or something."

"Don't think so, Willie, don't think so." Rick allowed himself a slight smile. At least Hudson seemed to be on his side. Rick might need his help, but he couldn't let on about his plans and he couldn't get Hudson implicated in anything. He had to tread lightly.

"Okay, my man, just watch out for yourself. I'm heading down to the chief's mess. Hear they've got a hot video 'bout ready to roll. You interested, Rick? It'll help you unwind."

"No thanks, Willie, I think I'll just hit the sack," responded Rick as Hudson left the berthing compartment. Rick paused for a few moments to ensure that the big chief was gone.

Rick stole out of the berthing compartment, wearing his heavy foul-weather jacket and carrying his almost-full parachute bag. It was a darkened ship and he knew these passageways well so he was able to proceed quickly, moving in the shadows, not drawing any attention to himself from the few *Coronado* sailors who were still awake at this hour.

As he slipped out onto the weather decks, Rick saw that the barge was just being made fast to the ship. He didn't want to get on until the fueling was done, but he couldn't afford to miss it either. He crouched low behind the motor whaleboat, securely set in its skid, as he waited for what seemed like an eternity. Finally the fueling was complete and *Coronado*'s engineers began to reel in their fueling hoses and other gear.

Rick had his move well planned out. Attaching a rope to a railing stanchion just above the barge at the farthest point away from the tug, he waited until the lines holding the barge to *Coronado* were slipped and the tug just started to pull away from the ship. Knowing that the tug-masters' attention must now be away from *Coronado,* he quickly hopped over the guardrail, slid quickly down the rope the forty feet to the barge, and curled himself up with his parachute bag right next to the gunwale. He had made it and now he lay low, as still as he had ever been in his life.

As the tug and barge moved away from *Coronado,* Rick allowed himself one furtive look at his ship. He didn't think he'd ever see it again.

CHAPTER 81

LAURA SAT IN A SMALL ROOM AT THE MILITARY POLICE Headquarters at Quarry Heights. She couldn't stand being in this place, certainly couldn't bear sitting down and not moving at all. She paced back and forth rapidly. She was having trouble holding it all together. She wanted to explode.

Laura had only been inside the Military Police Headquarters once—she had had to come down here to claim one of her young corporals who had torn the town of Panama City up the previous night and who had been turned over to the military police by the local gendarmes. She remembered the condescending look she had given the young man for being in this . . . this *place*. She remembered how the security guards had treated anyone held here as some sort of lower life-form. She hadn't liked it then and she certainly didn't like it now.

The room she was in wasn't really a cell. It was just stark. It had a metal table, old, beat-up; two chairs, equally old, with plain rough metal armrests where leather had once been; a cheap wooden bookshelf with no books; an overhead light that was unnecessarily dim; and a large mirror, very large, though she guessed maybe it was only a mirror for her—whoever was on the other side of that wall could probably see her. There was no window. The outside world was only accessible to her if and when someone came through that locked door.

No one had been through it in what seemed like hours. She kept looking at her wrist for her watch, but they had taken that from her when she entered this foul place. Watch, wallet, necklace, belt. Put everything in the bag, ma'am. Sign here. Yes ma'am. Yes, here's a receipt. Yes ma'am, just a precaution. Regulations, you know, ma'am. The way the military police sergeants at the desk had said "ma'am" every several words—not with a respectful tone, but with a condescending one that had shouted, *You're an inherently bad person to be here. We don't want to respect you but we have to*—had driven her to distraction. Keep your cool, she told herself. Don't let them see you break down.

But break down is exactly what she wanted to do. Murder? Andy Wilson? How could this happen? She had read books and seen movies where these sorts of things happened, but they had stretched the bounds of believability. And as bad as it was being arrested and thrown into this room, it was not knowing what was going to happen in the next few minutes, the next few hours, the next few days, that really made her nervous. She couldn't even contemplate being put on trial.

On the other side of Laura's mirror, Captain Fran Dawson looked at her lieutenant. She was almost as bewildered as Laura but couldn't show it. Not to her boss.

"Well, Captain, did you ever think it would come to

this?'' said General Walters. He was standing very close to her.

"No, General," she replied, taking a step away. "I still don't believe it. That is, I don't want to believe it. Are you . . ." She caught herself. She wished she hadn't said that.

"Certain? Am I certain, Captain? We've been through this already. Your loyalty to one of your subordinates is noted. You need to face reality and understand this isn't some half-baked case that some junior military investigator is trying to make. This is a major, major case. The evidence is overwhelming. The only way you can help your lieutenant now is to talk some sense into her and get her to tell us how she got drawn into this and start naming names. That's *the best* that you can do for her."

"I'm not sure how I can do that, General."

"You can go in and talk to her."

"Here? Now?" Dawson was caught off guard. She had come down here hours after Laura had been taken from her office, fully expecting to drive her back to the SouthCom headquarters once they had realized that this was all a big, big blunder. Now she was being asked to interrogate one of her junior officers. She couldn't. She wasn't prepared.

"Yes, Captain. Right here. Right now. You're her boss. What I'm doing is giving you an opportunity to question her in a, shall we say, nonhostile way. I've got other people standing by that can talk to her instead, but I can assure you they won't exactly be people she would enjoy discussing matters with." There was a particularly hard edge to General Walters's voice. Fran Dawson had heard this before when the general wanted results and when his patience was about exhausted.

"Yes, General, of course I'll talk to her. Is there anything in particular you want me to say?"

"Captain. If you can't figure it out, I'll spell it out for you. Wilson gets strung out with his little betting problem. Lots of money involved. Looking for a way to get some ready cash. They're shacked up. He needs money bad. Figures he'll use her. She's selling military secrets. Somebody gets cold feet. Somebody wants out. There's a fight.

Somebody gets popped. Her story doesn't wash. But who, Captain, who? That's what we don't know. What did she feed Wilson and who has he given that information to?"

Fran Dawson didn't like this at all, the idea of interrogating one of her junior officers, especially when she wasn't even sure if she believed everything General Walters was telling her. She was smart enough, however, to know that he was going to get what he wanted.

"Yes, General, all right," replied Dawson, with more resignation than conviction in her voice. "I'll talk to her. Right now."

Walters was pleased. Dawson's amateur interrogating would slow down the investigative process long enough to allow him to use Laura as a pawn to feed to Washington. It was coming together beautifully.

Laura jumped up as the door swung open. The bright light coming through the door overwhelmed the room's dim light and for a moment she shielded her eyes and squinted, trying to see who was coming into the room. She was expecting the worst. When she finally made out Captain Fran Dawson's figure she was relieved.

"Captain, is that you? What are you doing here?"

"Well, Lieutenant, I don't particularly like them putting one of my officers in confinement. I wanted to come down here and see how they were treating you."

Oh, this wasn't working, thought Fran Dawson. She couldn't lie like this. She would have to go through the motions to placate Walters, but she knew she sounded wooden and that Laura would see right through this ruse.

"Treating me? Captain, they're treating me like a criminal. This is just so unbelievable. Do you really believe I could do any of this?"

Captain Fran Dawson knew the only thing she could do was try to calm Laura down. "Lieutenant, I think they just want you to tell them everything you know, that's all. I really think this will all blow over if we can manage to do that."

"Captain, there's nothing to tell," said Laura as she jumped out of her chair. There's nothing. *Nothing!* I can't believe this!"

Nothing Fran Dawson could say would mollify her. Of course, General Charlie Walters was watching this through the window with great delight. She had spurned him. Now she knew too much about Operation Roundup—how she knew it he still didn't know—and he worried that she might somehow be capable of letting the wrong people know something he didn't want them to know about Operation Roundup. He'd neutralize her and he'd have others do the dirty work.

After another fifteen minutes of talking to Laura, Fran Dawson came out of the interrogation room looking exhausted. The ordeal had drained her. General Walters moved quickly to her. "Well, Dawson, I didn't hear anything come out of her that I didn't know already. I thought you had some kind of rapport with her. Are all of your junior officers so distant from you?"

That stung. Walters had a way of touching a raw nerve with her. "General, as I'm sure you heard," said Dawson, now staring directly at the general with just the slightest bit of defiance in her eyes, "Lieutenant Peters still denies even knowing Andy Wilson casually, let alone having anything to do with him."

"Seems strange, given the other facts that we've found out. Wouldn't you say so, *Captain?*" said Walters in his most condescending tone, a tone that said, *Don't defy me or you'll pay.*

Dawson looked appropriately chagrined and, in self-defense, softened her tone. "General, I'm just saying that she's sticking with what she told us earlier, that's all. She hasn't shared anything new with me."

"So what are we to do?" asked Walters, for the first time seeming to value her contribution or opinion.

"Sir, do you think we must continue to detain her while there are still questions?" replied Dawson.

"Well, yes, of course," responded Walters, but in a much more understanding tone of voice. "But I'm not sure we have anyplace appropriate to lock her up here. This place is built to house soldiers, sailors, and airmen who get drunk out in town; not officers, especially not women officers." He paused and looked directly at Dawson.

"No, General, I mean, this is not very suitable, you're exactly right." This couldn't be mercy on Walters's part, could it?

"She's your officer, Captain. How do you propose to detain her without leaving her here?"

Dawson thought quickly. She didn't know where the general was coming from on this one. She couldn't psyche out an agenda, so she just went with her instincts. "General, I can have her restricted to her room in the BOQ while we look for someplace more suitable to detain her."

"The BOQ? Is that a secure place to put someone accused of this type of crime?" Walters was probing now and she knew it. If she didn't want Peters left in this wretched place, she had to take the lead on this.

"We can make it secure, General. I can have a lock put on the door, and I can have the door guarded twenty-four hours a day."

"I think guarding the door is a little conspicuous. It would alarm the other BOQ residents who aren't guilty of anything. Maybe a bit more discretion would be in order, Captain."

"Yes sir, I can make that happen," responded Dawson, surprised that she was holding sway with the general.

"Well, yes, Captain, that will be fine. I have important matters to attend to. I am placing Lieutenant Laura Peters in your custody. See that she stays in your custody. Understood?"

"Of course, General, of course," responded Dawson. But the general didn't hear her. He was already breezing out of the room.

Captain Fran Dawson stood motionless for a moment. She was perplexed. Nothing she had ever done had prepared her for this sort of eventuality. Talk about not being in the manual, she mused.

But Dawson had not built a career marked by excellence to be stymied by any professional challenge. She summoned the administrative officer she had brought along, a seasoned Army warrant officer, and began giving orders. The warrant officer wrote in his "wheel book" as quickly as he could and uttered a snappy, "Yes ma'am," as he turned and left the room almost as quickly as the general had a few minutes before. Confident that her orders were in the process of being carried out, she returned to the interrogation room, stared directly at Laura, and said, "Lieutenant Peters, get up and come with me. We are going to get you situated for the night."

"Captain?"

Dawson did not want to have a discussion with Laura. She just wanted to get her out of there before General Walters changed his mind. She had to let Laura recover at least a little bit of her dignity, and that wasn't going to happen here.

"Lieutenant, I'm waiting, let's go!"

Laura, standing, could only manage a weak, "I'm coming, Captain."

CHAPTER 82

RICK LAY MOTIONLESS ON THE DECK OF THE FUEL barge. He was at the forward end, away from the tug, pinned against the freeboard, facedown. A combination of the darkness of the night and the fact that it was so unbelievable that anyone should be lying on a Navy fuel barge had made him invisible. He clutched his parachute bag close to him, almost like a friend. Rick was wearing his Navy chief's uniform, with a foul-weather jacket over it. He thought he knew what it would take to blend into the base.

The lone tug was nudging the barge into position against the pier at the Rodman Naval Station. As the tugmaster moved his throttles and the powerful tug gingerly pushed the barge right into position, two linehandlers on the pier attached lines to the barge to make it fast to the pier. It was a chore that they had performed hundreds of times with little enthusiasm or interest. Duty at the sleepy base at Rodman, Panama, was not the kind of assignment that attracted the Navy's best and brightest.

Finally the barge stopped. The shouts from the linehandlers and the throttling back of the tug's engines told him they had finally come to rest. He hazarded a look up. The tall light poles on the pier cast down a pale glow through the light fog that seemed to be a permanent part of the evening landscape here in Panama. Seaward, he could dimly see the lights of ships anchored in the roads. Landward, he could see some details of the base. The ends of the piers. The Special Boat Unit craft fast along the seawall. The narrow road leading off the piers. The gentle hills surrounding the immediate area.

Their job completed, the linehandlers were beginning to walk away. Just this little bit of work had been a chore for them. Probably the enlisted men were going back to the BEQ to grouse about it. He'd just wait for them to pass out of sight and then slip off the barge with his parachute bag. Rick could see the linehandlers stopped at the end of the pier, where they looked like they were now engaged in a conversation with the lone pier sentry in his guard shack. Didn't look like they would be moving away anytime soon.

As the tug chugged away and back toward its own pier, Rick decided to make his move. He gently lifted his parachute bag over the gunwale of the fuel barge and rolled up onto the pier. So far, so good. Now, up on the pier but crouching low, Rick moved furtively toward the head of the pier. The pier sentry and the linehandlers were fixtures. They weren't moving. The pier was a secure area. Normal access on and off went directly in front of the guard shack, and liberal amounts of barbed wire ensured that there was no other way on or off the pier, save jumping into the water. That wasn't a route Rick wanted to go.

It was a strange situation. Here, at this most out-of-the-way military outpost, on this pier holding only an unmanned fuel barge, he was a virtual hostage to a bored guard and two equally bored sailors. Rick's frustration with the situation and desire to take action, *any action,* caused him to let caution take a back seat. He moved about three-quarters of the way down the southern side of the pier, away from the lights, looking for a way off the pier and around the men at the head of it.

Now he could hear the guard and the sailors talking.

"So you guys going out into town tonight? Still some fine ladies available. It's real early as far as that goes," said the guard with just a little bit of resignation in his voice. He'd be at his post for another five hours.

"Don't know, man. You know, still about half a week till payday. Not that I'm short or nothin', but it ain't as cheap as some of you all think," said the first sailor.

"He's right, ain't cheap. No way is these ladies cheap," said the other.

The guard pressed them. Hey, they could leave, he couldn't. "So what's the matter? You don't like the local ladies? Say, man, you prejudice or something—"

They all turned simultaneously. It wasn't a loud noise, but it was enough. It wasn't supposed to be there. Their eyes all seemed to find the spot at about the same time. Rick was clinging to the end of the barbed-wire fence separating the land at the end of the pier from the pier itself. Designed to make the piers secure from those who would try to get on them and perhaps onto a Navy ship, this fence was now keeping Rick on the pier. He froze, hoping he wasn't seen, but as the guard brought the beam of his flashlight around toward Rick, he knew he had been sighted. He tried hustling his way around the end of the fence but was moving slowly—too slowly.

One of the sailors blurted it out first. "Hey, stop, stop. Hey you, stop right there."

Rick kept working his way around the fence.

"Stop, stop," said the guard. He was out of his shack by now and starting to grope for his sidearm, a weapon he had once fired on the pistol range what seemed a long time ago. He started to move toward Rick, who was by now almost all the way around the fence.

"Hold it," said the second sailor, who, among the three of them, seemed the most animated and who actually started moving toward Rick. "Hold it, now. We just want to talk to you."

The guard joined him in closing on Rick, and then the other sailor followed suit, moving more cautiously than the first two.

Rick finally made it all the way around the fence and dropped down on the sand near the head of the pier. He looked at the approaching trio and tried to look like what he had just done was completely normal. The three men continued to creep toward him. Now just fifty feet away, he was sure they could make out his chief's uniform.

He'd bluff them. "Hey fellas, know that this looks a little funny. Tugmaster dropped me off, just trying to get to my plane at Howard. Going stateside on emergency leave, you know." He didn't sound convincing to himself. He hoped he had to them.

He hadn't. "Sure, there, well, okay Chief, let's just see some ID," said the guard. They continued slowly toward him.

Rick started to back away. "Well, hey, look now, if I don't get this plane, well, I'm not gonna make it—"

"He said let him see some ID," said one of the sailors, emboldened by Rick's excuses.

Rick was off like a shot. Putting his parachute bag under his right arm, he sprinted down the road leading from the piers. The three men froze for a moment, probably in total amazement that a Navy chief was running away from them. After a few seconds, though, they began to chase him.

The guard somehow felt that he needed to lead this group and continued to grope for his sidearm as he ran. He was not doing a very good job of either. The other two sailors followed close behind him. They might not be certain why they were doing this but seemed to be caught up in the action.

His fitness as a SEAL was paying off as Rick began to put some distance between himself and the lumbering sailors. These guys didn't have a chance. He was feeling more and more confident as his pursuers seemed to drop away. He was now in an easy stride, no longer straining, just moving.

Bam! At first Rick couldn't believe it, but it really was a shot! Startled, he dropped his parachute bag.

It must have shocked the two other sailors as well as the pier guard himself, because they all stopped dead in their tracks for a moment. In the perpetual fog that hung over the pier area, they made for a surreal tableau.

Holden spotted his parachute bag several feet behind

him where he had dropped it. He knew he could outdistance his frozen pursuers if he just left the parachute bag there, but he needed it—needed it now and surely would need it later. He made his decision in an instant.

As he moved to pick it up, the three sailors again began running toward him. One linehandler somehow gathered some inner strength and sprinted out in front of the other two men. He was just a few feet away when Rick finally straightened up from retrieving his parachute bag.

All instinct now. This guy was about to grab him and at least slow him down to let the other two catch up. Rick dropped his parachute bag, wheeled, and swung his fist into the man's jaw. The man went down like a rock, rolled, and just lay there, prone. Rick didn't think he had hit him that hard. Had he killed him? He couldn't stand here thinking about it. Rick picked up his parachute bag, turned, and ran as he never had before.

The other two men rushed up to the downed sailor, who was still motionless. Their zeal to pursue Rick diminished. They just shouted.

"Stop. Stop. . . ."

But Rick was now getting out of earshot. He was running as fast as he could, but where it would take him and how he would get there was still something he had to sort out.

CHAPTER 83

LAURA SAT ON THE EDGE OF HER BED IN HER SPARSE but comfortable BOQ room. So many days she had bounded out of this same bed eager to take on the world. But now, as she sat staring at the wall, she just wanted to melt into the bed, wanted to retreat from the world that had done this to her. She was innocent. And she had done her duty. To hold her prisoner, then, went against everything she had ever believed in.

Captain Dawson had explained it all to her on the way

over in the sedan. After, that is, the embarrassing pro-cessing at the police headquarters. Laura had gotten the strong impression that they were stalling there, but she was powerless to do anything about it. Having her sign in this log, then that one. Reinventorying her gear and per-sonal belongings. Taking her picture. Taking her finger-prints. Putting her name into God knows what kind of computer file. The captain had tried to be comforting on the ride over, but the more Captain Dawson talked, the more numb Laura became. She was beaten. It was all she could do to pour herself out of the sedan and, accompa-nied by the captain and a sentry, trudge up the single flight of stairs to her room.

Her home was no more than a cell now. Because she was an officer—and probably, she thought, because she was a woman—they had allowed her this form of house arrest rather than the indignities of a jail cell. Although there was no guard posted at her door, she knew the two men in the government sedan across the street would watch her night and day. A petty officer had arrived just an hour after she had been brought here with a small meal. She assumed that this would continue indefinitely.

She longed to talk to someone, anyone, but her phone had been removed and even her intercom with the BOQ front desk had been disabled. All she had were her books, a television, a small stereo, and her own thoughts. She was exhausted, but couldn't sleep. Her mind still raced with those agonizing questions: Why her? How had this happened? How could this tour of duty, which had started out with so much promise, go so wrong so fast? She couldn't stand to look out of her front window at the men in the car watching her. Her back window offered her the only acceptable view of the world. As she stared out this second-story vantage point, she longed for the freedom as she never had before.

At another end of this sprawling base, Rick Holden crouched in a small wooded area and evaluated his situ-ation. His years of work as a CIA professional and train-ing as a Navy SEAL coalesced now as he tried to plan his next move. The only two things he was sure of were that he wanted desperately to complete his mission and that he was worried about Laura Peters. In many ways it was duty that drove him. His duty to do the right thing. His duty to try to snatch some good out of what was a horrible situation. And his duty to Laura was growing as well.

Rick found her attractive and very appealing in a number of ways. But his primary thoughts about Laura revolved around insulating her from the fallout of Operation Roundup. He knew she was in a vulnerable position and sensed that she might be in more trouble than he knew of. He was determined to alert her to what he was doing—certainly to the fact that he had gone AWOL—and tell her what he had told General Lovelace. He owed her at least that much. He hoped it would be enough.

There was the issue of the men who had been chasing him. Rick knew it could go either way. On the one hand, they might just forget about the whole thing. After all, he was a Navy chief. He might have a reason for doing what he did. The senior man among them was only a third-class petty officer, certainly not senior enough to have much of a say in anything. And there was the quite embarrassing fact that the three of them had let him get away. Certainly it was something that could easily fall into the category of letting sleeping dogs lie. On the other hand, they might feel duty-bound to report the incident to the base military police. They might think this was all designed as part of one of the seemingly endless base security drills to see if they would report just such a thing. He just didn't know, and the fact that he was perplexed bothered him a great deal.

Rick decided to take the prudent course and plan for the worst-case scenario. He would keep a low profile about the base as he first found Laura and told her, then moved on; he wasn't sure where to, but that would come in due time. After walking awhile and getting his bearings, Rick thought he had come up with a good way of blending in. He noticed small groups of men, and a few women, walking toward a bank of phones at the exchange and seven-day store just a short distance north of the piers. These phones were one of the only places where sailors who were assigned to a ship here for a few days could make a call stateside. The Navy base commander had collocated the phones here at this small exchange complex so most of a sailor's basic needs could be met in one stop.

Rick came upon the bank of phones, carrying his parachute bag casually, trying to blend in and look like just another chief petty officer in transit to or from one of the ships in Rodman that evening. Fortunately for him, the count of ships was just right. Enough to make his presence seem completely normal, but not enough to jam the waiting lines for the phone booths beyond reason. Rick stood in line chatting amicably with two very young sailors who were clearly on their first-ever deployment. They had big hopes for tonight—but first they each had to call their girlfriends back in the States. Interesting view of the world, thought Rick.

Rick finally got his turn at the phone. He wanted to call Laura first. It was a weekday night, so she probably wouldn't be out. Rick had to get the base operator first, who then provided him with the number for the BOQ. The phone rang several times and then a sleepy-sounding voice offered, "BOQ front desk, Petty Officer Aguillar speaking."

"Yes, Petty Officer," said Rick, actually a bit startled by the petty officer's quick reply, "I need to contact Lieutenant Peters, Lieutenant Laura Peters, please."

"Do you know what room she is in, sir?"

Sir. Not bad. Play along with that. "No, I don't, sorry."

Resignedly, like a man being asked to support the weight of the world on his shoulders, Petty Officer Aguillar offered, "Yes sir. I can look it up in the computer. Just hold on. Please. I am checking people in and I am the only one here."

Rick waited. Finally the petty officer came back on the line. "Sir, there's a Lieutenant Peters staying here in Room 216 but she doesn't have a phone connection."

"No phone? Are you sure?"

"Oh, yes sir, quite sure," responded Aguillar, now sounding just a bit agitated that Rick didn't believe him.

Rick was baffled. "But doesn't everyone in the building have some sort of telephone?"

Aguillar was now clearly annoyed. "Yes, *sir,*" he said curtly, "but you see, I have in the passdown log that the phone for the lieutenant was disconnected just today. Therefore, she doesn't have a phone," Aguillar finished with a flourish. If it was in the passdown log, it must be gospel, was his implication.

"Thanks," said Rick, hanging up. Rick didn't need great instincts to sense that something was terribly wrong here. His next move had now become decidedly more difficult.

Although there was a line of impatient-looking sailors standing behind him waiting to use the phone, Rick knew he had to make one more phone call. He knew it would be the most important call he ever made. He would have to say just the right thing to convince them that this was a serious matter. Even then, they might not be able to help. He took out his calling card and dialed the number.

CHAPTER 84

"SHIT," SHOUTED SENATOR JAY LINDSEY AS HE STARED at the copy of the *Washington Post* on his large desk in the well-appointed Senate office building. "Shit." His chief of staff, Tom Watson, came in knowing why he was angry and, as an experienced Washington hand, also knowing what he had to do.

"Senator, you've seen Liz Kennedy's story, I see."

"Yes, goddammit, I've seen it. You know what that prick Campbell is trying to do, don't you? He's trying to force our hand, isn't he? He's goddamned trying to force our hand on this one before we're ready. Why can't he just let us run with it?" Lindsey was still shouting but not specifically at Watson or at anybody else. In the way of the Hill, he was just shouting.

What he was shouting at, of course, was Liz Kennedy's story this morning in which she was picking up the trail again on Operation Roundup. Filled with information—

undoubtedly supplied by General Campbell—on the failure of the operation and alluding to a Pentagon investigation, it was designed to accomplish a number of things. Most importantly to him, however, Campbell was using it to force him to rush ahead with his investigation before he was organized, rather than proceed at a reasoned pace with hearings by his Senate Intelligence Oversight Committee, hearings that he would control and string along for his own best political exposure. Now, if he didn't get the committee moving right away, he could lose his leverage and risk having his hearings get overtaken by events. His committee could even be marginalized altogether. Shit!

That Kennedy woman could write—she really laid it out. He knew exactly where she came up with such detailed information for her stories. And how she had gotten it. Although Lindsey didn't put it past the general to "capitulate" if she could serve him in turn.

He was finally broken out of his musings by his chief of staff. "Senator."

"What?"

"How do you want to proceed with this, Senator?"

"Tom, I want an all-staff meeting of the committee by ten this morning. Round up all the staffers, supplement them with some of our personal staff if you have to. We need to get rolling."

"Already in the works, sir," said the always-efficient Watson. "They'll have position papers prepared to brief you on the options." Watson allowed himself a slight smile. He felt he had things well in hand for his boss.

"I know what the goddamned options are, Tom. Anyone can see that," said Lindsey, now clearly on the verge of completely losing his temper. "We have to convene the committee immediately. We have to start hearings on Operation Roundup. I won't have us hung out as nonentities because we can't move fast enough to be major players in this. Get the press secretary in here now!"

Tom Watson exited quickly as Lindsey began to pace around his office.

*   *   *

Liz Kennedy was trying to stay ahead of the power curve too. Howard Campbell was feeding her more and more information and her story was on a fast boil. Her natural instincts as a reporter were taking over and she was anticipating where the story might go and what she might do with it. She thought she'd try fishing with some of her other sources. She pulled one number out of her Rolodex and dialed. She barely had finished asking for her room when she got an earful from Petty Officer Aguillar. Strange, thought Liz, very strange indeed. Time to seek out another source.

Whatever his other faults, Jay Lindsey was not afraid of hard work. As he sat at the long oak conference table in his well-appointed Senate office, Lindsey was more colleague than boss to both his press secretary, Jodie Colville, his chief of staff, Tom Watson, and a few other select personal and committee staffers mustered to begin to put together the all-important press plan.

It was straightforward enough, thought Lindsey, but detailed and worthy of their full attention. First, leaks to the press that his committee had already been caucusing in secret to review very sensitive Pentagon documents. Then a call for more empowerment for the committee. Then a call for formal hearings. Then those splendid days and perhaps weeks of his august self presiding in statesmanlike fashion over the committee—hearing evidence, dismissing those he no longer wanted to hear from, waxing wisely on the administration's foibles and on the military's lack of competence. Oh yes, it was going to be quite a ride.

It was approaching midnight when he and his exhausted staff finally got up from their task and got ready to leave, the leftovers from their Chinese takeout meals littering this once-tidy office. He had authorized a number of well-crafted leaks throughout the day that Jodie Bayliss had dutifully passed to their most favored journalists. But the pride of the evening's work stared back crisply from the computer monitor on his desk and was just now coming out of the laser printer on his bureau:

UNITED STATES SENATE—Senator Jay Lindsey, Chairman of the Senate Intelligence Oversight Committee, has called for immediate hearings on Operation Roundup. Calling the Administration's intelligence program "a deadly catastrophe of entrenched bureaucracies, non-secure communications, lackadaisical procedures and unacceptable performance," the Senator from South Dakota had set the processes in motion which will result in a timely and thorough review of the factors that led to this disaster, as well as the overall competency of the Administration to collect, analyze and utilize the intelligence necessary to support America's fighting men and women. While not wanting to compromise the procedures of the Committee, key Committee staffers have indicated that the Committee's investigation will be "extremely broad in scope, and will investigate the Administration's policies and procedures from top to bottom." The Senator himself will be chairing every hearing and will leave no stone unturned in preserving and protecting this country's intelligence capability.

Satisfied that he had more than adequately captured the moment, Senator Jay Lindsey, soon to be projected into tens of millions of homes across America, smiled as he handed the still-warm paper to Bayliss.

"Jodie, you know what to do."

"I do, Senator, I do."

CHAPTER 85

RICK LEFT THE PHONE BOOTH WITH A RENEWED SENSE of determination. Although his phone call with the Agency had, of necessity, been a bit elliptical, for the first time in a long time he felt he was not completely alone in his efforts. His contact would set the appropriate wheels in motion and he set up a near-term communications window with Rick. At this point, that was all he needed.

Rick was familiar with the general layout of the base, but wasn't exactly sure of the best way to get to the BOQ from where he was. Several blocks away he saw a crowd of sailors alighting from a white Navy bus and heading toward the pier area. From the looks of the group, they had just arrived from stateside—they were all in their white uniforms, carrying their seabags, and they looked awfully young. He needed to know where that bus came from. Rick approached them casually.

"You fellas look like you just had a long trip," said Rick.

"Sure have," said one of the sailors. He was the only petty officer in the group; the rest were seamen and looked even younger up close.

"What ship you boys headed to?"

"USS *Reid,* Chief," said one of the younger sailors with a genuine sense of excitement in his voice. "She's outta San Diego, down here on counterdrug ops. We just got on the bus at Howard. Said she's supposed to be right here at pier two."

"They told you right, son. Hope you like tin cans that rock and roll. She's no deep draft, that's for sure. Think you'll find her on the pier waiting for you. Say, that broken-down-looking bus zip you out here directly from Howard?"

"You kiddin', Chief?" said the petty officer. "This junker is definitely a local. We were the only passengers but the old-timer driving this hulk stopped every two blocks once he got on the base here. Must be getting paid by the hour."

"Yeah, he drives like my gramma," chimed in one of the other sailors, sparking a nodding of heads by the others and a chuckle or two.

"Know what you mean, fellas. Been there myself plenty of times," said Rick sagely. He hadn't intended to get caught up in this light banter with these sailors, but Rick almost relished the conversation. He hadn't had a normal conversation with another person since he encountered Chief Hudson in the berthing compartment back aboard *Coronado.*

"Say," said Rick, "did you remember if the bus went by the BOQ, up at the other end of the base?"

"I've got no clue, Chief. Never been here before. All I can tell you is that it made plenty of stops. Except for two old gals—probably ladies that worked cleaning up something or other, from the looks of them—nobody but us got on or off the bus the whole time," said the petty officer, accompanied by more head-nodding by the others.

"Well, thanks," said Rick. "Guess I can just hop on and see what happens."

"I guess so, Chief," said another of the sailors. "We better get to our boat, get checked in, and pull some liberty. Where's the best place to go for a little action on this base, Chief?"

"Yacht Club's for you," replied Rick with a wave and a smile, but he was already striding purposely toward the bus stop.

After what seemed like an interminable wait for the bus, and after dealing with the clearly noncommunicative Panamanian driver, Rick finally alighted a block from the BOQ complex. As the bus sped away, sputtering and coughing and spewing fumes as only these relics that the military couldn't stand to get rid of could, Rick assessed his situation. It was almost midnight. Laura might be asleep. He didn't want to wake her up, but he had to tell her, and this phone business was beginning to worry him more and more. How could he let her know what was going on without alarming her too much? It was not a task he felt well prepared for.

Rick hadn't had much luck earlier talking on the telephone with the officious Petty Officer Aguillar. He decided it would be best to go in person. He walked into the front lobby of the BOQ, and to his delight, found not Petty Officer Aguillar, but another petty officer manning the front desk, Petty Officer Mary Osborne.

Osborne was absorbed in a magazine, trying to while away the hours on this boring watch, and did not notice Rick immediately.

"Good evening," said Rick, hoping that this person might be more cooperative.

"Oh, hello, Chief," said Osborne, shuffling a bit to try to look like she was really paying attention to her job. "What can I do for you?"

Rick was on unfamiliar ground; he knew he had to be cautious. "Well, Petty Officer Osborne, I needed to come by here to deliver something to one of my officers. Believe that she is staying here in your BOQ. Lieutenant Peters's her name."

Osborne wanted to be accommodating but thought that this was a little odd, a full chief acting as a delivery boy. "Is the lieutenant expecting you, Chief?" she said.

"No, I don't think so," replied Rick.

"Well, did you call first? Does she know you're coming?" asked Osborne.

This wasn't going well at all, thought Rick. He needed to get to Laura and his patience was really being stretched. "No, I don't think so. Just need to make a quick drop-off and then get back to my duty at the headquarters." Rick was specifically vague as to what headquarters he was referring to.

"Do you want to just leave it with me?" offered the petty officer, trying to be helpful but becoming more puzzled.

"No, sorry there, Miss Osborne, can't do that. Classified material and all that, you know."

"Well, all right, then," replied Osborne, "I think you should have called an officer first before you came up, but I'll just buzz the lieutenant on the intercom. What did you say the lieutenant's name is?"

"Peters, Lieutenant Laura Peters. I believe she's in Room 216."

Osborne looked surprised that a chief would actually know what room an officer lived in, and dutifully checked her roster. "Oh yes, here it is, Chief. You're right, 216. Here, if you're sure that it's important I'll buzz her room. Oh wait, wait." Osborne sounded alarmed. "Chief." Her voice grew much softer. "There's a big problem here. . . ."

"Problem?" asked Rick.

"Yes," said Osborne, leaning closer to Rick. "Says here in the log that her intercom has been disconnected . . .

along with her phone. No wonder you couldn't call her!" She sounded surprised that this could happen.

Damn logbook, thought Rick. He tried to make the best of it. "Well, looks like I may just have to go up to her room and deliver it," he said.

Osborne leaned much closer to Rick and whispered in a conspiratorial tone, "Not unless you want to be noticed by them." She jerked her head ever so slightly toward the Navy sedan parked discreetly—as discreetly as you can make a Navy sedan look—across the street from the BOQ. "The name didn't hit me at first, but when I looked at the log it all came back. Word around here . . ." she said, leaning even closer, "word is that the lieutenant is under some kind of house arrest. Only person going to and from the room, they tell me, is someone bringing food. Those guys out there in the car look like some kind of cops and they sure have been watching the place continuously. Kind of gives me the creeps." Osborne backed away from Rick and raised her eyebrows knowingly. She tried to look busy and normal so as not to draw attention to herself. They might be watching her too.

Rick was upset with himself. How had he not noticed the now-obvious sedan and the two very NIS-looking agents in the front seat? He couldn't afford to make mistakes like that. He glanced at the car again. So Laura was being watched, and there was no way he could knock on her door without being seen by them. He needed to regroup, but first he needed to disengage from Petty Officer Osborne.

"Well, Miss Osborne, doesn't look like anyone wants to have us mere mortals communicating with the lieutenant. House arrest. Sounds kind of funny, don't you think?" said Rick, hoping for more information.

Osborne didn't disappoint him. Clearly, she was not above snooping around a little bit. "Don't know all the details myself, Chief. But, you know, some male officer got shot on the base yesterday. Killed. Some folks around here think the lieutenant there"—she jerked her head in the direction of Laura's room—"is the one who did it. Some talk that they were *doing it*." Osborne actually winked at Rick, then feigned shock. Clearly she was relishing passing along the gossip. It validated that she knew more than anyone else.

Here was a complication Rick never could have anticipated. It was almost too much for him to absorb.

"Thanks, Miss Osborne," said Rick with a wink back. No telling when he would need her help again and charming her a little couldn't hurt. "I guess I won't complete my mission. I'll go on back to headquarters and tell 'em to come up with another plan."

"Good luck, Chief," said the still-smiling Osborne.

"Thanks," said Rick. He strode purposefully out of the lobby and moved in a direction away from the ominous sedan. But he didn't go far.

CHAPTER 86

TAYLOR CALHOUN BELIEVED HE WAS A PATIENT MAN, but as usual the act of waiting was driving him crazy. None of his advisors had been able to tell him anything concrete. Elliot Higginson *thought* there was an officer at SouthCom who was passing sensitive information to the Maradona cartel. Ray Weaver *thought* he had a lead on why Senator Jay Lindsey was pushing so hard with his Senate Intelligence Oversight Committee. Other advisors *thought* this and *thought* that, but Weaver didn't feel like he was getting the straight word from anyone. He was more than annoyed. He was angry and getting worse.

What bothered Calhoun most was that he couldn't focus on who the enemy really was, let alone what wolf was closest to the sled. He had read the press release that Senator Lindsey's office had put out, and that was certainly cause for alarm. But he had also had this issue of a possible "officer spy" dropped on him. It wasn't making sense.

The insistent buzz of the intercom broke him from his thoughts. "Mr. President, the chief of staff to see you, sir," Debbie Van Pelt said.

"Send him in," replied Calhoun. He welcomed the break. Damn, I'm depressing myself just sitting here, he thought.

"Hello, Mr. President," said Carter Thomas as he entered the room. The chief of staff looked serious but buoyant. Calhoun hoped he was bringing good news—but at this stage of confusion he would settle for literally any news.

"Hello, Carter," said Calhoun. "How's the weather?"

"Perhaps a small break in the clouds, Mr. President. Nothing brand-new, but some useful clarification." Thomas sounded upbeat. "I should tell you first of all, Mr. President, that Elliot Higginson has really taken control over at the Pentagon. He fully recognized your dissatisfaction with our uniformed leaders and therefore he has taken charge of communicating directly with you on these delicate matters."

"Fine, that's good," replied the President. Taylor Calhoun was less sanguine about this fact than was Carter Thomas. His long association with the military made him painfully aware of the fact that—no matter how smart and sound a Secretary of Defense might be—he could never totally crack whatever ways of doing business the military's senior officers cared to pick. It was definitely an insider's game. The only control he, or Congress, for that matter, had, was the power of the purse. Take away their precious appropriations and you might make them humble. But once things got into the operational realm, they wanted to remain a law unto themselves. That was abundantly clear.

"Mr. President, Elliot reports that there has been an officer murdered at SouthCom, a Lieutenant Commander Andrew Wilson, and that another officer, a female intelligence officer, a Lieutenant Laura Peters, is under house arrest and is implicated in his murder—"

Calhoun interrupted. "That's all very well, Carter, but what does that have to do with Operation Roundup, with the questions Senator Lindsey's committee is asking, with anything?"

"Mr. President. It seems that this Lieutenant Peters had access to some very sensitive information about Op-

eration Roundup at SouthCom headquarters and that she
provided it to Wilson—who was married but having an
affair with her—who sold it to agents for the Maradona
cartel—"

"What the hell is this all about? This sort of stuff
doesn't happen. There's no Cold War. Why would anyone
do this sort of thing?"

"Mr. President, the plot thickens, as they say. Seems
that this Wilson fellow had some pretty heavy gambling
debts and was behind, way behind, in paying them off.
We . . . I mean Elliott, doesn't have all the details yet, but
it sounds pretty plausible, under the circumstances." Carter Thomas clearly believed this story and was doing his
best to sell it, so he related it to the President just as Elliot
Higginson had related it to him, just as he had heard it
from General Campbell.

The chairman hadn't provided Higginson quite the level
of detail that he had provided to Liz Kennedy. No, he
wanted to dole it out, telling who he wanted to hear it,
exactly what he wanted them to hear, exactly when he
wanted them to hear it. Elliott Higginson had bought this
sop hook, line, and sinker. Campbell was sure he would
feed it to the President. He was not disappointed.

CHAPTER 87

RICK CROUCHED IN THE BUSHES IN THE BACK OF THE
BOQ, biding his time and getting ready to execute his
plan to rescue Laura Peters. From the moment he left the
BOQ lobby after his revealing conversation with Petty Officer Osborne, he knew Laura was in danger if she remained in the BOQ and within reach of those at
SouthCom who had put her there. It never occurred to
him to ponder whether she wanted to be rescued—but
with every fiber of his being he knew she needed to get
out of there.

He had been keeping an eye on the Q for over an hour

now, waiting for most of the lights in the rooms near Laura's to go out. He had decided that shimmying up the wall of the building to Laura's window on the back side of the BOQ was the only way to reach her while avoiding the scrutiny of those in the sedan out front. One by one, the lights in the adjacent and nearby rooms went out— but so did Laura's. He would have to wake her and that would complicate things.

It was just after one A.M. when the last light that Rick was concerned with went out. He waited about ten minutes for that room's occupant to lapse into sleep—a comfortable time, he thought—and then he began to make his move. Slipping quietly up to the base of the building, he left his parachute bag right next to it and then quickly worked his way up the wall, the large, dissimilar bricks providing near-perfect hand and foot holds. In short order he was perched right outside of Laura's window, clinging to the window frame to keep his balance.

Suddenly Rick was beset by doubt. What had seemed moments ago to be a straightforward, important thing to do now began to consume him with doubt. What was he doing? Who had asked him to be her protector? He was in enough trouble as it was. He knew he had a greater goal to inform the proper people about what had really happened in Operation Roundup. Would he derail that mission by his too-eager attempts to help Laura? And what would this young, very professional officer think of a Navy chief trying to direct her to do something totally out of character with her entire professional life?

Then there were his feelings for Laura. Rick had never really forced himself to focus them before now. In a way the two of them had a lot of history, going back to UVA days. Certainly he found her attractive, even beautiful. It was almost impossible not to be attracted to her. But Rick had never thought of her in that way. He wasn't prudish, and he certainly wasn't celibate. But Rick had always put women like Laura on a pedestal. They were the kind— his mother had always said—that you wanted to marry someday. But someday always seemed very far away.

Then Rick decided the issues simply: He disregarded

them. Hanging on to the side of a building, totally exposed, was not the time for mind games.

He drew a deep breath and then rapped on Laura's window.

No response.

He rapped again, harder now.

Still no response.

Rick tapped on the window still harder, three firm taps. Damn building. Damn Panama heat. Place was obviously air-conditioned and the windows were shut to keep the sticky night air out. Maybe this last rapping would rouse her.

He waited . . . no response.

Rick was struggling to keep his balance now. It took some effort to hold himself there and that effort was having a cumulative effect, weakening him. He knew he couldn't stay up on this ledge indefinitely. Convinced that Laura must be a heavy sleeper and that the constant, low-pitched drone of the building's air conditioners were probably drowning out his tapping, Rick seized on another idea, the often overlooked obvious. Gingerly putting his full hand on the window to her room, he pushed up on it.

It moved. Slowly, gingerly, Rick moved the window up bit by bit until it was up all the way. He called once, "Laura," then again, a bit louder: "Laura . . . Laura." But he was really worried that he'd be heard by someone else. Finally, not so much making a decision as going with the only option that seemed to remain, he quietly slipped into her room. There she was in her bed, curled up with the covers pulled around her. Everything in her room seemed in place and squared away, but she looked to Rick innocent, feminine, vulnerable. He knew he had to wake her, but if she screamed the watchers in the front of the BOQ, just outside her window, might hear her. That would be the worst possible thing.

Rick slipped over to her bed and cupped his hand over her mouth. She awoke instantly. She stared, wild-eyed, trying instinctively to move, but Rick held her down with the weight of his muscular arm, while with his other hand he put his forefinger on his mouth, signaling her to be silent. Her eyes told him she recognized him and that she understood. He removed his hand and backed away, ready to receive what he knew would be a barrage of questions.

"*Rick!* Are you crazy? What are you doing here? How did you get in here? You scared the hell out of me! What—" Laura had a wild stare as she tried to make some sense out of this sudden appearance by someone she thought she'd never see again.

"Shhh, Laura, shhh. I'll explain everything if you give me a minute. Just be quiet, that's all," said Rick.

· "Rick, I don't know how you got here from *Coronado,* and I don't really care, but it has been one hell of a few days. Sit down, there in that chair," she said as she pulled a light bathrobe around her. With that, they each poured out all that had passed and all they had learned since they'd last spoken. They talked almost nonstop for a half hour.

Rick was flabbergasted by her story. He didn't know what to say, but he was now certain what to do. "Laura, we've got to get you out of here. We've got to get you out of here now."

"Rick, I can't just run away. Then they'd be certain I was guilty. I'd prove their case for them."

"Laura, you have to, don't you see? This is all a frame-up against you. It doesn't matter how you *look.* The point is that *nothing* you do can convince them you're innocent."

"But I've never run away from anything."

"I know that, but you've never been up against forces like this. You're really standing between them and their own self-preservation. There's no way they could take the pressure off you even if they wanted to."

"Rick, if we . . . I mean, if I ran . . . where would I go? I can't exactly run to the other end of the base and wait for things to blow over."

"No, and you were right the first time . . . where would *we* go? We need to get off this base first, then eventually out of Panama, then back to the United States. Somehow we've got to expose what they're doing. That's the only way we can clear ourselves."

"Rick, you keep saying *we,* and I dearly appreciate it, but this is my mess—"

He cut her off. "It's our mess, Laura. I think I may have some proof as to why Operation Roundup went bad and as to who was involved—if I can just get it to the right people. I've also got some contacts that are . . . are . . . let's just say outside of military channels. But we can talk about that later. Are we moving?" Rick said the last few words cheerfully and with a big smile on his face, trying to goad Laura into trusting him and trusting his plan.

"Okay, Rick, I'm really, really, worried about this, but I agree. We've got to get away. Let me throw a few things together, okay?" Laura sounded more resigned than anything else, but Rick wasn't worried about her state of mind right now. He just wanted them to move.

"I've probably got to get out of this uniform. It looks a little conspicuous. Can I duck into your head here and change?"

"Sure, Rick," said Laura. She allowed herself a small smile. Here was a man who was putting himself on the line for her, yet he was still modest enough to not want to change clothes in front of her.

She forced those thoughts from her mind and, while Rick changed, put together a small bag with just a few necessary items. She had never imagined she would have only a few minutes to gather her life's possessions.

Rick emerged from the head, changed out. Laura was still fussing with her things, picking up an item, then rejecting it. Putting another into her duffel bag. He wanted to hurry her but didn't—didn't want to make this any more painful than it already was. Finally, she put the last item in her bag and closed it up. She was as ready as she could be.

Laura stood in the middle of her room with a duffel bag slung over her shoulder. She tried to look brave—tried to look resolved—but just looked scared. Rick didn't think, but did what his instincts told him he needed to do. He walked across the room and embraced her.

Laura melted. Her arms wrapped around his neck and her body went limp. First she sobbed, just muffled, deep sobs, but then they grew in intensity until she was bawling uncontrollably. Rick just held on to her and let her cry, cry unashamedly, until there were no more tears, holding her tighter and tighter, feeling more responsible for one human being than he ever had in his life. Finally she stopped and backed away.

"Well so much for being professional," sniffed Laura, her eyes red and face puffy. "I must be quite a sight. Don't run away."

"Never," whispered Rick, knowing he meant that with intense conviction. "Now let's go." He was welling up himself and he knew that if they didn't start moving right away he would be in the same state as Laura.

"Okay, Laura, I'll go out the window first. The bricks are pretty easy to climb down. Just take it slow and easy. I'll be there to support you if you slip."

"All right, Rick, I'm ready."

With that, Rick took Laura's bag and dropped it carefully out the window and onto the ground below. Then he clambered out the window, moving slowly enough for Laura to see exactly how he was doing it. She followed quickly and within moments they were standing on the ground. They both froze and listened, wanting to be sure the two agents in front of the BOQ had not heard them. There was no other sound.

"What now?" whispered Laura.

"We're going to move around the back of the Q and up this road. Gate's not far off."

"What then, Rick?"

"Just gonna take it a step at a time, Laura," replied Rick, trying to sound reassuring, but recognizing that their plan was not exactly well evolved.

They moved quickly away from the BOQ, out of sight of the agents and the sedan, and along a path through the greenbelt behind the BOQ, paralleling the road that led to the gate at that end of the base. Rick was coming up with a plan while they walked.

"Okay, Laura," he said, "when we get to the gate here's the way I think we should play it. I'll show 'em my ID card. No one should be looking for me in particular, at least I hope not. If they ask, I'll tell them you're my girlfriend from back home, you came down here and we spent some time together, and now I'm taking you back to the airport to fly back to the States. They're usually real reluctant to hassle civilians. Civilians are more likely to drop a dime on 'em for being rude or something than those of us in uniform."

"I think I can run with that."

"If they ask you questions you'll have to really hide the fact that you're in the military or they will think you're running from something. They may have discovered you are missing already. Don't use any military jargon. Look at the gate guards with a little bit of disdain—"

She cut him off. "Okay, okay, I got it." Laura didn't mind Rick leading on this, but he was being almost patronizing now. "I'll follow your lead, but don't worry, I can handle myself."

They caught sight of the gate at the end of the road and slowed down to a more leisurely pace. Laura was carrying her bag, but Rick reached over and took it and slung both it and his parachute bag over his right shoulder while he took Laura's hand with his left and walked along with her. As they got closer to the gate they popped out on the road and walked leisurely toward the gate guards.

The two gate guards, who were far more focused on vehicles and people coming into the base, looked at Rick and Laura with studied indifference. As Rick and Laura got closer to them and moved toward the pedestrian walkway, the guards looked directly at Laura but did not move to challenge them. The longer they looked, the more nervous Rick got. He decided that winging it would be the best approach.

"Morning, fellas, got to put my lady on the big bird back to the States. Got a general's sedan handy or do we have to jump into one of these third world taxis?" said Rick with an impish grin that suggested to the guards that they'd been shacked up for a long enough time to keep Rick happy.

Still frozen in place, one of the guards, smiling, responded, motioning to the ever-present taxis waiting just outside the gate, "Gee, we must have misplaced the general's car, buddy. You're on your own with those kamikazes."

"Thanks anyway," replied Rick, turning loose of Laura's hand long enough to give them a friendly wave, and then moving on to the first cab in the queue.

The second guard gave a friendly wave with one hand as he slapped at mosquitoes with the other. This pair was the least of their worries. In a few more hours they would be off duty for two days. Both had plans for some R&R. They were outta here.

Rick walked up to the cab on the driver's side and gently shook the sleeping cab driver.

"Good evening, señor," said the cab driver, a little bit surprised at the sight of a man and a woman together. His normal fares were just men going out on the town. "Where can I take you and the señorita?"

"Panama City."

CHAPTER 88

SENATOR JAY LINDSEY HAD SET THE WHEELS IN MOTION for the deliberations of the Senate Intelligence Oversight Committee and now he had the pleasure of sitting back and watching his staffers—all hand-picked from the best, brightest, and most aggressive, and molded in his own image—formalize the process of holding hearings and preparing for the work of the committee.

The senator had continued his planned releases—as well as the inevitable inside-the-beltway leaks to the press—regarding the venue for the proceedings of his committee. The process by which he would sustain the visibility of these hearings read like a battle plan for an invading army—staffers assigned to take care of formal press releases, other staffers assigned "ghost" leaks to favored journalists, still others set to talk to retired military officers who would testify as to how deficient the military's intelligence apparatus was, some who would gather information from contractors who had this black box or this whiz-bang gizmo which was better, cheaper, smarter,

faster than whatever the military was using today. He
saved his top, most experienced staffers for direct but discreet liaison between General Campbell and himself so he
could be absolutely conversant on the specific issues that
had brought about the failure of Operation Roundup.
Lindsey had already assured himself a long run on the
major network news shows as he got to the bottom of this
maze in his most statesmanlike manner.

Howard Campbell was always in control. He had built
his four-decade career on being in control. But the erup-
tion from inside his office was staggering. Both his executive assistant and his aide actually cringed as they heard
the stream of expletives that permeated even the heavy
oak door that led to his inner office.

"Charlie, now tell me again, from the beginning, just
how the hell you let your prime suspect in this case escape. This is so unbelievable, I want to hear each and
every word!"

On the phone Walters had just finished telling him that
Lieutenant Laura Peters was no longer in her BOQ room
under house arrest. Everything had seemed normal until
0700 that morning when the corporal bringing her breakfast had not heard her respond to his knock on the door.
He had quickly summoned the agents in the sedan, who
had opened the door to find her missing. The word was
passed quickly to General Walters, who had called General Campbell immediately.

Campbell had never emphasized his seniority to Walters as much as he was emphasizing it now. But Walters
had thought this through and, determined to make the
best out of a bad situation, had patiently endured the be-
rating Campbell was handing out until the chairman had
finally finished his multiple tirades. Finally Walters
spoke—calmly, reassuringly, with strength and conviction.

"Mr. Chairman," he began, "we may be able to turn
this event to our advantage." Walters was in this all the
way. The only real vulnerability he felt was, of course, the
unfortunate little incident with Lieutenant Commander
Andy Wilson. He had managed to deflect that to Laura
Peters, but he was concerned with his ability to perma-

nently make her the scapegoat. Now, the fact that she had escaped from house arrest made her look totally guilty. Why had she run? he wondered. She probably panicked, he thought—women; didn't really have a place in the military, except for his convenience. This just confirmed his worst prejudices. Now he was home free. He could feed her to the chairman.

"How's that?" grumbled Campbell.

"Mr. Chairman, don't you see? I let events here run and they tended to implicate Lieutenant Peters in the failure of Operation Roundup. No really hard evidence, just circumstantial up to now. However, add to that circumstantial evidence the fact that she's now fled and, don't you see, the case becomes almost compelling. We can point to her as the source for all the leaks and for everything else. You might even feed this to the White House to get them off our backs," said Walters, clearly pleased with himself that he had such a tightly wound plan.

"I'm beginning to see your point, Charlie. That may work. Of course, now you've got to catch her. Have you got your people looking yet?"

"There's really no place to go, Mr. Chairman, no place to run and hide. I'm certain she's hunkered down on the base somewhere. When she gets cold, tired, and hungry enough she'll turn herself in."

"Fine, but I want you to look and look hard anyway, hear?"

"Of course, Mr. Chairman."

"And Charlie, there's also the matter of Lovelace. I know he's contacted the White House at least once. What are you doing to take him out of the picture? He could be more than an inconvenience, you know that."

"Mr. Chairman, I've already anticipated that problem. I know we need to keep him off the nets, especially with his penchant for going directly to the White House with his story. I've just put *Coronado* into total EMCON and sent them south on a 'secret' mission. We've actually done this kind of thing before, send the JTF Eight flagship to a predetermined spot to try to intercept a seaborne drug shipment, so you can run with that cover story inside the beltway. I'll keep it real down here. Absolutely nothing is going on, but they'll be out of the picture for almost a week—surely enough time for us to have things solidified the way we want to. I figured that it was just a prudent precaution."

"Well, Charlie, I'm glad you've taken care of that," said Campbell in a more conciliatory tone. "I was getting blindsided by the calls Lovelace was making to the White House. We needed to put a stop to that. You say we won't hear anything at all from them for a week."

"That's right, Mr. Chairman, no one will."

"Perfect, Charlie, just perfect."

CHAPTER 89

RICK AND LAURA SAT IN THE VINTAGE TAXICAB AS they pounded along the Interamerican Highway toward Panama City. This was the second time they had been in a taxi together—what incredibly different circumstances accompanied the two rides. Rick stole a glance at Laura, who was staring straight ahead. Clearly the events of the last several days—and especially the past few hours—had shaken her, and shaken her badly. He wanted to say so many things to her, but he perceived, correctly, that she just needed some time for what was happening to sink in.

As the cab careened down the highway, blithely passing every other vehicle it could, he reviewed his plan. First and foremost, they had to get out of Panama. Those who had set up Laura and put her under house arrest would not—could not—stop at anything to track her down.

Rick leaned forward to instruct the taxi driver. "We're going to the Westin. You can find it, right?"

"Of course, señor, I know how to get there, very quickly too. I will not delay you and the señorita," replied the driver in near-perfect English. Panama had had an American presence for over a century and English was very much part of the language of commerce here.

"No need to hurry. Just get us there safely."

"Of course, señor, of course."

That settled, Rick leaned back and relaxed. Laura still sat up, staring straight ahead, looking almost brittle. He knew he needed to help her deal with this. Instinctively, he put his arm around her shoulder and pulled her gently and ever so slightly toward him. She responded with relief, gradually slumping onto his shoulder and letting much of the stress drain out of her body. Rick was poised to say something comforting, but within a minute she was asleep, gently breathing, protected by his arms.

The cab driver stole a glance in his rearview mirror. He was worldlywise enough to know that here were two lovers that he was taking to their destination. It made him feel good.

At his headquarters at Quarry Heights, General Charlie Walters *did not* feel good. Yes, he had not lied to Howard Campbell, and the chairman would be able to turn the fact that Laura Peters had escaped to *his* advantage. This would allow him to deflect much of the heat regarding Operation Roundup away from the Pentagon, keeping most of it on the President and off the chairman, yet offering a plausible explanation as to why things had gone wrong. But now that Laura Peters was on the loose, who might she call? he thought. Look at who she had called already. For a while he considered having all of the phones to and from the base disconnected but thought better of it—might be perceived as being too panicky. No, just go out and find her. That was his first order of business. Maybe he would have to interrogate her personally. That would be interesting. It might make her wish she had been a bit more accommodating with him. It might not be too late.

For now, though, he had to focus. Direct his command to find her. Although he had the entire Southern Command at his disposal, he tasked only his military police unit, supplemented by NIS and some other special agents, to comb this expansive base to look for her. Realizing that she might have slipped off base, he also used his well-established connections with the Panama police and paramilitary groups to be on the lookout for her. He set the wheels in motion and then sat back, anticipating that it wouldn't be much of a challenge to track down one very scared young woman.

CHAPTER 90

HOWARD CAMPBELL HAD DUCKED THREE CALLS FROM Liz Kennedy in less than eight hours and he knew his string was about to run out. He knew why Liz was calling, but he also knew he did not want to talk with her, at least not yet. He hadn't decided whether he really wanted to use the information he had, especially the pictures in the thick manila envelope that had arrived by special military courier from General Charlie Walters at SouthCom. His aides had told him that the courier had been put in the back seat of a military fighter and had flown directly from Howard Air Force Base to Washington, refueling in flight to make the long trip. He might feed this to Liz—but he might wait too.

The chairman was also wrestling with the dilemma of how to exterminate the bugs in his plan, and his thoughts now returned to Laura Peters. What Charlie Walters told him about her had begun to make more sense. The story had plausibility: naive young female officer (they were all naive, weren't they?); powerful, older male naval officer; gambling debts; chance to make "easy" money without hurting anyone; plenty of cash that the cartel had to splash around—it all could be made to make sense. Yes, Lieutenant Laura Peters would be a good one to take the fall for this operation.

But there was still one huge loose end that troubled him deeply. Lovelace. He knew Lovelace had communicated with the President and knew absolutely where his loyalties were. Charlie had done the right thing and put him on ice for a while with this bogus mission and the radio silence, but in time he would return and then it was only a matter of time before he challenged their story and did it with authority. The chairman had to destroy his credibility too and he had to do it quickly. Now Charlie had provided him the means to do it, he thought, tapping the manila envelope, and to do that he would have to pull Lieutenant Laura Peters even further into the abyss.

Liz Kennedy did not hide her annoyance when Howard Campbell finally took her call. That fact that she was almost entirely at his mercy with respect to feeding her story on Operation Roundup was beginning to trouble her greatly. She would have liked to have more sources, someone else she could turn to for additional or alternate views of what was going on—even if Howard was already as highly placed as they come. She was also beginning to worry if her charms were still having an effect on him.

"Hello, Liz, nice of you to call. How are you, dear?" said Campbell in his most conciliatory tone.

"Fine," said Liz, with enough of an edge to let him know it wasn't exactly fine, but not too much to really make him mad. Whatever her relationship with him now— or whatever it might be in the future—as a reporter, Liz was totally motivated not to lose a source, particularly one as well placed as Howard Campbell.

"I really need to talk with you about this Operation Roundup story," Liz continued. "What you have given me has been great, but I think it's played out. Now that Senator Lindsey has started his hearings, I'm almost obliged to use what he and the committee are doing as my lead. I think our readers are getting tired of the issue. I'm having to promise more and more just to get my editor to keep the story alive. I think the whole story will just have to go underground until the committee hearings actually begin. I know that from your perspective it's a big deal, but it's just not that newsy anymore, Howard."

Campbell picked up on the opportunity. "You're right, the attention span of the American public and all that. Now that all of the 'official' stuff is running, perhaps they're looking to be titillated a bit, wouldn't you say?"

"Absolutely!" she answered, happy he was understanding her point of view. "Not all of our readers are political science majors. We would never say we compete with the tabloids, but you know the real answer, I'm sure."

"Indeed I do," he replied. "Your timing is perfect, because this case is bringing up some interesting things. As a matter of fact, I've just come into possession of some photos I think you'll find very interesting—and that will probably be a big hit with your readers."

"That may be just what the doctor ordered, Howard. Thanks."

"You're welcome, dear. I'll have them couriered right over. We do need to get together soon, you know."

"We will, Howard, we will."

His plan set in motion, Howard Campbell slid back into the manila envelope the photos of General Ashley Lovelace and Lieutenant Laura Peters walking out of the BOQ, smiling and laughing. Sergeant Brooke had done exceptionally good work. He scribbled a short note to Liz providing some details of the photos, then pushed the intercom.

CHAPTER 91

RICK AND LAURA ALIGHTED FROM THE CAB IN FRONT of the Panama City Westin, arguably the finest hotel in this city. Located directly across from the massive Panama City Convention and Cultural Center, the fifteen-story hotel was an imposing addition to the city skyline. Rick tipped the driver generously. He had kept his promise of getting them there quickly and Rick wanted to buy some insurance. "And señor," Rick said as he pressed a large bill into the driver's hand, "you understand that you have never seen us, understood?"

"Oh yes, señor," said the surprised but pleased driver. "You are like ghosts to me, and you should know, I do not believe in ghosts."

As the taxi rolled several yards away to pick up a fare that had just come out of the Westin, Rick took Laura's arm and walked into the lobby. Passing through those thick glass doors, he found it difficult to remember that he was in sticky, sweltering Panama and not in some American city. We do our damnedest to make every place we can look exactly like America, he mused.

Laura seemed to perk up a bit as they entered the bright, airy lobby. She had slept for the majority of the cab ride, stirring only when the driver hit a particularly bad pothole or other road hazard. She looked directly at Rick and said, "I feel free. For the first time in days, I feel free."

"I'm afraid we may be a long way from being free Laura. That's why I thought we'd come here, to try to get our bearings, to plan our next move," said Rick as reassuringly as possible, although he was still unclear as to what their available options were.

"Rick, I'm still not sure I did the right thing by running away, or that you are doing the right thing getting tangled up with me. There's got to be some justice. Sooner or later they'll discover that this is all a mistake."

"Laura, there *is* no justice. You might take the fall for this, and running's not going to get you in any worse trouble. As for me, I've made my own problems. I chose to leave *Coronado*. They have every right to come after me, once they discover that I'm missing. I hope that won't happen right away. The only chance we have is to get back to the United States and blow the cover off what's happened to Operation Roundup. That's the only way we can clear ourselves and stop whatever else these scum have planned. Any people who could have consigned over a hundred brave young men to their deaths are capable of anything, don't you see?"

"I'm not sure what I think," said Laura. "But I am glad I'm with you. I'm not afraid anymore."

Rick was glad for that. In some ways he and Laura were so alike, but in others they were so different. Although they both had similar upbringings, strong middle-class parents, good Christian values, and jobs with the "establishment," early in their professional lives they had diverged. Laura still firmly believed in playing by the rules, staying within the system, doing as she was told, and trying to make as few waves as possible. It had nothing to do with being a woman; she just had a strong and abiding faith in doing what the system—what the military, what the Navy—wanted her to do, and doing it cheerfully. It made coming to grips with the fact that senior officers in the military might be conspiring against their government and were not above using her as a foil so hard to comprehend.

Rick, on the other hand, had moved away from that, moved to a willingness to go against the grain. He was comfortable with operating independently without waiting for approval, comfortable going with his instincts and not just with the "party line." He knew where the change had come. Operating in Eastern Europe for the Agency, he had seen cross and double-cross, seen men and women sent on missions without a clear picture of their senior's real agenda. He himself had sometimes felt vulnerable and exposed and unconvinced that, in spite of their assurances that they would not let anything go awry, they were willing, or sometimes even able, to go the extra mile to ensure the safety of their own people. Sure, they had rescued him when his last operation had gone terribly wrong, but he thought this was more designed to protect the Agency than to extricate him. He might never know the truth, but those experiences gave him enough of a hard edge to go his own route when it became necessary, the rules be damned.

Fortunately, in a way, their current plight was reducing some of the natural tension surrounding their very dissimilar views of the world. They had both run away, and although Laura's pursuers currently seemed to have the most compelling need to find her, he didn't think it would be too long before he became just as hunted. There was only one thing to do in what may be their last stationary moment for a while.

"Laura, let's eat," said Rick.

"Rick? Here? Someone might come here looking for us. I don't think it's safe," replied Laura.

"Laura, I think we're hours ahead of anyone who might be looking for you. You have to eat anyway."

"You're right. I guess I'm just paranoid."

"You'd have every right to be if you were."

They strolled across the lobby and toward the hotel restaurant. They were surprised to find a sign saying CLOSED, OPEN FOR BREAKFAST AT 6:00 A.M.

"Time flies when you're having a good time," offered Rick, trying to sound upbeat. They had left the BOQ shortly after two A.M. and it was now approaching four A.M. They were surprised that they hadn't picked up on the fact that the hotel lobby and environs were virtually deserted.

"Rick, we can't just stand around here like this. Do you think we can check into a hotel room and at least get out of sight?"

The suggestion surprised Rick for a moment until he realized it was the only logical move. "Sure, I'm certain that we can," he said with a bit of hesitation. It was one thing to be on the run with Laura, but checking into a hotel room seemed to take things to another level. Clear your head, Rick, stop thinking and start acting, he chided himself. "Just wait here for a minute," he said as he led her to one of the plush chairs in the middle of the lobby and put his parachute bag and her duffel bag down beside her. "Watch these."

Rick walked up to the reservations counter across the lobby. At this hour of the morning the hotel clerk was sitting in a tiny office just behind the banks of counters. Rick cleared his throat to get the man's attention, then said, "Good morning, señor."

"Good morning. Welcome to the Panama City Westin, señor." The clerk was straightening himself a bit. He'd been snoozing in the office and it took him a moment to get his bearings.

"Yes, well, I'd like a room for the night, please."

"Certainly. Reservation?" asked the clerk, although at this hour of the morning it was unlikely that Rick had one.

"No," said Rick. "Just got into town."

"I see," said the clerk, now waking up a bit more. "How many people?"

"Two."

"I see." As the clerk replied, he looked up past Rick

and saw Laura sitting across the lobby. The faintest hint of a smile came to his face.

"And how long will you be staying, señor?"

"Just one night."

"Ah. And how will you be paying?"

"Cash," said Rick. The clerk's smile broadened a bit and he took pains not to look directly at Rick. He had seen this scenario played out many, many times before. In some ways he took a prurient interest in having the early morning desk shift. You saw it all during this time.

"Very good, that will be a hundred twenty dollars, please . . . and a hundred security deposit. Just fill out the registration form, if you will, please."

Unaccustomed to moving in these circles, Rick was a bit taken aback by the price, but he peeled off the amount unhesitatingly from the wad of bills in his pocket. He had prepared for almost any eventuality and carried a lot of cash with him when he left *Coronado*.

"Thank you, señor." Then he said slowly and with some flair, "Do you need any help with your luggage?"

"No, not at all," said Rick a bit tersely. This man cannot be trusted, he thought.

"Good, señor. Here is your key. Enjoy your stay."

"I . . . we will, thanks," said Rick as he turned to get Laura. She was almost asleep in her chair when Rick reached her.

"Laura, here we go," he said.

"Well, a gentleman asking me up to his hotel room? Perhaps you should declare your intentions," said Laura, smiling now for the first time since Rick climbed into her BOQ room.

"Laura . . . I . . . well . . ." Rick didn't know what to say.

"Relax, Rick. I think you're safe tonight." She sighed. As she wearily grabbed his arm, they made their way toward the elevators.

They were silent as the elevator climbed toward the third floor. As the door opened, Rick grabbed both bags in one hand and put his other arm around Laura as they walked toward their room. Rick slipped in the key and allowed Laura to go in first.

"What, not gonna carry me over the threshold, Holden?" Laura was grasping for whatever small bit of humor she could conjure up to keep her spirits up.

Rick picked up on it. "No, but if we're caught in a rainstorm, I'll throw my coat over the mud puddle," he replied with a smile.

"Thank goodness chivalry isn't dead," she said, relieved by even this slight lighthearted banter.

Rick put their bags down in the closet and surveyed the room. Great place. Too bad they weren't here under other circumstances.

Laura sat on the edge of the bed looking at the room service menu. "You get off cheap tonight, Holden. How about ordering us up some room service? I'm starved."

"Can do," said Rick, immensely pleased that Laura was coming alive again. "What'll it be?"

"You pick. I'm just going to close my eyes until it gets here," she said, lying down on one side of the queen-sized bed.

"Don't crash too hard on me, Laura. We've got to think this through."

"Uh-huh," she replied.

Rick hesitated a few minutes before calling room service, then thought better of it. Laura was gently breathing, rhythmically, almost purring, already sound asleep, and he was exhausted too. He turned off the lamp, lay down on the extreme other half of the bed, and soon was asleep too, dreaming of what might have been.

CHAPTER 92

GENERAL CHARLIE WALTERS SAT AT HIS DESK AT HIS headquarters building at Quarry Heights, gazing out the window. Although it was midmorning, he had yet to tackle his burgeoning in-basket. He had let his deputy run the morning staff meeting, something he rarely did, so that he could have this time alone. He wanted to make sure he was doing everything he could to tighten the net he had cast for Laura Peters.

Walters had certainly turned this sometimes sleepy base upside down as he set the manhunt in motion. He had unleashed the entire base police force, all shifts, stripped down the numbers of men and women guarding the base gates to the absolute minimum, totally done away with all traffic patrols, and taken the security patrols away from the base housing complexes. They represented a large force. Additionally, he had called in the local director of the Naval Investigative Service and asked for all of his agents to immediately get involved in the search. After initially balking, the director was persuaded that he really did want to put all of his agents out in the field looking for Laura. Other agents, such as the local Drug Enforcement Agency and the rarely noticed FBI agents, were summoned and the importance of tracking down this murderer and probable traitor was impressed upon them in no uncertain terms.

Walters cast his net beyond the base too. As SouthCom commander, he had complete control of the eleven-thousand-plus military personnel permanently stationed in Panama, as well as every Navy ship that called in that country. A base curfew of any sort could seriously damage the economy of Rodman, Panama City, and the surrounding communities. The local officials were painfully aware of this awesome power and went out of their way to co-operate with him. By evening, every Panamanian police vehicle would have a picture of Laura Peters affixed to its dashboard.

The general did not fret or worry; he knew the forces he had unleashed would scour the base and the surrounding area and would find out what happened to Laura Peters. It was almost a game with him now, he the hunter, she the hunted. It wasn't much of a challenge.

The intercom buzzed. "General, Major Lang to see you, sir."

"Send him in," replied Walters. Major Rocky Lang was his deputy security officer and personal point man on this hunt.

"Major Lang reporting, General," said the tall, lanky

officer, looking sharp and extremely official in his starched uniform.

"Well, Major, tell me what you've turned up."

"Actually, General, we have found out some interesting things regarding Lieutenant Peters. I personally interviewed Petty Officer Aguillar at the BOQ. He's the day desk clerk. He tells me he knows nothing about Peters leaving, but he did field a call from an unidentified male earlier that same day who was very insistent that he wanted to talk with the lieutenant. He didn't remember the time exactly, but had it pretty close, so we pulled the phone record and found that the call was made from the phone banks down on the piers." Lang paused, letting the information sink in with the general.

"Go on, Major. So far none of this is particularly extraordinary," said Walters with a tinge of impatience in his voice.

"Certainly, General. I had some of my men check the pier areas and pull in anyone who was on watch around that time. Seems one of the pier gate guards had quite a tale to tell." Lang paused again.

"Were you a drama major, Major? Get on with it."

"Well, this young petty officer was a little reluctant to tell us at first, but seems that he chased, and actually fired at, a Navy chief petty officer who was coming from the pier and tried to work his way around the security fence. He was carrying a large parachute bag and the speculation was that he came off a ship somewhere."

"Well, what ship was at the pier?" asked Walters, just wanting Lang to get on with it.

"That's just it, General, there was no ship there, but there was a refueling barge that had just tied up. It had been out fueling up the *Coronado*."

Walters sat bolt upright. "Did you say the *Coronado*?"

"Yes sir, General. Of course, we can't follow up because the ship is in some sort of radio silence—must be a drill, we figure. We'll follow up on it when we can get in touch with them." Lang sensed that the general was now a lot more focused on what he had to tell him.

"Well, Major, we'll look into that. Now let's get back to the BOQ. How about the NIS agents parked in front and the desk person on duty when we think this escape took place?"

"We have it pinned down to an approximate time that she escaped. Petty Officer Osborne was on duty, but she went into Panama City today on liberty. We're looking for her, though."

"Any guards on any gates see anything?"

"Not that we've discovered so far, General, though some of the guards at some of the gates are on liberty and we haven't reached them yet. We're pulsing that one pretty hard and will get to anyone who could have seen anything," said Lang.

"All right, Major, keep looking," said Walters as he rose, signaling Lang that he was finished with him. "But keep looking hard. So far you don't have much. I'm not really interested in hearing about who you can't talk to because they're on liberty or whatever. I want her found. After all, she's wanted in a capital case. If you don't find her within twenty-four hours I'll get someone who can," said Walters, his voice rising and his face turning red. "You're dismissed, Major Lang," he said, as if Lang needed reminding.

Stung by the criticism, Lang actually backed away. "Yes, General. We'll find her, and find her soon. You can count on it."

As Major Lang left, General Charlie Walters returned to staring out the window, feeling no better than he had earlier. Someone from *Coronado*. Was this the person who had been exchanging phone calls with Peters? That could be a major complication, one he was not prepared for. Was that where this "chief" was really from? Who had really called Lieutenant Laura Peters in the BOQ? He had put *Coronado* in radio silence, he could take them out of it, but not without putting the plan at further risk. Was it worth it?

CHAPTER 93

RICK AWOKE WITH A START, MOMENTARILY DISORIented by his unfamiliar surroundings. He looked at the clock by the bedside. It was ten-thirty in the morning. He looked at Laura. She was still sleeping. Quickly he put his mind in order. They had to come up with a plan.

First, he called room service and asked for one of just about everything on the breakfast menu. He was famished and he figured that Laura was too. He went into the bathroom to shower and let the warm water envelop his body for a few minutes. He dressed quickly, and when he anticipated that room service would arrive any moment, he gently shook Laura awake.

When she gazed up at him she seemed to be at ease for the first time. She stretched and rolled over, clearly not ready to move yet.

"No fooling, Laura. We really can't stay here forever. I'll work through both our breakfasts if you don't turn to," chided Rick, feeling that they needed to spring into action, but not overly anxious to spoil this moment.

"Okay, okay, spoilsport, just give me a minute," purred Laura, who, at the moment, didn't have any of Rick's sense of urgency about the situation.

There was a knock on the door. "Room service."

"Hold on," said Rick, reaching for his wallet. He walked to the door, took a long look through the peephole, then opened it guardedly, allowing the attendant to wheel in the cart covered with food. "Thank you, señor," said Rick as he paid him, tipping him generously.

As Rick wheeled the cart near their table, Laura slipped out of bed. She moved noiselessly to the table. He wondered why she had bothered to dress for bed but then forced himself to stop wondering. Stay on focus, he told himself.

They launched into an idyllic breakfast. The tropical breeze blew off the ocean and they could see the azure blue water from where they sat. Laura looked absolutely ravishing. Her tousled hair and sleepy eyes made her all the more appealing to Rick. Had she been trying to send Rick a signal last night that he just hadn't picked up on? He might never know.

Had they not been on the run, this could have been perfect. But they were, and they began to discuss ways to leave the country.

"We've got more than a few problems," Rick began. No passports, for openers. They're definitely looking for you, maybe for me too. Not many ways out of here, land, sea, or air."

"I know," said Laura. "Don't suppose we'd get very far if we rented a car and tried to drive north."

"No chance of that. Too risky to use a credit card and with no passports we'd never get through all the countries we'd have to go through."

"Air?" offered Laura.

"Passport problem would be too hard to crack, plus the airport's too easy to watch. If they're doing their job, they probably have it well covered already."

"Sea's the only answer," said Laura, arriving at the only potentially logical conclusion, "but how?"

They talked for a long time, but no really good possibilities leaped to mind and they kept going over and over the same ones, hoping one would suddenly make sense. Laura felt an impending sense of doom. Each rejected plan filled her more and more with dread. Rick wished he had a way to buoy her spirits.

Hoping some fresh air would inspire him, he got up and walked out on the balcony and gazed at the port of Panama City and the Pacific Ocean beyond. Laura sat, still pondering their fate. It was almost silent, only the occasional chirp of a bird, the whisper of the breeze, the distant pounding of the surf to disturb their thoughts. Suddenly Rick's gaze was riveted. Spontaneously, he called out, "Laura."

CHAPTER 94

PRESIDENT TAYLOR CALHOUN HAD SUNK TO THE depths of depression. He was not without his information sources and what was happening was beginning to gel. He was now firmly convinced his military leaders were out to ruin him and that his Secretary of Defense was powerless to stop them. Senator Lindsey had a burr up his butt with these Intelligence Oversight Committee hearings—they were going to be bloody, no doubt about it. Then there was this reporter, Kennedy. Junior gal, all of a sudden elevated to national prominence with information that the military had to be feeding her. She couldn't find that much out by herself. Hell, they were making her look like Woodward and Bernstein. She was blistering him, his administration, Lovelace, anyone he was close to. She was worse than the Russian mafia. The polls were plummeting and the editorials were all brutal. Worst of all, there was a lot of loose talk on the Hill that Lindsey's hearings were going to be a prelude to impeachment hearings. He had never had a blacker day in his life.

Several miles away, hard by the George Washington Parkway at CIA Headquarters in Langley, Virginia, three men sat at a table in a secure office in the Crystal Palace and attempted to deal with the unexpected. Tucked discreetly between the Parkway and Route 123 in upscale McLean, Virginia, the headquarters for the world's most well-known intelligence agency went unnoticed by the thousands of commuters who used these roads to travel to and from their jobs inside Washington's beltway. Those who worked there liked it that way.

"I thought we had told him to go underground and stay underground," said the first man.

"We had," said the second man. "But under the circumstances, don't you think he did exactly the right thing by calling us from Panama?"

"I'm not so sure," said the first man.

"Hold on," said the third. "Neither of you actually puts stock in this wild-ass tale, do you?"

"He's been with us awhile. Oh sure, underground for the last few years, but absolutely solid. Do you think he's making all this up?" said the second man, somewhat incredulously.

"No!" shouted the first. "No, I don't. But look, he isn't in a position to know these sorts of things. And yes, it's such an incredible story that he has to be misinformed. Maybe someone found out about him on this Navy ship and wanted to discredit the Agency. God knows we're under enough fire. Maybe that would be the straw that broke the camel's back."

"He's right," added the third man. "It's too incredible to be true. He must have gotten knocked off track by some bum data. He hasn't exactly been up on the step in this Navy disguise you put him in."

"*We* put him in!" countered the second man. "We put him in there to hold on to him for further service. I don't give a damn about what specific instructions we gave him. He's just trying to do his job and if just half of what he suspects is happening is true, *we've* got our job to do and we'd better do it now!"

"All right," said the third man, his voice indicating he wasn't so much agreeing with his colleague as placating him. "All right. We'll give him a chance to tell us some more. Are we manned up for when he calls again?"

"As always," added the second man, responding to what should have been a rhetorical question. "We're prepped and waiting for his call twenty-four hours a day."

"Good," said the first. "I want to put Team Charlie on this now. Absolute discretion. No reports up or down the chain, not until you have my specific approval. Start out with bios, then let's do some discreet interviews with the people on this list we have. Then we need to look at this reporter, what's her name?"

"Kennedy," offered the second man.

"Right. Kennedy," said the first man. "Finding out

where she's getting her information could be a key. Let's tap the usual methods for that, but *discreetly,* understood?"

There was a general nodding of heads. The three of them were the handlers for this case and none of them could quite believe everything Rick was telling them. When he called again they would have some pointed questions.

CHAPTER 95

MAJOR LANG TOOK OFF HIS GLASSES AND RUBBED THE bridge of his nose hard. He had just completed his last personal interrogation after his men had done all the preliminaries, and he had what he felt was a complete story to tell General Walters. It hadn't been easy putting all of the pieces together, and he had taken some liberties with his methods, but the general wanted results and he would not disappoint him. He was "in zone," the military's euphemism for up for selection, for lieutenant colonel later this year, and the efficiency report the general would have his deputy write on him would make or break his chances for promotion. Lang was unwilling to risk that by worrying about anyone's sensibilities.

"Lipman," he called to the Marine corporal who was manning the desk immediately outside of his spartan office, "call General Walters's secretary and see if the general is available. Tell her it's urgent that I see him."

"Yes sir," barked the corporal, already dialing the number.

Lang got up and began adjusting his uniform. His well-honed instincts told him General Walters would be seeing him soon.

"General, Major Lang here to see you," said the general's secretary as she showed him in.

"Major," said the general, rising out of his chair, "come in. I understand you have some information for me."

"I do, General," he replied. "We've contacted all of the people we were after and persuaded them to cooperate fully." Lang was really embellishing his efforts to curry favor with Walters, but this was one of his few opportunities to grab the limelight and he wanted to make the most of it.

"Go ahead, Major."

"Yes sir. We talked to Petty Officer Osborne, the BOQ clerk on that night. She said a Navy chief petty officer came to the Q asking for Lieutenant Peters. Said he had something to deliver to her. She thought it sounded strange, and she offered to take it, but he refused. Then she blew it. She told him that she—Lieutenant Peters, that is—was under house arrest. She said he looked really shocked when she said that."

"What did he do then?" asked Walters.

"She said he just left right away."

"Then what?" queried Walters a bit impatiently.

"Well," continued Lang, "we took the description of the chief that Osborne gave us. I had one of the NIS gents bring in a police artist, and went back to the pier sentry who fired the shots. He, and two other sailors that he identified to us, as we suspected, all identified the same man, confirming our suspicions. We even canvassed the ships in port, rounded up the entire ship's company, and showed each and every man this picture. Several of them remembered him at the phone bank. We also found the tug operator who brought the fuel barge to the pier they said this chief emerged from. He confirmed that he had just taken the barge out to the *Coronado* earlier that evening. Said he didn't see anyone or hear anything unusual, though. Finally, we talked to the gate guards at the gate closest to the BOQ. They confirmed that this chief, though he was then in civilian clothes, and the lieutenant, walked out the gate carrying some bags a little after two in the morning."

"Walked out the gate?" said Walters, incredulous.

"Yes, General, just walked out."

"Do we let people just stroll through our gates?"

"Not exactly, General. We check everyone on the way in, of course," replied Lang. "But people just walk out the gate here, just like anywhere else. The gate guards said he spoke to them. The chief said he was putting his girlfriend back on a plane to the States. They said he sounded really normal."

"Great! We'll see about that later," said Walters, his face growing red. "What did they do then?"

"They got in a cab and disappeared."

"Have we found the cab driver yet?"

"No, but we're looking."

Walters was boiling. What Lang had told him confirmed his worst suspicions and added a new, inconvenient wrinkle. Instead of a young female lieutenant running scared, she evidently had a companion who was helping her—and worse, someone with apparently enough moxie and with the wherewithal to make the escape effective. But who was he? A Navy chief? That didn't make sense. For a moment he thought he couldn't be more upset. He was wrong.

Lang piped up. "Oh, and General, there is one more thing. I almost forgot it."

"What?" said Walters, now glaring at the major.

"When we interviewed the sentry who fired the shots, he mentioned something strange."

"What?" said Walters again, now wanting to be rid of the major, who was no longer doing him any good.

"Well," continued Lang, "while they were chasing this chief, he dropped this large parachute bag that he was carrying and some things rolled out."

"What things?" asked Walters. The major still had this annoying habit of pausing just too damn much.

"They weren't sure exactly, said they were large, cylindrical, containerlike objects. We quizzed 'em pretty good," continued Lang with conviction in his voice. "From the description these sailors gave, it occurred to one of my sergeants to show them some pictures. They sort of think they could have been Stinger missile launch tubes."

"Stinger missiles!" exclaimed Walters.

"Well, yes sir, General. Not the missiles themselves, of course, just the spent casings."

"In this chief's parachute bag?"

"Yes sir. Seems like an awfully strange thing to be carrying around, don't you think, General?"

Silence.

"General?"

"That's all, Major. Give me a moment, would you?"

"Of course, General," said Lang as he wheeled and departed the general's office. He had worked closely enough with Walters that he knew when he was dismissed.

For the first time in a long time, General Charles Bigelow Walters, commander of the U.S. Southern Command, was filled with dread. He could wait no longer. He pressed the intercom and got his secretary.

"I need you to place a call right now."

CHAPTER 96

PROPPING THE PHOTO OF GENERAL LOVELACE AND Laura Peters against her desk lamp, Liz Kennedy struggled with how to work with this rather startling information that Howard Campbell had just provided her. It sounded really juicy, could play into her story, she thought, but really wasn't a perfect fit. She debated the need to keep the story alive versus the need for it to have internal consistency, then considered how she could turn the story toward the general. He had, she realized, escaped a great deal of scrutiny by being at sea.

She was shaken out of her musings by the insistent jingling of the phone on her desk. The light told her it was her private line. Few people had that. Very few.

"Kennedy," she answered with her usual salutation.

"Liz, dear. Howard here. How is my favorite reporter?" said Campbell, his voice fairly dripping with charm.

"How nice to hear from you here at the office, Howard. Where are you, love? Still at work?"

"Yes, of course," replied Campbell, suddenly sounding impatient.

Howard was getting a little stressed, thought Liz. At

first the information he had passed her came during evening dinners, romantic vignettes that combined business with pleasure. Of late, though, he had become more and more, well, careless. Now he seemed almost cavalier, calling her directly from his Pentagon office, seemingly oblivious to the possibility that his lines could be monitored—the military did that to a fault, didn't they? His demeanor had changed too. The charm was wearing thin. He seemed rushed, abrupt, sometimes almost a little panicky. Howard Campbell? Chairman of the Joint Chiefs of Staff? Didn't make sense. Her instincts told her to be cautious. She wanted first to calm him down.

"Well, Howard, I understand you must be terribly busy there." She was always careful not to say where "there" was. "I know you're calling about something important."

"I am, Liz, something that, I'm sure, will add to the importance of that package I sent over. I trust you received it."

Liz was starting to think Campbell was leading her just a bit too much. He had done very well by her, and in some ways had almost written her stories for her. But she didn't want to lose control of them completely. Just give me the facts, Howard, she thought. I'll decide what fits and what doesn't. She held her tongue and just responded, "Great."

"Well, dear," he continued, "the young, *attractive* lieutenant in the picture with General Lovelace? Lieutenant Laura Peters?"

"Yes?"

"They found the officer she was having an affair with."

"Where?"

"On his back, Liz. Dead."

"How?"

"Shot. They had Peters under house arrest. That is, until she escaped. But here's where it gets interesting, Liz, and where it may tie into that picture of Peters and General Lovelace back to this murder."

Here he was, leading her again. "Tell me more, Howard," she said, interested but wanting to hear it on her terms.

"Peters murdered Wilson, we're sure of that. But the link with Lovelace makes this more complex. Seems the reports—that's why I sent you those pictures—are that they were an item when they both were stationed in Washington. When he showed up in Panama, they went at it again, if only for a night or two. Anyway, he's on the command ship, *Coronado,* hears that she's locked up—"

Liz interrupted. "Howard, how does he find out about something like that while he's out at sea?"

Campbell continued the deception. "Liz, the commander of anything has a vast information network that he can tap into. Lovelace had reason to want—need—to stay very connected. He had his ways of finding out."

"So he knew that Peters was locked up—where's the connection?" said Liz, now clearly puzzled.

"This is it, Liz," said Campbell. He was enjoying this ability to manipulate her. It was even better than their sex. "She escaped, but didn't escape alone. As we walked this back, we found that a Navy chief was spirited off *Coronado* and slipped into the base at Rodman and broke her out of the BOQ."

"A chief from *Coronado*?" said Liz, now confused.

"Yes, Liz, don't you see? Lovelace was concerned about her. Didn't want her to take the fall on this."

"That's kind of incredible, Howard. I mean, he's just having a tryst with this little honey. If she takes a fall for something else, he moves on to greener pastures, right?"

"Well, almost, dear. Except that, if she's held on a murder charge, you know they're going to interrogate her until the cows come home. It's funny how other things come out in these interrogations. Lovelace is under the gun for screwing up Operation Roundup and we have General Walters running an investigation on that as it is. I'm sure General Lovelace wouldn't want it known, especially to General Walters, that he had an additional foible of shacking up with Navy lieutenants. Wouldn't want it known to Mrs. Lovelace and the three very nice Lovelace children back in northern Virginia, either."

"But what would he do once he got her out of confinement?" said Liz, now starting to put the pieces together.

"Just get her out of there. Her situation was so desperate with the murder investigation that she'd no doubt jump at the chance to escape. Where to is just a matter of logistics. Like everything I've told you, dear."

"I'm starting to understand now," said Liz.

"Darling, I've got to run," said Campbell, "but I will give you more as soon as I have anything."

"I'm sure you will, Howard," said Liz. "I'm sure you will."

As she put down the phone, she started to order her thoughts. This would be a capstone piece. She swung her chair around and faced her word processor. Her hands flew over the keys. After more than an hour, she pushed her chair back and stared at the screen:

UNITED STATES SOUTHERN COMMAND—In the wake of the disastrous outcome of Operation Roundup, military investigators continue to look into allegations that two junior military officers passed details of the operation to Costa Rican drug lords. One of the officers, a Lieutenant Commander Andrew Wilson, has been murdered, and the other officer, a Lieutenant Laura Peters, implicated in his shooting, has escaped from house arrest in her quarters at the Rodman base, in the company of an unidentified man, believed to be a Navy chief petty officer.

In a related matter, Lieutenant Peters has also been linked to General Ashley Lovelace, Commander of Joint Task Force Eight, embarked in USS *Coronado*. Seen here alighting from the Bachelor Officers' quarters in Rodman with General Lovelace, just days before the General directed the ill-fated operation, Peters is rumored to have been linked romantically to the General while they both were stationed in Washington, D.C., last year. Officials at the Southern Command suspect that General Lovelace may have been somehow involved in Lieutenant Peters's escape.

These latest revelations come against the backdrop of a worsening strain between the White House and the Pentagon—exacerbated over the failure of Operation Roundup. Pentagon officials are becoming increasingly vocal about the break-

> down of the chain of command and the orchestration of the failed operation directly from the White House; directly, some say, from the President to his close personal friend and Washington and Lee classmate, General Lovelace.
>
> Meanwhile, the latest polls . . .

Not a bad effort, thought Liz, especially with a story that she thought was all but dried up just a short time ago. Funny the way this had worked out, she thought.

At Senator Jay Lindsey's Senate Intelligence Oversight Committee hearings, it was anything but funny. Witness after witness presented himself or herself before the committee. There were a parade of officials from the Central Intelligence Agency, the Defense Intelligence Agency, the National Security Agency, the National Reconnaissance Office, the Defense Mapping Agency, the National Security Council, and others.

Throughout the hearings, Senator Lindsey was spellbinding. He did not speak frequently, allowing junior members of the committee, or even staffers, to handle most of the questioning. However, he saved his sharpest questions for the highest-ranking administration officials. What started out as an omnibus look at the nation's entire intelligence apparatus quickly focused in on the Calhoun administration and its hands-on running of the U.S. intelligence process. Although the senator took great pains to appear statesmanlike and totally unbiased, close observers of the process detected a hard edge to his questioning of senior administration officials, particularly those closest to the President, and a constant return to the theme of the President ignoring intelligence that should have caused him to stop Operation Roundup. His questioning of National Security Advisor Brian Stavridis was particularly pointed.

"So, Mr. Stavridis, could you tell us again about the methodology for collecting and consolidating intelligence at your level at the National Security Council?" began Senator Lindsey.

"Yes, I can," said Stavridis, already defensive. "The

other agencies all have set procedures to gather and disseminate all-source information. Since the volume of data is so enormous, we work on a 'pull' system where we ask for, and get, only the data we actually need in a particular situation. Then—"

Lindsey interrupted, "So you need to know in advance what information you will need—before you get the actual information?" The senator paused for dramatic effect, his expression incredulous, and looking directly at the cameras.

"Well, yes, in a way," said Stavridis.

"Seems a little arrogant," continued Lindsey.

"Senator?"

"What I mean, Mr. Stavridis, is you presuppose an infallibility at your level. Do you consult with all intelligence agencies first?"

"Of course, Senator," continued Stavridis, a little off balance now. "We work closely with all intelligence agencies on a daily basis."

That was the answer he wanted. Senator Lindsey again looked directly at the cameras and raised his eyebrows. Turning slowly to the National Security Advisor, he continued, "So, if we were to use Operation Roundup as one example, would you say that you had access to all the other intelligence agencies and activities in that case?"

"Yes, I would say so, but—"

Again Lindsey interrupted, now turning more hostile. "So it's safe to say that you knew, in the White House, at least as much as any of our military commanders, wouldn't that be so?"

"Yes, but—"

"I should remind you, then, Mr. Stavridis, that those military commanders have already testified before this committee that they had ironclad information that an ambush awaited our brave soldiers and Marines and that"— he paused again and looked directly at the cameras—"in spite of their earnest pleas to stop the operation, the 'go' signal was given directly from the White House to General Lovelace, purposely and explicitly bypassing a long chain of command that would have stopped the operation if they had known that a 'go' order had been given!" Lindsey was almost yelling. Enunciating, his speech coach called it.

"That's not how it went, Senator."

"Not how it went! Not how it went!" boomed Lindsey, not screaming, but clearly bullying. "No, Mr. Stavridis, that's *exactly* how it went. This committee oversees the almost thirty billion—that's billion—dollars spent on intelligence by this country every year. We got you that intelligence, sir. Got it to the military commanders. Got it to the White House. Why on God's green earth did you order those boys to their deaths?" Lindsey was on a roll now. The cameras were rolling and the reporters were scribbling.

"If you'd just let me finish—" said Stavridis, clearly wilting under the intense interrogation.

"Oh, we'll let you finish sir, we'll let you finish. You'll get to finish with this committee, but somehow I think that this won't be the last one you—or the President—will be seeing."

"Senator—"

Again Lindsey cut him off. "Our committee is in recess until tomorrow." Satisfied that he had played his roll and played it well, Senator Jay Lindsey allowed a faint smile to color his stern expression. Now it was time to pass the baton.

CHAPTER 97

IT NOW SEEMED SO CLEAR TO RICK. JUST AN HOUR AGO he and Laura had been frustrated beyond words, trying to think of a way they could escape from Panama. They had ignored the obvious: a cruise ship entering the harbor.

"Laura, this is it. We can get away on one of these cruise ships!" began Rick, unable to contain his enthusiasm.

Laura was more cautious. "Rick, I don't know. I mean, we aren't registered passengers or anything. Surely they check identification of some kind. How do we get on in the first place?"

"Getting on is easy. I've had friends go on these cruises before. There's always a big gaggle of well-wishers on board before they sail, saying good-bye to the passengers. At some point they tell all guests to leave. We just don't. We'll fade away somewhere into the ship. Between the two of us, we should be able to find our way around, don't you think?" Rick was almost beaming.

"I still think it's risky," cautioned Laura.

Rick put on his game face again. "Look Laura. There's probably no perfect option for us. This plan may not be foolproof, but compared to the alternatives, it's the best one we've got. Besides, we don't know how fast the net is closing around us. I say we have to move, and move fast."

As much as she didn't want to think about the possibilities, Laura saw the handwriting on the wall. "Okay, Rick, if you've got a good feeling about this, I'll follow your lead."

But Laura was troubled beyond the urgency of needing to escape from Panama. She had prided herself all her life on doing a man's job in a man's world, neither asking for nor receiving any special favors or consideration. She had held her own in the toughest of circumstances. She'd never flaunted it; she'd just been quietly efficient and effective. But that was changing, and changing suddenly. She felt herself being pulled along by Rick. He was definitely in charge. Protective. He listened, but he always had the plan formalized in his own mind before he discussed it with her. For a woman who prided herself on her professional accomplishments, this was a big leap. She was in turmoil.

Something else bothered Laura too. The longer she was around him, the more attractive she found Rick. He was, in less than professional terms, a hunk. When her mind wandered she fantasized all manner of things—they said it was healthy to fantasize, didn't they? She had been drawn to Rick at the Westin, but she was unsure of his feelings toward her. She didn't know what to do. She didn't consider herself that worldlywise, and she felt Rick

was going to be a gentleman first and foremost. She didn't
feel comfortable with the role of the seductress in general—and especially not under these conditions and in the
situation she now found herself in. She was just trying to
keep it together.

Rick was happy that she was going along with the plan.
"Okay, Laura, here's what we'll do to limit our exposure.
I'll call the concierge. He'll have the cruise ship sailings.
We'll wait here until a few hours before one sails, then go
down and mingle with the visitors and well-wishers. Once
we're aboard, we'll take the next step."

"Do we have a preference as to where this ship might
take us?" said Laura with just a hint of skepticism in her
voice.

"I say we go for the first one," replied Rick, more concerned with just getting away.

"I'm not so sure," said Laura, weighing in more now to
assert some equality in the partnership as well as out of a
real concern with where they went. "I think we ought to
look a few steps ahead. Once we get out of Panama we're
still on the run. We can't go just anywhere. I say we have
to get to the States if at all possible."

"I agree with you," Rick said. "Maybe, if we don't have
to pass up too many, we should try to get one that's going
toward the East Coast, as close to Washington as possible.
Don't see us accomplishing much in California or anywhere else on the West Coast. Do you?" He couldn't tell
her that D.C. not only was the best place to find someone
to talk to about Operation Roundup, but was where the
Agency was focusing its efforts to help him.

"Not really," said Laura, her spirits lifted now that Rick
was taking her ideas into consideration.

"It's settled, then. I'll call the concierge and ask for the
first cruise ship going through the canal."

Rick made the call and found out there was a cruise
ship, the *Stattendam*, that was already in the harbor at
Panama City and that was making the transit of the canal
that evening. Now that so many cruise ship patrons had
been through the canal at least once, the new attraction
being offered was a nighttime transit. *Stattendam* had orig-
inated in Los Angeles, stopped in Acapulco and Mazatlán,

and—best of all—was heading to Fort Lauderdale via Curaçao. She would depart her dock at five-thirty that afternoon. It was now after eleven-thirty in the morning. A leisurely lunch—room service again—get packed up, taxi down to the wharf area, and they were gone. .

After his next call to room service, Rick and Laura sat on the balcony of this now very familiar room. Both their minds—and especially Laura's—were somehow at ease now that they had a plan. They said nothing as they ate, still hungry in spite of their huge breakfast. They didn't talk much. Just enjoyed the ambience, each thinking private thoughts. Thinking about what might be.

Rick and Laura hopped out of their taxi at the wharf area at about two P.M. Passengers and well-wishers were streaming onto the *Stattendam*. Rick and Laura watched for a while and it didn't seem that anyone in authority was making an attempt to stop anyone from going onto the ship. Rick wanted some insurance. He took Laura over to one of the many vendors crowding the pier.

"Señorita needs a hat," he told the vendor, as he started to pull some small-denomination bills from his pocket.

"Rick!" said Laura.

"Oh yes, and that bag, and these beads, yes, yes, and this hat for me, and . . ."

Rick was on a roll, and Laura soon realized there was a method to his madness. They were going to be attired like the many tourists who had shopped all day in the markets of Panama City. Laura thought he was going a little bit overboard, that he really was beginning to look incredibly tacky—but there were many who looked worse. Finally, he bought them both disposable box cameras—yellow, gaudy—and hung one around each of their necks.

"Rick," said Laura, trying to be a good sport and find some humor in their situation, "you're going to have the fashion police after us."

"That's the idea, my dear."

There was one last problem. Laura's bag was fairly innocuous. Rick's military issue parachute bag wasn't, not with its contents of several spent Stinger launch tubes. Surely they'd raise some questions and draw attention to them. That was the last thing he wanted or needed. Rick thought he was stuck. Then, looking around, he saw the piles of bags that passengers had set on carts waiting to be loaded aboard the ship. A set of golf clubs in an over-sized bag caught his eye. Perfect. Discreetly as he could, without even telling Laura what he was doing, Rick walked over and casually picked up the golf bag. No one noticed. He walked back toward Laura and grabbed his parachute bag. He took both into a nearby restroom. He emerged with a bulging golf bag with some clubs emerging from the inside of the bag.

"Fore," he said as he smiled at Laura.

She just rolled her eyes.

After watching the crowd stream onto the ship for a little while longer, Rick thought he had the routine pegged pretty well. Some passengers stopped on the fore-deck and presented some sort of identification to the attendant there, others on the far side of the gangway just waved or simply pushed ahead. Security didn't seem to be a big deal. In any event, he thought he had a good plan.

Rick and Laura eased into line with the others, many geriatrics, he thought—too bad you have to wait that long to have the money to take one of these cruises.

"Nervous?" Laura said, giving his arm a mock clutch.

"We got it covered."

"Sure?"

"Indeed we do, Mrs. Allen." Rick, beamed, with a gleam in his eye.

"Mrs. Allen?"

"Yes, my love. Mr. and Mrs. Harvey Allen. Married in Newport Beach just last week. Honeymoon, my dear. Now act lovestruck."

"Rick, I don't know."

Now they were on the gangway. They couldn't turn back now without really standing out. Rick edged Laura toward the far right side of the gangway, away from the attendant only twenty feet away. A few elderly people right in front of them were holding on to the railings. Ten feet away now. Almost on the ship. As one older woman a few feet in front of them grasped the railing tightly and stopped to catch her breath, Rick put his golf bag on his left shoulder, pulled Laura close to him with his right arm, and kissed her deeply.

Laura was too shocked to respond. She almost went limp. As they shuffled forward, they held the kiss. An elderly man standing to their left arched his eyebrows and said out loud, "Newlyweds." That set off some agreeable murmuring among all the people on the gangway. As they shuffled up to the foredeck, Rick paused long enough to wink at the attendant as he rubbed Laura's shoulders in a very affectionate way. The attendant just smiled back. He couldn't break this up.

Rick and Laura continued along with the stream of people, some going up, some going below. It was still over an hour to sailing. They'd have to move along and blend in some more. Rick's self-congratulation about getting on the ship was broken by Laura's voice.

"Suppose you want to explain that, Holden?"

"Thought you told me back in the hotel room to declare my intentions," he said with an impish smile.

"Oh, indeed I did, Rick."

"No, Mrs. Allen, it's Harvey. We've been married a week. I'd think that you'd get it right by now."

"Right, Harv," countered Laura as she popped his shoulder with her fist.

All business now, Rick and Laura started looking around for places where they could blend into the ship. They were going to be here for a while. They needed good cover.

CHAPTER 98

MAJOR LANG KNEW HE HAD TO STAY ONE STEP AHEAD of General Walters. Walters had an agenda, that was certain. Lang desperately wanted to please—no, placate was a better word—the general. He doubted that the general would take any excuse for his not coming up with Laura Peters, and coming up with her in a hurry.

He was learning more and more, it seemed, every moment. They had finally tracked down the cab driver who had picked them up outside the gate. It took little questioning, and just a few dollars, to determine from him that he had taken them to the Panama City Westin.

"Oh, yes, señor," he had eagerly told them, his pockets fatter thanks to them. He was a romantic man, but also a poor man. "There were two, a señor and a beautiful señorita. Yes, they had two bags. The señor's was quite heavy and rattled a lot when he placed it in the trunk." He allowed as how he thought they were much in love.

Tracking down the night desk clerk had been a little tougher; they only had an address in the outskirts of Panama City. They arrived at his house just hours after he had gone off duty, and in spite of his wife's protests that her husband was sleeping, Lang and his agents rudely rousted him. He confirmed the description. Yes, they had stayed at the Westin. Paid cash. Lovers, he assumed. She was a pretty one, he recalled.

The day clerk was no help. No, she was certain that that room had not checked out with her. Magnetic card key was just left on their desk in the room. No outstanding bill. They'd evidently paid cash for everything. Room service confirmed that, and that they were delivered lunch sometime before noon. No, didn't look like they were in a hurry to go anywhere. Questioning of all the cab drivers who serviced that area was ongoing but was going to take some time.

"Send him in," said Walters over the intercom when Major Lang was announced at his headquarters. Lang's visits were so frequent now that he didn't even call and make an appointment. The staff knew to usher him in right away whenever he arrived.

"Major Lang reporting, General," said Lang as he stood at rigid attention just two feet in front of Walters's massive desk.

"At ease, Major," said Walters. The more officious

Lang was, General Walters had noticed, the less effective would be his report.

"Yes sir."

"Well, what do you have for me this time?"

Lang explained what they knew, and more importantly what they didn't know. He waited. It didn't take long. Walters exploded.

"Goddammit, Major. What in the hell *can* you and your people do right? All you've managed to do with this case is to stay two steps behind a pair that is making you all look sick. I don't want to know where they've been, do you hear me? I want you to find Peters and whoever is running with her. Get out there and do it. No more goddamned excuses. No more."

"But General—" Fatal mistake, thought Lang.

"But . . . but . . . no, no goddamned buts! Get your ass out there and find her now!" Walters was up out of his chair and literally sputtering. He was almost incoherent. Lang practically ran from the office.

Lang and his people dutifully retraced their steps, hoping to find something they had overlooked in their search. They continued to focus most of their efforts at the Westin, the last place anyone had seen Rick and Laura. They camped there throughout the night and into the next morning, interrogating hotel employees as they came in to work, some for the third or fourth time. The interrogations were so all-encompassing—no shift was spared—that the hotel guests were being deprived of even a modicum of service. Some of the hotel employees who lived a distance from the hotel were difficult to track down, so Lang determined to question them immediately as they showed up for work. One of the last people he questioned was the morning concierge, who showed up promptly at six-thirty A.M. After only a minute or two of questioning, the man's eyes lit up.

"Señor," he piped up, "these may not be the people you are looking for. But in the late morning I received a call from a man in one of the guest rooms asking about cruise ship schedules. I could tell by how basic his questions were that he did not know much about these ships."

Interested, Lang said, "Well, what did he ask, and what did you tell him?"

"He asked what ships were leaving port today, and when they were leaving," he continued cheerfully, obviously hoping that once these inquisitors had what they wanted they would leave them alone.

"And you told him?" probed Lang.

"I told him that there was one leaving in just a bit, but I didn't think he could make that, and another leaving about five-thirty P.M."

"And?"

"And he thanked me, señor."

"What ship was that?"

"The one I tell him. The *Stattendam.*"

Without even thanking him, Lang and his men were off toward the wharf area. They raced through the streets of Panama City, darkness falling now, radioing their headquarters with their status—a strange procession of marked and unmarked military police vehicles of every kind, seemingly racing each other. They knew *Stattendam* would be gone, but they hoped to find out if she had left on time, when she was scheduled to go through the Panama Canal, and where she was going next.

The wharf was nearly deserted when they arrived, save for a few vagrants, the type who always seemed to frequent these areas. No one had come to work yet and there was no one to answer their questions. They were about to drive off in frustration when one of Lang's men called to him.

"Sir, I think I found what we're looking for."

Lang walked over to the man. There, in his hand, he held one of those ubiquitous flyers that almost all cruise ships produce, showing where they were going and what they were doing. It showed that *Stattendam* had a night transit of the Panama Canal scheduled and that she had cleared Cristobal breakwater an hour earlier. It also said her next stop would be Curaçao.

"That's all we need to know. Let's go," said Lang, as they jumped back into their cars and sped away back toward Rodman Naval Station.

CHAPTER 99

SENATOR JAY LINDSEY HAD MADE ONE MISCALCULA-
tion. He had thought that his hearings would take several
weeks, assuring him of continued media attention for a
protracted time period. However, the hearings had been
so high-powered, and had cut to the chase in such rapid
fashion, that they looked as if they would be over in days,
not weeks.

This was not all bad. Although the quantity of media
attention would be diminished, by all accounts the quality—quality being defined as positive impact on the long-
term political aspirations of Senator Jay Lindsey—of the
hearings exceeded even his highest expectations.

His grilling of National Security Advisor Brian Stavridis
had been just the tip of the iceberg. Little by little, the
senator had preempted other scheduled inquisitors and
conducted more and more of the interrogations personally, his success attributed to the quality of his staff and
the spadework they had done, as well as his mastery of
the issues. Yes, these "Lindsey Hearings," as they were
now generally referred to, had exposed a critical failure
in the operation of the administration's intelligence apparatus.

But the ramifications of the hearings went beyond just
the failure of one small part—albeit an important one—
of the total operations of the Executive Branch. What
Lindsey and his committee were able to come up with was
sworn testimony by highly placed military officials that the
White House, and by very strong implication the President himself, had driven Operation Roundup, called all
the shots, and demanded that it kick off in spite of known
intelligence that an ambush was waiting. And why? Presumably, Lindsey concluded out loud on a number of oc-

casions during the hearings, because the President was sinking in the polls and wanted to try a high-risk ploy to bring his administration back into favor with the American people. It was a disgrace, Lindsey pontificated. An absolute disgrace.

Lindsey was saving the best for last—his questioning of the chairman of the Joint Chiefs of Staff, General Howard Campbell. In spite of the understandable desire of many other members of the committee, as well as most of the committee professional staffers, who wanted to hear Campbell's testimony early in the hearings, Lindsey had persuaded Campbell to be "unavailable" until the tail end of the hearings. So by the time Campbell was brought in, interest in what he had to say was at a fever pitch. Lindsey had arranged a special late afternoon session, designed to fold into the networks' evening news programs. They were the perfect venue.

As General Howard Campbell entered, arrayed in his precisely starched uniform with row upon row of personal decorations and campaign ribbons, a silence descended on the packed committee hearing room. Campbell was as distinguished-looking a man as anyone in the room had ever seen, and it was as if he had rehearsed for this role and this entrance his entire life. Every step a statement, every move purposeful, he strode toward the witness table with a sense of conviction and purpose.

Once he was seated and sworn in, Senator Lindsey addressed the general.

"General, good afternoon," began Lindsey. "The committee appreciates your taking the time out of your busy schedule to speak with us. I hope we are not taking you away from pressing duties at the Pentagon."

"Not at all, Senator."

"Good. General, do you know why the committee has called you as a witness today?"

"I believe so, Senator."

"Would you tell us in your own words, then?"

"Senator, it is probably an open secret at all levels—*all levels*—" he said, pausing for dramatic effect, "that the fact that there was an ambush set for our brave men who landed in Costa Rica during Operation Roundup was well known before the operation commenced. My Unified

Commander, General Walters, commander of the United States Southern Command, explicitly told the on-scene commander, General Lovelace, not to start the operation without his permission."

Lindsey was doing a masterful job of making it seem like he and Campbell were meeting for the first time during this "interrogation." The senator just trying to get to the bottom of things, the General just doing his duty, their incredulity over why the administration could do such a bizarre thing—for something that was so well planned and well rehearsed, it all came across so naturally, so convincingly. They were pros.

Lindsey said, "General Campbell, do you mean to tell me that his immediate military superior told General Lovelace not to begin the operation?"

"Yes, precisely, Senator."

"And why do you think he proceeded?"

"We strongly believe that General Lovelace had direct orders from the White House to begin the operation."

"What do you base this belief on, General?"

"In any theater of operations the military commander must set up communications monitoring capabilities. We know there were several transmissions between the White House and USS *Coronado* in the hours leading up to the operation."

"Do you know what those communications entailed? What was said?"

"No," the general lied, as prerehearsed with Lindsey. "Our monitoring equipment is not that sophisticated, unless we just happen to be up on the correct frequency, which we weren't in this case. All we know is that these communications took place and what time they occurred."

"Then why are you so certain the White House directed the operation to begin? Couldn't General Lovelace have decided this on his own?"

"Anything is possible, Senator!" exclaimed Campbell, buying some insurance for their ruse by pretending to be a bit hostile toward Lindsey. "But other factors mitigate, as they say."

"And what other factors would those be, General Campbell?" said Lindsey, reinforcing the ruse of hostility.

"Senator. When I was summoned to the White House

by the President, he showed me the press release saying
that the operation was a huge success. He said he had
gotten this directly from General Lovelace. He then went
on to harangue me, and by extension General Walters,
for being overly cautious. He emphasized that he had had
to go over our heads to get this done by talking directly
to General Lovelace. I tried to tell him that we were getting different reports from his, but he would not listen."

"What did he do then, General?"

"He threw me out."

"Threw you out."

"Yes, Senator."

Lindsey paused until the murmuring in the hearing
room died down. "Why do you think he threw you out?"

"I suppose he didn't like the news I was trying to bring
him."

"And how do you suppose he got the incorrect information that the operation was a success?"

"We know for certain that General Lovelace told him
that."

"Did General Lovelace make that up?"

"No, Senator, General Lovelace was evidently duped
by the druggies and a simple communications deception
ruse. They got into our communications nets and reported, falsely, that we were winning a big victory."

"Why would they do such a thing?"

"It's really very simple, Senator. They had to know
we'd have reinforcements ready. If they made it seem like
we were winning, they would dissuade us from using those
reinforcements as unnecessary. This misinformation
would give them an edge that could prove to be decisive.
It actually makes a lot of sense, tactically speaking."

"And General Lovelace was fooled by this?"

Campbell sighed. A heavy, prearranged sigh of resignation. "Yes, he was."

"You seem particularly bothered by that, General."

"Only that, well, you see, Senator, General Lovelace
was not our—I mean the Pentagon's—first choice for this
assignment."

"Why did he get it?"

"The President placed him there."

The questioning of General Campbell continued for another hour, Lindsey feigning surprise at each revelation. As the session ended, both men looked spent from doing their duty. Lindsey mustered the energy for a closing flourish.

"General Campbell. Is there anything else you would like to share with the committee?" said Lindsey, staring directly at Campbell for a moment, but then turning his head directly at the cameras.

"Only, Senator," Campbell intoned in his stentorian voice, "that someone should tell the parents of those poor boys who died how very, very sorry he is."

A short way away on Capitol Hill, in the chambers of the Speaker of the House of Representatives, Representative Bobby Wilcox, this dramatic moment was not lost. The Speaker had virtually no interest in military matters, but his party had been chafing for three years under the imperious rule of Taylor Calhoun's White House. He had been a huge thorn in their side. This might be the opportunity to remove that thorn permanently.

CHAPTER 100

HOWARD CAMPBELL WAS HAVING A GREAT DAY. HIS testimony before Lindsey's committee had been riveting. Press reports had commented on his "expansive knowledge of military intelligence," on his "commanding presence during committee deliberations," and of his "obvious intellect to go along with his unbridled patriotism." Not bad, thought Campbell, not bad at all. All of those comments, as well as others like them, would be shining pearls for future political contests. The possibility had crossed his mind more than once. He wasn't planning on passing quietly into retirement on the completion of his tour as chairman of the Joint Chiefs of Staff—no, the country should not be deprived of his services.

The intercom buzzed. "Mr. Chairman, General Walters for you."

"Yes, put him through," said Campbell. Just like Charlie, doing a great job of keeping him updated. He guessed that Walters was calling him to tell him they had Lieutenant Peters back in custody. That would let him tie up one damn annoying loose end.

"Good afternoon, Mr. Chairman," Walters began. Campbell detected a weariness in his voice.

"Good afternoon, Charlie. What's the report from the field?"

"I'm afraid it's not good news, Mr. Chairman."

"Oh!"

"Yes sir. It seems that Lieutenant Peters has escaped off the base and may be out of our grasp."

"Out of your grasp. Out of your grasp! Dammit, Charlie. I hope you know that you're empowered to go out into that town and tear that third world shithole apart until you find her."

"Actually, Mr. Chairman, she's no longer in Panama. We're virtually certain that she's escaped onboard a cruise ship."

"A cruise ship."

"Yes, Mr. Chairman." Walters was sounding obsequious now. He knew he was going to get blasted. "And what's more, we know that she's in the company of one man and we're also pretty sure that this man was slipped off USS *Coronado* to help her make good her escape."

"Keep talking, Charlie," said Campbell, barely able to hide his rage.

General Charlie Walters poured out detail after detail to General Howard Campbell. He wanted Campbell to have the complete story, partially to absolve himself, but also because he knew that, if his worst suspicions were confirmed, Campbell would soon have to take up the job of finding Peters and her companion.

His story complete, General Charlie Walters waited. And waited. And agonized.

Finally, Campbell spoke. "Well, Charlie. I liked your plan when you presented it to me a while ago. So she escapes. Makes her look guilty. Solidifies our plot.

Sounded great! But now you've screwed it away and with the additional wrinkle of someone from *Coronado* helping her escape. Did you get in touch with *Coronado* and see if they admit to having anyone missing?"

Relieved by the chance to speak, Walters quickly said, "Mr. Chairman, if you recall, we put *Coronado* in radio silence to take General Lovelace out of the picture, at least until the hearings were over."

"I damn well remember that you did that, Charlie, don't patronize me. Find out a way to find out! We need to know who that is!"

"Right now we're portraying it as someone who was sent to spring Lieutenant Peters—to help her escape."

"I know, and we're playing the sex angle with Lovelace and Peters. That's all well and good, and we'll keep playing it. But I want to know who in the hell is running with her. Now!"

"I agree, Mr. Chairman, but you might also consider that we can now further implicate Lovelace in this plot. Portray it that he aided and abetted Peters's escape by sending his man in to assist her. I think we can totally destroy his credibility."

"And what would that gain us?"

"You see, Lovelace is the last possible leg propping up the President. If we feed the White House Peters and her companion, we can even turn the President against Lovelace. Remember, he's got to be still smarting because Lovelace fed him that initial false report. At a minimum we can make him think Lovelace is panicked and that these are dangerous folks on the run who need to be eliminated."

"Eliminated?"

"Eliminated, Mr. Chairman," said Walters with conviction. "Eliminated, or this entire thing may be blown wide open. This is no time to get cold feet, Mr. Chairman."

"No one is getting cold feet, Charlie," countered Campbell, stung by the criticism that he might be soft here.

Their exchange could have continued on and on, each man measuring the other, but Campbell was in no mood for sparring.

"This cruise ship that Peters is on—where's it going?" Campbell said.

"It has already gone through the Panama Canal, Mr. Chairman, and is in the Caribbean."

"What's its next port of call?"

"Curaçao, Mr. Chairman."

"I assume that you have a plan, Charlie."

"I do, Mr. Chairman," he lied. Charlie Walters had thought that Howard Campbell would take matters into his own hands at this juncture, but he hadn't. All right, he'd do it himself, dammit. "I'm still putting the last pieces together, but I can assure you, when that ship leaves Curaçao, Peters and her companion will be in our hands."

"I know they will, Charlie. I know they will."

But what Charlie Walters did not know was that Howard Campbell *was* going to take things into his own hands. He'd let Charlie try to catch them, but he'd have a backup plan too. Two loose ends now. This was too important to leave to amateurs. He was going to have to call in the men who had made things happen for him in the past. There was no other way. He buzzed his secretary.

"Alice, get me Colonel Bleich on the line."

CHAPTER 101

WHAT STARTED OUT AS ALMOST PARALYZING FEAR HAD soon become an almost pleasant challenge. Rick and Laura had boarded the MS *Stattendam* and they had—at first—constantly looked over their shoulders waiting for someone in authority to confront them, to ask them for some sort of identification, some proof that they belonged on the ship. That had not happened yet and two days out of Panama, when they reached Curaçao, their only stop before arriving in Fort Lauderdale, they were actually starting to let down their guard and not spend every minute absolutely paranoid. Upon entering the channel to the harbor at Willemstad, the capital city, they had even decided to go ashore, not only to relax, but because the ship would be berthing there overnight. They would be very conspicuous without a cabin to go to. Their relief, however, was at best premature.

By the time the ship reached the inner harbor and the tugs took over, nudging it alongside the seawall, the ship's tour directors were already out about the decks in force, signing scores of passengers up for this tour or that, selling package programs, making hotel reservations. The convenience of wireless telephone communications was making what was usually a laborious, rushed task a pleasant one: "A room for two at the Van der Valk Plaza? Certainly, please wait—ocean view or mountain view? Yes, of course—will the eighth floor be satisfactory? Yes—twin beds—certainly, no problem. And for you, sir—how many in your party? Yes, I think that the Avila Beach Hotel will be your best bet—yes, they have a pool . . ."

And so it went, and while they did not—could not—make a reservation in that manner, Rick was able to overhear enough to determine what hotel would be their best bet. They had stashed Rick's "clubs" and Laura's bag for the back of a large maid's closet so they were free of any encumbrances. They had discussed taking the bags with them but didn't want to run the risk of getting them back aboard again. They would just have to hope for the best and trust that they would be there when they got back.

Once the gangway was open, the passengers poured off the ship like sailors who had been at sea for months. Funny, thought Rick, these folks pay a small fortune to make these cruises, then scurry off the same cruise ships as soon as they hit port. Rick and Laura waited awhile for the throng to thin out a bit, then worked their way off the ship and onto the pier. From the time they left the upper deck Laura had been silent, shuffling along next to Rick, holding his arm with both of hers every time they were jostled by a passerby, stopping when he stopped, moving when he moved again. She looked up at him from time to time, saying nothing.

Once they were on the pier, Rick chided her, "Come on, sailor, you're on liberty. Let's see some spring in your step and a smile on your face."

"Oh, I'm looking forward to it," she said absently, but with a smile.

Rick grabbed her arm in a way that said, *Come on, let's go,* but Laura wrapped both of her arms around his and edged closer.

Rick missed the signal, focused as he was on picking a cab out of the chaos. He finally saw one. "Laura . . . over here . . . quick, a cab." He absently let go of her arm, taking no notice of her intertwining grasp.

As Rick trotted up to the cab, Laura was just a few steps behind. He peered into the window and said, "Holiday Beach Hotel, please."

"Of course, sir, please get in," replied the taxi driver.

Rick ceremoniously opened the right-hand back door for Laura. "Ma'am, your chariot awaits."

"I'm honored, sir," she said with a smile that melted him.

As he gently closed the door and rushed around the back of the cab to hop in himself, he felt some of the reserve and uncertainty that he had about Laura melting away.

Nervously he said with a chuckle, "So I guess we'll be shacked up again. Another one-night stand, eh, Peters?"

Laura did not chuckle, or even betray the hint of a smile. Her eyes met his and she held him in her gaze, held him as intently as she had ever looked at anyone. "I guess we will be." But when she stopped talking she was still gazing deeply into his eyes. To Rick, it was as if she were looking deeply inside him.

The taxi wheeled away with Rick and Laura secure in the back seat. She finally broke their gaze and cuddled next to him, her head resting gently on his shoulder. Naturally. Without reservation. As the driver worked his cab through the narrow, winding streets of the Otrobanda section of Willemstad and outward toward the Holiday Beach Hotel, a feeling of tranquillity neither of them had felt in days came over them. For a moment, they felt there was nothing that could touch them. Nothing that could hurt them. Neither noticed the car trailing loosely behind them.

CHAPTER 102

"THEY'RE WHAT?" TAYLOR CALHOUN SCREAMED, AND shot out of his chair. His staffers had debated during the early morning hours as to who should brief him and take the full brunt of his rage. Courageously, his chief of staff, Carter Thomas, decided that he would be the one to break the news to the President. The official announcement would come from Congress later that morning, but their sources had let them know what to expect. Thomas had already mobilized the staff—and especially Press Secretary Ray Weaver and his people—to begin an all-front counterattack.

For now, Thomas endured the barrage of presidential wrath, dealt out as only Taylor Calhoun knew how to deal it out, bravely being the focal point of the President's wrath, buoyed only by the knowledge that the attacks were not directed at him personally. The President needed to lash out, and Thomas's loyalty to his President was such that enduring this barrage was merely a validation of that loyalty. That was the least he could do for a man who was being victimized by what was now unfolding as one of the most elaborate and well-orchestrated attacks—short of assassination—ever conducted on a head of state, let alone on the President of the United States.

The President stared directly at Thomas, a look of total incredulity enveloping his face. "I can't fucking believe it, Carter, I can't fucking believe it. What are they thinking about? They can't do this! They can't do this!"

But he knew they could, knew that with the Intelligence Oversight Committee hearings as a backdrop they could just about do anything they wanted to do. Oh, these bastards couldn't wait. They just couldn't wait.

"They can try anything they want to, Mr. President.

361

We'll fight them, and we'll win," said Thomas, attempting to mollify the President by any means possible, but knowing that the deck was stacked heavily against the President.

The Intelligence Oversight Committee hearings, of course, had been a catalyzing force. Hell, thought Calhoun, if half of what they were saying he did were true, *he'd* vote to turn it over to the House for impeachment hearings. God, they were awfully good damned liars, the lot of them.

What had gotten this asshole Lindsey all fired up anyway? Taylor Calhoun knew he was an ambitious son of a bitch who saw a whole lot of visibility coming his way from the hearings. But somebody had to be feeding him. Campbell. That had to be it! He was watching the net widen and he was feeling less confident that he could escape.

The whole impeachment process was looking a little too contrived as well. The House Judiciary Committee took a smooth baton handoff from the Intelligence Committee and they were using most of the same allegations. It was all too damn convenient.

Calhoun realized he was ignoring Thomas as he went through his mental anguish. "Okay, Carter," he began, "now let's get our shit in one sock. We need to take the offensive against these sons a bitches. You got a game plan?"

"As you might imagine, Mr. President, we've been working continuously since we got the tip shortly after midnight. We elected not to wake you, sir. We just had snippets of information over the first few hours, but by 0530 we had a fairly complete picture—"

Calhoun interrupted him. "Carter, how long were you going to wait to tell me all of this?"

Carter Thomas knew the question was almost inevitable. "I know we could have awakened you, Mr. President, or contacted you when you were dressed and breakfasting in the family quarters, but, in conferring with the Vice President, he—I mean we believed—I mean—we really felt that you would want to be in the Oval Office when you received this word."

They knew him well, thought Taylor Calhoun. "Well, I

appreciate that, Carter, and I know you all had things that you needed to do without me badgering you with questions. But let's talk about that game plan."

They talked for a long time—first the President and his chief of staff, then one by one with the President's other key advisors, and then as a group. Each contributed a little bit to the puzzle—a little more news—another suggestion as to how to proceed. They all supported him, he did not doubt that, but they were spending too much damn time analyzing this and not enough time planning the counterattack that must come if he were to rescue his presidency.

On Capitol Hill, Congress was in turmoil. The Speaker of the House had moved against Taylor Calhoun with a vengeance. In calling for Judiciary Committee deliberations as a prelude to impeachment hearings he had polarized the House membership. The split went primarily along party lines and the President was paying dearly for the previous year's midterm elections where his party had lost heavily.

Beyond the normal political antipathy that existed between powerful figures of opposite parties, Bobby Wilcox felt no particular animosity toward Taylor Calhoun. He had not contrived a chance to strike out at him, but he was not wont to let an opportunity lapse. He was no fool and he had no desire to commit political suicide. The Lindsey Hearings had been damaging—hell, by themselves they were almost fatal. Then there was all of this appearing in the press. That Kennedy woman sure must have a well-placed source. The allegations about the President directing it all from the White House—shades of LBJ and the Vietnam War, he thought. And then there were those pictures of Calhoun's man Lovelace and that Navy lieutenant they were now trying to hunt down.

That meddling-with-the-military business was the final straw that galvanized the Speaker into action. He was from a district in the Deep South, one of the dwindling pockets in the nation where military service was still an honorable calling and high-ranking military officers still were trusted almost above all others. Bobby Wilcox had no desire to enrage the always-fickle, ever-patriotic voters

in his district who had finally returned him to the House
enough times for him to rise in seniority to have real
power! After being a political nobody and sucking it up
for almost two decades to get where he was, he wasn't
about to jeopardize that just because in his heart of hearts
he didn't think what he was doing was exactly the right
thing.

The Speaker had thought about how he was going to
do this for a while and had come up with a good plan. He
had turned the matter over to the House Judiciary Committee and instructed the committee chairman, Representative Linda Cohen of New York, to conduct "the most
thorough possible hearings into this most important matter." Cohen had needed little urging and bolted out of the
starting blocks determined to capture the attention of the
nation.

On the appointed day, the Judiciary Committee began
its hearings. As the other Congressmen were taking their
seats in the hearing room, she walked the corridor to take
her seat with them, her mind focused with blissful clarity.
By the end of the hearings, Representative Linda Cohen
would be a household name throughout America.

CHAPTER 103

As the taxi pulled up to the Holiday Beach Hotel after only a short ride from *Stattendam*, Rick and
Laura were taken by the lush surroundings. Willemstad
was a quaint town, but gave little hint of what awaited on
the south side of this small island. Just thirty miles north
of Venezuela, Curaçao was more tropical than most places
in the Caribbean. The prospects of spending a day and a
night in this spot with Laura began to excite Rick in a
particular way. For Laura, she was beyond excitement.
She knew what she wanted and she was at peace with that
thought.

As they alighted from yet another taxi, Rick wished for

a moment that they had some luggage. Here at the front entrance to the Holiday Beach Hotel, with families and children streaming in and out of the hotel lobby, a man and a woman checking into the hotel without any bags sent all the wrong signals. Somehow he felt particularly exposed in their current situation. He'd try to finesse it as best he could.

"Good afternoon, sir," said the desk clerk.

"Good afternoon," replied Rick. "We're just in port for the night with the MS *Stattendam*. The ship's people gave your hotel the highest recommendation. We're interested in a room for one night."

"I think that we can accommodate you," replied the clerk, already punching the computer to see what rooms were available. "Here, I've had a cancellation. Would the fourth floor be satisfactory?"

"I suppose so," replied Rick. Then looking at Laura, almost as an afterthought he said, "That all right with you, dear?"

"Perfect," she said.

As they walked up the three flights of the outside stairwell to their room, it was impossible not to be taken by the island. The warm breeze, which blew gently, making the ubiquitous palm trees sway. The faint scent of suntan oil wafting up from the pool, which sparkled below them. The flutter of birds, which flew from tree to tree. The ambience of this hotel: not new, not modern, not glitzy, but comfortable, appealing, inviting. Whatever mood they were in upon arrival, whatever feelings they might have had, this place only encouraged them.

When they reached their room, 403, Rick said, "This must be it."

"Of course it's it," Laura gently chided.

"Right."

The key in, he slowly turned the knob. The world seemed to pause for a moment. What awaited them in that room? What awaited them beyond it?

The answer to the second question was waiting on the far side of the hotel parking lot. Naval Investigative Service Agents Lee Robinson and Harry Bennitt had gotten out of their car at a discreet distance from where Rick and Laura had left theirs, and positioned themselves where they had a good view of the entire hotel. They had watched Rick and Laura go into and then come out of the hotel lobby, climb three flights of stairs, and enter their room, which, conveniently, faced towards them too.

"Should we call now?" said Bennitt.

"No, let's watch them for just a minute. They may pop right out and we'll have to move again," replied Robinson, clearly the senior agent of the two.

"I'm not comfortable with this," Bennitt continued. "We had strict instructions. If they're here, call for backup immediately."

"Yeah, I know all that," replied his partner, clearly annoyed. "That's the bureaucratic response we're always going to get. And I'm going to call, in just a minute. But hell, are you saying we couldn't take these two if we needed to? Come on, we could take 'em, cuff 'em, tie 'em up, and have 'em for lunch in the time it took the rest of the gang to get their lazy butts out here."

Robinson and Bennitt had been sent here by Major Lang and General Walters first to see if Rick and Laura were on the cruise ship. They wanted to be certain of that before they committed a large number of assets and caused a diplomatic rhubarb by flooding this small island with agents, soldiers, and the like. Walters didn't want to use military people in the initial search for Rick and Laura. He wanted to keep it low-key by using agents who worked the counternarcotics effort in and around Central and South America and the Caribbean. Robinson and Bennitt had traveled extensively in this area and were perfect point men for this mission. To ensure that these agents raised absolutely no suspicion and carried out their mission in a completely low-key fashion, General Walters had insisted that they not carry weapons of any kind. Backup help was on call—they were just the scouts.

The plan was simple. The two NIS agents had arrived by commercial flight yesterday. They were to determine if Rick and Laura were aboard the *Stattendam*. As soon as they found out, they were to call for reinforcements. If the two fugitives never got off the *Stattendam*, they were to leave them alone and wait for the ship to get to Fort Lauderdale. If Rick and Laura got off the ship, they were to call for reinforcements and a mixed team from SouthCom's security branch was already earmarked to arrive on a "training flight" on a T-39 military jet, which was on strip alert at Howard Air Force Base. Once captured, the tricky part would be spiriting them off the island. The plan was to have another T-39 "training flight" arrive on the island and take Rick and Laura back to Panama. It would take a little finesse, and some local officials would have to be enriched just a bit, but this island had a reputation for being the place where you could get things done for a price. The plan had no holes.

No holes save actually capturing the two. While Bennitt paced, Robinson reviewed his options. Hell, he finally admitted to himself, if that's the way they want it done, I'll do it. Better to keep the peace. Sounds like overkill, though. The two of them against two scared people on the run—and one of them a woman to boot—those were odds he could live with. He could—but they couldn't. Damn bureaucrats. He told Bennitt to keep a sharp eye out while he made the call.

"Done," Robinson said as soon as he had completed the call back to Panama. "They'll be here late this evening. Any activity?"

"Nothing I can see from here, but hey, no bags, still up there. You tell me," replied Bennitt.

They remained there for hours, thinking they knew exactly what was going on in Room 403 of the Holiday Beach Hotel, letting their prurient imaginations run wild. All they could do was to sit and wait, wait as they were told. Backup better damn well get here on time, Robinson thought to himself. At least he had his own contingency plan tucked away if they didn't.

At Howard Air Force Base, the crew chief stood in front of the roaring T-39 as the jet tried a third time to run up its second engine. The pained look on his face matched that of the pilots as one of them finally gave the cut signal to shut the jet down. Disgusted, they threw their headsets down and stalked down the ladder and out of the aircraft.

"Dammit, Staff Sergeant," the first pilot said. "Can't get near full power."

"We'll check it out, sir," replied the crew chief.

"Hurry it up, would you?"

"Yes sir."

Turning to his copilot, he said, "Better tell our passengers there will be a delay while we either get this one fixed or get another aircraft. Why don't you get an updated weather brief and refile our flight plan for a later departure?"

"Will do," said his copilot as he rushed off toward base operations.

"Sir," said the crew chief, who had overheard this conversation as he was removing the cowling for the recalcitrant engine, "it's fix this one or forget it. Only other T-39 here right now is torn apart in the hangar for a phase inspection. All the others are out on missions. First ones due back late tonight from a three-day operation. No telling what shape it'll be in."

"Work it hard, Staff Sergeant," he replied. "Sounds like I better pass this news up the chain. They're really gonna like this."

As Rick closed the door behind him, Laura drew the curtain on the room's window that faced out on the pool. They were now two people moving with one purpose. No words were necessary. It was as if both of them were propelled toward this by forces bigger than themselves. They stood facing each other in the center of the room, the only light the faint glow of sunlight that slipped around the corner of the curtain.

Finally, she made the first move. "Rick," she almost shouted as she wrapped her arms around him as she had done at the Westin. But this time she did not go limp, did not collapse in his arms. Instead, she grabbed his face in her hands and kissed him. First a peck. Then, her lips still closed, a long full kiss. At first gently, then with more and more insistence, she forced her tongue inside his mouth, moving slowly at first, probing, waiting for a response. It was there. Responding eagerly, Rick matched her, their kissing more and more passionate, probing each other more rapidly now, releasing deep feelings and pent-up passions.

Each time it seemed they could not kiss any more deeply, they surprised themselves by finding new avenues of pleasure, each one taking the lead, then passing it off, then taking it again, until they were like one mind. Hands moving more and more rapidly too, first touching, then caressing, then pulling, almost crushing, then almost tearing off each piece of clothing, each responding to the other, until there was nothing left, just a pile on the floor and both of them drinking in each other, enjoying every aspect of the other's body for just an instant, for that was all they would allow themselves to stop kissing, by now so deep that they gasped for breath.

Laura finally pulled back and held him in her gaze. "Rick?"

"Yes," was all he needed to say.

She pushed him down on the bed, gently but with authority, her passion going full-tilt now, wanting him, needing him inside her. Rick pulled her to him, kissing her deeply again. She pulled back a little, then tilted her head back and pulled Rick ever so slowly up. He caressed her breasts for a moment, then his mouth was eagerly on them, kissing, drinking her in, responding as she moved his face from side to side, moaning with pleasure.

Now she pulled away once again. Oh, to continue this for hours, kissing and caressing each other, but their passion was too intense now. Laura was sitting on top of him, looking into his eyes, saying nothing but saying everything. With one motion she slid up toward him and then pushed him inside her. They both hesitated for an instant, then Laura began, rising up and sliding down, first slowly, controlled. He matched her, their rhythm perfect. Then her eyes widened, the rhythm became less and less controlled. She was in the full throes now, rising and falling, Rick matching her, the rhythm now gone, the intensity surprising them both, both gasping.

Finally they both went rigid, suspended in space and time. One with each other. Too enveloped by each other to say anything. Laura just closed her eyes and rolled her head back. Rick closed his eyes too as if to freeze this moment in his brain. She rolled off of him, flung her arm across his still-heaving chest, and then curled up and buried herself in his side. Words were not, could not, be there. Soon they were asleep, dreaming, of course, of each other, but also dreaming of freedom.

Still in the parking lot of the hotel, Robinson and Bennitt were getting more and more impatient. They'd held up their end of the bargain. Where the hell was the cavalry?

CHAPTER 104

THE GROUP OF CONGRESSMEN SITTING IN THE HEARING room waiting for Committee Chairwoman Cohen were a grim-looking lot. Mercer from New York's Fifteenth District, Carmichael from Kentucky's Fourth District, Allison from California's Thirty-second District, Harrison from Minnesota's Sixth District, Chambers from Oregon's Fourth District, Rathborne from Colorado's Third District, Coyne from Michigan's Twelfth District, O'Doyle from Connecticut's Second District.

There was no animated conversation. No collegial bantering. No last-minute deal-making on this bill or that. They were about to conduct grim business. Regardless of their party affiliation, regardless of their professional or personal feelings toward Taylor Calhoun, they all recognized that if they were here doing this, then the system had broken down, and broken down terribly.

They rose as the chairwoman entered. Linda Cohen motioned for them to be seated, motioned gracefully in a way that suggested that they needn't have gotten up in the first place. She sat down and got right to the point. Pleasantries had no place in this room.

"Ladies and gentlemen, you all know why we are here.

We have the very unpleasant task of determining whether or not there is sufficient reason to call for the impeachment of the President of the United States. I don't have to remind you, I am sure, that this is a matter of the utmost gravity. Proceed without proper deliberation and without proper caution, and we do a great disservice to the President and to the nation. Proceed too slowly, and we shirk our duty to do the right thing and do what we are charged by law to do. I want all of you to put your other weighty duties on hold while you are performing this critical service to your nation."

There was a moment of silence as her colleagues considered her remarks. Then, as Cohen would relate later, all hell broke loose.

Coyne, of Michigan, spoke first. "Madam Chairwoman, I in fact *don't* know why in the hell we are here."

Harrison, from neighboring Minnesota—and, like Coyne, a member of the President's party—jumped in. "That's right, Madam Chairwoman. This charge against the President is the thinnest of all possible reeds. It just doesn't add up. We have *got* to find out more before proceeding one bit further. I make a motion that the Judiciary Committee dissolve immediately. I'm sure we all have pressing matters that we're involved in."

"I agree," said Coyne. "Let's dissolve, and let's do it now!"

Congresswoman Linda Cohen looked at each of them impassively as they spoke. She motioned as if she were going to speak, but then, as scripted, she demurred as one of her colleagues from her party rose to speak.

"Madam Chairwoman," began Lawrence Allison, the distinguished-looking Congressman from California. "I know that my colleagues from Michigan and Minnesota have very important matters to attend to. I empathize with their dilemma. We are all busy, and I am sure that if the gentlemen want to be excused from this committee, that can be arranged." Allison paused for dramatic effect and met the glares directed at him by Coyne and Harrison, holding them in his gaze as if to burn right through them.

Again, as if on cue—and it was, for Linda Cohen was

one of the House's consummate political insiders and had had a premeeting to discuss their strategy to oust the President—Congressman Billy Carmichael of Kentucky rose and cleared his throat. "Madam Chairwoman, I must agree with the distinguished gentleman from California. This is certainly no rush to judgment. Senator Lindsey's committee revealed some shocking details of the President's meddling in military affairs. We certainly need to give our Commander in Chief sufficient latitude to fulfill his duties, but he is not a military man and has no business directing military actions!"

Coyne leaped from his chair. "No business? No business! He has every business doing just that! He's the Commander in Chief. But the mistakes here were made in the field, not in the White House. Surely you know that every military operation incurs risk!"

"Oh, I know that!" replied Carmichael, now clearly seething with rage. "I know that all too well. So do the families of the three boys from Kentucky who died in that ambush, especially the family of Harold Ashby of my district. Harold was all of nineteen. Risk! You explain risk to Harold's widowed mama, who raised him all by herself since he was three. You explain that to Harold's two baby sisters, who carried a picture of Harold in his Marine uniform with them everywhere they went. You explain that to Harold's seventy-eight-year-old widowed grandmother, Mrs. Alice Baker, who also lives in my district and who will never have a grandson again. You tell them, Mr. Coyne, why your President sent Harold and all these other boys to their deaths just to try to convince all of us he was tough on drugs and just because he wanted to raise his standing in the polls!" Carmichael was in full fire now, stabbing his finger at Coyne spitting his words out.

Linda was enjoying every minute of this. Yes, it would all go the way she and the Speaker had orchestrated it. She just needed to keep a semblance of order—for the record. Even though these hearings were closed, the ever-present secretary was there dutifully taking down every word, preserving these hearings for history.

"Gentlemen, *gentlemen,*" began the chairwoman. Then, almost forgetting the lone other woman on the panel, Jessica Mercer of New York, she added, "And lady. I'll remind you all that we are colleagues. We are supposed to be about the business that the nation has charged us with. I know that you all feel strongly about the things that are transpiring, but we must conduct these deliberations in as dispassionate a manner as possible. We must decide, on the facts and on the facts alone, if there is sufficient evidence that the President of the United States committed high crimes and misdemeanors in his actions with respect to Operation Roundup. That is the matter before us. Now, I assume that you all read the numerous depositions that have been placed before us. Congressman Rathborne," she said, addressing her party's fifth-term congressman from Colorado, "not wanting to put you on the spot"—but of course she wasn't, for this too had been rehearsed—"have you had an opportunity to go over all of the depositions that have bearing on this situation?"

Rathborne rose. "I have, Madam Chairwoman."

"Do you have a general sense of what they are telling us?" said Cohen. She had used the word *general* purposely and knew that Rathborne would seize this opportunity to add punch to his response.

"Oh, I have much more than a *general* sense, Madam Chairwoman. I have spent days and nights poring over these depositions, with the help of my staff, of course, and I have a *precise* sense of exactly what these documents tell us."

"And what would that be?" asked Cohen, working mightily to portray herself as a dispassionate neutral, a Solomon-like arbiter who had no agenda but to do what was right for the nation.

"These documents," replied Rathborne, "and especially the depositions of our military men—men, I would remind my esteemed colleagues, who have no political agenda, no ax to grind, no purpose in life except to serve the nation and protect the young men who they lead—tell us a disturbing story."

"How so?" said Cohen.

"They show," continued Rathborne, enjoying the limelight Wilcox had promised him, "that the 'system' worked exactly as it should have. You know full well, Madam

Chairwoman, as do all of our colleagues, that we appropriate over thirty billion dollars a year—*thirty billion*—for
intelligence of all kinds, much of it military intelligence
and other intelligence directly related to national security.
I believe that we mostly get our money's worth. However,
the key is that this intelligence must be used. In this case,
the military commanders in the Pentagon and in the field
had the information, used the information, and then
passed very strong recommendations to both the White
House and to the President's personal appointee as JTF
commander, General Lovelace, that an ambush awaited
our brave men. Clearly, convincingly, according to these
depositions, as well as other information available for our
deliberations, this sound military advice was ignored, with
catastrophic results. This evidence is so damning, so convincing, that any reasonable man—or woman—would recognize that we have only one recourse."

The discussions went on for hours, while every word
was being dutifully recorded. Congressman after Congressman—those who were recognized by Cohen—was afforded an opportunity to get up and speak as Rathborne
had spoken. Cohen strove mightily to preserve her image
of mediator and she was largely successful, although occasionally she had to bully one or another member of the
President's party into truncating his remarks, citing the
need to keep the hearings moving. All in all, it was an
impressive, well-staged performance.

CHAPTER 105

"GOOD MORNING."
     Then louder.
     "Good morning."
     Rick sat bolt upright in the bed. Instinctively, he looked
down at Laura. She was there. She was safe. Still sleeping.
He thought he had never seen anyone as beautiful in his
life.

His eyes moved quickly to the door and met another set of eyes. The tiny Venezuelan maid had opened the door a discreet crack—opened it has she had done hundreds of times—in order to see if it was okay to come in and make up their room.

Rick remembered that they had failed to put the DO NOT DISTURB sign out and just gave the maid an embarrassed wave. She understood instantly—most in her trade had seen and heard just about everything and they had learned as a matter of professional survival to be discreet—and pulled the door closed behind her.

That mini-crisis over, Rick looked down again at Laura. The night had been indescribable. Making love to Laura and being one with her was something he had dared not think of before—now it overwhelmed his very being. This was not a conquest. No, she was so different, so unlike anyone he had ever known, so unlike anyone he had ever imagined. Although their intimacy had been total bliss, a more important aspect of it was that it sealed the bond between them, a bond that had been growing stronger by the hour.

The time! Had they missed the MS *Stattendam*? As he slipped out of bed and pulled on his shorts, he looked around frantically. No clock. Where was his watch? As he almost frantically tossed piece after piece of clothing aside looking for it, Laura stirred.

"Hey, what's up, you?" she said sweetly.

"Good morning. Didn't mean to wake you," he replied.

"You're moving awfully quickly. Why so rushed?" she said as she sat up in bed and the covers slipped away. Rick stared at her. She was incredibly beautiful. Here. This morning. Not in the passion of the night, but in the harsh light of the day. Rick could not believe that anyone could be so beautiful—or so desirable. But that was not what he was about now. He had to find his watch.

"Laura, I've—I mean, we've got—"

But she didn't let him finish. She rose out of bed and came toward him in a rush. No pretensions, but with full abandon, she pulled him to her. He felt himself go limp, melting into her arms, this goddess who totally enveloped him, kissing, caressing, then letting go and pulling him down onto the bed. Almost instantly out of control, ripping off his shorts, now on top of him. Eager, insistent. More passionate than he could ever imagine anyone being. Powerless to resist, he let himself be drawn in.

After what seemed like an eternity—a blissful eternity—she rolled off Rick and lay beside him. He gathered his wits and started to speak.

"Laura, we—"

"Shhh."

They lay beside each other for what seemed another eternity. And for the first time in his life, Rick Holden—model son, CIA agent, Navy SEAL, a man who lived his life in total control—had no control, and it did not bother him.

Laura finally let reality slip back into the picture.

"I know that you're going to tell me we have to get back aboard *Stattendam* before it sails. What if I don't want to? What if I just want to stay here? In bed. With you."

"I'd say that's an idea worth pursuing," said Rick, meaning it more than he thought he dared.

"Oh no, you wouldn't. You'd tell us we have to move along—but thanks for saying that."

"I meant it, Laura."

"You're a dear. And you're something else," said Laura with a knowing wink and arched eyebrows. The sex had been incredible for her too and she wanted Rick to know it for certain. Wanted him to know it for a lot of reasons.

"You are too. I don't think we really have a choice, though. *Stattendam* is our only sure way out of here, and I've got to think that Walters is going to keep pursuing you, so we've got to stay ahead of him and his henchmen. Where the hell is my watch? Aren't they sailing at one P.M?"

Across the parking lot of the hotel, NIS Agents Robinson and Bennitt were in a foul mood and were more than a little bit worried. They had stood the watch here as the balmy tropical evening had slowly degraded into a cool, then cold and rainy night. They had taken turns trying to sleep in their crammed compact car while the other carefully watched the hotel room, but it was uncomfortable at best, torture at worst. Even the principal on watch couldn't be certain that he had remained awake every moment.

And then there was the fiasco back in Panama. The other agents and military personnel—the "hit squad," as Major Lang called it—that had been assembled to back them up had now gone through two T-39s, both of which had severe enough maintenance problems that they were deemed unflyable. Powerless to do anything about it from their position, Robinson and Bennitt had cursed the fates and were more than a little suspicious that this group didn't really want to embark on this mission anyway. Leave it to the military, in particular, to come up with some lame excuse as to why they couldn't participate in an operation. After the last particularly heated phone call, Robinson and Bennitt were starting to come to the conclusion that they might be on their own on this one. But on their own to do what?

Robinson looked at his watch. "Jesus, Harry, it's eleven forty-five. Do you think we missed 'em?"

"No, no . . . at least, I don't think so. Kinda hard to see the hotel room clearly all night, especially through the rain. But no, I think they're still in there," Bennitt replied, but without full conviction.

"I do too," said Robinson, "but they must really be going at it. Think they're planning on getting on the *Stattendam* or just shacking up here indefinitely?"

"Hard to say. When do you think those assholes back at Howard will finally get some help to us?"

"Don't know. We just gotta plan to do it all ourselves if it comes right down to it."

"We need to get instructions," Bennitt replied, now questioning the senior agent. He wasn't accustomed to freelancing and was uncomfortable enough with this hurry-up and hush-hush mission as it was already.

"We gotta complete our mission. And if the drones back at Howard can't get us reinforcements and can't even decide exactly what they want us to do, we have to call an audible."

*   *   *

"Laura, it's almost noon. We've got to get back to *Stattendam*," said Rick, trying to push her along without seeming to push her along.

"Sure you don't just want to stay here for the duration?" she replied. She smiled in a way that let him know she knew full well that they had to get back aboard the ship, but that the alternative of staying with him was much more appealing.

"Sure," he said, "we could be islanders. Maybe set up a bead shop down in town." He started picking her clothes off the floor.

"Okay, I get the hint. Let me throw my things together and we're out of here."

As he watched the hands of his watch come together, then apart, Agent Lee Robinson could stand it no longer. "Harry, I'm not sure they're there anymore. We've got to find out."

"How do we do that?" replied Bennitt. The junior agent was clearly dissatisfied with this entire arrangement and his patience was wearing thin.

"Simple," replied Robinson. "We'll move in and ask the desk clerk if they've checked out yet."

"Do we identify ourselves?"

"Of course not. We have no jurisdiction on this island anyway. We'll just tell them we're friends who are on the cruise with them. Say we rented a car and we're offering to give 'em a ride back."

"Okay, maybe they'll buy that."

"I don't see why they wouldn't," replied Robinson, now getting a little bit agitated that the junior agent was not fully enthused about his plan.

They drove their car around the outside of the parking lot and up to the entrance to the hotel, keeping a wary eye on room 403 the entire time. They left the car idling outside as Robinson approached the desk clerk and Bennitt hung back, still scanning the landscape for any sign of Rick and Laura. Robinson had just started telling his tale to the clerk when Bennitt moved toward him.

"Lee."

"I'll be right with you, Harry," said Robinson over his shoulder. "Let me finish with this gentleman first."

"Lee!"

"Harry, I said—"

As he turned, Robinson saw the reason for Bennitt's interruption. Rick and Laura had emerged from their room and were heading quickly toward the staircase that would lead them to the front desk. The agents knew it was time to blend back into their car and trail them again.

Rick looked toward the lobby as they made their way down the steps but took no particular note of the two men near the desk clerk or the idling car just outside. As Rick and Laura proceeded toward the lobby, Robinson and Bennitt slipped into their car and drove away slowly. He didn't give them another thought.

Rick went straight up to the desk clerk. They weren't in a panic, but they didn't have any time to waste. Speaking crisply, he said, "We're checking out of 403. Wonderful hotel. Sorry if we're a few minutes late checking out. We'll need a cab to take us to MS *Stattendam*, please. Will cash be okay?"

"Cash will be fine, sir. I'll call a taxi for you. It will be here within minutes. Your friends were just here asking if they could give you a ride back to the ship."

"Our friends?"

"Yes. Two gentlemen. Said that they had rented a car and would take you back to the cruiseliner. We were having a nice conversation, but they left abruptly."

"Are you certain they were asking about us?"

"Well, I think so. They mentioned your room number, although not your name, Mr. Allen. Thought they might have missed you. I told them you hadn't checked out but that you might be out touring around. Then they left suddenly."

Rick feared the worst. "Fine. Thanks. We won't wait for them to come back. Really would like to get that cab now."

"Of course, sir. Right away."

Rick stepped away from the desk and toward Laura. She had heard the entire exchange and now she too feared the worst. They were being followed. He pulled her toward him and pulled her head down onto his shoulder.

"It's okay. It's going to be okay."

"I know it is. Let's just get back to *Stattendam* and get out of here."

"We will."

After waiting what seemed like an eternity, the taxi arrived and Rick and Laura jumped in. "We're going to the MS *Stattendam*. Please hurry or we'll miss our ship."

"No worries, my friend," said the driver. "Only a short hop. Have you there in a flash."

They had only gotten a block away from the hotel when Rick's fears became a reality. A car eased into the traffic stream right behind them, the same car that had been idling in front of the hotel. Rick strained to look in the rearview mirror and try to see if the same two men who had been talking to the desk clerk were in the car. Laura did not say anything, but took Rick's hand and held it tightly.

Rick decided not playing it sly would get them nowhere. He leaned forward and pressed two twenty-dollar bills into the driver's hand. "I need you to *really* make good time to *Stattendam,* and I'd appreciate it if you would lose that fellow trailing us."

"Traffic laws are pretty strict around Willemstad."

Rick pressed two more twenties into his hand. "This should take care of any infraction you might get."

"I think that it might," replied the driver as he stomped on the accelerator and blasted down the road. This driver did not need much encouragement, it seemed.

Rick's mind was now in overdrive. What to do now? They would get to *Stattendam* in ample time, that was not an issue. Would the car behind them keep up? As Rick looked into the mirror, he confirmed that they had not lost their "friends."

"Think they'll stay with us to *Stattendam*?" Rick asked Laura.

"Looks like they're doing a great job of keeping up," she said, loud enough for the cab driver to hear her, hoping that he might somehow be shamed into working harder on losing them.

"Do you think they'll follow us aboard *Stattendam*?"

"If we could figure a way to get aboard, they probably can too."

"I kinda agree."

"Then what?"

"Well," replied Rick, "that would be the worst case on all accounts. We'd never know when they'd strike and then they could always call for reinforcements once we get to Fort Lauderdale. No, I think our choice is clear."

"I don't know, Rick," replied Laura. "It's sure not all that clear to me."

But it was to Rick. They were only a few blocks from the cruise ship. The driver was moving as fast as he dared through the narrow streets, but they had not lost their pursuers. Rick pulled Laura close to him, held her face in his hands, looked deep into her eyes, and spoke.

"Laura, when the taxi stops we're only a few blocks from *Stattendam*. Run for it for all you're worth. Don't stop. Don't look back. Just get aboard and blend in. I'll find you," he said with great urgency and conviction in his voice.

"Rick, no . . ." she said, but he wasn't listening.

Rick scanned right and left up and down the streets of Willemstad. He spotted his opportunity. Leaning forward and putting his face right next to that of the driver, he said, "Next right. Turn into that alley. Do it."

"But—"

"*Do it!*"

The driver needed no further urging. As he approached the corner he barely slowed the taxi and wheeled into an alley barely big enough to fit his cab. The two- and three-story buildings with their muted colors and deep-set wood-framed windows were almost close enough to reach out and touch. The cabbie began picking up speed again, then Rick reached up and grabbed his shoulder.

"Stop. *Stop here!*"

The driver hit the brakes immediately, barely keeping the cab straight. As it jolted to a halt, Rick flung open the door and pushed Laura. "Now, Laura. Run. Run ahead of the cab. Do it!"

Laura gave him a look that said she hoped she could trust him and took off like a shot. Rick and the driver sat frozen, watching her make her escape. Then Rick looked in the rearview mirror and saw what he expected to see.

Surprised by the taxi's sudden turn, Robinson and Bennitt overshot the alley in their car, but quickly backed up and roared down it. Then they saw into the alley. The taxi stopped ahead of them.

"Geez, Lee, hit the brakes, hit the goddamned brakes!" screamed Bennitt, although Robinson was only inches away in their cramped car.

"I am, Harry, I am!"

"What now?" Bennitt screamed as the car clipped a wall and jerked to a halt.

"We take 'em, goddammit, that's what!" said Robinson. But although his senior partner screamed it back with conviction, Bennitt wasn't sure if he really knew what they were doing.

The alley fell quiet. Laura had scampered out of the alley and was gone. In the taxi, Rick just held onto the driver's shoulder, the unmistakable body language conveying, *Just wait. Just wait one minute.* In their car, Robinson and Bennitt did not jump out, having seen there were people in the taxi. Eerily, even at midday, there were no pedestrians in the alley. It was as if anyone who saw even part of this scene knew enough to drift away.

Finally, Rick made the first move. Pressing several more bills into the driver's hand, he said, "I'm getting out and walking toward that car. Just wait here a moment and then drive slowly, very slowly, away and turn away from the cruise ship pier."

"Yes sir," said the driver. He seemed willing to go along with Rick, although he was not sure precisely why.

As Rick exited the taxi, his mind was racing with the possibilities. Did they see Laura? Were they armed? What did they intend to do? He stood stock-still for a moment, looking at the car, trying to determine if Robinson and Bennitt were the ones he had seen at the Holiday Beach Hotel. They looked very much like they were. He kept walking toward them. Slowly. Not threateningly. Closer now. They stared at him. Then Robinson got out of the car. Bennitt followed. The cab started to drive slowly up the alley. Rick knew they were the ones at the hotel now. Robinson and Bennitt hesitated momentarily when the taxi started to move, but then Rick kept moving slowly toward them.

"Whoa, friend," Robinson said, raising his arm. "I think that's close enough."

"You were chasing my cab. Why?"

"Just thought something was amiss. Say, your cab is going away."

"I'm through with it."

"Kind of odd he dropped you in this alley. Lost?"

"No—shopping," replied Rick, momentarily emboldened, thinking that this might not be as tough as he had feared.

"Shopping. I see," said Bennitt. "You alone in the taxi?"

"No, the driver brought me here." Rick was seeing how far they would let him go. So far, there were no limits.

"I see," replied Bennitt. "No young lady?"

"If I had a young lady I sure wouldn't be in this alley talking to you two."

"Oh?" said Robinson. "Not now, you mean. But wasn't there one with you when you left the hotel?"

"The hotel?" said Rick.

"The Holiday Beach Hotel."

"You fellas been following me since there? Say. I don't owe either one of you money, do I?" Rick was on a roll now and for a moment he almost thought he could talk his way out of this.

Bennitt snapped, "No, wiseass. Now how about some ID?" Robinson winced. That wasn't the smart play.

"ID?" replied Rick. "Are you fellows with the authorities?"

"You're damn right," began Bennitt, growing enraged. "Let me—"

Robinson cut him off. "Okay, fella, we'll make this all very clear to you. But first you tell us where the young lady is who was in the cab with you. There was a young lady who embarked with you at the hotel, wasn't there?"

"Oh yes," said Rick. "Yes, of course. Another guest I met casually. Wanted to share the cab. Several blocks back, I dropped her to do some shopping at the floating market. Didn't you see her get out?"

"No," growled Bennitt.

"Yes, she did. Well, sorry for the confusion. I'll be on my way."

Rick's plan was evolving by the second. It now looked like Laura would get safely back aboard *Stattendam*. These goons seemed content for the moment to waste their time talking to him. But what then? When would he have to break off and sprint for *Stattendam* himself? Would they follow? Almost surely yes. This could not go on forever.

"I'm afraid that won't be possible," said Robinson as he reached out to grab Rick's arm.

In an instant it was all clarified for Rick. He began to pull his arm away as if to merely break the man's grasp but then quickly grabbed Robinson's arm just above the elbow and flung the older man into the side of the building. He slid down in a heap. Rick wheeled and faced Bennitt, who was frozen in disbelief. Rick started toward him and Bennitt took a wild swing at Rick. He easily dodged the agent's blow, then countered, hitting him once, twice, then again and again. They weren't wild, maniacal blows, just the steady pummeling of a man who knew he must subdue the other.

Suddenly Rick felt a weight on his back. Robinson had picked himself up and had jumped Rick from behind, trying to restrain his arms. Rick flung his shoulders wildly trying to dislodge him and it gave Bennitt enough time to recover. He started punching Rick, mainly in the body, occasionally finding the range and hitting him in the face. Rick finally flung Robinson off his back and attacked Bennitt again. Now tasting his own blood, Rick began to deliver blows repeatedly to Bennitt's head, striking out at him with abandon. Finally the man slumped on the ground. He was motionless. Was he dead? Rick didn't know.

He looked around again. Seeing Bennitt dropped like that had taken away all of Robinson's zeal. He was standing on the far side of the narrow alley, still just a few feet away from Rick with his back pressed up against the wall and his arms outstretched in front of him, clearly signaling Rick that he wanted no more. Rick looked around. No one else had entered the alley, and although he saw a person occasionally pass by one end or the other, it didn't appear that anyone was going to come and stop them. Had someone called the police, though?

Rick approached Robinson menacingly, his fists up. "Who are you?"

"Listen, we don't want to hurt you. We just—"

Rick lunged at him and put his right hand on Robinson's throat, pressing him against the wall of the building. The man was terrified, Rick could see that. He had to use that to his advantage. "Last time before I snap your neck. Who sent you?"

Robinson was as terrified as he had ever been in his life. Damn Lang and damn General Walters for making them leave their weapons behind in Panama. "Low-key." What a joke. Now he was letting it all hang out. He assessed him as capable of anything. He had no desire to give his life in the line of duty.

"We ... we ... well ..."

Rick increased the pressure on his neck and now lay his left forearm into Robinson's chest, shoving him even tighter against the building. Robinson felt as if every rib would snap. "*Now!* Don't bullshit me, friend, or you'll end up like your partner!" screamed Rick, trying to break the man right there, right now.

"We're ... we're NIS. Sent from Panama. The woman you're with escaped from confinement. Sent to bring her back. Unharmed. Totally unharmed. That's all it is."

Robinson went limp, as if telling the story had drained his body of the last bit of energy it possessed.

Rick knew all he needed to know. He relaxed his grip but then quickly spun Robinson around and flung him to the ground. "Don't move. Don't move a muscle."

He was contrite now, but in five minutes? Looking around for a solution, Rick looked down on the still-motionless Bennitt. He knelt down next to him and rolled him over, taking his light sport coat off of him. The man was still breathing, but unconscious.

Sport coat in hand, Rick returned to the cowering Robinson, who looked like he was trying to crawl into the wall. In a fluid motion, Rick grabbed the supine Robinson and used the sport coat to tie his arms behind his back. Robinson groaned with the pressure on his arms and wrists, but Rick wanted to ensure that Robinson would not escape.

That done, Rick stood up and gathered his wits. Still no passersby. He patted each man down, extracting their wallets from their pockets. NIS. Clearly. Identification. Robinson hadn't lied. Special Agent Lee Robinson, age fifty-two. Special Agent Harry Bennitt, age thirty-five. Other ID confirmed that they worked out of Panama. The picture was becoming very clear. Pocketing the wallets, he returned to Robinson and, putting his hand roughly on his neck again, demanded, "Who else is on this island with you?"

"N-no one," stammered the terrified Robinson. Was he going to kill him after all? "No one."

"Bullshit!" screamed Rick, determined to elicit the truth from this terrified man.

"No. No. We were supposed to wait for others. There was a plane. It went down with mechanical problems. We couldn't get anyone else here. We just were trying to do our job—"

Rick cut him off. "Do your job for who?"

"The security officer at Rodman. This is what we do— we track down people who are AWOL or whatever. Routine, really routine."

Robinson was whimpering now, clearly afraid that Rick would kill him.

"Enough," said Rick. He had to complete this job. Reaching down around Robinson's waist, he pulled his belt off. He stuffed the handkerchief he had pulled out of Bennitt's pocket in Robinson's mouth and secured it roughly with the belt, causing Robinson to groan again. Then he returned to the still-unconscious Bennitt and stripped off his belt, tying his arms behind him with it, while pulling his shirt up over his head and jamming the bulk of it into his mouth.

Rick stood up. Couldn't leave them there. He dragged Bennitt into a doorway and then grabbed Robinson and duckwalked him to the same spot, throwing him down on his partner.

"Don't try to move. And if you come after me, I'll kill you."

With that, Rick sprinted for the MS *Stattendam*.

CHAPTER 106

CHARLIE WALTERS THOUGHT BACK TO A SIMPLER TIME, a more straightforward time. He thought back to the time—it seemed like just yesterday—when he was still J-5 with the Joint Chiefs and when Howard Campbell had told him of his plans and enlisted his support as they sat on the clubhouse rooftop at Army-Navy Country Club in Arlington. As he closed his eyes, the general remembered every detail of that day vividly—the lush golf course laid out before them, the shouts of the children frolicking in the swimming pools, the resounding whap of the tennis balls being stroked on the club's many courts, the smell of the gardenias proliferating on the club's lush grounds. Howard had picked the spot well. It was a perfect venue to broach such a subject.

Major Lang had just left. This time Walters had all but thrown him out of his office. What had started out as a simple tracking down of two people on the run had grown incredibly complex. Planes had broken down. Two agents were doing what they damned well pleased. About the only thing he did know was that Peters and her companion were in Curaçao. That was small recompense, because they were soon to be beyond his reach.

He had to report all of this to the chairman—a task he did not relish. He knew General Campbell was under enormous stress and that he did not intend to ride roughshod over him, but the recent attacks had stung nonetheless. He found himself wondering if he had embarked on the right path, as he buzzed for his aide to get Campbell on the line.

"Hello, Charlie," Howard said when they were connected. "I've been waiting for your call. I assume you have Lieutenant Peters and her friend in hand and have them on their way back to your headquarters in Panama."

"Not exactly, Mr. Chairman."

"How so, Charlie?"

"We're still pursuing them."

"Still pursuing them? How many people do you have on that little island anyway?"

"Just two, Mr. Chairman."

"Two?"

"Yes, two. But they're two very well qualified NIS agents. I have—"

Campbell cut him off. "What the hell is the problem, Charlie? You got a whole fucking Unified Command at your disposal. All I'm asking you to do is to catch up with two people on the run on a little island that's barely more than two dozen miles long and not half again as wide. Do I have to call out the reserves and maybe the fucking National Guard to help you?"

Charlie Walters knew there was no reasoning with General Howard Campbell. He was now just taking perverse delight in kicking him around. He'd had enough.

"Mr. Chairman, clearly we've botched it at this end. You'll have to pick it up when they get to Fort Lauderdale. It's just over two days' sail. I can have my people let yours know exactly when they'll be arriving and—"

Again Campbell cut him off. "No, Charlie, don't bother. I'll buy a fucking Fort Lauderdale newspaper and figure that out. Thanks anyway."

With that the line went dead. On the other end, after listening to dead air for one incredulous second, Walters slammed down the receiver.

Sitting alone in his Pentagon office, Howard Campbell didn't worry whether he had offended his friend's sensibilities. That loose end, *that damned loose end*, was now driving him to distraction. If Charlie couldn't catch these two, he sure as hell could. Goddammit.

Less than an hour later, after a flurry of phone calls and a number of aides and assistants coming in and out of his office, Howard Campbell was secure in the knowledge that the two fugitives would be in his hands as soon as they reached Fort Lauderdale. You didn't get to be chairman without having ready assets.

He leaned back in his chair and picked up his copy of the *Early Bird*, the Pentagon's clip sheet of all important articles that would appear in that day's national newspapers, and gazed contentedly at the *Washington Post* article on the first page. The byline was by reporter Liz Kennedy:

WASHINGTON—Speaker of the House Wilcox has confirmed that the House will move ahead with impeachment hearings against the President, charging him with "high crimes and misdemeanors" in interfering directly with Operation Roundup, going around senior military commanders and giving orders—unlawful orders—to the commander in the field. The President is being afforded every opportunity to have proper representation, but Speaker Wilcox had indicated that proceedings must begin by next Thursday in order to afford members an opportunity to begin the congressional recess period on time. Members of the President's party have been thus far unsuccessful in blocking these hearings on procedural grounds. Additionally, there are increasing defections from the President's party, particularly from congressmen representing promilitary southern states where public opinion is running heavily against the President . . .

The story went on inside the other pages of the *Early Bird*, and Campbell read them all with relish. He had succeeded exactly as he had planned. And after he tied up that loose end, he would be able to relax and let the system do what it was going to do. Two people on the run— people without the wherewithal to muster any forces against him—were powerless to stop him.

*   *   *

A short drive up the picturesque George Washington Parkway, other forces were starting to coalesce. The three men had found out a lot more than they knew just a short while ago and had come up with a course of action.

They walked along the long, tortuous corridor that would take them from one wing of the CIA's "Crystal Palace" headquarters building to the other. The corridor wound with abrupt angles, reminding them of a rat maze every time they passed through it. As they exited the corridor and passed in front of the guard station where the agency guards carefully checked every bag and parcel brought into the building, the men were in a foul mood. They had developed their own agenda and own sense of urgency regarding what to do with the information Rick had provided them, as well as what to do for Rick. But they had not yet gotten the key people in the Agency who had to sign off on their plan, to agree. They paused in the lobby area by the guard station before entering the rat maze beyond it en route to the office of the assistant chief of the Operations Directorate. It was as if they needed the open space to clear their minds and prepare to tell their story.

"Even if this story is half-true, it needs to come out."

"Yes, but this entire program is black. Only a half-dozen people in the agency know it exists. Even the assistant operations director isn't read in—"

"You're not sure of that."

"No, I am sure. I'm quite sure, and there is no way we can compromise that part of the program."

"I can't believe I'm hearing this."

"You know, our man hasn't called back after the first contact."

"Maybe he's not in a position where he can call back."

"True enough, but we're going to be asked to make an assessment on the validity of the call. I, for one, am not prepared to go out on a limb and say with certainty that all this is true."

"No one's asking you to do that. We just need to alert the system."

"Sure, that sounds easy. But have you thought about how many conspiracy theories are floating around out there? Our job is to separate the wheat from the chaff, to stay unemotional about the whole thing."

"No one's getting emotional."

"Aren't we? He's our man. Maybe we should be."

"Look, we've got a job to do. Let's get on with it."

And so it went. Standing there in the inner lobby area of the CIA's imposing Crystal Palace, the three men argued. Framed by the aqua-green windows surrounding them on all sides and looking at the earnest men and women who plied this building, they wrestled with issues that were as old as time—bureaucratic inertia, not wanting to stick one's neck out, trying to balance sounding alarmist against waiting too long to alert the system that something was amiss. Finally they reached a tentative consensus and one man emerged as their spokesman.

"It's settled, then. We can't push this tale up into the organization; too much else is at stake. We can help Holden, though. Get him into town, have someone waiting for him, ensure that he completes his mission. But he's got to know, it's his mission. No one else's. Strictly covert on all other aspects of this. Anything anyone does to support this, they do because a favor was called in. No other reason. I want to talk to him personally the next time he calls, no matter where I am. Understood?"

The other two men nodded that they understood and their plan was sealed. They hoped it would be enough, given the potentially devastating consequences their failure might bring about.

Back at his headquarters at Quarry Heights, General Charlie Walters had not moved from his office for hours. For the first time he could remember in his long and illustrious career he was shaken, and not because he had let Peters get away, but because Howard Campbell had seemed to step away from him. He didn't know what to do about this. What he did know was that he felt himself stepping ever so slightly away from Howard Campbell. He felt himself thinking more and more about his own survival. Team play was only good as far as it went. His agenda might have to change and might have to change quickly.

Walters began to rehash the entire plot in his own mind. Campbell was in Washington pulling the strings. Down here in Panama, he had no insight into what moves were being made, who was going out on a limb, who was taking the blame. Charlie Walters didn't want to go after anyone else, least of all Howard Campbell; no, that would be ungentlemanly at best, unseemly at worst. He just needed to take some commonsense precautions to limit his own exposure. That was reasonable, wasn't it? Hell, you weren't really tracking to be the next chairman, anyway, he thought. Finishing it off with four stars and a more-than-comfortable pension, directorships in a few key companies that did business with the military—that wasn't so bad. He knew he was rationalizing, but he also understood he had to hang on to whatever thread of stability he could. Oh yes, he would be well insulated.

He pushed the intercom: "Executive Assistant, get in here."

Even though the Secretary of Defense had been sent by the President to rein in the generals and admirals, Higginson was reluctant to tread too heavily. With Calhoun gone, either through impeachment or through the next election, he would no longer be Defense Secretary. Few former Secretaries of Defense had a political future, but most had worked their way into the still-vast military-industrial complex, either as vice presidents of this corporation or that, or as directors of companies doing significant business with the military. Campbell, the other chiefs, and most of the other senior officers in the Pentagon were well networked into that arena. Did he want to totally foreclose any ability to tap into that lucrative career as soon as his stint here was over? He didn't think so. He would do what the President had directed him to do, but he would proceed cautiously when he met with the chairman that afternoon.

At exactly the appointed time, General Campbell was ushered into Secretary Higginson's large office. Higginson was reserved but polite, walking a fine line.

"Good afternoon, General," he said while motioning

the chairman to sit down. "It certainly seems as though we are all working later and later in this building."

"It certainly does, Mr. Secretary," began Campbell, proceeding carefully, but correctly sizing up the Defense Secretary's motivations and discomfiture in talking with him. "But these are times that try us."

Campbell knew that his stock with the President could not be lower, and he was determined to no longer communicate with him directly—not that Taylor Calhoun would talk with him at this point anyway. The chairman did have confidence in his ability to communicate with the Secretary of Defense. Although Higginson was a political appointee of the President, he appeared to Campbell and the other senior military leaders in the Pentagon to be "less political"—whatever that meant—than many of the others. They had all worked diligently to co-opt him into seeing things their way and conducting "business as usual"—their euphemism for no civilian interference in the normal course of events in the Pentagon—and had, Campbell thought, largely succeeded.

"Indeed they are, General. I know you are busy, and you know that I am too. What was it you wanted to discuss? My executive assistant said you had some interesting information. Can't say that that's really too specific."

"I know it's not, Mr. Secretary. As you might imagine, there was only a limited bit that I could have mentioned over the phone, even over lines that we believe are secure," continued Campbell.

"I appreciate your candor, General. Now, what is this interesting information?" He was anxious for it and Campbell could sense it.

"Mr. Secretary, we—by that I mean those of us in the Pentagon, but especially the SouthCom commander, General Walters, and I—have pieced together a great deal about Operation Roundup. It seems that the evidence that this Lieutenant Commander Wilson did, in fact, sell military secrets, specifically precise details of what was to happen with regards to Operation Roundup, to the Maradona cartel for a substantial amount of money, is compelling indeed. That is known and we have recovered a sum of money apparently left over after he paid off his gambling debts . . ." Campbell paused to let it all sink in. He was not only stretching the truth now, he was fabricating it completely.

"Go on," said Higginson.

"We have, as you know, tied this Lieutenant Peters to him and know now, convincingly, that she killed Wilson. General Walters had her in custody, and, Mr. Secretary, please understand that Charlie is a good man, but he's been under a great deal of stress lately. Anyway, he got himself talked into keeping her in custody in the BOQ instead of in their police facility—"

"In the BOQ?" said Higginson. "In the goddamned BOQ? Who the hell authorized that?"

"Sir, General Walters did. Now, I know this seems irregular, and I, for one, don't put any credence in these rumors about the general and this lieutenant—"

Higginson interrupted him again. "What rumors?"

"Well, it seems that she and General Walters were regular squash partners. Now, Mr. Secretary, these are just rumors, of course."

"This lieutenant really gets around," said the secretary. "And we think she had a fling with General Lovelace too?"

"Yes sir, Mr. Secretary. Of course, that's another matter."

"Damn right, it is. Now what about her confinement in the BOQ and about her escape? Hasn't General Walters found her yet? I was briefed yesterday that he had a wide search under way and that we thought he would have her by now."

"He won't find her."

"Won't find her? What are you saying, General?"

"Please don't misunderstand me, Mr. Secretary. I'm not saying that General Walters was not conducting this search vigorously, just that there were many breakdowns and that he is no longer in charge of that search. I am."

"Fine, General. Basically, no one really gives a damn who finds her, just that she is found."

"Of course, Mr. Secretary. Then there is the matter of her companion, who is aiding her escape."

"Yes, supposedly someone from USS *Coronado*."

"Yes, Mr. Secretary. But we now know that for certain. Over a week ago a Chief Holden, Richard Holden, disappeared from the ship. We know that he and Peters had communicated frequently and suspect that there may be more that we haven't learned yet."

Higginson had no time for the chairman's posturing. "Knowing your current relationship with the President, I'm sure this is not just a friendly FYI. What do you want?"

"We may need coordination with other federal agencies and even with local officials. I'd ask for your support in securing that coordination for us."

"Of course. You have it, General. Just catch them so we can get to the bottom of this." With that, the secretary looked at the papers on his desk as a way of dismissing the general.

As Howard Campbell left and walked back toward his office with his aide in tow, he marveled to himself how cleverly he had woven this web.

CHAPTER 107

THE LAST OF THE SHIP'S PASSENGERS WERE MOVING briskly up the gangway of MS *Stattendam* as the linehandlers, crane operators, and others prepared to make the ship ready for sea. High on Lido Deck, Laura craned her neck for a sign of Rick. What had happened in that alley? Had he been captured by those two men? Every possible fear ran through her mind and she leaned toward the worst now that Rick had become so important not just to her freedom, but to her heart.

She should have insisted more forcefully that he not stay behind to divert them. They could have taken their chances driving right up to the *Stattendam*. Maybe their pursuers wouldn't have followed them onboard. She had the ship's emblematic shirt and hat that Rick had had the foresight to buy in the ship's store, so she blended right in with the last-minute crowd streaming aboard. The men couldn't have gotten aboard after them. After all, no matter who they were, they had no jurisdiction, no clout here. They could ask for them by name, but that would obscure them even more. Hold the ship from sailing? Doubtful. Oh Rick, why, why did you do it this way?

Then in the distance she spotted him, running along the long quaywall, making his way toward the ship. Even at a distance he looked battered and disheveled. She offered a silent prayer and then she moved.

The last of the passengers were onboard and the gangway was already attached to the small crane that would move it aside. As Rick approached, running at breakneck speed, those on the pier gave him curious looks. He too had his emblematic shirt, although it was ripped and bloodstained. Suddenly Laura appeared on the foredeck.

"Oh, thank God," she said as she grabbed the mate. "It's my husband. Thank God. We were shopping. I came back early because I was feeling ill. He must have been mugged. He was carrying a lot of cash. Oh, my God. Harvey! Harvey! Over here."

Rick looked up and managed a weak wave.

"Your husband almost missed the ship. What did you say your name was, ma'am?" said the mate on the deck, now more than a little perplexed.

"Allen. Mrs. Harvey Allen. We're on our honeymoon, you know," she said, beaming at him and smiling her most effervescent smile. "Oh Harvey, Harvey, come here."

Rick played along, staggering across the foredeck. "I'm all right, dear. They got my wallet and all my identification."

"We can get those replaced. Just thank God you're alive."

"Would you like us to call the authorities, ma'am?"

"No," blurted out Rick. "I didn't get a good look at them. Probably kids. Came up behind me. It's my own fault. I had my wallet out in the store and paid for something with a lot of cash. No, I'll never see that wallet again."

"Are you sure you don't want us to do something, sir?"

"No, thank you. I'll settle it all when we get to Fort Lauderdale."

"Very well, I'll have the attendant see you to your cabin."

For an instant they were panic-stricken, then Laura jumped in. "No, thank you. Harvey is a little claustrophobic as it is. I think he wants to stay outside for just a minute while he gets his wits back together. Thank you, though. You all are so kind."

"Yes, thank you," said Rick, working mightily to play the poor, victimized tourist.

"Very well, folks. Just let us know if we can be of service. And sir, I apologize for your incident. Curaçao has traditionally never been a problem for our guests aboard *Stattendam*."

"I understand, and it might not be the next time we come here. I was just careless, that's all."

"We do want to replace your *Stattendam* shirt, Mr. Allen. I'll have it delivered to your cabin."

Rick began to say no, but before he could finish, the mate had moved off to more pressing matters, secure in the knowledge that he had made these two honeymooners as happy as he possibly could.

The *Stattendam*'s ship's whistle sounded one prolonged blast to indicate she was getting under way as her powerful screws began to whip up mud from the bottom of the harbor. Rick explained every detail of his encounter with Robinson and Bennitt to Laura as she looked at him in wild-eyed amazement. All the while, Rick kept his eye on the pier, waiting for them to emerge in pursuit of him. Were they still in that alley? Had he killed Bennitt? Now that Rick was free, at least for the moment, he was overcome by remorse for what he had done. The two NIS agents weren't the enemy. They had been sent on this mission, probably against their will, and had no personal animosity toward either Rick or Laura. Rick had to do what he had done, but nonetheless, had he killed a man? Had he beaten a man to death in a rage? The possibility disturbed him deeply. He had never killed another man before. Laura had listened to his entire story and sensed his concern.

"Rick, you did nothing wrong. They tried to subdue you any way they could."

"I know Laura, I know. But I hit him. I hit him again and again. I wasn't in control."

"Rick, it's not a controlled situation. It was a fight in an alley."

"It was a fight I started. There could have been another way to escape, there just could have."

Laura realized she couldn't pull him out of this, so she just stood there and eased next to him, putting her arm gently around his waist and her head on his shoulder.

Rick and Laura stood on the Sports Deck on *Statten-dam*'s port side as the ship headed outbound under the Queen Julianabridge and the eighteenth century facades of Handelskade hove into view ahead of them. They were free—for the moment. But they were also bonded in a way that they never imagined they could be. Now, truly, they were one mind with a common purpose.

CHAPTER 108

TAYLOR CALHOUN SAT IMPASSIVELY IN HIS HIGH-backed leather chair in the Oval Office. He felt like a virtual prisoner there. All the news was bad. Every avenue of recourse seemed to be closed off, except one. He would try his best to exploit it.

Brian Stavridis broke him out of his daydreaming. "Mr. President, they're ready for us in the Cabinet Room."

"Fine, Brian. Thanks. Do we have everyone assembled?"

"Yes, Mr. President. I think this will be a short meeting."

Perhaps not, he thought. "What's on the agenda?"

"We do have some interesting developments regarding the people we think are responsible for Operation Roundup's failure. At least that's what the Pentagon has provided us with."

"Who in the Pentagon?"

"Why, the Secretary of Defense, of course, Mr. President. I know you've lost confidence in General Campbell, and, quite frankly, Mr. President, I have too. I know that he's served the nation for four decades, but he's not serving you. Secretary Higginson has taken control over at the Pentagon and I'm convinced that he's put the generals and admirals in their places."

"That's good, Brian." Calhoun wasn't convinced that this had really happened, but he had no other path than to agree with his advisors at this point.

"Shall we, Mr. President?"

Like a doomed man on his way to the gallows, armed only with the hope that he would make the rope snap, Taylor Calhoun rose slowly and followed his National Security Advisor toward the Cabinet Room. Ironic, thought Calhoun. He'd been a party to any number of financial irregularities in office, like most people in government, but now he could be brought down by something he didn't do.

"Gentlemen, the President." His advisors rose as Taylor Calhoun entered the well-appointed Cabinet Room. Damn their looks, he thought. They wanted to be supportive and sympathetic, but they clearly pitied him. He didn't know how long he would be able to stand it.

"Thank you all for being here," the President said as he sat down heavily in his seat. It was not an auspicious start.

Chief of Staff Carter Thomas began. "Mr. President, we have two primary things to cover: the House impeachment hearings, of course, and also some additional information regarding the officer and now a companion who have escaped from Panama. With your permission, sir—"

Calhoun cut him off. "Let me make it easy for you. We're not going to stand around and wait for these impeachment hearings to bury us. I mean, we're not!" The President rose up out of his seat, something his advisors had never seem him do in this forum. "I'll tell you what we're going to do."

With that, the President began to lay out what he thought of, but didn't reveal, as Operation Lifeboat. Obviously he had done a lot of legwork, with his closest personal staffers—a lot of phone calling, a lot of lobbying, a lot of calling in of favors. He laid out his plan impassively, with two young staffers holding up pressboard after pressboard showing which House members were clearly and firmly in their camp and which other members these loyalists, in turn, had been assigned to convince to side with the President. Since so many of those likely to vote for impeachment were in the opposing party, some of these efforts were incredible long shots. For others, however, where there was a fence-sitting opposing party member or a defector from his own party, Calhoun had assigned—and personally spoken to at great length—a key senior member of his own party. The plan was a bold one—if a long shot—but Calhoun had fought his way to the top, and he would fight even harder to stay there.

Less than two miles away as the crow flies—but many more by every other measure—Howard Campbell sat in his Pentagon office and reviewed the details for capturing Rick and Laura.

He had been badgering the deputy and assistant Secretary of Defense for the authority to coalesce an enormous amount of power into his hands and gain recognition as the one man who was protecting the nation from these criminals. Campbell put only his best—and most trusted—personal aides in charge of the details of apprehending Peters and Holden. His most important ally was FBI Director Douglas Van Tine. Knowing that Tine's agency had been stung by criticism for botched operations with militia groups, Campbell astutely worked with him to have him agree to let Campbell use military people to apprehend Peters and Holden when they arrived in the United States. Van Tine, in turn, assured the overextended Fort Lauderdale Police Department that if they went along with the plan they would get ample credit for the bust, including, Van Tine assured them, extensive national media coverage.

So really, the takedown would be simple. He'd flood the area with his handpicked people, have them all in unmarked cars, with all of their communications networked together and tied into a mobile command post that had been designed for contingency operations. He'd heard the story about how this Holden had beaten up two NIS agents and escaped—damn amateurs—and was determined not to let that happen this time. They'd let them get off the ship and start moving somewhere. They'd probably check into some hotel, he figured. His agents would watch them continuously, and then, when the fugitives had let their guard down, would round them up and have them brought back to Washington. He'd already reserved a place, at the stockade at Quantico Marine Corps Base, only an hour south of Washington—close enough to be convenient to him and his people, but far enough from the prying Washington press corps—to interrogate them fully and elicit the "truth."

And that "truth" would show exactly what his plan—but not necessarily General Walters's plan—needed to show.

No more than a mile from the Pentagon, a nondescript Maryland National Guard C-130 Hercules aircraft lifted off of Bolling Air Force Base. The pilot had filed a flight plan to Homestead Air Force Base, Florida. One more small step in Campbell's plan.

CHAPTER 109

THE ATMOSPHERE ON MS *STATTENDAM* WAS FESTIVE IN the early morning sunshine. Her passengers lined every conceivable vantage point to catch a glimpse of the Florida coastline near Fort Lauderdale. Like sailors returning from a month's-long deployment, the cruise ship passengers strained to see something that was familiar—a building, a hill, a bridge, a causeway—anything to convince them that they had arrived at their appointed destination. It was not as if they really had any doubts, but it was a ritual carried out on every cruise ship that ever put to sea.

For Rick and Laura it marked the end of an agony of waiting, waiting to see if they'd been discovered, or if Robinson and Bennitt had told the proper people, who had told the ship, whose crew might then be trying to locate them. They had taken extra pains to blend in with the passengers, staying up until all hours gambling, striking up conversations with willing passengers who were always eager to talk with the "honeymooners." When they decided to finally submit to sleep, they had covered themselves with blankets and settled into some out of the way deck chairs for a few hours. Thus far, they had not been confronted, and now they had only hours to go until freedom, at least the momentary freedom of being on United States soil again. Then the race to expose the truth would kick into high gear again.

As the ship turned and entered the harbor, most of the passengers went over to the starboard side of the ship to get a better vantage point. Rick and Laura hunched over the Sports Deck railing reviewing their plan.

"Laura, I think we need to be careful when we get off the ship. There may be another pair like Robinson and Bennitt out there. Let's cling to a big group and move together with them, at least until we can see if there's any immediate danger."

"Okay, we can do that. What should we do about our bags? You know they have to clear customs. We've got no passports, no identification saying who we are. And we can't just abandon them."

"No, no, we can't. We need what's in my golf bag."

"Except you'll never clear customs."

After a few moments of thought, Laura added, "Wait. Not all of these bags are carried off by the passengers. Some of them just aren't capable. Can't we declare in advance, pay whatever tariff there is, and have them delivered somewhere?"

"You may be right," replied Rick.

Rick had had the foresight to put a tag saying, MR. & MRS. HARVEY ALLEN on both bags, removing the tags of the actual owner, and he and Laura set off in search of the ship's concierge, first to set up a hotel reservation, and then to arrange to have their bags delivered there. They worked their way quickly from their vantage point on the Sports Deck, down five decks to the Promenade Deck and the shore excursions center. Laura wandered through the atrium and the photo gallery, looking at the hundreds of pictures taken of *Stattendam*'s passengers that were now for sale, while Rick waited his turn at the desk. He felt uneasy having Laura out of his sight for even these brief moments, but she needed this bit of freedom, these snippets of time to feel confident about herself again. He would not linger here long.

The couple ahead of him completed their business and Rick was next.

"Good morning, sir, how may I help you?" said the friendly and vivacious hostess manning the desk.

"We'd like to book a hotel room in Fort Lauderdale."

"For how many?"

"Two. Just my wife and I." Rick was surprised at how easily those words came out of his mouth.

"Any particular hotel in mind, sir? Fort Lauderdale is a beautiful place and we have quite a few options."

"Perhaps something close to where we pull in. Something nice."

"Let's see what we have." She ran her fingers quickly over her keyboard.

"Well, sir, you're in luck. I can get you a good view room in the Hyatt Regency Pier Sixty Six. It has a commanding view of the intercoastal waterway and is just a stone's throw from where we pull in. May I make that reservation?"

"Yes, certainly," said Rick, distracted now a bit as he strained his neck to catch sight of Laura. Damn, I wish she'd come back so I could stop worrying, he thought.

"Very good, sir. A great choice. How many nights?"

"Just one for now," said Rick absently.

"Certainly. With our Holland America corporate account I can get you in for $239 a night. Shall I put that on your credit card, Mr. . . . ."

"Allen, Harvey Allen," offered Rick, now not looking at her at all.

"Allen, yes . . . Allen?"

Rick caught himself. He couldn't let her get into the

computer and discover no Mr. and Mrs. Allen. "No, hold it—I mean—what did you say the price was?" he stammered.

"I mentioned that I can get you our Holland America rate of $239, sir. It's an excellent room and that's a fabulous rate."

Rick was backpedaling now. "Well, I'm sure it is, but, well, you see, we're honeymooners." He grinned sheepishly. "We're on a little bit of a budget. Could you look at some other options?"

The woman was a professional who had been trained to deal with just this type of situation. "Of course, sir. No need to bust that budget just yet. Let's see. I have the Best Western Marina Inn, just east of the Brooks Causeway and A1A. It's very nice. Clean. Less than a third the price of the Hyatt. I'll still need to reserve with a credit card."

"Could they just put it on a six P.M. hold?"

"Well, we can request that, sir. It's a bit unusual, though. Our network with these hotels works best when we just use the same credit card you used to pay for your cruise. It's in our computer and all."

Rick was scrambling. "Well, yes, but, you see, my wife's parents paid for this honeymoon. This stay in the hotel here is just a side trip—you know how it is." Rick winked, trying to exude as much charm as possible. "We didn't think it fair to have them absorb this cost, so we wanted to pay it out of our pocket. We'd really appreciate your understanding."

"I'm certain we can do that, sir. Now, the room won't be guaranteed."

"That's all right. We'll just hustle over there. Oh, and can we have our bags sent there instead of carrying them off?"

"Of course. Have you filled out your customs forms?"

"No."

"Very well, the bellman will provide some to you and then he will fetch the bags from your cabin. Cabin number?"

"Oh, no, we've already packed them and dragged them out. Thought we were going to carry them off. They're my golf clubs, you see. And I was going to play a round right away. But then . . . it's a long story."

Rick's story was getting stranger and stranger, but the line behind him was lengthening and the hostess felt some pressure to keep things moving. "All right, sir. I'll let you and the bellman work out the situation with your bags. What name shall I put the reservation under?"

"Allen," replied Rick. "Mr. and Mrs. Harvey Allen."

"Very good, Mr. Allen. Enjoy your stay in Fort Lauderdale."

"We will," replied Rick. "And thank you, thank you very much."

She didn't respond but merely smiled sweetly—sweetly, but with a slight disdain she reserved for those less well-heeled passengers.

Rick rushed off toward the atrium where he had left Laura. She wasn't there. Frantically, he walked quickly to the photo gallery. No Laura..He was near panic. Why had he left her? Why? He paced quickly up and down the port side of the forward Promenade Deck, peering into the empty Van Gogh Lounge. No Laura. Walking back to the Java Café. Still no Laura. Back to the atrium. Where the hell was she?

"Harvey." Then, louder and more pointedly when Rick didn't hear the call, "Mr. Allen!"

Rick turned to see Laura at the entrance to the ladies' room on the starboard side. Rick felt a weight drain from his body. Then he got upset.

"Where have you been?" he said loud enough to make several passengers turn their heads.

"Well, I think that's obvious, dear. And lower your voice, please," she scolded.

"I was worried, that's all."

"Okay. Easy. It's okay." Laura knew how she might have reacted had she not been able to find Rick. She didn't think she would ever get used to this cloak-and-dagger stuff.

"Okay. Got it. Listen, I have to get our bags out of that maid's closet. They'll deliver them if I'll take them to the bellman."

"*We'll* take them, Rick. Let's just stay casual."

"That hostess asked a lot of questions. I had to tell her our names to reserve the room. I don't think she went into the computer, though."

"I'm sure she didn't," said Laura reassuringly.

"I know I'm paranoid, Laura, but I was sure someone had grabbed you. I panicked. I'm sorry."

"No, no, you're a dear." She leaned up and kissed him deeply. "Now I want to know about our next love nest. Tell me everything," she teased.

"I'll do it while we get our bags. Let's go."

They headed back up to the Lido Deck to the maid's closet where the bags, Rick saw, remained undisturbed, then back down again to the Promenade Deck, where they filled out all of the required customs forms and deposited the two bags with the bellman with instructions to deliver them to the Best Western Marina Inn as soon as the *Stattendam* docked. Rick tipped the man generously while mentioning casually that it would be great if they could get them as soon as possible.

"Of course, Mr. Allen. We'll do our very best."

That settled, Rick and Laura returned to the Sports Deck, which offered the most commanding view of their entry into Fort Lauderdale Harbor. Beyond the Brooks Causeway, the beach skyline of Fort Lauderdale was arrayed ahead and to their right, while aircraft departing Fort Lauderdale–Hollywood International Airport climbed into the sky directly behind them as *Stattendam* made her way directly into the Port Everglades Channel. They had made it.

As the tugs made up to *Stattendam* and began easing her into her berth at the cruise ship terminal, Laura said, "That's one crisis behind us. Now we need to start preparing for what comes next."

"I know. We'll get to the hotel and get checked in. I've got contacts I can check in with and find out what repercussions, if any, this whole Operation Roundup failure has had. Once we get a sense of that, we'll know if, or how quickly, we'll have to move."

"I think we need to move right away," she continued.

"But we've got to keep you protected. We can't assume that something has spontaneously happened to clear you and so we have to believe the Navy is still looking for you. Do you have anybody in the Navy you really trust that you can call to see which way the wind is blowing on this?"

"Not off the top of my head, no, no one comes to mind."

"Well, keep thinking along those lines. We may need to pulse the system."

Stattendam was against the pier now and her passengers were all crowding toward her gangway. As the ship finally tied up, Rick and Laura joined the long line of passengers and made their way down the gangway. Both of them were alert for anyone suspicious watching them, but with the throng of people—passengers, family members and friends greeting them, vendors, Holland America Line workers, and the like—it was impossible to really get a sense for anyone out of the ordinary in the crowd. Fortunately, they were unencumbered by luggage, and so were able to make their way quickly toward the waiting line of taxis. A moment later Rick put Laura in one, took a last look around, and slid in behind her.

"Where to, Mac?"

Displaced New Yorker, thought Rick. "Best Western Marina Inn, thanks."

"No problem. Should be able to see it in just a minute or two."

"Sounds good," said Rick. "Say, what's the news in Fort Lauderdale? We've been away for almost two weeks."

"Here? Nothing. Same old, same old. Impeachment's taken over the front pages. That's the talk."

"Impeachment?" said both Rick and Laura in unison. "What impeachment?"

"You *have* been gone for a while. But have you been in outer space?" He thought better about that statement, didn't want to hurt his tip. "The Speaker of the House, what's his name, Watkins, Warlock, something like that, he's having that congresswoman from New York—Cohen, that's it—hold these hearings to impeach the President. Some people say that President Calhoun will beat it, but me, I don't much know." He stopped with a flourish and with that self-assured punctuation that seems unique to those who drive taxis in any major American city.

"How long have these hearings been going on?" said Laura.

"Oh, for three or four days now."

Rick and Laura sat in stunned silence. Things were much worse than they had imagined. What would have given them more cause for concern was the small army of nondescript cars arrayed around the Fort Lauderdale cruise ship terminal area, one of which was following their cab now, none of which would follow it for more than a few blocks, all of which were equipped with instantaneous communications. This was no amateur Robinson and Bennitt bumbling.

The taxi pulled up to the Marina Inn and the couple hopped out. Rick scanned the area but did not see anything or anyone at all suspicious. Then they hustled into the lobby. His exchange with the desk clerk was short and to the point.

"Hello. Allen. Harvey Allen. Just off *Stattendam*. I believe I have a reservation with you."

"Allen. Yes, here it is, sir. Two people. Just one night?"

"Yes. Just one night."

"Very well. How will you be paying, sir?"

"Cash . . . if that's okay."

"Cash is fine. Our check-in time isn't until three, but we always try to accommodate our Holland America clientele. Let's see if I have a room made up already. Yes, here it is. Room 212. Nice view of the intercoastal waterway. Can we help you and Mrs. Allen with your luggage?"

"No, actually, not yet. They are sending it over from *Stattendam*. Will you notify us when it arrives?"

"Of course, and enjoy your stay at the Marina Inn."

"I'm sure we will," replied Rick, but he was already shepherding Laura toward the elevator. Suddenly he stopped and, recalling the conversation with the taxi driver, ducked into the lobby gift shop and bought a *Miami Herald*. Tucking it under his arm, he rejoined Laura and watched as the blinking lights showed that the elevator was heading toward the lobby. Had he taken the time to look at the paper, he would have seen that there

was only one story above the fold, and that the headline
was exceptionally prominent:

JUDICIARY COMMITTEE IMPEACHMENT
HEARINGS HEAD TOWARD SECOND WEEK
CONGRESSIONAL LEADERS PREDICT
PRESIDENT'S FALL

As Rick and Laura entered the elevator, they sensed
that within the next few hours the course would be set for
what they would do to accomplish the mission they had
set out on. They thought they were ready for anything.

In the parking lot of the Marina Inn, four men met in
a dark, out-of-the-way corner and talked in hushed tones.
They were the point men of the considerable force that
had been brought to bear to capture Rick and Laura. Four
blocks away, in a normal-looking Winnebago that served
as the group's mobile command post, Colonel Kendall
Bleich presided over a group of six specially trained men
from all of the services who had been assembled to perform the seemingly simple task of bringing in two un-
armed and unalerted fugitives. He knew he was more than
up to the task and that the men in the motor home, as
well as the almost dozen others on the streets outside,
would have no trouble whatsoever bringing in Rick and
Laura. He turned to Major Pete Gallo, his second in command, and shared his confidence.

"Looks like this is unfolding according to plan, Pete,"
said Bleich, exuding the confidence that had helped get
him selected for this assignment by the chairman of the
Joint Chiefs of Staff.

"I think it is, Colonel. They're trapped now. That hotel
might as well be a prison," replied Gallo.

"When they come out, however long it takes, they come
into our custody."

"What if they try to fight it out, Colonel?" said Gallo,
voicing just a hint of concern.

"Then let the games begin," replied Bleich.

*   *   *

Rick and Laura alighted from the elevator on the second floor. As they walked toward their room, Laura was in a playful mood.

"Another one-night stand, eh, Holden? My father warned me about sailors like you. I should have listened to him."

"You should have," said Rick, smiling back at her. "Here it is, 212. Our 'no tell motel,' I guess."

"Right," said Laura.

Rick opened the door and let Laura in. He followed, and as soon as the door closed behind him, he took Laura in his arms and kissed her, kissed her deeply. She held his kiss for several moments, then pushed away.

"Okay, Romeo," she said with a wicked smile. "I'm thinking the same thing you are. But we've got work to do. We have calls we've got to make."

CHAPTER 110

THE SECOND MAN RAN THROUGH ONE OF THE RATLIKE mazes in the CIA's Crystal Palace. Such strange activity turned heads in this staid organization. But the news he had was urgent. The senior man had to know immediately.

He was just getting up from lunch in the cafeteria when the second man found him.

"Our mutual friend just called. I have him on the line, but he doesn't want to hold for long."

"You could understand why. Let's go."

They left the cafeteria at a jog. Nearing the office, they were joined by the third man and entered the small, windowless room where the lone phone—black—was in its cradle with the top left-hand light blinking, indicating that someone was on hold. The senior man picked up the phone.

"Epicenter here," he said tersely, using his prearranged code name.

"This is me," replied Rick, using no name at all—again, a prearranged system that they had developed long ago.

"I have been briefed on your situation. Do not tell me where you are now. We will make that determination via the usual methods."

"Okay."

"Are you being followed?"

"Can't tell at this point. Initial look is no, but I've— we've—been surprised before."

"Just two?"

"Yes."

"Do you have a clear path for your mission?"

"No. No, I don't. It's starting to shape up, though. I've seen the papers with respect to what we have been discussing. What is your take on that?"

"The assessment here—by that I mean our private assessment—is that it will go through, that it will happen."

"Official support for me from the Agency?"

"None. You don't exist vis-à-vis us."

"Understood. Other support?"

"We have several operatives who can assist you in getting to your destination. They'd be under very deep cover."

"Where would they weigh in?"

"Definitely inside the beltway. That's the only way that Stovepipe"—another code name—"would buy into this."

"How would they help me—help us?"

"That depends strictly on what you intend to do, how you intend to approach this. Have you firmed that up yet?"

Epicenter was sounding impatient, as if he expected Rick to have a fully worked-out plan already. Easy for him to say, Rick thought, sitting in his air-conditioned office at Langley, not on the run, not out of touch.

"No. No, I don't. I—we—have to work that out."

"Yes. I see. Now, with respect to your companion. You should know that she is the subject of an extensive manhunt by the Pentagon. The word is that the chairman himself is directing the search for her. You may have to consider jettisoning her to complete your mission."

"Jettisoning?"

"Yes."

"I don't think that's an option." Laura was listening to Rick's half of the conversation, and he was being careful to avoid alarming her. He couldn't believe he was hearing this.

"It may have to be."

"You don't understand. I said that that's not an option."

"Look. We didn't call you. You called us. You surfaced. There's no documented evidence for anything you're telling us. I know we've worked together for a long time before the incident. I'm not saying I don't believe you. I'm only saying that, under the circumstances, it's impossible to get any official support on this. I'm going way, way out on a limb to get our group to support you in the way we are. You are running solo on this. It's your operation."

Rick was staggered. They were talking about an assault on the highest office in the nation, an assault on the Republic itself, and the Agency was not willing to stand against it. Unbelievable. Rick was seething.

"All right. Done. The next call you get from me will be my plan and the minimal support I'll need from you. Agreed?"

"Agreed."

Rick slammed down the receiver and looked at Laura.

"Well, you heard one-half of a rotten conversation," he said, looking defeated.

"Was the other half of it as bad?" she said.

"Worse."

"Hey Holden. Don't fade on me now. You pulled me out of a big mess. We're in this together now. We're gonna make it turn out right."

"I hope you're right."

"I'm am."

Laura was determined to do her part and had decided that she would take the risk and make a call of her own. Yes, she would call him. It was a stretch, but there was a chance—just a chance—he could help make this right. They had met only briefly, yet long enough for her to think that he was loyal to a fault—loyal to his service, loyal to the nation, loyal to the President. She would push on that really hard and see where it would take her.

Rick was less sanguine about their situation. The fact that they *hadn't* seen anyone following them to the Marina Inn bothered him. He would rather have seen pursuers and known that he had to deal with them. And he felt like he was getting blown off by the Agency. The CIA had always had a reputation of being a conservative organization, but this was carrying that a bit too far. And the part about jettisoning Laura disturbed him. She was as much a part of this as he was. Sure, he might have taken the same position had he been at Langley, but he wasn't. He was here. In the crucible.

Howard Campbell put the receiver down in its cradle and leaned back in his oversized chair. Colonel Bleich had just delivered the news that he was waiting for. He hoped he hadn't sounded too anxious in the way he pumped the colonel for information. The important thing, though, was that the trap was set and that his people only awaited the word to put it into motion. He would give that word imminently.

CHAPTER 111

USS *CORONADO* STEAMED INTO RODMAN ROADS AS she had done many times before. As the ship approached this now-familiar area in the morning mist, her crew went about their tasks with anxious anticipation. They were to proceed through the Panama Canal in midmorning, joining up near the end of the stream that was positioning to go first through the Milaflores Locks, then the Pedro Miguel Locks, then steam down the long, narrow Gaillard Cut and the continental divide, break out into vast Gatun Lake, and step down through Gatun Locks, before finally exiting into the Atlantic Ocean at Cristobal.

The Atlantic Ocean! Home! How different it had been

a few short months ago when they had made this trip in
the opposite direction. So full of hope. So innocent in
many ways. They were off to a new mission in the other
ocean. It was a prospect that had filled every man, from
the JTF Eight commander to the lowest seaman, with anticipation and excitement. Now, as they approached the
canal from the West, they had totally different emotions.

This last mission had put an explanation point on their
frustrations. Sent south on a "secret mission," in total radio silence—the "penalty box," as some shipboard wags
were now calling it—they had done absolutely nothing.
Bitch as they might when they were busy working eighteen hours a day, sailors always found some great recompense in actively doing something useful, even if it was
difficult. Steaming around in circles just off the coast of
South America had driven them to distraction. As onerous as this radio silence was to the ordinary sailor, it was
many times more onerous and particularly bothersome to
her leaders, especially General Ashley Lovelace and Captain Pete Howe.

To add one more wrinkle to their frustration, they had
had another loss that bothered them deeply. On the first
afternoon of the trip south, during a routine man-
overboard drill, one of those seemingly endless drills that
Navy ships at sea conduct, they had discovered one of
their men missing. Chief Rick Holden, assistant platoon
leader for the embarked SEAL platoon, was nowhere to
be found. They had mustered the entire ship to join the
search, but to no avail. The captain was beyond despair.
The loss of even one sailor brought back frustrating memories of the Operation Roundup debacle. With Chief Holden, the loss was especially acute and particularly ironic—
he was the man who had risked his life in the field to save
his comrades. It wasn't fair. But what was almost worse
was the reaction that Howe's reporting of the events had
gotten from the JTF Eight staff. Sitting in his large chair
on the starboard side of *Coronado*'s wide bridge, Captain
Howe reflected on that exchange less than a week ago.

After his chief master at arms and executive officer had
reported to him that the search for Holden had failed, he
took them in tow and walked down the two decks from

Coronado's bridge to General Lovelace's cabin. Once there, and after an exchange of the usual pleasantries, he began to tell his story to the general and his chief of staff, Colonel Conrad Hicks.

"General, Colonel, I'm afraid I have some bad news to report," began Howe.

"Is it about the possible missing man?" asked the general.

"Yes, General, I'm afraid it is. We are quite certain that Chief Petty Officer Rick Holden is not on board and fear he may have been lost at sea."

"Holden? Chief Holden? That SEAL who brought back those Marines from the field? How? When did this happen?" said General Ashley Lovelace.

"We knew he was on board the night we refueled in Rodman Roads. But he was missing this afternoon. Even though it's getting dark, I recommend that we reverse course and try to find him," replied Captain Howe.

"Yes, of course. We've got our mission, but—"

Colonel Hicks interrupted him. "General, our top-secret orders were quite clear. Proceed south at best speed—"

Boldly, the captain spoke up. "Of course, Colonel, but we have a responsibility to our men—"

"That's all well and good, Captain," Hicks snapped at him, "but let's face a few facts. What time did you have your man-overboard muster drill?"

"Why, right after lunch, 1300."

"Fine, and what time is it now?"

"Exactly 1922, Colonel." Howe was getting visibly agitated at the colonel's condescending tone.

"And, well, I'm not a Navy person, but it would seem to me that *if* he fell overboard sometime *before* 1300, even if we reverse course immediately, *in absolute contradiction to our orders,* we'd never spot him at night. So then, there we are tomorrow morning, searching God knows how much ocean area, and with currents and the like there's just no chance that we could find anyone, assuming, of course, General, that this man did, in fact, really fall overboard." Colonel Hicks looked directly at the general as he finished his remarks with a flourish.

Howe opened his mouth to speak, but General Lovelace raised his hand. Howe remained silent.

"*Assuming* that he fell overboard, Colonel Hicks, I think that's the only logical conclusion we can make." Lovelace was almost sounding defensive now in backing up the ship's captain. Holden had been here, right here in his cabin telling him an unbelievable story about a conspiracy, and he in turn had related that story to the President. Now this man was missing. Fell overboard? That was too much of a coincidence. And it was all too convenient that Conrad Hicks was trying to wave this away as just one of those things. He had his suspicions about the colonel and this exchange was fanning those concerns.

"Well, certainly, General," said Hicks, backing off a bit. "I mean, we can certainly go back and search as the captain suggests, but our orders—"

"We'll see about those orders, Colonel. We'll see."

Captain Howe shifted uneasily in his chair now as he thought about what had happened in the aftermath of that conversation. General Lovelace had broken radio silence and contacted General Walters, asking for permission to turn around and look for his missing man. Although Howe did not hear the conversation between the two generals, he suspected the worst. Less than a half-hour after telling Colonel Hicks that he'd "see about those orders," Lovelace had called both of them into his cabin. He was ashen-faced and visibly shaken. He reported that General Walters had directed them to proceed on their mission as ordered but that he would initiate a search for the chief using air assets stationed at Howard Air Force Base, as well as Navy and Coast Guard ships then at Rodman. Howe suspected that Walters had chewed him out royally for breaking radio silence.

Now that they were in the Roads, they were within an hour of the time when they were allowed to come back up on their radios. He hoped against hope that he would hear that Chief Rick Holden had been found by one of the units sent to search for him. He feared the worst.

CHAPTER 112

WASHINGTON, D.C., IS A COMPLEX CITY. SEAT OF GOV-
ernment, media center, international melting pot, tourist
mecca, and a host of other descriptors make it a city where
multiple stories fight it out day in and day out for front-
page status in the city's premier newspaper, the *Washington Post*. On any given day, as many as a dozen stories
could legitimately compete for the two or three above-
the-fold headlines.

On any given, normal day. But these were not normal
days. The complex city, so cosmopolitan, so urbane as well
as urban, so full of itself sometimes with its ability to jug-
gle complex issues, was singularly focused on only one
thing: impeachment.

After the completion of the Judiciary Committee's last
round of deliberations, the hearings had been moved from
closed sessions to open ones. Although Chairwoman Cohen would have preferred to continue the closed sessions,
the clamor to open them had been overwhelming. She had
reluctantly agreed, and then, on the advice of her public
relations people, became an impassioned advocate of the
open sessions, citing the need to "keep the American people, the real stakeholders in this process, fully informed."
It was a masterful job of telling them exactly what they
wanted to hear. The hearings had been ongoing for several days now and had been riveting. Not since the Anita
Hill hearings, or the O. J. Simpson trial, had all of America been so glued to their television screens. All of the
testimony had been powerful as public figure after public
figure had testified either for or against the President. In
a lateral arabesque to, in some small way, thank him for
starting the hearings that made these impeachment hearings possible, the Speaker had directed Linda Cohen to
ensure that Senator Jay Lindsey was called as a witness

to talk about the findings made by his Senate Intelligence Oversight Committee. Lindsey was well prepared and well situated for his testimony. He sensed that he, the Speaker, and the chairman had similar agendas and that they may have had some of the same people as confidants.

Taylor Calhoun and his people worked their strategy to the fullest extent of their capabilities. The Congressmen from their own party were active, calling in favors from their colleagues not only from past events but for promises of future work on their behalf. There was a full-court press of gigantic proportions that had never been seen inside the beltway. The President and his men were sparing nothing. If they went down, they would go down with all guns blazing and all flags flying.

In spite of their heroic efforts, it did not appear that it would be enough. The Congressmen firmly in the camp for impeachment were as solid as they were numerous, and large numbers of the "fence-sitters" were not fence-sitters at all, but merely those who, for one reason or another—and usually because they wanted to be courted just a little bit longer—didn't want their vote accounted for too early. By any realistic estimates, it appeared that, when the final tally was made, Taylor Calhoun would be impeached by the full House of Representatives, the same House that he had served in proudly for so many years.

CHAPTER 113

ABOARD USS *CORONADO*, FAST AGAINST THE PIER IN Rodman, Panama, linehandlers were standing by to cast off the ship's heavy mooring lines as steam escaped from both stacks and the ship made ready for sea and her transit through the Panama Canal and imminent return to the naval base at Norfolk, Virginia. It was perhaps the oldest routine in the Navy, getting a ship ready to go to sea, and *Coronado*'s crew had probably done it at least a thousand times in her three decades of service. However, it was still an evolution that occupied the attention of virtually every sailor on the ship.

In *Coronado*'s spacious flag cabin, other matters were occupying the staff of JTF Eight. General Ashley Lovelace sat impassively and stock-still reading the document that lay in the center of his desk one last time. Only his flag secretary, Commander Ted Steuer, who had prepared the document in accordance with the guidelines of the Uniform Code of Military Justice, stood in the cabin with the JTF Eight commander. Together, they had drafted earlier versions of this document, and now, with a final version on command letterhead, with the various serializations and other indicators of official military correspondence, Ashley Lovelace pondered it one last time before going on with the proceedings. Finally, he was ready.

As he turned in his large black leather chair to gaze out the porthole on *Coronado*'s port side, he thought back to the series of events that had led him to this decision, and to another that he was about to put into action. In hindsight, it all seemed so clear now, the coolness of the staff upon his arrival, the hair-trigger reactions of his chief of staff during their initial meetings, the messages that never reached him, the way in which Hicks had been willing to let him shoulder the blame, the information that he had finally extracted regarding the frequent trips the colonel had been making to Radio Central, his argument with the ship's captain regarding Chief Holden's disappearance, that disappearance itself—it was all too compelling. He sensed what would happen if he alerted his superiors as to his proposed actions—so he didn't. He knew what he must do. Asking permission could only impede or even derail his actions. He'd have a lot of explaining to do after the fact, but that was far better than failing to act. He knew he could never live with failing to act.

Someone rapped loudly on the cabin door. "Permission to enter," called out the master at arms.

The master at arms then entered, along with the staff legal officer, Commander Jerry Zigler; the operations officer, Colonel Sam Perkins; and the chief of staff, Colonel Conrad Hicks. All but Hicks stood there impassively, looking at General Lovelace, waiting for him to speak.

After a few moments, Hicks could stand it no more. "General? You wanted to see me? This is awfully unusual, sending the master at arms to bring me here. Is there something wrong?"

Lovelace looked directly at him. "Wrong, Colonel? Should there be anything wrong?"

"No, General, of course not. I've been here hundreds of times. This is the first time I've been escorted here." Hicks was treading carefully. He might have been more perplexed, or even alarmed, had General Lovelace not been in such a strange mood over the last few days. Hicks thought he was about to crack, so he was careful not to send the general over the edge by being too aggressive about what he thought was a damn stupid way of doing business. And what were these other people doing here? Probably had some soldier or sailor on the staff who was in trouble again. Ops was here, probably one of his guys. Too bad. He'd be doing a rug dance. He was growing tired of these petty personal problems of the staff members and wanted to get this over with. He looked back at Lovelace. "So, General, what can I do for you?"

"You can listen, Colonel."

This is really strange behavior, thought Hicks. It's a good thing we're going directly back to Norfolk. The general's definitely losing it.

"Colonel Hicks, I am placing you under military arrest for treason. I have evidence that you have done a number of things prejudicial to national security, but most egregiously you directly interfered to cause Operation Roundup to fail. I'm removing you from the ship and having you held in the brig at the Rodman Naval Station until the Department of the Army and the Department of Defense inspector general decide how and where to conduct your court-martial."

Hicks went white. His jaw hung slack and he just gaped at Lovelace. He always knew there were risks in taking the actions they had told him to take; he had dealt with risks his entire career. What did Lovelace know? He couldn't possibly know that much. More importantly, what could he prove? He had nothing, nothing at all.

"General? Is this some sort of a joke?"

"I assure you, it's no joke, Colonel."

"Treason? What are you basing this on?"

"I think you know fully, Colonel Hicks. The charge sheets will be hand-carried to the base commander by Commander Zigler, who will stay behind to represent this command should legal proceedings start here—"

Hicks interrupted him and the master at arms moved a step closer to him. "General, look. I know you have been under a lot of stress—"

Lovelace shot back, letting him know that he was out of line. "Stress, Colonel? Oh yes, there's been stress, all right. You've seen to that. But how about remorse? Got any of that, Colonel Hicks? Remorse for all the Marines you sent to their deaths in this ambush?"

"General, I—"

"Shut up, Colonel. I know everything. You're through. My only question is how far up the chain this goes. Anything you'd like to tell me?"

Although it didn't seem that Conrad Hicks could get any more pale, he did just that. If Lovelace knew everything, he could nail the colonel to the wall. Treason? Hell, he'd be lucky if that was the only charge. He pondered his next move. Was Lovelace bluffing? Was he asking him to give up his coconspirators? Hicks made up his mind in an instant. He'd play hardball.

"General, I am completely baffled by your actions. You have the power to do anything you wish to. We are all accountable and I tell you, in front of these men, that I have done nothing wrong. I can explain all of my actions to you en route to Norfolk—"

"Enough, Colonel. Even if I let you stay aboard, I won't be making the transit myself. I think the brig at Rodman will be just perfect. That is, unless you'd like to share your thoughts with me—in private if you prefer—regarding who's masterminding this plot. No offense intended, Colonel, but it defies belief that you could run with this all by yourself. Well, your thoughts on sharing some information with me?"

"General, there's nothing to share," said Hicks, forfeiting his last opportunity to slither off the hook.

"Very well, Colonel. Have it your way. I hope your

colleagues thank you for your largesse in taking the rap for them, even though you're just a bit player. Master at Arms, escort the colonel off the ship."

"Aye, aye, sir," responded the master at arms as he walked the colonel out of the room.

Ashley Lovelace continued, "Commander Zigler, you will accompany Colonel Hicks to the brig with all of the paperwork. You will give the paperwork to the base commander, Captain McHenry, and only to him. I have already communicated with him and he will cooperate. Colonel Hicks is to have no phone calls and no visitors and you are to tell no one except Captain McHenry that he is there. Colonel Perkins, you are now the acting chief of staff. You will follow the instructions that I briefed you on while the ship transits to Norfolk. Do either of you have any questions?"

"No sir," they replied in unison. Lovelace had chosen them well.

One deck below and all the way aft on the ship's portside quarterdeck, Captain Howe stood next to the ship's officer of the deck, Lieutenant Junior Grade Alex Tan. The captain wanted to ensure that the general's instructions were followed to the letter and that Colonel Hicks was not afforded the usual military honor of having the word passed on the ship's announcing system, "Staff, departing." It was one last nail in Hicks's coffin that Lovelace wanted to hammer in. As the master at arms escorted him past the quarterdeck, Hicks snarled at the captain.

"Your general has lost his mind. As commanding officer you have paramount authority on this ship. I insist that you stop this madness."

"You're the one who's mad, Colonel. Just leave."

"This isn't the last you'll hear of this," shouted Hicks.

"I'm sure someone will want to read your book after all this is over," said Howe. He was just turning to walk back toward his cabin when General Ashley Lovelace appeared, his aide, Major Carl Gerken, following closely behind with several bags. The captain looked quickly down on the pier and saw a white staff car with a petty officer in his crackerjack whites standing next to the door.

"General, are you leaving?"

"Yes, Captain. I know this is a bit sudden. My staff will backbrief you. Colonel Perkins is in charge. I have every confidence that he will be able to discharge the duties of my staff during your transit back to Norfolk."

"But General—"

"Captain. I know that this is perplexing to you and that you have many questions that need to be answered and deserve to be answered. I regret that I can't do that at this time. Now, as I said, what I'm doing will be back-briefed to you by my staff once you are under way. There will be no mention of my departure in any OPREP or SITREP, is that understood?"

"But General, we have—"

Lovelace interrupted him. He liked Howe and wished he could tell him more. Wished he could keep him in the loop. But he couldn't. It was just too chancey as it was. "I know the regulations, Captain. Let's just say we're going after a greater good. You'll see why in good time. I'm still your commander and I can issue you an order to do this if it makes you feel more comfortable."

"No, General. That won't be necessary. I understand completely. Have a safe journey—wherever it leads you. We'll take good care of your flagship."

"I know you will, captain—and thank you."

As Ashley Lovelace started from quarterdeck, Howe knew he shouldn't use the IMC system to announce his departure, but he wanted to extend that courtesy to him somehow. He called for the general and met his turn with a salute. The general returned it. "Joint Task Force Eight, departing," Howe said.

The general nodded and hurried to his staff car. As he drove away, a perplexed Captain Howe turned to Lieutenant Junior Grade Tan and said, "Let's get under way son."

Tan looked back at him. He had never called him son.

The canal pilot and other workers came aboard and the linehandlers cast off their lines to get under way and transit the canal. Theirs would be a somber journey home.

CHAPTER 114

LAURA THOUGHT RICK'S CALL EXCEEDINGLY ODD FOR a SEAL. "Rick," she asked, "who are you working with? Your calls have been kind of convoluted. I don't want to pry into every aspect of what you're doing, but I think I need to know."

Rick knew how secretive the Agency was, and how they did not want him to let anyone know about his situation. But these were extraordinary times. And it wasn't as if the Agency was cooperating fully with him now anyway.

"Laura, I shouldn't be telling you this, but I used to do some work for the CIA and I've still got some contacts there. I'm trying to get them to help us, but all they'll do is work with me on a strictly unofficial basis. That's almost no help, but I think they can help us reach whatever destination we decide to try to get to. Other than that, it's a dead end."

"That's just it, Rick," she replied, understanding she shouldn't press him to reveal more about his background. "I don't think we're really sure about what we think we can do."

"I thought I had some ideas, before that taxi ride and before seeing this paper. I'm not sure we have many options. Do we have any options?"

"I think we do, Rick. Look, this entire operation was designed to fail, no doubt by some fairly highly placed people. I know the military brass didn't much care for the President—no, that's not right—they really despised him. Even General Walters occasionally let it slip when we played squash. You know, nothing really specific, just a general sense that he really didn't like the President or the changes he was making. You don't think he orchestrated this, do you?"

Rick thought for a moment. "No, I don't think Walters could have pulled it all off from down there in Panama. Had to be some connection in Washington too. That's where the real action is."

"But General Walters is really pretty senior. Do you think someone above him was pulling the strings?"

"Only one military man who has more clout than a Unified Commander."

"Who?"

"The chairman of the Joint Chiefs of Staff, General Howard Campbell."

"Do you think he's involved too?"

"Can't say for sure. That would certainly be a powerful force if the two of them were working together."

"Wait," said Laura. "General Walters just came from the Joint Chiefs. J-5 Directorate. He'd have worked closely with General Campbell while he was there."

"You bet."

"Rick, we need to find out more. Can't you get your CIA contacts to find out more than they have?"

"I don't think so. Besides, they don't move in those military circles. About all they'd know about the military and what's going on in the Pentagon is what they read in the papers."

"Not much intelligence help, then, huh?"

"No, 'fraid not."

"Wait, Rick. Maybe there's a way to find something out. We've got Navy Intelligence. Our organization would be tapped into what was going on. Maybe they wouldn't have the entire story, but they'd be pretty tuned in. I worked for the director, Rear Admiral Phillips, when I was on summer duty during my first-class summer when I was a midshipman. He was deputy director then. He wrote a really good efficiency report on me. Several years later, when I first made lieutenant, I interviewed with him to be his aide. I didn't get the job, but he was very complimentary and said he'd be sure I got a great set of orders my next time being detailed—which I did. I know it's a stretch, but I really think I can call him—"

"What would you say?" Rick interrupted. "Hi, Admiral, you probably don't remember me, but I worked for you almost a decade ago and, oh by the way, I'm on the run, charged with murder, you know."

Laura ignored the flip remark and continued. "No. But you see, we're a really small community. Everybody knows everybody. Even lowly lieutenants."

"Okay, Laura, I follow you. What do you plan on saying to him?"

"I'm not exactly sure, but, well, he just struck me as a really straight arrow, someone who will do the right thing because it's the right thing. I've got to think that he's pretty well connected in Washington. I don't know, Rick, I just think he could tell us what to do and where to go with our information."

"All right, Laura. I agree it's worth a try. See if you can contact him."

"Is there anyone else you can think of that can help us?"

"No, not really. I'll talk to my contacts at CIA, but don't expect much."

"You know, I may call Liz Kennedy too. You remember, that reporter for the *Washington Post* who broke the story about Operation Roundup."

"Are you sure you can trust her?"

"I think so. I'll go slowly and feel her out."

"Great. I've got one other contact to try too. It might pay off."

"Flip you for the phone," said Laura.

"Take it," said Rick.

The next several hours were some of the strangest they'd spent together. Each had to make several phone calls, some of which might pan out and some of which probably wouldn't. There really wasn't time for each of them to give the other a lot of background on who they were calling or why, so each of them listened in on just one-half of the other's conversation, trying to pick up the gist of what was transpiring, an always difficult task.

Laura put down the receiver last. "Rick, I think we've got a path." She was wrung out but had a glow. She felt that she had a breakthrough.

"Glad you do. None of my sources really panned out, and the CIA group is only going to help us in their 'unofficial' way."

"I think we can work with that," she continued. "Once I got through the bureaucracy and got to speak with him—I swear, if I hadn't met him before, I never would have gotten through—Admiral Phillips listened for a long time. He said he couldn't talk too much over the phone, but that a lot of what I was telling him tracked with some suspicions and speculations that they've had at the Office of Naval Intelligence."

"Good, but what does he want us to do?"

"I told him we were followed once and may be followed again. I told him about being on the run—of course he knows all about that because the NIS is looking at Andy Wilson's death, and ONI has been brought in to assess what secrets may have passed into the wrong hands."

"Does he think you're implicated?"

"I don't know. I'm sure he's not going to go out on a limb and back me up based on what I've told him in one phone call. But he listened and he was empathetic. I don't think he wants to lock me up and throw away the key."

"I don't know, Laura, he could change his tune once he gets hold of you."

"He could, but he gave me his word he wouldn't. He said we needed to get to Washington to talk with him in person—somewhere where we wouldn't be seen. In the meantime he's going to press really hard to see if our suspicions are true. He's got a reputation for being a bulldog, so I don't think he'll be able to be deterred."

"I hope not. But when does he want us to come to Washington?"

"As soon as possible, but as safely as possible. He really recommended against flying. Said it's too easy to watch the airports. That leaves us driving or taking a train or bus."

"I'm worried about renting a car. One of us would have to show a driver's license and if there's a manhunt under way we'd be easily tagged."

"Bus? Train?" she said, letting Rick lead with this.

"I don't know much about bus routes between here and Washington. But Amtrak runs up the eastern seaboard. We could check and I think that it would only be a day trip. Do you think that would get us there soon enough?"

"Maybe. From the paper, it looks like that entire impeachment process may run its full course through the House in the next day or two. After that, all it has to do is get voted on in the Senate and it's over."

"I agree that it's critical we get there right away, but I think the train may be our safest bet."

"You may be right."

"Hungry?"

"Famished."

"Room service?"

"You're on again, you cheapskate. Am I the cheapest date you've ever had, or what?" said Laura, kidding Rick. He appreciated her more and more now. She was propping him up, lifting his spirits.

Rick called room service and sat down on the bed, exhausted. There was a knock on the door. Rick looked warily at Laura. He motioned for her to be silent. Surely this couldn't be room service already.

Rick approached the door carefully. "Who is it?" he said.

"Bellman, Mr. Allen—with your bags from *Stattendam*."

He looked at Laura. Was this a ruse? Had they been tracked down? Rick carefully approached the door, motioning for Laura to be silent and to stay on the other side of the room. He brought his head up to the peephole and looked out. Looked like a bellman, and there was his golf bag and Laura's bag. He passed the duck test.

Rick opened the door a crack. "Hello. Thanks for bringing these up."

"You're welcome, sir. They just came over from the ship moments ago and we brought them right up. You and the Mrs. have a nice stay in Fort Lauderdale." He beamed expectantly.

Rick gave him a once-over, then opened the door more, fished a bill out of his pocket, and tipped him. "Thanks."

"You're welcome, sir," replied the bellman. As he left, Rick closed the door and smiled at Laura. Another minor victory.

A short while later, room service delivered their food. They enjoyed a late lunch looking out on the intercoastal waterway, chuckling about their paranoia. This seemed to

THE CORONADO CONSPIRACY　　429

be a routine with them. Room service with a view, Laura called it.

They discussed how much they would need the help of the director of Naval Intelligence. Otherwise, who would believe two Navy people on the run, one of whom was a chief AWOL from his ship and the other who was a lieutenant wanted for murder? They felt they had put all the pieces together and that they had a compelling story to tell, but it would be hard to tell it as they were being cuffed and taken away. They needed someone to champion their case, and right now Admiral Phillips was the only game in town.

As they discussed it further, they realized what a long shot this was, and how desperate their plight was. Who would believe them? They probably would be treated as two criminals who would say anything to anyone to extricate themselves. They thought eventually the truth would come out, but who knew what would happen if the President was actually impeached? If they could believe the paper, and the little bit that Admiral Phillips had shared with Laura, it looked like the Senate had already made its mind up that the President was guilty and that the required two-thirds of the Senate was predisposed to convict him and remove him from office once the House delivered its article of impeachment to the Senate. The only place they could stop this train wreck was in the House of Representatives.

Optimistically, they thought that once they got to Washington, Admiral Phillips would listen to their story, see the evidence Rick carried in the golf bag, and then talk with ever more senior officials until a critical mass formed of people who believed what Rick and Laura were saying. Then, somehow, this information had to be made known to the House leadership, perhaps to Speaker Wilcox himself, so that he would stop the hearings.

They finally arrived at a consensus. Laura said, "All right, Rick, it's settled, then. We get on the first Amtrak train out of here heading to Washington. Once there, I'll contact Admiral Phillips and we'll get further instructions."

"Sounds good." Within minutes he had called and gotten the Amtrak schedule.

"Laura, they have only two trains a day. We've already missed the 2:02 P.M. out of here. The next one is 8:09 tomorrow morning. It gets into Washington at 5:30 the following morning. I think we should take that."

"Okay. I just hope we're not too late. . . ."

Around the hotel, Bleich's men were fanned out waiting for further instructions. The game plan had changed since he left General Howard Campbell's office and flew down from Bolling just a few days ago. At the meeting, the chairman had graciously empowered him to be in total command of the operation, putting his full trust and confidence in him. But the general had changed drastically since then. He was virtually camped out in his Pentagon office now, and insisted on being called every several hours with progress reports, even if there was absolutely nothing of significance to report. Bleich was spending more and more time just speculating what to tell the general to keep him off his back.

After several calls back and forth, they had decided to wait. There was no value added in storming into the hotel and yanking them out of their rooms. Too much visibility, he'd argued. The agents had an unobstructed view of Rick's and Laura's second-floor room. They would see them leave—and see them check out. Once they came out on the street, probably to get a cab, Bleich's men would roll up in an unmarked car and stuff them in. Just in case, Bleich had a half-dozen cars and a score of men backing up this operation. This couldn't fail.

The general had seemed satisfied with this plan—satisfied, that is, after he had asked what seemed like the millionth question. Bleich was chafing at the inquisition, but he was smart enough not to let it distract him. He knew his stuff, knew the mission, knew the stress the general had been under. He'd get it done and he'd get it done right. That star that the general had promised him if he pulled this off would be on his collar next year.

CHAPTER 115

HOWARD CAMPBELL CONTINUED TO PACE IN HIS OFFICE. He was now a virtual prisoner there, as were his legions of assistants who he insisted on keeping around just in case he needed them. They saw the stress on his face and empathized with him, but even his closest and most trusted aides and advisors were beginning to get worn down by the general's constant questions and accusations. He had become very secretive too, calling people, some in civilian clothes, into his office for one-on-one sessions, routinely dismissing his executive assistant, who usually always was there taking notes and acting as his alter ego. They thought his actions very strange indeed, but none had the nerve to confront him.

His secretary was starting to get involved in some puzzling calls. The chief of Naval Operations, Admiral Boomer Curtis, had been insistent on seeing him immediately that morning. Soon after that visit, which included the usual hangers-on, he gave a private audience to Rear Admiral Warren Phillips, the DNI, director of Naval Intelligence. His aides thought it particularly strange, not just because it was a private audience, but because the DNI was not in the circle of people he usually met with. ONI supported the Navy directly, and not the Joint Chiefs. No one could think of any personal affiliation between the two. Very strange indeed. His personal staff really didn't know what to make of it. What they did know, because it was impossible to miss, was that the chairman was seething when the DNI left. He immediately returned to his office, instructed them to leave him alone and to keep the phone lines clear. He thought a moment before making the call. It was a drastic step, so sudden, so violent. But it was about *that damned loose end,* and nothing gnawed at him more.

*   *   *

The line of people outside the Capitol had started the night before, and by morning it had swelled to the hundreds. Citizens all, from the curious to political junkies, they lined up faithfully, hoping to be one of the few that could be squeezed into the House gallery for the first day of the House impeachment hearings for President Taylor Calhoun. To a visitor from another country, and perhaps even some U.S. citizens, it was quite astounding that such a serious matter could be open to the public—to the masses—but this was the essence of American democracy. In spite of determined efforts by Speaker Wilcox, the media were allowed to bring a limited number of cameras into the House chamber. There was just too much national and worldwide attention to keep them out. Although they protested mildly that the "dignity of the proceedings" would be diminished, each representative secretly relished the extensive media attention he or she would receive during these hearings.

The full House had been following the proceedings of the Judiciary Committee for the past several days and knew full well that an article of impeachment would arrive for their vote. That was no surprise. They also knew that, strong as the sentiment against the President was in the House, it was mild compared to the Senate. Most of them believed that if the President were impeached by their body, he would be found guilty by the Senate and then found disqualified to continue to hold office. In accordance with the Constitution, the chief justice of the United States, Justice James Purtell, certainly one of the President's severest critics, would preside over the proceedings. Therefore, the entire House was in a particularly somber mood as they contemplated what they were about to embark upon. Even those who disliked the President personally, or disliked what his party stood for, or hated what he was accused of doing with respect to Operation Roundup felt a sense of dread about removing their Chief Executive from office against his will. They all felt that their country would be diminished in the eyes of the world.

And the entire House was there, save for Representative Wesley Monroe of Oklahoma's Second District, who was recovering from triple-bypass surgery. Even some of the more senior members could not recall when the chamber had been this full, surely not in this decade. Other than a powerful sense of duty to be here, missing a vote on the impeachment of the President of the United States was not something that would be easy to explain to one's constituents back home. The entire membership was poised to do their duty.

The President's grand scheme to have his party loyalists lobby their colleagues to sway their votes to him had been almost for naught. The evidence against him, particularly after the Judiciary Committee's thorough hearings, had looked so overwhelming. There was even more defections from the President's own party and only one or two fence-sitters had been swayed to consider—only consider—siding with the President. The Judiciary Committee hearings had been incredibly damaging, particularly the testimony of General Howard Campbell and the other Joint Chiefs who were overridden by Taylor Calhoun as he lunged forward with Operation Roundup. This was now something that went beyond party lines; it was a bipartisan ground-swell.

The gallery was filled to capacity as the House members arrived at their seats. There was none of the amiable bantering that usually ensues among men and women who work so closely together and who direct the course of their government. They just filed in and took their seats, going out of their way to avoid talking with their colleagues. Some of the younger members stared incredulously at the full chamber, something they had never seen. Still others gaped at the packed gallery of citizens sitting and ready to become fully engrossed, not the typical noisy rustling of tourists who passed through for a few minutes at a time just to "check the block" that they had been there.

Speaker Wilcox mounted the platform and intoned, "The House will come to order," banging his gavel several times for emphasis. After the usual acknowledgments he began to speak to the matter at hand. The reporters in the press pool clicked on their tape recorders and began to furiously scribble notes.

"Ladies and gentlemen, we are gathered together here, every member of this body save one, to consider a matter of the highest national urgency. The Judiciary Committee, chaired by Representative Linda Cohen of the great state of New York, has delivered its decision to us that the President of the United States is guilty of impeachable offenses and has recommended that an article of impeachment be adopted in the case of the President. You have a copy of those proposed articles before you, and I will have Representative Cohen read them shortly. After this reading the floor will be open for debate. I will recognize members one by one. The debate will continue in accordance with our normal rules with one exception: There will be no filibuster. Furthermore, there will be no posturing, no grandstanding, and no manifestos. This is a serious matter and will be treated as such. Just do your duty. I yield to the representative from New York."

Wilcox left the podium and Linda Cohen got up. A diminutive woman with a typical New Yorker's moxie, she was in her element.

"Thank you, Mr. Speaker," she began. "The Judiciary Committee met for a total of six consecutive days to hear testimony and consider evidence as to whether, as laid out in the Constitution, the President should be removed from office on impeachment for, and conviction of, treason, bribery, or other high crimes and misdemeanors. I can tell you that we heard extensive testimony and considered a wealth of evidence. After deliberating thoroughly, we have concluded that the President is guilty of high crimes and misdemeanors. Specifically, he overrode the advice, I might add insistent advice, of his highest-ranking military officers and ordered the start of Operation Roundup, which led directly to the deaths of over one hundred of our brave young boys. This is the single article of impeachment that we recommend to you and urge you to adopt it."

As Linda Cohen left the podium, the House sat silent, letting her remarks sink in. Even though they knew this moment was coming, actually hearing the recommendation delivered, with the full House assembled, increased the gravity of it in all of their minds. They knew that things would now move quickly.

Bobby Wilcox continued. "We will now begin the debate on the recommended article of impeachment."

Then in very learned and statesmanlike tones and with all cameras focused directly on him, he laid out the very structured rules and regulations, the procedures and the protocol, that these hearings would follow. As soon as he finished his instructions, he began to recognize his colleagues—in accordance with his prearranged script that favored allies and disempowered enemies.

The hearings wore on for hours. The cameras kept rolling. The gallery stayed packed as few observers left, and their places were taken immediately. The membership stayed in their places, each and every one of them knowing that the cameras were rolling inexorably.

It was now ten P.M. The full House had been assembled since eight-thirty that morning. The debate had been heated, often strident. Bobby Wilcox surveyed the sea of exhausted faces before him and determined that going on any further this night would be futile.

"Ladies and gentlemen. The House stands recessed until nine tomorrow morning. We will attempt to conclude our debates and deliberations then. Thank you for your work today."

CHAPTER 116

THE JINGLE OF THE PHONE STARTLED RICK. "FIVE forty-five A.M., this is your wake-up call." He put the phone back in its cradle. Just five minutes, he told himself. Laura's arm lay lightly on his stomach. She was still fast asleep.

The night had again been incredible. Rick couldn't believe that their intimacy could be that strong or that . . . well, wild. He and Laura had been all over each other, insistent, insatiable, totally enveloping each other. Rick drifted with those thoughts for a few moments.

Then Rick looked at the clock again and couldn't help shouting out. *"My God! Laura!"* It was almost nine A.M. Rick's five-minute rest had turned into a sleep of several hours.

"Rick? Rick, what?" said Laura as she awoke with a start. "Are you all right? What's the matter?"

"Laura, I went back to sleep after the wake-up call. I was just going to snooze for five minutes. I can't believe I did this. It's completely irresponsible. I can't believe it. I just can't."

"Rick, it's okay. Look, we'll get the afternoon train. It will be almost the same thing. Actually, it may be better. If we took the morning one we would get in at five-thirty the following morning. We'd probably have to lay low for a while before we'd have to meet with Admiral Phillips. Let's relax. I'm . . . well, I'm still thinking about last night," she said as she smiled and gently stroked his face.

Rick caught her gaze. What had he done to deserve a woman like this being close to him? She was right too: The afternoon train would work. Now they'd have plenty of time to get themselves together and travel the twenty minutes to the Amtrak station. They'd also have more time to continue to define their plan, which thus far was still a little sketchy.

"I am too," he replied. "Laura, you're just fantastic. After this is all over—"

She didn't let him finish. "After this is all over, Holden, you're going to have to either leave town or make an honest woman out of me."

"Laura, I—"

Again she stopped him. "Okay, Rick, let's keep our eye on the ball. We've got a lot to do. Order us up some breakfast and then I'm going to call Admiral Phillips and update him on when we're going to be arriving in Washington."

"Okay. I'll only be a minute."

After Rick had called room service, Laura took the phone and called the office of the director of Naval Intelligence. It was still too dangerous to use her real name, so using the same alias she had used the day before when she worked her way through the admiral's secretary, she began again.

"Yes, good morning. Captain McClain for Admiral Phillips."

"Good morning, Captain," responded the secretary with a bit of caution in her voice. "Is the admiral expecting your call?"

"Oh yes," responded Laura. "We spoke yesterday and I had some follow-up information for him. I definitely think he's expecting my call."

"Yes, Captain, well, you see, the admiral is not here at the moment. Perhaps if we could return the call. What organization did you say you were with?"

Laura was caught off guard. "Yes, oh, I'm with . . . with the Fleet Intelligence Support Center in San Diego. I know I'm calling rather early, my time, but we come in early out here. No, I won't be at this phone for too long. I'll have to call back. Did I miss the admiral before he started on his busy round of appointments?"

Laura was so convincing that the normally wary secretary opened up to her. "Actually, Captain, he hasn't come in yet. I have appointments that he's missed so far stacking up in our waiting area. I'd suggest you call back much later in the day."

"Of course, of course," said Laura. "Thank you anyway."

She hung up the phone and looked at Rick. "Rick, the DNI didn't come into work today. His secretary has no idea where he is."

"Strange," said Rick.

"I'll try to reach him later. For now, let's get our stuff together and maybe go to the station a little early."

"I don't think that's a good idea. We're safe here. There may be someone out there looking for us. Let's sit tight until about one. That will give us plenty of time to get there, get our tickets, and get out of here."

"If you really think so . . ."

"I *really* do," replied Rick. "Curaçao wasn't that long ago. They really were after us, Laura. I can't believe that they'd just give up. They know *Stattendam* went to Fort Lauderdale. There's not that many options for us."

So they stayed in Room 212, enjoying each other for several more hours. Tender now, everything slow and easy. Daring not to fall asleep again.

At his command center, Colonel Bleich was trying to decide which course of action to take before the next call to General Campbell and some more gratuitous advice.

He had his men everywhere and felt that he had the area around the Marina Inn totally blanketed. Arrangements had been made with the Fort Lauderdale police to let his men work the area without their assistance, so his mobile command center, all his cars, and the men on foot had carte blanche to go where they wanted to go and do what they wanted to do. For those local police who couldn't recognize Bleich's men, a single code word— "takedown"—had been devised.

The chairman had insisted that they stick with their plan of not grabbing Rick and Laura until they emerged from the hotel, even though the wait was becoming interminable. Bleich felt that he had to apologize to the general because the two had not emerged from the Marina Inn yet. Hell, General, he wanted to say. If you think you can do a goddamned better job, you come on down here and do it yourself.

As the day wore on past noon, Bleich's men on the scene were becoming impatient too. He wanted this to be a fail-safe operation, and therefore he didn't switch watch stations or provide relief for any of them. Whoever picked up a position once Rick and Laura were in the hotel stayed right where they were. It was a perfect plan for a few hours, but now that their prey had been holed up for over twenty-four hours, it was beginning to break down.

Fink and Hillis, sat in their sedan less than a hundred yards from the lobby of the Marina Inn and had an unobstructed view of Rick's and Laura's room, as well as the hotel lobby. Benham and Lewis were backup and were only another two hundred yards away from them. Nimitz and Baldwin were on foot. Dressed, as best they could, as street people, they alternately sat at a bus stop, checked out Dumpsters, and panhandled people for money. Fink had been leading Hillis $3.75 to $2.37 before Bleich told them to knock it off.

Of course, all of them felt that this was ridiculous overkill. They had been given a pep talk about how dangerous Rick was, about his actions in Curaçao and the guy still in intensive care. But hell, those were NIS agents. Civilians. Barely better than rent-a-cops. Wait until he—they—tried to deal with the real military. The only tough thing was deciding who would actually grab them. This was just not going to be hard at all.

It was approaching one P.M. Rick had arranged for a late checkout with the hotel and had also had them deliver a newspaper. The *Miami Herald* covered the impeachment hearings extensively, providing a verbatim transcript of the previous day's debate. One thing was obvious: There was little support for the President. Even those party loyalists speaking on his behalf were cautious, trying not to go too far out on a limb, couching their defense of Taylor Calhoun in often elliptical phraseology so as not to get themselves too closely connected with the man who most pundits thought was well on his way out of office. This betrayal made Rick and Laura only more determined.

Rick hefted his golf bag over his shoulder and picked up Laura's bag with the other hand. "Ready to go?" he said.

"Sure," she replied. "How are we getting to the Amtrak station?"

"When I called the front desk to arrange a late checkout, they told me to just come down to the lobby and in the time it takes us to check out they can have a cab right over here."

"Sounds like you have it covered. I'm concerned about the DNI not coming in to work. Maybe I should call again."

"Maybe we can call from the train station. We're cutting it a little close on time as it is," said Rick.

"Okay, Rick, fine. I imagine that if he's there I might not get put right through to him anyway."

Then, with one last kiss, he ushered her out of the room. As he did, cellular phones lit up.

"Bleich . . . Hillis. Subjects emerging from room, luggage in hand. Heading for lobby."

"Bleich, roger. Benham, Lewis, you have them in sight too?"

"Roger, clear view."

"Nimitz, you there?"

"Roger, other side of parking lot, about fifty yards away."

"Baldwin?"

"On the other side of the hotel now. I'll move closer."

"Baldwin, negative. You stay put for now."

"Roger."

"Nimitz."

"Roger."

"You stay right where you are and surveil. Only approach the subjects after Fink and Hillis get within a few yards of them. Don't make a direct approach but come around from the side. Fink and Hillis are primary. Repeat, Fink and Hillis are primary."

"Hillis, roger. I got it. Tell us when."

"Let them get into the lobby and pay their bill. I assume they'll call a cab. Let them walk out of the lobby and then as soon as they start to get into the cab, Fink, grab Holden first; Hillis, you assist him. Nimitz, you grab Peters. Baldwin, once the action starts—not before then—you approach and help out where needed. Benham and Lewis, you move in much closer but stay in your car, repeat, stay in your car until I give you other word. We're not using weapons—not appropriate here. I expect you to overpower them with overwhelming physical force. I want it all to end quickly." His detailed instructions complete, Bleich added, "How copy?"

"Hillis."

"Nimitz."

"Baldwin."

"Benham."

While their transmissions were being made, Rick and Laura had made their way down the exterior staircase and were approaching the lobby. Both were scanning the landscape carefully, looking for danger, but saw none. Bleich's men had done their job well and were inconspicuous.

Nimitz edged a little closer to the lobby but was still well hidden. Fink and Hillis started to drive slowly toward the hotel lobby, their car partially obscured by a low fence. In the command post, Bleich sat tensely, waiting for the next bit of information to come over his phone.

Rick and Laura entered the hotel lobby. "Checking out, Room 212."

"Ah, yes, Mr. and Mrs. Allen," said the clerk. "I do hope you enjoyed your stay at the Marina Inn."

"We did, and we'd like a taxi to the Amtrak station."

"Certainly," said the clerk, simultaneously picking up the phone.

After a moment he turned back to Rick and Laura and said, "Five minutes or less. Now, I see you have paid in advance with cash last night. Would you like to still pay cash or put it on a credit card?"

"Cash will be fine."

"Certainly. That will be another twenty-two-fifty for long-distance calls. Cash too?"

"Yes," said Rick, peeling the bills off of his now-dwindling roll of money.

Rick and Laura thanked the solicitous clerk again, assuring him a third time that they had enjoyed their stay and that, yes, they would recommend it to their friends and that yes, they would be back another time. The banter got so idle that they decided to wait outside for the taxi. They wanted to get some of that Florida sunshine, they told him.

"Subjects coming out of the lobby," said Hillis over his phone.

"Roger," said Bleich. "Any sign of a taxi?"

"Negative. Not yet. They're just standing outside, though."

"Roger. Wait."

"Roger."

Time seemed to stand still. For everyone. Rick and Laura actually gazed at the sun for a few minutes, enjoying its warmth. They occasionally looked around warily, but their tension was easing. Maybe they were home free.

Fink and Hillis were itchy. Twenty-four hours had been a long time to wait.

"Colonel." That was a slip. They weren't supposed to use military ranks, remembered Hillis.

"Say again," replied the angry voice.

"Still no sign of a taxi. Subjects still just standing outside of the lobby. No passersby. Request permission to move in."

"Negative."

Hillis was more insistent. "I say again. We have a clear path to the subjects. No other personnel in the area. Request permission to move in!"

Bleich thought for a moment. Maybe this was as good an opportunity as any. The taxi might be in the way, anyway. "Hillis, Fink, move in. I repeat, move in. Nimitz, continue to close. Baldwin, stand by. Benham and Lewis, start to close. Acknowledge."

They did, and with precision, Bleich's men began to move in.

Fink and Hillis pulled closer to the lobby, warily eyeing Rick and Laura. Hillis was the smaller man and he was driving. Fink would get out first and subdue Rick. He was a large man with the build of a linebacker and was an expert in the martial arts. He wore false black horn-rim glasses and had on an ill-fitting sports jacket, hoping to project a bookish, harmless image. Though smaller, Hillis was also a martial arts expert and had, like Fink, been specially selected for this detail in large part because of his physical skills. They'd be more than a match for one man and one woman.

Closer now, they cruised up as if they were going to check into the hotel. Fink would enter the lobby and approach the desk while Hillis stayed in the car. Then, once Rick and Laura had forgotten about him, he'd come up behind Rick. Hillis would jump out of the car and help his partner. Nimitz and Baldwin would approach the lobby on foot from different directions and grab Laura. Piece of cake.

As the car pulled up to the lobby, stopping just fifteen feet from where they stood, Rick and Laura looked at it.

Rick automatically went through a mental checklist in sizing them up. Two businessmen. Salesmen, no doubt. These guys needed some sun. Nothing remarkable about the car. One guy checking in. The other waiting, probably going to park as close to their room as possible. Fink walked past them, neither making eye contact or acknowledging their presence. Rick eyed him over his shoulder as he approached the front desk. Still nothing remarkable. Not a really expensive suit. This wasn't the cheapest hotel in town, but it was probably at the upper limit of their expense accounts. Fink disappeared out of Rick's scan. Damn, where the hell was that taxi? he thought.

"Laura. Wait right here. I'm going to check with the clerk and see where our cab is."

"It will be right along. We're okay for time."

"I hope so," said Rick. "Be right back."

As Rick entered the lobby, he noticed that the man in the suit was still there. He wasn't at the counter, though; he was just standing off to the side looking out of place. It didn't feel right. Rick went through his mental checklist again. Big guy. Suit. Haircut a bit short. Shoes. *Shoes*. Not right. Military issues, that was it.

Outside, Hillis was getting worried. This wasn't in the script. What was going on in there? Did Holden recognize his partner? No, of course not. But was he suspicious?

Laura was looking at Hillis casually. He probably thinks his buddy is taking too long, she thought. Probably thinking that he could do it better and faster himself. Type A, no doubt. And was that phone ringing coming from his car? Why wasn't he picking it up?

Inside, Rick eyed Fink warily. Fink was avoiding eye contact, first reading the brochures on the sideboard, then looking at the list of church services. He's in here doing nothing Rick realized, and his buddy's still outside. What about Laura?

The sound of a car moving caught Laura's attention. It was their taxi. Laura waved at the cab and then called for Rick.

My God, she's in trouble, thought Rick. He eyed Fink,

who was now looking at him. It all came together in a flash.

Rick ran out of the lobby and toward Laura. "Are you all right?"

Startled, Laura started to answer, but now it was all happening too fast. Hillis jumped out of the car and grabbed Laura. Fink, a few steps behind Rick, ran after him out of the lobby. Laura screamed as Hillis grabbed her and immediately started kicking and screaming. Nimitz saw what was happening and started toward the group. Each second seemed like an hour.

Rick saw Laura in Hillis's grasp and went into a rage. He rushed at Hillis as Fink rushed up behind him.

Laura saw Fink before Rick did. "Rick, look out."

Rick turned and saw Fink. He wheeled and sent a blow into the man's stomach. It slowed him, but he didn't stop. He still came at Rick.

Laura continued to struggle in Hillis's grasp. She was fighting for all she was worth, but couldn't shake free.

Nimitz was now only twenty feet away, waiting to jump into the melee. Fink now had his hands on Rick's throat and was trying to choke him to the ground. In their car, the phone continued to ring, a frustrated Colonel Bleich on the other end trying desperately to get his men to check in.

Meanwhile, the taxi driver who had been summoned saw what appeared to be a couple being attacked by two large male assailants. An older Cuban man, he was too old and too worldlywise to get involved physically. He wanted to drive off. But the girl, she might be raped. And the bigger man was now pummeling her companion. And there, another was coming to join in.

Something stirred inside him too. This was too good a country for citizens to do nothing; that had been Cuba's downfall. He was too frail to try to take them on, though. He came to a solution before he even realized he had. It happened so fast it was beyond conscious thought. The Cuban turned his cab toward Fink's and Hillis's car, then picked up speed.

Fink and Hillis were entangled with Rick and Laura,

but they caught the taxi in their peripheral vision. It was unbelievable. What was that crazy old man doing?

The taxi crashed into the car and sent it skidding sideways across the parking lot. Fink was momentarily startled and relaxed his grip on Rick long enough for Rick to wheel and level him with one blow.

Hillis recovered momentarily and rushed Rick, tackling him around the waist and pushing him against the now-wrecked car. Rick hit it with a resounding thud.

Rick and Hillis went at it, fists flying, neither man thinking for a second about defending himself, only about subduing his adversary.

Nimitz moved in closer to Laura.

She didn't wait, but rushed him. It was not the reaction he expected. He saw her as a woman. She saw herself as a naval officer.

Nimitz reached out to grasp her and subdue her, but as Laura approached, she drew her right knee up and planted it in Nimitz's groin with her full force.

Nimitz went down like a sack of potatoes, moaning.

Their melee had momentarily startled Hillis, just long enough for Rick to deliver a blow to his jaw that dropped him too.

Baldwin was approaching.

Rick and Laura had seconds to make their decision.

"Rick, the bags."

In one motion, Rick scooped up his golf bag and Laura's duffel bag and threw them into the cab, then he opened the driver's door and pulled the dazed Cuban out of the taxi.

"Sorry, pops. You don't want to be with us now." Then, realizing that he didn't know where he was going, he had the presence of mind to ask, "Where's the Amtrak station?"

"What, señor?"

"Amtrak. Amtrak. The train. The damn train. That's where you were going to take us. One second." As Baldwin leaped at Rick, Rick reached into the car, yanked a nine iron out of his bag, and before Baldwin could see it coming, cut it across his skull. Baldwin collapsed. Rick looked around and saw a car coming toward them. "Hurry. The train!"

"*Sí,*" said the driver, still dazed but understanding enough. "Over the bridge," he said, pointing to the A1A, or Brooks Causeway. "Go to Highway 1—Federal Highway. North to Broward Boulevard. It's within sight of where Broward meets I-95." It was a struggle for the Cuban to blurt all that out, but he knew Rick and the girl were in terrible trouble.

"Thanks . . . for everything, señor," said Rick as he gently relaxed his grip on the man. "Please, please, señor. Don't tell them where we are going. These are evil men. You saved us once. Save us again."

The Cuban just looked at him and nodded. Rick knew he could trust him to be silent.

"Laura, get in."

She needed no extra urging. Laura jumped in the passenger seat and Rick slid into the driver's seat. The car driven by Benham and Lewis continued toward them, picking up speed.

Back at the command center, Colonel Bleich was wild with rage. Now every transmission was a scream. Almost no one was talking to him.

"Fink. Come in, dammit."

No answer.

"Baldwin. Baldwin!"

No answer.

"Lewis. Lewis!"

"We're here. We're in pursuit. They're getting away in a cab."

"Catch it, dammit. Catch it!"

Benham and Lewis needed no urging. They were hot after Rick and Laura as they sped out of the Marina Inn parking lot. Rick was accelerating quickly, wanting to put as much distance as possible between them and their pursuers.

"Laura, help me navigate. What did he say to do first?"

"Over that bridge there," she said, pointing toward the Brooks Causeway—or 17th Street Bridge, as it was more commonly known. He kept glancing over his shoulder at their pursuers, but Benham and Lewis were still right behind them.

Rick went up the ramp and onto the bridge causeway, while Laura did her best to navigate. It had been wishful thinking to imagine that they were no longer being hunted, but this was unbelievable. "Four men in the parking lot," Laura said. "Another car after us now. And one didn't answer his phone. Someone must be giving instructions. How many more do you think there are?"

"No idea. Let's hope none are at the train station, though. There's the sign for Highway 1. Looks like this just blends right into it. Get ready to make a right."

"Got it," replied Rick, confident that Laura had remembered the directions better than he had.

"Okay, we just passed Route 736. Broward can't be too far along up here," she said. "Yes, there's a sign. Half-mile. We go left."

"Got it," said Rick. As he looked in the rearview mirror, he saw Benham and Lewis not far behind them. He suspected they were just told to follow them and that reinforcements from other quarters were coming after them too.

As he approached Broward Boulevard, Rick turned left hard, hoping to lose Benham and Lewis, but as he came out of the turn they were still there. He could see Lewis on the phone, talking to someone who was sure to join the chase soon.

As they crossed Andrews Avenue and approached 7th Avenue, Laura spotted the sign. "Rick, there it is. I-95. The Amtrak station should be right there."

"I know," replied Rick, still looking at Benham and Lewis in pursuit, but his head starting to clear a bit. "But if we get there, they'll be able to catch us on the train and they'll also call their buddies. It's not a good option."

"Well, what do we do?" said Laura, now a bit panicky since she wasn't on the same wavelength with Rick.

"We've got to disable them. They can't know we're going to get out of here on the train. How's our time?"

"It's coming up on 1:45, Rick. Train is at 2:02."

"Okay, it's our only chance, Laura. Hang on!"

Laura didn't know what chance that was, but did as Rick told her to do, clutching the handle over her door.

Rick was going almost eighty. They were only 150 yards from 7th Avenue. He braked hard while whipping the wheel to the right, going over into the far right lane and barely missing a van. Benham and Lewis responded and stayed with him. Rick whipped the taxi right onto 7th Avenue. He hit the brakes hard momentarily, then coasted. Passing 2nd Street, he slowed to about thirty. Approaching 4th Street, he slowed to almost ten.

Benham and Lewis couldn't believe what they were seeing. Then it dawned on Benham. "They're out of gas. Goddammit. They're out of goddamned gas!" he said, fairly screaming with glee. Ahead they could see Rick pounding on the steering wheel, venting his frustrations.

"Call the colonel and tell him," said Benham as he slowed his car to stay a few dozen yards behind Rick and Laura. Lewis did as he was told, telling him their location.

Benham and Lewis were perplexed now. What would they do? Go pull them out of the car? Wait for reinforcements? After seeing Rick take on their buddies in the Marina Inn parking lot, neither of them was anxious to tangle with him.

As the taxi came to a complete stop just north of 4th Street, Benham and Lewis decided to come up to a few yards of the taxi. It was stopped, all right. Holden and Peters were not getting out. Benham and Lewis started discussing contingencies if one or both of them got out of the taxi and started to run. They left the motor of their car running and waited for additional instructions from Colonel Bleich.

"Hold on, Laura," said Rick. "Hold on for all you're worth." Laura still didn't know why, but gripped the handle tightly and pressed herself into her seat.

Suddenly, Benham and Lewis were flabbergasted as they looked up. The taxi was getting bigger. The goddamned out-of-gas taxi was getting bigger. Benham groped for the shift handle, trying to find reverse.

Too late. The trunk of the taxi slammed into their car, snapping their heads forward and then violently back. Benham's hit the wheel with great force, Lewis's the dashboard. Both airbags inflated. There was an instant hissing sound as steam escaped from the broken radiator. The horn blared as Benham's head continued to lean on the steering wheel. He was out cold. Lewis was conscious but dazed. Instinctively, he reached for the phone.

Rick looked at Laura. "You all right?"

"I think so."

"I think we stopped 'em. Let's go."

Rick continued straight ahead on 7th Street. The car did not follow. Several more blocks straight ahead. The car looked like it still wasn't moving. Now sure they weren't being followed, Rick stopped hearing his heartbeat. "What time is it now?" he said.

"It's ten to two."

"Gonna be close." He sped ahead another block, trying to work his way back to the Amtrak station. He turned left on NW 16th Street. One block. There was NW 9th Street, State Road 845. Left on it, major road, going the right way.

"What do you think now, Laura?"

"Find I-95. Find I-95." Laura was almost screaming, willing them to get to the Amtrak station.

Back at the command post, Colonel Bleich was almost blind with rage. This couldn't be happening, goddammit. It couldn't be.

"Lewis."

No answer.

"Lewis."

Still no answer. He flung the phone down in a rage. Yelling at the man closest to him, he screamed, "Get a car. *Get a car now!*"

They were going south, the street numbers were getting smaller. Rick had slowed down to something near the speed limit. Trying to balance getting to the Amtrak station on time and not attracting the attention of the state police.

"There," said Laura, "turn right on 838. Bet that will lead us to I-95."

She was right. As soon as he got on Route 838, Rick saw the sign for I-95, one-quarter mile ahead. He pulled into the right-hand lane to get ready to head south on the interstate. He still found himself looking in the rearview mirror, but so far, so good. No Benham and Lewis. No other pursuers.

"Rick, there," shouted Laura. A sign for Amtrak.

"I see it," said Rick, almost gleeful. They had made it.

"Rick pulled off the interstate and followed the signs. The Amtrak station was only a few blocks away. Still no pursuers. Then he said, "Laura, they know what this cab looks like. We can't leave it right in front of the Amtrak station. Here," he said as he fished his roll of bills out of his pocket. "Get us two tickets to Washington. I'll take this a few blocks away and try to hide it. Then I'll meet you."

"Rick, we only have a few minutes."

"I'll make it. We've got to try to make sure they don't know for certain that we're on Amtrak."

"Okay, but hurry."

Rick wheeled the taxi right up to the main entrance. Laura hopped out and ran into the station, lugging both her bag and Rick's golf bag. No one offered to help her. A sign of the times, she thought.

Rick turned down SW 3rd Street and drove one block, then another. Finally, at the corner of SW 3rd Street and SW 24th Avenue, estimating that he could barely get back to the Amtrak station on time, he pulled the cab over to the side of the street and got out, leaving the keys in the ignition with the hope that some enterprising amateur car thief would help himself to the cab. Then he broke into a sprint. He'd done his best to cover their tracks. He hoped it would be good enough.

Laura had found the ticket counter and cajoled her way past two waiting customers to get to the front of the line.

"Two tickets to Washington, D.C."

"That'll be three hundred sixteen dollars."

Laura gasped. Resignedly, she peeled four hundred-dollar bills from Rick's thinning roll of money. "Here."

"Thank you, ma'am. Better hurry. Train's boarding."

Laura hurried toward the gate. Rick would probably come right to the train. Please, Rick, she thought, hurry.

Now just a block from the station, Rick was running as hard as he could.

Laura stood on the platform next to the last door on the last car on the train.

"All aboard."

Laura gaped at the conductor, panic-stricken.

"All aboard," he intoned again.

"*Sir! Sir!* My husband. He's paying the cab. He's coming. He's coming."

"*All aboard.*" The conductor had been doing this for twenty years. This wasn't the first time he'd heard this. And never once had he given a damn.

Laura put one foot on the step of the train and kept the other firmly planted on the platform.

"*All aboard. All aboard.*"

Suddenly he came into sight. "Rick! Rick!" she shouted, waving frantically.

He didn't return her wave, but just bore down, reaching down deep inside to pick up even a little more speed.

The train's whistle blew. Laura's eyes grew wide as the train began to move. She had to get on.

Just a hundred feet away. Reaching down for one last burst of speed, Rick sprinted the last few yards as fast as he had ever run. Finally, he jumped up to the step Laura was on. She grabbed him and held him as tightly as she ever had held anyone. They had made it.

CHAPTER 117

GENERAL HOWARD CAMPBELL'S SECRETARY HAD A very short list of callers she was permitted to put through. Colonel Bleich was one of them. Less than a minute after she had sent his call in to the chairman, she heard a blood-curdling yell. Simultaneously, instinctively, his secretary, executive assistant, and aide, all of whom he had strictly admonished to leave him alone, burst into the office, thinking they would find him dead of a heart attack. Instead, they found the general screaming into the receiver.

"*You fucking incompetent. I can't believe you fucked*

this away. You worthless piece of shit. I'll have your ass in Leavenworth for this. I can't fucking believe you—"

He stopped his ranting in midsentence to reward them for their concern.

"Get out. Get the fuck out of here. I told you to leave me the hell alone. Out, dammit. Out!"

They needed no further encouragement and escaped to the temporary safety of the outer offices. Out in the passageway, on the hallowed and subdued E-Ring, people a full corridor away turned and stared in the direction of the chairman's suite of offices. It was an unbelievable clamor. Even people too far away to hear the exact words uttered somehow got the unmistakable gist of what was going on. Every seasoned Pentagon hand knew enough to head in the opposite direction of the sound. A few visitors actually edged closer—cautiously—to the offices, their curiosity in overdrive.

The chairman looked back to the phone receiver. Anyone watching his expression and demeanor wouldn't have known whether he was going to speak into it, smash it on his desk, or throw it as far as he could. Finally, he started in again on Bleich, whose staff had already endured his own tirade.

"Bleich! You goddamned well better find them, and find them now! I mean it. I'll have your ass for this!"

"Yes sir, General." He had not expected a pat on the back for letting Rick and Laura escape, but he had not been prepared for the full fury of the general's wrath. It seemed for a moment that the chairman would come right through the phone and attack him where he stood. As combatwise and as street-savvy as Bleich considered himself, he had never tangled with anyone like Howard Campbell. He knew only one response would be even mildly acceptable.

"General, we're regrouping," he began. "I have my men fanning out in all directions from where he smashed his cab into our men. The cab will be easy to track. I guess my only question, sir, is whether we want to bring the metropolitan Fort Lauderdale police into this yet or not."

"No," said Campbell emphatically. "No outside help

yet. We *ought* to be able to track down *and* catch two very scared people on the run, shouldn't we?"

"Absolutely, General," replied Bleich.

"Good. Get to it. Call me before dark to tell me of your progress."

"Yes sir," was the only thing Bleich could say.

Howard Campbell had not needed that piece of bad news. He had wanted to be left alone to enjoy the ongoing impeachment hearings. This is what he had worked for. This is what he had planned for. Incompetents like Bleich couldn't ruin this for him. No, they couldn't. If only Bleich had been as capable as Clubber, he wouldn't be in the foul mood he was in right now.

The elimination of the DNI; that had been a "pop-up target," as they say, but it had been one that had been handled with dispatch. Clubber had been one of his men a long time ago. He'd actually been a key operative in training the Contras and done a hell of a job. The man could get the job done and he was ruthless. But then there was the rape charge on the Air Force base—Clubber had gotten carried away, and the military judge had gotten self-righteous about making an example of him. Campbell had intervened, avoided the dishonorable discharge, gotten Clubber a quiet retirement at twenty-two years with a nice military pension. He'd even gotten Clubber placed in a security firm. Clubber had pledged his undying gratitude—and since Clubber was a man of principles, the chairman fully intended to take advantage of that gratitude someday.

It had actually been blissfully simple once he had made up his mind that this needed to be done. What the DNI was threatening to do could be damaging, and once he had crossed that bridge, he had no trouble calling Clubber. The man understood instantly what needed to be done. There was no negotiating, no convincing, no agonizing over why, no guilt over the family that would be left behind, no emotion at all. It was business. The only time Clubber had even hesitated an instant was when the question of when came up. Campbell had insisted that Clubber do it that night. That caused the man to have to scramble a bit, but that was not the chairman's problem.

He had such complete faith in Clubber that he didn't even have him report back that the job was complete; damn, that was a long way from what he had to go through to micromanage that idiot Bleich. He imagined Clubber would nab him as he returned home from work that night. It was sure to be dark by then. He probably wouldn't have time to really dispose of the body properly, so knowing Clubber, Howard Campbell supposed that he'd take all of the DNI's valuables and make it look like a mugging. Hell, in the murder capital of the United States that was about as plausible as it got. Eventually someone would find the body, they'd eulogize his three decades of service with the Navy and the nation, cluck again about the unsafe city such fine, dedicated military people had to work in, and that would be it.

Thus far, the body hadn't been found—Clubber was going to make the search at least a little challenging—but the fact that a relatively high-profile flag officer had just not come to work was already creating a mild, low-level buzz in the Pentagon. Of course, the intel types were so damn secretive that they hadn't seen fit to tell anyone about this, but he had his network. There was nothing he didn't know.

It was time to get back to enjoying the impeachment hearings. After calling his secretary in and chewing her out for invading his privacy like that, he assured her that his screaming over the phone was just a necessary part of a very important thing he was doing. He told her to expect a call from Colonel Bleich again and to put him through immediately when he did call. Somehow, he knew that Bleich had gotten the message loud and clear that he'd better accelerate his efforts to find Holden and Peters. He'd get it done—eventually.

At Langley, the three met and went over their progress. The last call from Holden had been specific enough that they were able to get the right people lined up to do what was needed to be done. They were committed to this plan now, even if it wouldn't be finalized until Holden gave them the last details he had promised. Then they would activate their operatives and put them in position. Holden wasn't really asking for that much in some ways—just wanted to level the playing field, keep those he knew would be after him from grabbing him before he could complete his mission. They owed him at least that much. Once that was done, they would all fade away, neither taking the limelight nor sharing in the credit. That wasn't what they were about.

Bobby Wilcox was presiding over the second day of impeachment hearings. As the day wore on into afternoon, it was becoming apparent to him that any hopes he had of wrapping this all up today were gone like the will-o'-the-wisp. It wasn't that the outcome was in doubt. What was taking so long was a phenomena that borrowed a euphemism from football—piling on. No member of the House—servants of the American people all—was going to miss the opportunity to be telecast into the homes of over a hundred million of his or her fellow citizens. Hell, the election was less than a year away. Every member had an agenda and a game plan, all somewhat different, but all similar once you peeled away the rhetoric: Appear statesmanlike; eulogize those brave young men who had died—it was always helpful to name those from your state who had died, and their hometowns, the smaller the better; pontificate on the need for checks and balances, especially congressional oversight to make sure that nothing like this ever happened again; allow that the President was a fine man, a man who had served his nation admirably in the past—but that was then, this was now; say just as firmly that he had now crossed the line and must be turned out, that something like this could not stand.

Bobby Wilcox did not need to give them any further urging. They all knew how to run with it. His position now became an enviable one—he got to decide who would be recognized, who would benefit from this powerful media exposure, and who would just continue to sit in their seats with their 434 other colleagues. If there was nothing else that made being Speaker of the House of Representatives worthwhile, this was it. He was able to reward those who had been his allies in the past as well as reward those who promised to be his allies in the future. Hell, thought Wilcox, this was as close to the medieval practice of fealty as it got in twentieth century society. Just as importantly, maybe even more so, he was able to punish those who had been on the wrong side of the aisle on too many issues, too many times. Somehow he took particularly perverse delight in seeing them, sitting there in their best— their most powerful power suits, recently coifed, maintaining that statesmanlike demeanor—while he knew that it had been a waste of time, because they would never have the opportunity to get in front of the cameras. Oh, how he loved it!

Still, he could not delight in this forever. There were more pressing, practical matters. As chairman, he had the responsibility to get closure on the hearings. If he let them drag on indefinitely, he would lose too much political capital. Even though the Judiciary Committee deliberations were "secret," the word was out via these debates as to how thoroughly Linda Cohen's Judiciary Committee had done their job—they'd almost done it too well. Some commentators were already calling the full House impeachment debates "pro forma"—a necessary closure on something that was essentially decided already. He couldn't leave this hanging much longer. He'd let them run with it into early evening tonight—time to pass out a few dozen more favors—then he'd force them to a vote tomorrow.

CHAPTER 118

NEITHER RICK NOR LAURA COULD REMEMBER WHEN they had been silent for this long. As the Amtrak train sped northbound, the steady clicking of wheels on track sounding like a mantra, they just sat close together and let the tension drain out of their bodies.

Time passed as the train made its way north along the eastern seaboard of Florida, passing city after city, town after town, the Atlantic Ocean on their right, the setting sun to their left. After a long time they finally began to stir and talk, feeling more comfortable now, able to think ahead and not merely behind. Neither Rick nor Laura had thought of themselves as particularly brittle, especially vulnerable to panicking, or being unable to cope, but they both were realistic enough to know they had reached the limits of what they thought they could be.

Rick looked around furtively, checking for what seemed the thousandth time to see if their pursuers were on this train. "I think we're safe for now. My contacts at CIA said that they'll be in place to level the playing field for us in D.C. if it gets to the point where someone is going to grab either one of us. That's about the best they can offer right now. It's still all unofficial."

"I think that's fine, Rick. I think that will be a lot of help."

"I'm sure the DNI will get you to the right people right away. He must have a tremendous amount of clout."

"If he's there. I never got a chance to call his office. We have to know if he ever came in."

"I'm sure he did. We'll be able to call one of these times when the train stops."

"I hope so, Rick. I hope so."

Normally a man who was difficult to deal with, Bleich was in an especially irate mood after being chewed out by General Howard Campbell. The chairman had issued more than an ultimatum, he had made finding Rick and Laura the single focus of Bleich's life. So he had mustered every last man on his detail in his command to pass on his new religion.

"All right, people, I'm going to make this easy. We stubbed our toe on this, stubbed it badly. We're going to start our search from the point where these two wrecked Benham's and Lewis's car and we're gonna fan out in all directions until we find them."

He paused to look out on the sullen faces before him.

"We're going to find them, dammit, if it takes every one of us searching twenty-four hours a day. We're not allowed to fail. We won't fail."

Wouldn't fail, he thought, if he could run it the way he

wanted to run it. This fantasy of the chairman's, to do it only with his people, wouldn't work, couldn't work. He needed to bring in the local police at a minimum, the state police, perhaps. He knew Campbell didn't want that, but hell, what was he going to do, chew him out? This wasn't going to be a love-in in any event. The chairman had made it clear he wanted results; he probably wasn't going to quibble with Bleich's methods as long as he got the job done.

The colonel seized upon a way to do just that. Holden and Peters had stolen a city cab and had assaulted the driver. He knew the city police would want a piece of that one. As Campbell had prearranged with the FBI, he had already presented himself to the chief of police—not using his real identity, of course—and told them that he and his men were after two escapees from military confinement. The upscale citizens of Fort Lauderdale wouldn't want that element running loose in their neighborhoods. They'd worked out an arrangement in which the Fort Lauderdale police would stay on the sidelines. That had sounded like the best arrangement then. But he needed them now. Bleich made the call.

Bleich's men were not waiting for anything. Assisted, in force, by the Fort Lauderdale police, they had fanned out at three P.M. and searched every possible nook and cranny for the missing taxi. It was now early evening. Helicopters had been brought in, which greatly expanded the search area. The taxi company had also joined in the search; if the police were going to put this much effort into finding one of their stolen cabs, they would help too. The Cuban cab driver was even featured on one of the local TV channels telling his story—he called the couple "crazy" and had no idea where they'd gone—and the public was urged to provide the police with any information they had.

At about seven-thirty P.M. Bleich got a call.

"Colonel," said the man excitedly, "we've found the taxi."

"Where?" he replied.

The man told him. "I'm over here now. It's the right one, all right. Back end's pretty smashed up from where they backed into our guys."

"Anything else?"

"Nothing else that we can find so far. They sure didn't leave anything behind. We've got some folks from the Fort Lauderdale police here already and they're going to dust it for prints."

"Okay," replied Bleich. "I'll be right over."

"Oh, Colonel," the man said. "There's one more thing. They left the keys in the ignition."

"That's strange. Maybe they hoped someone would take it."

"Could be. It's pretty smashed up, though. Maybe that's why nobody took it."

"What else is near there?" said Bleich.

"I don't know, sir. Wait, I'll ask the police officer." Bleich heard muttering. "Colonel, he says the Amtrak station is just a little over two blocks away."

"I'll be right there."

He had been burned before, so Colonel Bleich had done some more checking, had gotten his story fully together, and had finally gotten through to Howard Campbell. It was after nine P.M. and the general was still in his Pentagon office.

"Well, Bleich, what do you have to tell me?"

"General, we've located the taxi that Holden and Peters stole only two blocks from the Amtrak station here. We found out that there was a train that left Fort Lauderdale at 2:02 P.M. en route to Washington."

"They've been on a train since two o'clock and this is the first we're finding out? What the hell have you been doing?"

Bleich had been expecting a pat on the back. It didn't look like that was going to happen. He continued, "General, we just found the taxi less than an hour ago. Once we found out about the train schedule we checked with the Amtrak people. The ticket agents on duty then are off shift now. We're looking for them, but the records show that several tickets were purchased for travel on this train all the way to Washington." Bleich was actually proud of the thoroughness of the information he was providing to the chairman.

"Anything to ID them? Credit card receipts? Checks?"

"No sir, we've checked for that. However, the records

do show that two tickets for one-way travel to Washington were purchased with cash less than five minutes before the train departed. So I would bet they're on that train."

"Right."

Bleich was expecting the chairman to pull it all together, to start acting on this information. He didn't. Bleich decided to lead him.

"General, the train gets to Washington tomorrow afternoon at one-thirty. There's plenty of time to get someone on the train anywhere along the way. It stops many places. I think you should have someone intercept them before they get to Washington."

Colonel Bleich didn't get the full picture, thought Howard Campbell. He'd been able to bring a number of forces together, but there was no way he could mobilize enough men to guard every station. He'd told Higginson the fugitives were dangerous, but such a mobilization could only create too much visibility for him to deal with them quietly after the arrest, and create possible suspicion as well.

"Colonel," replied Campbell, "this is your ball and you're gonna run with it. Your group is it. You've started this and you're going to finish it. Get your men assembled. Pick the half-dozen best you've got. I'm sending a T-39 down to pick you up. You'll fly up here and intercept the train before it gets to Washington and grab Holden and Peters—if they are really on the train, that is."

"General, I'm sure—"

Campbell cut him off. "No Colonel, we're not really 'sure' of anything at this point. But we're going to pull out all the stops. Now, where does this train stop before getting to Union Station?"

Fortunately for him, Bleich had done his homework. "General, it gets to Richmond shortly after eleven A.M., then Fredericksburg at about twelve-fifteen P.M., then Alexandria at one P.M., then Union Station at one-thirty P.M."

"I think you and your men—not a whole crowd, just you and two others—should get on at Fredericksburg. Find them on the train and then call me to let me know they're there. Then, just before you get to Alexandria, grab them and get them off the train there. We'll have vehicles waiting for you. We'll take them to Quantico as we've planned."

Bleich was glad the general was engaged, but there was one thing he didn't like about the plan.

"General, this Holden's a tough character. He took on several of my men and got the better of them. I'd like to put more men on the train."

"More men!" replied Campbell. "Colonel, you and two of your best don't think you can take them?"

"Yes sir, we do, but just in case—"

"Colonel, we're beyond 'just in case.' You've got to do something right for a change. I want just you and two others on that train, period. I'll have you and your two dropped off at the Fredericksburg airport. Vehicles will be waiting to take you to the Amtrak station. The rest of your folks that I pick up with the T-39 will continue on up here. They'll man the vehicles at Alexandria and will also report to my people in the building as backup should we need them here."

Bleich knew it was pointless to argue. "Yes sir, General, we'll be standing by for the T-39 when it arrives."

"Good, Colonel. Don't let me down."

"I won't, General. You can count on us."

Howard Campbell wasn't sure he could count on anyone anymore. He'd have to go with the colonel for now, though.

"Good hunting, Colonel. Stay in touch." Howard Campbell hung up the phone for just a second. He had several more calls to make. He was going to back up this plan as best he could.

The sun had come up by the time Bleich and his two men landed at the Fredericksburg airport. A nondescript rental car, driven by an uncommunicative driver, picked the three of them up and drove toward the Fredericksburg Amtrak station. They felt hamstrung. Despite Bleich's protests, the chairman insisted on no weapons of any kind. All they had were handcuffs to put on Holden and Peters after they subdued them. Though Bleich had called some audibles in Fort Lauderdale, going the route of having weapons after the chairman had given him explicit instructions not to carry any was one bridge he didn't want to cross.

The Amtrak train approached Richmond for its scheduled fifteen-minute stop. Rick and Laura had already decided what to do there.

"Rick, as soon as the train stops, I'm gong to call the DNI and let him know we're coming. Do you want to call your contact at the Agency too?"

"I don't think so. I think I've given them enough to go on for now."

"Okay, then, why don't you just get us a paper so we can see how the impeachment hearings are playing out?"

"Done. Don't you miss this train before it leaves."

"Won't happen." She smiled. They noticed that their words were now more and more brief, their body language conveying all they needed to know.

As the train pulled into the station, most of the other passengers were gathering their things. It looked like almost everyone was planning to at least get off the train and walk around the platform for a few minutes. For the first time during this entire trip, Rick and Laura felt like they were in a crowd. Somehow it made them just a little bit wary.

After debarking, Rick headed inside the station while Laura looked for a phone. Unfortunately, several other passengers had the same mission as she did during this brief stop. No doubt their calls were important to each of them, but if they only knew her urgency, perhaps they'd yield it to her. Then again, perhaps not.

Laura was still waiting her turn behind an elderly woman calling her daughter collect to pick her up at Union Station when Rick found her. He didn't say anything. He just held his paper up in front of her and pointed to an article:

DIRECTOR OF NAVAL INTELLIGENCE FOUND DEAD

WASHINGTON—The director of Naval Intelligence, Admiral Warren Phillips, was found dead last night just blocks from his home. Robbery is suspected, as the admiral's wallet, watch, and rings were missing. The admiral had departed his office about 7:30 P.M. and had indicated that he was heading directly home. When he failed to arrive on time, his family contacted the police.

Admiral Phillips is the first high-ranking military official to be killed in the Washington, D.C., area in recent memory. The neighborhood where he was found was not known for a high level of criminal activity, but according to officer Ted Monroe, youthful gang members are ranging further and further out to victimize those living in supposedly safe suburbs . . .

Laura just looked at the paper wild-eyed. Finally she spoke. "Rick, that couldn't have been a mugging. He had to have been murdered by the same people that derailed Operation Roundup. Oh, if I hadn't called him . . ."

Rick shared her shock and rage. He also knew where this was going and he had to stop it. "Laura, you can't blame yourself. I agree that it's highly unlikely this was a mugging, but you can't blame yourself for something the DNI decided to do because he wanted to do it."

"Oh Rick, this is getting too awful. I don't know if we'll ever be able to do any good."

"Laura, you can't think that way. Now maybe it's more important than ever that we do something."

The elderly woman had finally completed her call and was leaving the booth. Laura picked up the receiver, then put it back softly. Her call couldn't be answered, she realized.

"All aboard," intoned the conductor. "All aboard."

What they needed to do became crystal clear to Rick. "Laura. Give me the phone. Get close to the train and don't let it leave without me. This will only take a minute."

Laura followed his lead. She was perilously close to being in shock. She stood at the bottom of the steps leading into the Amtrak car closest to the phone as Rick spoke. She couldn't overhear his conversation, but could tell he was excited.

"All aboard. *All aboard!*"

Rick hung up and ran over to the train. He and Laura were aboard just seconds before the train chugged north.

After they returned to their seats, Laura looked at Rick, waiting for him to tell her who he had called. He was silent for a moment, then spoke.

"I've given my contacts at the Agency a chance to step up. Let's hope they do it."

The train pulled into Fredericksburg station at 12:25 P.M., just ten minutes behind schedule. Colonel Bleich and his two men got up from separate benches and joined the stream of people moving toward the train. They blended in innocuously and fanned out separately to three different cars. Their plan was to locate Rick and Laura, but not to do anything until just prior to pulling into the Alexandria station. The others would be waiting there, ready to whisk Rick and Laura off to Quantico.

After a bit of searching, they located them. Bleich and the men huddled together in the next car.

"All right," the colonel began. "I like where they're sitting. No one in the opposite seat. Close to the door. Should be able to whisk them off the train without too much fuss. Webb."

"Yes sir," replied the first man.

"You take the seat two forward of them. You block any attempt they make to get off in that direction."

"I can do it."

"Stevens."

"Yes sir, Colonel."

"You take your newspaper and sit down in the seat opposite to them. Pretend to read it intently. Peters is sitting next to the window. That's good. About two minutes out of Alexandria I'll come up behind Holden and pull him back with me. You move immediately next to Peters and hold her down. No really rough stuff. Just let her know that it's useless to struggle."

"Got it, Colonel."

"Webb, if Stevens has to help me with Holden, you move in take care of Peters."

"Piece of cake, sir."

"Let's not get too confident. Clearly this wasn't a piece of cake in Fort Lauderdale. Let's just do it right."

"Yes sir," they said in unison.

In the next car forward, Rick and Laura stared out on the rolling Virginia landscape. Rick continued to try to console Laura that she wasn't directly responsible for Admiral Phillips's murder. Finally, he could see that it was having no effect.

"Laura, for whatever reasons everything happened, we've just got to go through with this and make it work."

"I know, Rick, I know. What did your contacts say they'd do?"

"They're going to help us do the only thing we can do now. They're going to help us break what happened in Operation Roundup directly to the Congress, directly to the only people who can stop what the generals are about to do to the President and to the nation."

"Rick, how?" she said. "I mean, you can't be talking about just walking into the Congress and telling our story."

"That's exactly what I'm saying, Laura," he said with more conviction than she had ever heard him use. "Who but us knows the entire story? Who but us has at least some evidence that would help prove what happened?"

"Rick, we'll never pull it off. We'll never get in."

"I'm counting on my Agency people to help us do just that. That's probably the only way they can help, but that's exactly what we need right now."

"Fine, but assuming we get in, and assuming we get to tell even part of our story, what if they don't believe us?"

"That's always a possibility. Even if they do tend to think we're telling the truth, they'd have to check out our story anyway. But remember, the newspaper said these are open hearings. The gallery will be full. News media will be there. If we're telling the truth, someone will investigate further and it will all come out."

"Rick, I hope you're right."

"I hope I am too."

*   *   *

The cooperative conductor had promised to tell the three men when the train was less than five minutes out of Alexandria and he didn't disappoint them. Armed with that knowledge, the three began to move toward Rick's and Laura's car. They moved individually, first Webb, then Stevens, then Bleich.

Now, less than two minutes out of Alexandria station, they were all in position. Rick and Laura did not notice them. They were gazing out the window, looking at the countryside. Rick looked up and had an intuitive sense that something had changed, but as he did, he felt a hand on his shoulder. He froze. Colonel Bleich whispered in his ear. "Cooperate and the lady won't get hurt, *understood*?" With the word "understood" the squeeze on his shoulder became much tighter.

Rick nodded that he understood. His mind raced. This had to be them. They had finally hunted them down. How? That didn't matter. The threat against Laura continued to freeze him.

"Get up slowly," Bleich said.

Rick obeyed, with Bleich guiding his movement with his hand. Rick didn't dare move his head but made his eyes dart around. Was this man the only one? No, that one, and that one too; they weren't here a few minutes ago. Was that all? Were there any more?

For now, all Rick could do was cooperate with Bleich. Laura was looking out the window, but glanced at Rick as he was getting up.

"Rick, this isn't a full stop. You're not planning on getting off for a just a minute, are you?"

He didn't answer. Then she saw why. Her eyes grew wide. Just then, as instructed, Stevens slid over in the seat beside her.

It was all happening too fast. Rick was walking docilely toward the rear of the car. This man was just sitting there looking at her for now. There was another man in front of them who hadn't been there before. The train started slowing down to enter the Alexandria station.

Rick had to make decisions, and make them quickly. It looked like there were three men, maybe more. He didn't know whether they were armed. It looked like they intended to take him and Laura off the train at this station, and if that were the case, they undoubtedly had other people standing by with transportation to take them to places unknown. He knew there was only one way to keep the odds even close.

As he and Bleich got to the end of the car, Rick saw in his peripheral vision that Laura and the man next to her were starting to get up, no doubt to leave the train soon. These men had evidently coordinated their actions in advance; they were purposeful and well choreographed. Seeing Laura start to move, with that man standing menacingly close to her, triggered Rick into action.

As he got to the end of the car, the train lurched as it started to slow to a stop. Rick jerked away a bit, appearing to catch his balance on the side of the doorframe. Then he came back up suddenly, kicking his right leg with full force, nailing Bleich in the groin.

"Ahhhh," Bleich screamed, doubling over, contorted in pain.

"Rick!" screamed Laura, instinctively knowing that Rick was going against too-tough odds.

It all started happening with lightning speed. The train entered Alexandria station, Stevens saw Rick's attack and started back toward them. As instructed, Webb moved quickly into the seat next to Laura, grabbing her and pinning her against the window. She struggled to get free, but Webb's bulk was too much for her.

The other passengers in the train had heard Bleich's scream and knew something was amiss. One elderly couple in the back of the car near Rick and Bleich just hunkered down, hoping that this robbery, or whatever it was, would pass them by. Several people with children who were nearer the front of the car scooped them up and moved forward, as far away from the violence as they could. A college student, sitting three rows and across the car from Laura, came back toward the action. Seeing Laura pinned by Webb, he moved toward him.

"Hey, leave her alone," he said, menacing Webb with balled-up fists.

Webb was up in an instant, pushing off on Laura to keep her down. He let the college student get to within

two feet of him, then swung at him. His measured blow
landed directly on the bridge of the student's nose. Blood
shot everywhere and the man went down, holding his face
and screaming in agony.

At the same time, Rick was moving after Bleich, ready
to finish him, when Stevens lunged at Rick, driving him
back toward the car's rear door, ready to push him out
and move him off the train. Webb grabbed Laura and
started dragging her in that direction. She fought valiantly,
laying into him with body shots from both fists, but her
blows were barely affecting the powerful Webb.

Rick knew they had to keep fighting and, most importantly, had to keep from getting dragged off the train. The
train was now fully stopped and the doors were opening.
At the front of their car, passengers now poured off. Rick,
Stevens, Bleich, Webb, and Laura were all bunched up in
the very rear of the car. The elderly couple near them
scrambled forward to get away. Bleich was starting to
straighten up and get back into the fight.

The train hissed as it paused only long enough to let
passengers get off and let others get on. Two cars away,
on the station platform, two men waited patiently for
Bleich and the others to emerge from the train. Behind
them, several other men stood by, and farther back still,
three dark black sedans waited to whisk them all away.

Rick struggled with Stevens, trading blows with him.
Laura went totally limp, forcing Webb to drag her, then
reached out and grabbed one of the seats, making it impossible for him to get her any farther back. Angered,
Webb let go of her for an instant so that he could bend
down, pick her up, and carry her off the train.

Laura wasn't an exceptionally strong woman, but she
had military training. As he bent down to pick her up, she
rammed her fist into his groin with all her might. Webb
went down like a ton of bricks. Laura scampered up and
moved a step back from him. As he started to move, she
kicked him in the head—hard. He went flat on the ground
and started to try to crawl. She kicked him again and
again, harder each time, grunting with each effort. Finally
he was motionless.

Now she moved back, toward Rick, who was still struggling with Bleich and Stevens. Laura was in full rage now, her mind a blank, not thinking, only reacting. She started toward Stevens and grabbed him from behind. Surprised, he stopped struggling with Rick and tried to shake free of Laura. Given a momentary advantage, Rick turned all of his attention to Bleich.

The train started to move out of the station. The men on the platform who had expected Bleich and his men to emerge from the train with Rick and Laura were perplexed. Not caring about being discreet anymore, they began to run up and down the platform, looking for them, looking into the train as it pulled away, trying to see if they could see anyone familiar. They couldn't. One of them almost bumped into the elderly couple who had been in the midst of the fight. They were shaking.

"Sorry, ma'am," said the man abruptly.

"It's . . . it's . . . all right," she managed. "There are men in there . . . fighting."

"Where, ma'am?" said the man, his interest piqued.

"There on the train . . . they . . . they're beating the man—"

"I'm with the police, ma'am," he lied. "Please come with me."

Within minutes they knew that Rick and Laura were still on the train and headed for Union Station.

Rick continued to struggle with Bleich, who now fought with a rage of his own as he realized he had failed again. Stevens struggled with Laura, trying to use his weight and bulk to subdue her as she continued to try to beat on him with her fists and kick at him. Some sense inside of him held him back from delivering a blow to her—something about really striking a woman that hard didn't fit into his psyche. It was unfortunate for his psyche that he'd never met a woman like Laura before.

Rick was going blow for blow with Bleich, each man giving his all, each trying to give better than he got. The struggle ebbed and flowed. For a while they were almost wrestling, then trading blows, then grappling again. The train continued to speed toward Union Station. Stevens continued to block Laura, hoping to overpower her quickly so he could help Bleich with Rick. Webb continued to lay motionless on the floor of the car, a trickle of blood emanating from his ear.

Finally, Rick got a momentary advantage and rolled on top of Bleich, taking up the entire aisle, trying to pin him so he could really lay into him.

Stevens saw what was happening and turned Laura loose. He leaped on top of Rick and grabbed both his shoulders, trying to wrestle him off of Bleich. All three men banged into the sides of the seats, making them even more bruised and bloodied as they continued to struggle.

Laura knew Rick was unlikely to survive the two men pummeling him, so she leaped up and jumped on top of Stevens. In one quick motion she dug her teeth into the back of his neck, biting down hard, tearing into his flesh.

"Arrrgggh," bellowed Stevens. He stood up and shook Laura off him. She was rocketed back into a seat and slumped down from the shock.

Freed of Stevens for a moment, Rick knew he had to finish off Bleich. He rained his fists down on him.

As the train continued north, Stevens moved toward Laura. He had held back before, but he wouldn't anymore. Laura saw the crazed look in his eyes and knew what was coming. Desperately, she kicked at him, flailing her legs, not really aiming at anything in particular, just trying to fend him off. He kept moving toward her, trying to knock her legs out of the way with his arms.

Finally Bleich stopped moving. Instantly Rick leaped up to see that Stevens was now on top of Laura and starting to hit her. It drew out a hidden resource of strength. Although battered and bloodied, he leaped on top of Stevens, dragging him off of Laura and flinging him against the seat on the opposite side of the train.

As Stevens recovered, he looked left and right. He saw that Webb and Bleich were both down and not moving. He was on his own now.

In one final burst, he leaped at Rick. It was now one man trying to best the other. Laura was slumped in a seat, her strength totally sapped from the beating Stevens had delivered. Rick swung, Stevens swung. It was all a blur. Finally, Rick delivered a flurry of blows that were more than Stevens could handle. He stopped trying to hit Rick and started to just try to fend off his blows. Rick kept coming, hard. Stevens started to back down. More quickly now, Rick came at him. Stevens backpedaling, Rick charging. Stevens had given all he had. He turned around and ran toward the front of the car.

Rick started after him. Then he heard: *"Rick."*

He turned to see Laura trying to get up. Stevens disappeared out the front of the car.

"Laura?"

"Let him go. The train will be stopping soon. He's not a threat anymore. We've got to keep focused on getting to the Capitol."

The train hurtled on and Rick and Laura tried to lend strength to each other before they made their final push.

CHAPTER 119

THE TRAIN PULLED INTO WASHINGTON'S UNION STAtion shortly after one forty-five P.M., only fifteen minutes late, fairly good by Amtrak standards. It was none too soon for Rick and Laura. They both stood in front of the door, waiting for the train to stop, trying not to look around, hoping none of the other passengers would alert anyone about what they had done—but knowing that it was just a matter of time until they did. Rick and Laura were resigned to their fate—a dash to the Capitol. They had one shot and one shot only. There would be no second chances.

As the train lurched to a stop at the platform Rick and Laura detrained and ran down the platform toward the terminal, hoping to avoid anyone waiting for them there. Rick was toting his golf bag, but they had left Laura's bag behind so it wouldn't slow them down. They passed several porters and a few others who were waiting to greet people on this train. It was an eerie sight. Everyone was accustomed to people running to catch trains—that happened all the time, especially in busy Washington. But the sight of two people running *off* a train caught most people by surprise.

Rick occasionally looked over his shoulder to see if they were being chased by Stevens. He thought he caught a glimpse of him getting off the train and starting to run toward them, but they didn't slow down to wait and see.

When they reached the main station, they ran straight through the center of the magnificent rotunda, heading for the glass-doored exit. Outside, they jogged across the traffic islands, the small, square cobblestones almost tripping them up, and dodged taxis and the ubiquitous Old Town trolleys. They ran up onto the herringbone brick, past the three enormous flagpoles, around the Christopher Columbus monument, tasting the freedom of finally being here, finally reaching their destination.

"Laura, there it is," said Rick grabbing her arm and stopping her before she stepped into the traffic circle in front of them.

"I see it," she said, looking up. A few blocks straight ahead, but so imposing it seemed that they could reach out and touch it, was the Capitol.

They paused for a moment to get in sync with the traffic whipping around the circle; paused to see where their clear path was. "Let's go this way, up Delaware Avenue," said Rick, hitching his golf bag up under his arm.

"Okay," said Laura, remembering Washington well from her previous tour here. "We'll cross Constitution Avenue at the end of it and that will take us right up onto Capitol Plaza. I think that's the best way to get in."

They stepped off the curb and started across Columbus Circle, heading for Delaware Avenue. They were focused straight ahead, looking up the tree-lined street toward the Capitol, which seemed to be beckoning them.

Suddenly, out of his peripheral vision, Rick caught a car's movement that was unlike the other cars in the circle. Then he saw another, this one was moving left to right, *against* the flow of traffic in Columbus Circle. The cars were unmarked, but he could tell instantly what they were about. Then a third appeared on Louisiana Avenue, and a fourth came up First Street. Clearly, someone had called in the cavalry.

The cars came screeching to a halt, and men came pouring out, determined men in suits who were shouting and running toward them.

"Rick, there's too many of them," Laura said. She was clearly terrified.

Rick agreed. They couldn't get to the Capitol through these men. They had to find another way.

"Let's go!" he said, taking her arm tightly and running back toward Union Station.

They ran back through the sliding glass doors and into the station's main rotunda. Their pursuers were all still outside the station, maybe two hundred feet away, not rushing the station headlong, but forming into groups and starting to come toward it. They continued straight ahead, toward the Center Café. Then he saw the sign.

"Laura," said Rick, "this way!" He grabbed her again and moved sharply left. She did not know where he was taking her.

"Where?" she asked, but he just motioned her on.

They ran through the wing of the main station, out the automatic doors, and onto the street. Rick looked back and could see their pursuers entering the main hall. They had no other choice. The metro station was directly below. Rick pulled Laura onto the down escalator and they began taking the steps two at a time. They ran past the entry area, where dozens of people were lined up to purchase scrip for the trains.

"Rick!" Laura exclaimed as he ran past these machines and directly for the turnstiles.

"No time. Let's jump it!" he said. Laura went with him, leaping over the turnstiles and heading down the steps to the far side of the tracks where the sign read, TO METRO CENTER. They tried to ignore the stares and mumbled curses of the people they bumped into.

They cast furtive glances up toward the top of the station by the ticket booth, seeing if anyone was coming after them. Then they looked down the tunnel. There was the headlight of a train.

"Rick. It's got to get here. It just has to."

"Hurry, train. *Hurry,*" said Rick, now clearly desperate.

The metro train moved closer. The other people on the platform moved away from them.

"*Hurry.* God, please hurry."

Rick looked up at the top of the platform. First one, now another, then a third man appeared. Keeping his eyes fixed on them, Rick handed Laura his golf bag. No words needed to be exchanged. He would have to take them on until the metro arrived. Laura would wait for him until the last minute, but she had to be prepared to go if he didn't make it.

The train moved closer.

The first man came down the escalator. Rick allowed himself one last glance at Laura, then took off directly at the man at a full run. Now the other people on the platform started to run away from him as fast as they could.

Rick crashed into the man, knocking the wind out of him and knocking him down a few feet in front of the steps he had just come down. The second man, halfway down the steps, attempted to dive on top of Rick. Rick sidestepped him and the man came crashing down. Now the third man at the top of the steps paused. He was considering the best way to attack Rick. He came down the stairs more slowly, sizing Rick up. Rick waited at the bottom, his fists balled up, eyeing the man on the steps, but still checking the other two that had just attacked him. They weren't moving.

Laura just watched in horror, willing the train to arrive.

The man got to the bottom and stepped toward Rick. Ten feet apart now, they started to circle in. Five feet apart now. A fourth man now appeared at the top of the steps. He started down slowly, trying to get a feel for where to help out.

"*Rick!*" yelled Laura.

It was too late. The man who had leaped at him had come to and had grabbed Rick from behind. The man who had just come down the stairs responded by rushing at Rick.

It all happened quickly now. Rick struggled to get his attacker off his back as the other man joined in the fray, trying to wrestle him to the ground, reaching behind his back, looking for handcuffs.

The train was almost at the station. It would be greeted with a surreal sight: the passengers melted away except for three men struggling, another about to join in, and a woman standing nearby with a golf bag, looking helpless.

Then it all crystallized for Laura, a strange mixture of emotions: fear, rage, determination—and some she didn't comprehend.

Rick heard a sickening *thwack*. The man holding him slumped to the platform like a rag doll. He lay motionless.

Then he heard a *whoosh*, and the man pummeling Rick backed off. Another backed off further. The man now halfway down the stairs hesitated. Rick turned and saw Laura wielding a Big Bertha driver like a bat. Her eyes were wide. She moved toward the man, swinging the club, moving him farther away from Rick.

The train roared into the station now. The scream of brakes and wind rose around them.

Laura took another swing at the man, then she was attacking him wildly, Rick forgotten. She screamed savagely. The man halfway down the steps just froze.

"Laura!" shouted Rick.

She heard, but it had no impact. The driver's oversized titanium head hit the wall, cracking it.

"Laura!" She swiveled her head toward him. Their eyes met. Rick's look of desperation broke her out of her trance.

The train was almost stopped. Rick looked at the two men still standing. He looked at Laura. He looked toward the top of the stairs at the upper platform. No more pursuers . . . yet.

"Laura, come on. Get on the train," he said, almost softly, trying to break the rage, trying to get her to make escaping the goal, not killing the men who had attacked him.

She turned to him, almost in a trance, and followed. The train hissed to a stop. They rushed on. The two men's feet were frozen in their tracks, their eyes frozen on Laura still holding the golf club.

"Rick, the bag!" shouted Laura.

There on the platform, just a few feet from the door, was the bag. That woke up the men. They started to move slowly toward them. The train would be here in only seconds. Rick jumped off the train and grabbed the bag. He turned to get back into the car, Laura waving him on almost madly, but the doors were closing. Rick leaped at them, wedging his body between the two doors. The pressure was tremendous. The dozen or so passengers on the train looked on in disbelief. His arms wrapped around the golf bag, Rick struggled to get in the door.

Emboldened by his plight, the two men rushed at him. Laura pulled. Rick struggled. Closer now, the two men lunged at him, one catching the bottom of the bag just as Rick broke free of the closing door and fell into the car with it, and Laura tumbled backward against the opposite door. The train began to move. The two men pounded on the door in a rage, running alongside it, shouting.

The train picked up speed now. Rick and Laura slowly picked themselves up. They noticed the other passengers had melted away into other cars, and saw that missile launch tubes and clubs were everywhere, spilled out of Rick's bag as he hit the floor.

Silently, still not able to come up with any words, Rick and Laura began putting the canisters and few golf clubs back into the bag. The train was up to full speed now, roaring toward its next stop, Judiciary Square. Finally Rick spoke. "Laura—thanks."

"For what? You didn't think I was going to let them beat you to a pulp, did you?"

"No. I just mean, well, you were really going after them, like . . . well, like—"

"Like a madwoman? You bet. I don't know what came over me. I can tell you that there was never any question that I was going to let you get caught."

The train slowed down and entered the Judiciary Square station. Rick and Laura tensed. What surprise awaited them here? They scanned the station warily.

"Rick, how many of them do you think there are? Are we ever going to get away from them?"

They continued to look out on the station. The train slowed to a crawl. They mentally assessed each person on the platform. No one looked especially threatening. No one looked totally benign. As the passengers got on the train, those getting on the car with Rick and Laura saw how ragged they looked and avoided them. One couple simply backed off the train. It looked as if they were safe for the moment.

"Rick," continued Laura, "will this take us to the Capitol?"

"No, we needed to get away from them and this provided the best way. If we take this for two more stops and get off, we can get on the Blue Line and that will work us around west of the Capitol and we'll come up on it from the south. It's three or four stops on the Blue Line, I forget exactly how many."

"Do you think they'll be waiting for us?"

"I don't think they can move fast enough to get to one of these metro stations before we do. At least I hope not."

"Rick, where did they all come from? Who sent them?"

The train started to slow down again. Their antennae perked up again, ready to look for more pursuers. No other passengers moved toward them and they eased into the bench seat in the center of the car.

"Which station is this coming up?" asked Rick.

"Gallery Place, I think," responded Laura.

At Gallery Place, no one worth noting boarded, so they returned to considering their plight.

"Rick, who do you think is masterminding this chase? I mean, this just doesn't happen without someone controlling it directly."

"You're right. I don't think it's General Walters. He's too far removed from things in Panama. Someone higher up is doing this."

"Rick, General Walters is a four-star Unified Commander. Hardly anyone is higher up."

"The chairman of the Joint Chiefs is."

"General Campbell?"

"That's the only person it could be."

"You know, right before and right after Operation Roundup, General Walters was talking to General Campbell a lot. Nobody on the staff knew what the calls were about. They all were very private—and they usually aren't so. The executive assistants are usually always there—but the word gets out among the staff, you know."

"Didn't they used to work together too?"

"They worked together closely in the Pentagon. Also, General Walters used to let me know when we played squash that he had a direct line to the chairman. Yeah, I think they were tight."

"I think the chairman was just as unhappy with the President as General Walters was."

"But how, Rick? How could he bring all these people to bear against us? Soldiers follow orders, but what does he tell them?"

"He tells them you're an escaped murderer and I'm AWOL from a ship and an accessory after the fact. Maybe he tells them they need to track us down without a lot of uniforms getting involved in order to keep it from breaking as a military scandal. If he could do all that he's done, he'd have no trouble concocting a story about us. No trouble doing that at all. I think he's capable of anything."

"Including the DNI's murder."

"It seems like too much of a coincidence to me," replied Rick. He saw her go white. "You can't let yourself think that, Laura. Come on. We need to stay focused on what we're doing next."

The train slowed again as it pulled into the Metro Center station, just a few blocks east of the White House. The platform looked crowded. Many of the passengers in their car were already getting up to get off.

"Rick, this is where we connect to the Blue Line," said Laura, her memories of her previous tour in Washington now coming back. She had known the metro like the back of her hand, as had most military folks stationed in and around the Pentagon.

They got up and moved toward the door, still tense, warily eyeing the station platform. They got off and moved with the crowd toward a Blue Line train, which had just arrived. There were no empty seats, so they just stood near the center of the car.

As the train left Metro Center, they knew they had only a short time to finalize their plan.

"Laura, how many stops to where we get off?"

"Just four or five, I think. They come up really quickly. We get off at the Capitol South stop. It's just a block or two from the Capitol. Do you think they will be waiting for us there?"

"If they can figure out where we're headed, I think they will have enough time to get out in front and intercept us. Let's hope they just think we were running away from them."

The train slowed again and pulled into the Smithsonian station. A huge crowd, mostly tourists from the looks of them, was on the platform waiting for the metro. It would be almost impossible to spot anyone in this crowd that might be after them.

Some passengers got off, but many more got on and the jostling of bodies made Rick and Laura all the more uneasy. It would be so simple for someone to get to them here.

The train moved out of the station, jostling everyone as it did. There were too many people too close by for Rick and Laura to continue their conversation. They just stood there, waiting.

L'Enfant Plaza. A big group of tourists got off, freeing up some space on their car. Rick and Laura still stood in the center. It had cleared out enough now so they could at least talk again. They were feeling a little less uneasy as the train left the station.

Then Rick felt a hand on his shoulder. Every muscle in his body tensed. They had them. They had slipped onto this train and now had them trapped. Damn, damn, damn.

Years of training, and especially the events of the last few days and the last half-hour, all coalesced as the message went from his brain to his arm. They wouldn't take them. Not here. Not like this. He'd fight them off again. Maybe he could at least spring Laura. Come on, train, come on, get to the next station so Laura can get off as I deal with this, he thought. He shifted his weight, slowly, almost imperceptibly. The first blow would have to count. If he leveled the first one with one blow, maybe the others would back off and he'd have the advantage. How many were there this time? He continued to shift around. He balled his fist up, coiled and spun around, ready to strike.

"Rick! No!" screamed Laura so loudly she even startled herself.

As Rick finished wheeling around, he stayed his blow. A disheveled girl, no more than a teenager, stood there with stark terror in her eyes and a flat basket with roses in her hand.

The other passengers on the train stared at Rick—and particularly at Laura—in disbelief.

"I'm sorry. I'm sorry," said Rick. "I'm not going to hurt you. Here." Feeling guilty and ashamed, Rick fished a bill out of his pocket and gave it to the girl.

"Thanks," she said. She tried to hand him a rose, but he wouldn't take it.

"No, that's okay," he said. "You just keep it."

As the girl moved down the car, Rick and Laura realized just how frightened and paranoid they were. He had almost slugged some teenage girl. They were at the end of their rope.

"It's okay, Rick," whispered Laura, trying to reassure him. "It's okay. We'll be off this train soon."

"Laura, this plan—I know it's really a long shot. If someone had told me a month ago that we would be thinking about running into the U.S. Capitol, running out onto the floor of the House as hearings to impeach the President of the United States were going on, and were going to try to stop all that from happening, I would have told them they were crazy."

"I'm ready, Rick. I'm not going to flinch."

The train pulled into the Federal Center Southwest station. A few passengers got off, a few more got on. They measured each one. As the train left the station, Rick and Laura knew the next stop would be theirs. They were tense with anticipation about what would happen next. They thought the next half-hour or so would be a turning point. They had no idea how true that would become.

CHAPTER 120

BOBBY WILCOX HAD THOUGHT THAT HE WOULD BE able to wrap up these impeachment hearings before lunch. But it was not to be. Although he had cajoled all of his allies and friends in the House, there were a few Congressmen who insisted on getting up just one more time and waxing eloquently for the folks back home.

"Mr. Speaker," began Representative Tyrone Webster of the Fifth District of Illinois, "I think that it bears repeating that brave, brave men have died ..."

This is going to be good, thought Wilcox. Why can't we just get on with it?

"... brave men, courageous men, men who never had a chance who were sent to their deaths for political expediency! We cannot let this go unnoticed. We must take action. The President is unfit to serve."

"I agree," said Representative Alex Carroll of neighboring Ohio's Eighth District, undoubtedly on cue. He and Webster were great buddies, recalled Wilcox. "We have a responsibility to the nation ... to America ... to do what is right, to do what is necessary, to do what is, *imperative!*"

The Speaker was, on the one hand, visibly annoyed that this stream of wannabees was dragging this out the way they were. On the other hand, he empathized to some extent with where they were coming from. Hell, he'd been that junior once. They worried about getting reelected. They couldn't pass up the opportunity to be broadcast into millions upon millions of homes, insisting that the House of Representatives give the nation what the polls all said the majority of Americans wanted. That was too good an opportunity to pass up, in spite of cautions by their leadership. Hell, he'd give them their due and they'd

be allies for a long time, but for the love of God, he
wished they'd just cut the crap and keep it short.

Finally, as the hour approached two P.M., no more representatives stood up. Wilcox shook his head in amazement. Were they finally done? He looked around again to
be sure that no one else was going to ask to stand up and
be recognized. They weren't. He was on center stage.

Bobby Wilcox had rehearsed what he was going to say
next for a long time, for so long, in fact, that he was actually very worried it would all sound rehearsed. So he
had rehearsed making it sound spontaneous. He knew
that everyone knew these would be the last days of the
hearings. They knew a vote would take place today. He
knew that almost every TV in the country would be tuned
in to these hearings, carried on all the major networks and
half the cable channels. He knew they would all have to
hear him speak before they got to hear the vote. Millions
in campaign funds could not bring him as much publicity
as he would receive in the next ten minutes.

The Speaker moved in front of the microphone, de-
porting himself in his most statesmanlike manner. He de-
layed for a minute or so, adjusting the microphone,
arranging his papers, shifting from side to side, looking first
at one camera, then at another, making as much political hay
as possible from every precious second. Finally, he nodded
sagely at the House in general and began to speak.

"Over the last few days, we have listened to the evidence presented in this chamber. We have debated it at
length. I wish to commend each of you for doing your
duty, for speaking your mind—both pro and con—for trying to get at the truth, at the essence of what had occurred.
For making up your minds and for battling with your con-
sciences.

"My role as Speaker is simply to preside over this
House, to ensure that we conduct the matters put before
us. In no way have I tried to affect the presentation of the
evidence, steer the course of debate or influence your
votes, nor would I be so presumptuous as to think that I
could.

"However, I would be remiss if I did not share with you
first how I intend to vote. As the leader of this body, I
am accountable to you and to our nation. To wait and see

how the majority was voting would not be leadership at all. Indeed, I would be abrogating my leadership.''

Silence. No whispering among the members. No shuffling around in the packed gallery. Every camera was focused directly on the Speaker.

''I cannot express in words how difficult this is for me. If we are to do what we are to do, it is an admission that somehow our system has broken down. Reluctantly, regrettably, I must tell you that I, personally, in good conscience, no longer have confidence in the President's ability to continue to lead our nation. You all must vote your conscience, but you must not let empathy or sympathy color your view. The President has served the nation long and faithfully for decades. He served it with distinction while sitting in this very chamber. In spite of that, you must focus on the events of the last several weeks. There are some actions that are so wrong, so misguided, so *heinous*, that they go beyond the pale of what is acceptable for any human being, let alone our nation's highest-ranking elected official. I, for one, and with deep regret, intend to vote to impeach President Taylor Calhoun and to have the Senate of the United States bring him before that body for a full and fair trial.''

Still silence.

''Ladies and gentlemen, we will now have a roll call vote.''

CHAPTER 121

HOWARD CAMPBELL SAT ALONE IN HIS OFFICE WATCHing the impeachment hearings on his television. He had all but barricaded himself in. No staff members came in to talk to him or simply to deliver or pick up paperwork. No one buzzed him on the intercom to tell him someone was calling. No orderly came in and delivered lunch or even a cup of his favorite black coffee.

His staff had never seen him behave like this before.

He had sent his executive assistant away to meet with the vice chairman's executive assistant on some relatively trivial matter. He had sent his aide away to the far end of the Pentagon on some useless errand, actually telling him to go get a workout when he was through doing that. Only his secretary remained as the guardian of his bastion. She would not let him be disturbed. He could count on that.

He had one of his many phone lines shifted so that it rang directly in his office. The only indication his secretary had that a call was either being received or being made was the light on her phone that came on every time the chairman was on that line. It must be something intensely private, she thought. She dared not ask.

The chairman had gotten yet another call from Lieutenant Colonel Schriefer, Bleich's number two man, whom Campbell had brought to Washington while Bleich and two others had gotten on the train. It was the latest update of his attempt to stop Rick and Laura, another chronicle of failure. Campbell was enraged, but this time he didn't let loose. All he did was hiss, "Stop them, dammit, stop them. I don't care what you have to do, but you stop them and take them to Quantico, dead or alive."

Schriefer stared at the phone in disbelief. Catching them was his task. The dead-or-alive part was a new wrinkle. He couldn't believe the chairman was serious. Schriefer was so convinced he could bring them in alive that he discounted the chairman's directions. It wouldn't be necessary. Those two they were chasing had been incredibly lucky so far—and the pursuers had been incredibly unlucky. The last trap he was setting would be the one that brought them down. After all, he and Bleich only had to be lucky once.

Campbell put down the receiver, convinced that he had given Schriefer all the direction he needed, and all the empowerment to get the job done. There was one more person he needed to talk to just one more time. But he couldn't call him. He had to wait for the call. He knew he wouldn't have to wait long.

He watched the impeachment hearings with a great deal of interest and not a small amount of satisfaction. He had pulled this off. He was definitely a man of destiny, and he was just one phone call away from sealing that destiny.

But he felt a sense of malaise too. It wasn't the fact that he had sent all those men to their deaths. It wasn't even the fact that he was going after Taylor Calhoun and doing him in for something he didn't do. No, his concerns went deeper. They went to the heart of the American political system itself. He resented—yes, that was the word, actually *resented*—the fact that these elected officials, these *civilians*, who came into office for at most eight years, had the power to decide the fate of the nation, while men like him served at their pleasure, their whim. It was not right; it was not fair to the nation. But he would not let this stand any longer. He had the solution. He had only to wait for the phone call.

The television droned on with the impeachment hearings. The chamber was going with a simple roll call vote, and one by one, each representative got up and registered his vote to impeach or not to impeach. After only the first few dozen votes, the outcome seemed like a foregone conclusion. The votes crossed party lines and were running almost three to one for impeachment. It was only a matter of time, he thought, only a matter of time to let the string run out.

He was snapped out of his musings by the jangle of the telephone. He grabbed it on the second ring.

"Campbell."

"General, this is Mustang."

There wasn't anyone named Mustang. But a code word was necessary just in case these supposedly ultrasecure lines were tapped. Mustang was the code name Howard Campbell had given to Alex Paul, the Vice President of the United States.

"Good afternoon, Mustang. I assume you have the proceedings on."

"I do indeed."

"Have you now had time to thoroughly consider what we discussed?"

"I have."

"And?"

"There are some areas that, I, well—"

Campbell cut him off. Brutally. Without remorse. "There is nothing to discuss. You understand what is about to happen in the next hour or so. You know how that was made to happen. Having gone this far, you can't think that we won't replay this scenario again and again as many times as we need to. The offer still stands and your public power and prestige would be undiminished— even enhanced. Your sole promise is to allow us to do what we and only we can do and allow us to do it our own way."

"Yes, I am in basic agreement with that. I was only concerned—"

"Concerned? Concerned that things might not run as well? I think perhaps if that's the way you feel, then you're not our man—"

"No!" Now it was time for the Vice President to interrupt. "No, only concerned that this might be too much of a change for the country—for the people."

"Change? *Change!*" said the chairman as loud as he dared without being heard by his secretary just outside his office. "You are the ones who brought the changes. I'm— we're—just trying to put things back the way they were. The way they've worked for decades. We're not trying to *change* anything. You have just got to sign on to that."

"I will."

"You will, what?"

"I will agree with your plan. As we discussed during our meeting."

"Very good, Mustang. Welcome to the team. I'll be in touch with you. Enjoy the rest of the afternoon."

With that, the receiver went dead. Howard Campbell picked up the remote control for his TV and turned the volume back up, eager to hear all the details of the roll call vote. Now the circle was complete. He let his mind wander. It had all been fairly straightforward, he recalled. After he and Charlie Walters had concocted their plan, the natural question was, what would happen when the President was gone? Would it be any better?

The chairman had bided his time. He knew about Taylor Calhoun's and Alex Paul's backgrounds and motivations. He knew that their party ticket had been a marriage of convenience, not a melding of similar minds. He knew they had bickered frequently and that Paul had been silent in public only out of party loyalty. He studied the relationship and knew there was only the thinnest veneer of mutual acceptance.

As the crisis surrounding Operation Roundup began to unfold, he watched the relationship between the President and Vice President become more tenuous. He had heard through his most reliable sources that the two men had argued bitterly. After a National Security Council meeting to deal with a European Community issue, the chairman had stayed behind for a private word with the Vice President. They felt each other out, fenced for a long while, then Campbell told the Vice President of his "fears" that the President had meddled in Operation Roundup. To his pleasure, Paul was not shocked, nor did he attack Campbell for attacking the President. The chairman suggested a follow-up meeting and the Vice President agreed.

It had been only a week later, with the impeachment hearings beckoning and things looking very bad for the President, that Campbell and the Vice President had found themselves alone for a short while on an Air Force Two flight, returning from a state funeral. The chairman spoke in hypotheticals, but the message was clear. President Taylor Calhoun was going down because he had forced radical changes in the military. The Judiciary Committee Hearings which at that time were surely leading to impeachment hearings were no accident, no natural evolution of things. Calhoun had dared to go against the chairman and his cabal of generals. Now he was going away. Simple. Straightforward. Unemotional. Business. Just business.

The Vice President had listened intently and had worked mightily to show no emotion. He didn't know if he had succeeded or not. He did not want to let himself get drawn in too far—at least not yet. He worded his response carefully.

"I think I understand where you are coming from, General. I will give your proposal serious consideration. Change is not always a good thing. I assume you're describing an era of peaceful coexistence within the Executive Branch."

"That's precisely what I'm saying, and what I'm offering."

"Then we'll know more in a short while. Perhaps we can talk then."

"I suggest you give it *very* serious consideration, Mr. Vice President."

"You can count on it, General."

The meeting ended then, satisfactorily, Campbell thought. But the past was just prologue to the present. Now this phone call sealed the deal. Alex Paul was a cautious man. He dared not commit until the impeachment hearings were all but a foregone conclusion. Campbell had to admit to himself that he would have waited the same way himself. But the Vice President would play ball. As the new President, Alex Paul would run the country, if you could call that anything worth running. He, Howard Campbell, would be reappointed chairman and would run the most powerful military machine the world had ever known. He would run it his way. By his rules. It was a prospect that gave him the only joy he felt anymore. Now if Schriefer would only get the job done. Just get it finished.

Major Lang dared not come into General Walters's headquarters with this news. Lang had been decorated in battle in Panama and in the Persian Gulf. He thought himself more courageous than any other man, any other warrior. But seeing the general personally with this news wasn't courage, it was stupidity.

The secretary buzzed the general. "Major Lang for you, General."

He picked up the receiver instantly. "Lang! Where the hell are you?"

"I'm at the security headquarters, General. Just reading the latest dispatches and I have just finished talking with my informants. It seems, General, well . . ."

"Spit it out, goddammit!"

"All right, General. Holden and Peters have been sighted in Washington, D.C. They are being chased, we assume by General Campbell's people. They're near the Capitol. Word is that they contacted the DNI, and as you know, he's been found mugged, or so they say."

"Cut to the chase, Major. No one believes for a minute that he was mugged."

"Of course, General."

"So now we'll have to see if the chairman can catch these two. Anything else?"

"Yes sir."

"Well, what is it, man?"

"General Lovelace has also been reported seen in Washington."

"General Lovelace?"

"Yes sir," said the nearly deafened Lang, now holding the phone receiver away from his ear.

"What in the hell is he doing there? Why isn't he on-board Coronado? *Why didn't I know that he wasn't still aboard* Coronado?"

"I can't answer that, General."

"No, of course you can't. Where is he in Washington? Are your sources good enough to tell you that?"

"Yes sir," said Lang, relieved to be able to tell the man who still controlled his career and his destiny something that he wanted to hear. "He was spotted this morning arriving on Capitol Hill, in his uniform, heading for the Capitol Building."

The silence seemed like it would last for an eternity.

"General?"

No answer.

"General?" repeated Major Lang.

But Charlie Walters did not answer. He did not hear. He just slumped down in his chair, dumbfounded.

CHAPTER 122

AT THE CAPITOL SOUTH STATION, RICK AND LAURA bolted from the train and climbed the two escalators to the street two at a time, trying to save every second, ready for anyone who might be waiting to ambush them. Pausing at the top, they realized for the moment they were in the clear.

They ran up SE First Street, past more government workers and tourists, leaving the Rayburn Building on the left and the Madison Building of the Library of Congress on the right. As they crossed Independence Avenue and the park, they came up to the south side of the Capitol Building. But as they got closer, first one man, then four or five all told, appeared and advanced on them. This must be Howard Campbell's goal-line stand to stop them. They were doomed. They'd never fight off this many. Rick and Laura stopped in their tracks.

As suddenly as this group of men appeared, other men appeared, seemingly out of nowhere. Now the odds against them were impossible, thought Rick and Laura. But then they saw the second group was attacking the first group. There were so many in the second group that one or two men each were able to subdue each of the original group. It all happened very quickly. This second group was incredibly proficient—as if they had been trained to do this all their lives.

Rick and Laura stood dumbstruck for a moment, then Rick finally realized that the Agency had come through for him. They knew—at least his handlers did—that this was the right thing to do, the right thing to do for the nation. Inspired by what they were witnessing, Rick and Laura accelerated their sprint toward the Capitol Building, now only a few score yards away.

Crowds of tourists swarmed around the Capitol. Many were drawn by the impeachment hearings, while for others it was but one stop on a tour of the city. Rick and Laura were able to tell where the best place to enter the building was, but as they approached it, the inevitable Capitol security force guards blocked their path.

They knew from experience there was no arguing or cajoling these civil servants. There was no time, though, to try to queue up for the standard tour of the Capitol. Suddenly several of the agents who had just cleared their way appeared again. They moved close to each guard, flashed some sort of ID, then, talking very excitedly and convincingly, got the guards to shrug and wave to Rick and Laura to proceed toward them. No words were exchanged as Rick and Laura entered the Capitol, two CIA operatives preceding them silently.

As they approached the House chamber, more security guards got up to stop them. The two CIA men in the lead showed their ID, talked briefly, then led them through. As they entered the House chamber, with the roll call vote under way, the CIA men melted away and Rick and Laura found themselves standing in the middle of the floor of the chamber while the House membership stared at them and the spectators in the gallery began to buzz excitedly. The press was perplexed. Was this part of the script?

One spectator in the gallery didn't join the excited buzz. He was not there as a voyeur of the political scene. He was there on a mission. General Ashley Lovelace sat in an obscure corner of the gallery and patiently watched the proceedings. He was determined to make an opportunity to try to extricate the President from this crucible. He had come to the House chamber with an imperfectly formed idea of just how he would accomplish that—he knew he had to do something, he just wasn't sure what it was.

Rick's and Laura's sudden appearance on the House floor instantly crystallized the general's plan. Lovelace recognized Rick immediately and the entire chain of events—from Rick's return from the battlefield, to his mysterious disappearance, to the ensuing manhunt he had subsequently learned about—all made sense now. He had to act, and he had to act immediately. There was no other way.

Speaker of the House Bobby Wilcox couldn't believe

some yahoos would disturb such calamitous proceedings. He called for the guards to have them removed, but no one answered. He was about to take other steps when General Ashley Lovelace appeared out of the gallery and walked up the center aisle, resplendent in his starched and pressed uniform, bedecked with personal decorations and campaign ribbons.

"Mr. Speaker," began Lovelace, "I request to be recognized."

"Sir, return to the gallery. We are debating an issue of the utmost importance to the fate of the nation. How dare you interrupt these proceedings?" He banged down his gavel. Hard.

Wilcox did not recognize Ashley Lovelace, but several other representatives did. He had been a regular in the Washington social scene and he had done favors for some of them. Nothing extraordinary—a tour here, some free material—maps of the Capitol, posters from government events, stationery and other items—there, access to a military facility that was hard to get into. A clamor started as first a few of them, then many more, shouted, "Let the general be heard." Thus far, Rick and Laura were being largely ignored.

Lovelace began again. "Mr. Speaker, I realize we are deciding the fate of the nation. That's why I am here. That's why these two brave people are here," he said motioning to Rick and Laura. "I am General Ashley Lovelace, Commander of Joint Task Force Eight. I left my flagship, USS *Coronado,* just yesterday in order to be here and testify on what really happened with respect to Operation Roundup. I am here to tell you—no, *these two brave people* are here to tell you—what really happened to Operation Roundup. I only risked my career by leaving my flagship to come here and tell you this; they risked their lives to come here. Honor them with the opportunity to tell you the truth."

Bobby Wilcox didn't like this, but he was no fool. With a packed gallery and the media taking notes furiously, he dared not try to sweep this incredible entry under the rug. He looked directly at General Lovelace. "All right, General. If the House membership has no objection, I will give these individuals the opportunity to speak."

Overcome with curiosity, if nothing else, first a few, then dozens, then more representatives shouted their consent. Wilcox looked back to Lovelace and said, "General, please introduce these two people and have them tell us their story—briefly."

"I will, Mr. Speaker, and they will try to relate this briefly, but this is a very involved story. I present you Chief Petty Officer Rick Holden—a man, incidentally, who bravely went out into the field after Operation Roundup and personally rescued many of our wounded men—and Lieutenant Laura Peters, an intelligence officer on the staff of commander, Southern Command. They will tell you how you all happen to be assembled here today—how you were duped by some of the men who, I am troubled to admit, wear the same uniform that I do."

When Lovelace stopped, every eye turned to Rick and Laura. Rick began:

"I am Chief Petty Officer Richard Holden, with the SEAL team embarked in USS *Coronado*. Lieutenant Peters and I came upon information—independently at first, but then together—that convinced us that Operation Roundup was designed to fail by our military leaders both in the Pentagon and at SouthCom. . . ."

Rick related the story from the beginning, ignoring the Speaker's admonition to be brief. He poured out every detail, asking Laura to speak when it was important to convey the nature of their efforts. He was compelling, sparing nothing, speaking with emotion when he described caring for the wounded, speaking with conviction when he explained how he and Laura had been attacked a number of times on their journey here. Giving specifics, names, dates, places, times. Occasionally, when Rick said that he was puzzled as to what motivated these generals to do what they did, General Lovelace spoke briefly about his suspicions regarding General Campbell and General Walters.

The entire House sat spellbound. No one moved. Few talked, and those who did merely whispered to the member sitting next to them that such an incredible story couldn't be made up, it had too much passion, too much conviction. Most of all, it was frightening that military men could try to do this to the nation they were supposed to be defending.

Finally, Rick reached into his golf bag and produced the spent Stinger missile launch tubes. He calmly explained what they were, where they had come from, how these were very traceable to their point of origin, and then, most damningly, how he had watched the missiles that emanated from them destroy the helicopters and kill his comrades. It was an absolutely compelling performance.

"Ladies and gentlemen, I hope you believe my—our—story. We have no reason to tell it other than to tell the truth. I watched brave men die because our highest military leaders did not like the idea of a civilian—even a civilian with the title of Commander in Chief—telling them what to do with 'their' military. It's not theirs, it's all of ours. Lieutenant Peters and I are never prouder than when we wear our uniforms. We implore you not to make a mistake and put the blame for what happened in the wrong place."

There was a pregnant pause that hung in the air. There was no script for what anyone should do in a case like this. One congressman stood up and began to clap slowly. Then another did likewise. Then another. Then another. Now they were rising more quickly and clapping more loudly. Finally the entire House was on its feet, clapping loudly, some stamping their feet. Now the clapping was totally in sync, the members almost outdoing each other in enthusiasm. Rick and Laura were stunned and actually looked embarrassed.

In the duration of the clapping it all became crystal clear. There was only one path that this could take. The guilty would be brought to heel, the innocent would be protected. Bobby Wilcox was stunned, but he was no fool. He waited for the clapping to almost completely subside, then banged his gavel with authority.

"Ladies and gentlemen. These impeachment hearings are suspended."

EPILOGUE

THE HOUSE CHAMBER HAD BEEN CHAOTIC FOR SEV-
eral hours. Someone had had the foresight to whisk Rick
and Laura out of the House and take them over to the
Old Executive Office Building. There would be much to
tell.

With the impeachment hearings suspended, all chal-
lenges to the President and his authority were truncated.
Expectedly, there was a catharsis in rounding up those
guilty of the plot. Some, like General Charlie Walters and
Colonel Conrad Hicks, who realized what they had done
and were, at least, somewhat remorseful, came easily,
knowing what was awaiting them, resigning themselves to
their fate. Others, like General Howard Campbell, held
out until the bitter end, first protesting their innocence,
later trying to legally maneuver, but in the end being
bound over for trial and punishment.

The war against drugs continued as it had for so many
years, unsuccessfully, the twin demons of supply and demand thwarting all noble attempts to stop this scourge.
Money was still appropriated, sometimes in great quantities. High-profile operations were still launched, some of
which were mildly successful. Education programs were
announced, then initiated, only to fall victim to the same
hopelessness that nurtured the drug scourge in the first
place. U.S. drug czars, appointed to coordinate all national anti-drug efforts, served for shorter and shorter
terms as they recognized the futility of their mission.

Taylor Calhoun's standing rose in the polls as the nation
rallied around him in the wake of the tragedy of Operation Roundup and the diabolical plot against him. He was
enough of the politician to play the martyr and use it all
to his advantage. Just months before the election he had

at least an even chance. Vice President Alex Paul resigned suddenly, citing health reasons, and returned to his home state to live in virtual seclusion. The President appointed Secretary of Defense Elliott Higginson to serve out the remainder of Paul's term.

The President appointed a blue-ribbon commission and gave it an extraordinarily short deadline to make recommendations to effect changes to the operations and oversight of the military. These recommendations were quickly adopted by an aggressive Executive Branch and a compliant Congress. More checks and balances were put into place to ensure that military leaders were under increased scrutiny by their civilian masters.

Ashley Lovelace was given his second star and brought back to Washington to serve in a high-visibility job in the Pentagon. Captain Pete Howe finally got his aircraft carrier, the USS *John F. Kennedy,* home ported in Norfolk, Virginia, close to Washington. Within the CIA, several men were given new positions with increased standing, while a congressional committee initiated a comprehensive study to examine the organization and policies of the Agency.

Rick Holden and Laura Peters had come into the public spotlight like two blazing comets. Both wished to disappear from it as quickly as they had come. There were very private ceremonies where they both were recognized for their heroics. Then the senior leadership did an unusual thing—it listened to their requests and tried mightily to accommodate them.

Lieutenant Laura Peters returned to her work as a Navy intelligence officer. Keeping her at SouthCom was out of the question, and bringing her to Washington was too high-vis. Therefore, she was given an important billet in the very out-of-the-way JICPAC J-DET, the Navy Intelligence Detachment in Japan, supporting the commander in chief, Pacific Joint Intelligence Center. Located at Camp Zama, just outside of Tokyo, she was at the focal point of military intelligence regarding Japan, China, and the Korean Peninsula. She was happy professionally, and she began to try to deal with being apart from Rick Holden.

Rick Holden. Many midnight hours were absorbed in

trying to decide what fate would befall him. Everyone recognized that, singularly, he was the one man who had derailed this plot against the President. At every level and across every agency there was a universal clamoring to reward him. Many competed with ways to do that. Rick would have none of it. His first thought was to return to the Agency, to take up where he had left off, to blend in again among those hundreds of anonymous patriots who dealt with the minute details of what might, someday, become something vital to national security. But it could not be. Try as it might, the Agency could not find a niche where he could fit in. He was too well known. For an organization that dealt in anonymity, this was a nonstarter. Rick knew this, but he was disappointed nonetheless.

What then? The idea of moving out into the civilian world did not thrill Rick. He tested the waters regarding remaining in the Navy, continuing to serve as a Navy SEAL, as a Navy chief petty officer. When it was brought to the attention of the President, he would have nothing of it. We need men like this in the Navy, he said, but we need them in the officer ranks. The President called Rick in personally and told him that this was Rick's opportunity to continue to serve his nation—that the President was counting on him—and that in this way he could serve even more people, make a greater contribution. Rick was attentive and a pointed call to the Secretary of the Navy ensured an instant commission, which Rick gratefully accepted. The President himself, with Rick's parents—and Lieutenant Laura Peters—in attendance, read the commissioning oath and pinned on Rick's ensign bars in the Oval Office.

In West Potomac Park, just east of the Korean War Memorial, south of the Reflecting Pool and within sight of the D.C. War Memorial, a small but elegant monument was erected to the Marines who lost their lives during Operation Roundup. Although he tried to keep it low-key, it was an open secret that President Taylor Calhoun had been the most vigorous fund-raiser for the private foundation that was established to erect the memorial, and that he had used his considerable influence to have

its design and construction approved by the always-
bureaucratic Capitol Monuments Commission.

Half a world away, the Persian Gulf was again in turmoil. This time, their orders of battle fattened by military
sales from nations such as China, the middle powers of
the Persian Gulf were determined to control their own
destiny and truncate U.S. presence and influence in the
region.

AFTERWORD

WHILE THIS BOOK IS CERTAINLY A MEMBER OF THE
"military suspense" or "techno-thriller" genre, it is really
about power—about its ability to do good, and certainly
about its ability to do evil. Few will argue with the requirement for the military to have power, or with the requirement that the military have the ability to project
power in support of national aims, that the military retain
the ability to enforce the will of the people. However,
fewer recognize the enormous bureaucratic power vested
in our senior military leaders. Because military leaders are
charged with enormous responsibilities and vested with
extraordinary power to carry out their missions, the public
in general, and the nation's elected civilian leaders in particular, would be remiss in failing to understand just what
the military can do and ought to do, in much the same
way as they would be remiss in not listening to the leaders'
expertise regarding military matters.

Clearly, I have painted several military figures in this
book in broad, unflattering strokes. They are evil men. I
feel obligated to add that none of this represents, in any
way, any first-person experience that I have had in my two
and a half decades serving in the military. Rather, the
actions of these officers are hypothetical examples of the
enormous power for evil that men could have if they as-
cended to these lofty positions within any of the military
services. The secret to avoiding this, I am convinced, lies
not in additional rules and regulations or more congressional oversight, but in maintaining the military as a place
where honorable men and women want to serve their
country. Only by attracting the best and most ethically
sound professionals, and making it attractive for them to
serve long enough to rise to the top of the military, can

we ensure that the dismal scenario played out in these pages—or one similar to it—does not engulf our nation.

Captain George Galdorisi
Coronado, California
June 1997

Edgar Award Winner
STUART WOODS
New York Times Bestselling Author of
Dead in the Water

GRASS ROOTS   71169-/ $6.50 US/ $8.50 Can

WHITE CARGO   70783-7/ $6.99 US/ $8.99 Can

DEEP LIE   70266-5/ $6.50 US/ $8.50 Can

UNDER THE LAKE
70519-2/ $6.50 US/ $8.50 Can

CHIEFS   70347-5/ $6.99 US/ $8.99 Can

RUN BEFORE THE WIND
70507-9/ $6.50 US/ $8.50 Can